PRESTON
& CHILD

CITY OF
ENDLESS NIGHT

HEAD
ZEUS

First published in the USA in 2018 by Grand Central Publishing,
a division of Hachette Book Group, Inc.

First published in the UK in 2018 by Head of Zeus Ltd
This paperback edition published in 2018 by Head of Zeus Ltd

9 7 5 3 2 4 6 8

A catalogue record for this book is available from
the British Library.

ISBN (PB): 9781786696854
ISBN (E): 9781786697059

Printed and bound by CPI Group (UK) Ltd, Croydon, CR0 4YY

Head of Zeus Ltd
First Floor East
5–8 Hardwick Street
London EC1R 4RG

WWW.HEADOFZEUS.COM

CITY OF
ENDLESS NIGHT

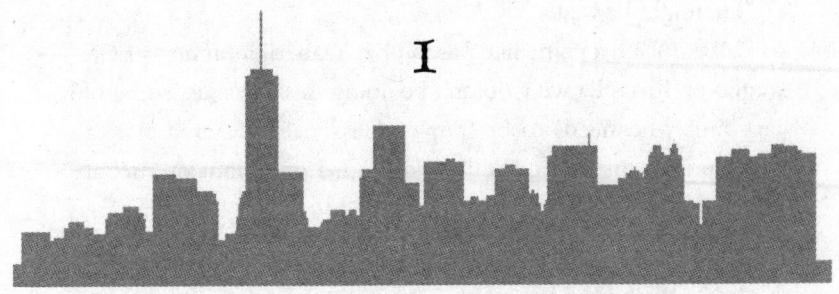

I

Jᴀᴄᴏʙ ᴡᴀʟᴋᴇᴅ ꜰᴀsᴛ, ahead of his little brother, hands stuffed into his pockets, breath flaring in the frosty December air. His brother, Ryan, was carrying the carton of eggs they'd just purchased at the nearby deli with money Jacob had stolen from his mom's purse.

"First, because the old man is a total asshole," Jacob said to his brother. "Second, because he's a *racist* asshole. He yelled at the Nguyens and called them 'slopes'—remember?"

"Yeah, but—"

"Third, because he cut in front of me at the C-Town checkout line and cussed me out when I said it wasn't fair. You remember that, right?"

"Sure I do. But—"

"Fourth, he puts all those stupid political signs on his yard. And remember when he sprayed Foster with a watering hose just 'cause he cut across his yard?"

"Yeah, *but*—"

"But *what?*" Jacob turned around in the street and faced his younger brother.

"What if he has a gun?"

"He's not going to shoot two kids! Anyway, we'll be long gone before the crazy old turd even knows what's happened."

"He might be Mafia."

"Mafia? With a name like Bascombe? Yeah, right! If he was Garguglio or Tartaglia we wouldn't be doing this. He's just some old fart-biter who needs to be taught a lesson." He stared at Ryan with sudden suspicion. "You're not gonna wimp out on me, are you?"

"No, no."

"Okay then. Let's *go*."

Jacob turned and walked down Eighty-Fourth Avenue, then turned right onto 122nd Street. Now he slowed and went onto the sidewalk, moving along easily, as if out for an evening stroll. The street was mostly single-family homes and duplexes, typical of the residential Queens neighborhood, and it was festooned with Christmas lights.

He slowed further. "Look at the old guy's house," he said to his brother. "Dark as a tomb. The only one with no lights. What a Grinch."

The house was at the far end of the street. The streetlights shining through the leafless trees cast a spiderweb of shadows across the frozen ground.

"Okay, we stroll along like nothing's happening. You open the carton, we unload a bunch of eggs on his car, then we beat it around the corner and just keep going."

"He'll know it was us."

"Are you kidding? At night? Besides, all the kids in the neighborhood hate him. Most of the grown-ups, too. *Everyone* hates him."

"What if he chases us?"

"That old geezer? He'd have a heart attack in seven seconds." Jacob sniggered. "When those eggs hit his car, they are going to freeze, like, *right away*. He'll have to wash it ten times, I'll bet, just to get them off."

Jacob approached the house along the sidewalk, moving cautiously now. He could see the blue glow in the picture window of the split-level ranch; Bascombe was watching TV.

"Car coming!" he said, in a whisper. They ducked behind some bushes as a vehicle turned the corner and came down the street, headlights sweeping along, illuminating everything. After it had passed, Jacob felt his heart pounding.

Ryan said, "Maybe we shouldn't…"

"Shut up." He emerged from behind the bushes. There was more light in the street than he would have liked, cast not only by the streetlamps but also by the Christmas decorations— illuminated Santas, reindeers, and crèche displays on the front lawns. At least Bascombe's place was a little darker.

Now they approached very slowly, keeping to the shadows of the parked cars along the street. Bascombe's car, a green '71 Plymouth Fury that he waxed every Sunday, sat in the driveway, pulled up as far as possible. As Jacob moved along, he could see the faint figure of the old man sitting in a wing chair, looking at a giant-screen TV.

"Hold up. He's right there. Pull your hat down. Put your hood up. And the scarf."

They adjusted their outerwear until they were well covered, and waited in the darkness between the car and a large bush. The seconds ticked past.

"I'm cold," Ryan complained.

"Shut up."

Still they waited. Jacob didn't want to do it while the old man was sitting in the chair; all he had to do was stand up and turn and he'd see them. They would have to wait for him to get up.

"We could be here all night."

"Just *shut up*."

And then the old geezer stood up. His bearded face and skinny figure were illuminated by the blue light as he walked past the TV and into the kitchen.

"Go!"

Jacob ran up to the car, Ryan following.

"Open that up!"

Ryan flipped open the carton of eggs and Jacob took one. Ryan took another, hesitating. Jacob threw his egg, which made a satisfying *splat* on the windshield, then another, and another. Ryan finally threw his. Six, seven, eight—they unloaded the carton on the windshield, the hood, the roof, the side, dropping a couple in their hurry—

"What the *hell!*" came a roar and Bascombe burst out of the side door, wielding a baseball bat, coming at them fast.

Jacob's heart turned over in his chest. "Run!" he yelled.

Dropping the carton, Ryan turned and immediately slipped and fell on some ice.

"Shit!" Jacob turned, grabbed Ryan's coat, and hauled him to his feet, but by now Bascombe was almost on top of them, the bat cocked.

They ran like hell down the driveway and into the street. Bascombe pursued, and to Jacob's surprise he didn't drop dead of a heart attack. He was unexpectedly fast, and he might even be gaining on them. Ryan began to whimper.

"You goddamn kids, I'll bust your heads open!" Bascombe yelled behind them.

Jacob flew around the corner onto Hillside, past a couple of shuttered stores and a baseball diamond, Ryan following. Still the old bastard chased, screeching, with that baseball bat held high.

But it seemed he was finally getting winded, dropping back a little. They turned onto another street. Up ahead Jacob could see the old shuttered automart, surrounded by a chain-link fence, where they were going to build apartments next spring. A while back, some kids had cut an opening in the fence. He dove for the opening, then crawled through, Ryan still following. Now Bascombe was really falling behind, still screeching threats.

Behind the automart was an industrial area with some dilapidated buildings. Jacob spied a nearby garage, with a peeling wooden door, and a broken window beside it. Bascombe was now out of sight. Maybe he gave up at the fence, but Jacob had a feeling the old fart was still following. They had to find a place to hide.

He tried the garage door; locked. Gingerly, he stuck his arm through the broken window, felt for the knob, turned it from the inside—and the door creaked open.

He went in, Ryan following, and carefully and quietly he shut the door and turned the bolt.

They stood there in the blackness, breathing hard, Jacob feeling like his lungs might burst, trying to stay silent.

"Dumb kids!" they heard shrilly, in the distance. "I'll bust your balls!"

It was dark in the garage, which seemed empty except for some glass on the floor. Jacob crept forward, taking Ryan's hand. They needed a place to hide, just in case old man Bascombe somehow thought of looking for them in here. It seemed the crazy old coot really would clobber them with that bat. As Jacob's eyes adjusted to the dimness, he saw a pile of leaves in the back—a large pile.

He pulled Ryan in that direction and he dug into the leaves, lying down on the soft surface and sweeping his hands around, piling the leaves over himself and his brother.

A minute passed. Another. No more shouting from Bascombe—all was silent. Gradually Jacob recovered both his breath and his confidence. After another few minutes he began to giggle. "The drooling old bastard, we got him good."

Ryan said nothing.

"You see him? He was, like, chasing us in his pajamas. Maybe his dick froze and broke off."

"You think he saw our faces?" Ryan asked in a quavering voice.

"With the hats, scarves, hoods? No way." He sniggered again. "I'll bet those eggs are frozen hard as a rock already."

Finally Ryan allowed himself a little laugh. *"Dumb kids, I'll bust your balls!"* he said, imitating the old man's high, whistling voice and heavy Queens accent.

They both laughed as they began rising from the leaves, brushing them away. Then Jacob sniffed loudly. "You farted!"

"Did not!"

"Did so!"

"Did not! He who smelt it, dealt it!"

Jacob paused, still sniffing. "What *is* that?"

"That's no fart. That's...that's *gross.*"

"You're right. It's like...I don't know, rotten garbage or something."

Jacob, disgusted, took a step back in the leaves and stumbled over something. He put out his hand and leaned against it to steady himself, only to find the leafy surface he'd been hidden against now yielded with a soft sigh, and the stench suddenly billowed over them, a hundred times worse than before. He jerked away and staggered back even as he heard Ryan say, "Look, there's *a hand...*"

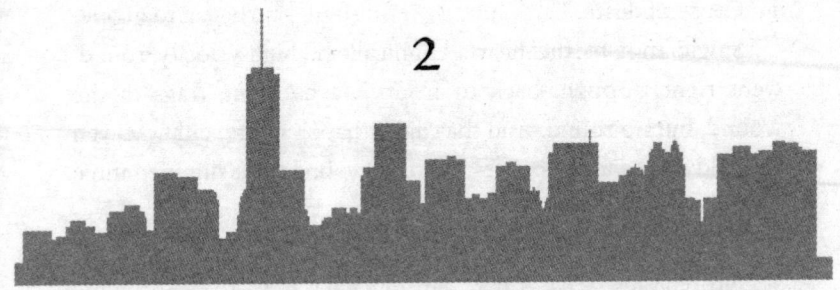

2

LIEUTENANT COMMANDER DETECTIVE Squad Vincent D'Agosta stood in the floodlights outside the garage in Kew Gardens, Queens, watching the Crime Scene Unit work. He was annoyed at being called out so late on the night before his day off. The body was reported at 11:38—just twenty-two more minutes and the call would've gone to Lieutenant Parkhurst.

He sighed. It was going to be messy, this one: a young woman, decapitated. He played around in his mind with possible tabloid headlines, something along the lines of HEADLESS BODY IN TOPLESS BAR, the most famous headline in *New York Post* history.

Johnny Caruso, the head of the CSU, emerged from the glare, slipping his iPad into his bag.

"What you got?" D'Agosta asked.

"These damn leaves. I mean, try searching for hair, fiber, fingerprints, whatever in that mess. Like a needle in a haystack."

"You think the perp knew that?"

"Nah. Unless he actually worked on an evidence collection team once. Just a coincidence."

"No head?"

"None. The beheading didn't take place here, either—no blood."

"Cause of death?"

"Single shot to the heart. High-caliber, high-velocity round, went right through, back to front. Maybe some frags in the wound, but no round. And that didn't happen here, either. Given the cold and so forth, best estimate is the body was dumped three days ago, maybe four."

"Sexual assault?"

"No obvious signs of it so far, but we'll have to wait for the M.E.'s examination of, you know, the various—"

"Right," D'Agosta said quickly. "No ID, nothing?"

"None. No documents, empty pockets. Caucasian female, maybe five six—hard to say—early twenties, toned body, obviously fit. Wearing Dolce and Gabbana jeans. And see those crazy sneakers she's wearing? Just looked 'em up on the web. Louboutin. Almost a thousand bucks."

D'Agosta whistled. "Thousand-dollar sneakers? Holy shit."

"Yeah. Rich white girl. Headless. You know what that means—right, Lieutenant?"

D'Agosta nodded. The media would be there any moment—and here they were, as if he'd conjured them out of his head: a Fox 5 van pulled up, then another, and then an Uber with none other than good old Bryce Harriman, the *Post* reporter, stepping out like he was Mr. Pulitzer himself.

"Christ." D'Agosta murmured into his radio for the spokesperson, but Chang was already on it, at the police barricades, talking his usual smooth stuff.

Caruso ignored the rising chorus beyond the barricades. "We're working on an ID, looking through the missing person databases, fingerprints, the whole nine yards."

"I doubt you'll get a match on her."

"You never know, girl like that: cocaine, meth. She might even be a really high-end hooker—anything's possible."

D'Agosta nodded again. His feeling of disgruntlement began to ease. This was going to be a high-profile case. That could cut both ways, of course, but he never shied away from a challenge and he felt pretty sure this one would be a winner. If anything so awful could be called a winner. Decapitation: that meant it was some sick, twisted perp, easily caught. And if she was some rich family's daughter, it would mean priority for the lab work, allowing him to cut ahead of all the piece-of-shit cases waiting in line for the notoriously slow NYPD forensic labs.

The Evidence Gathering Team, all gowned up like surgeons, continued to work, crouching here and there, humped up and shuffling about like oversize white monkeys, sifting through the leaves one by one, examining the concrete floor of the garage, going over the door handle and windows, lifting prints from the broken glass on the floor—all by the book. They looked good, and Caruso was the best. They, too, sensed this was going to be a big case. With all the recent lab scandals they were taking extra care. And the two kids who'd found the body had been questioned right on the scene before being released to their parents. No shortcuts on this one.

"Keep it up," said D'Agosta, giving Caruso a pat on the shoulder as he stepped back.

The cold was starting to creep in, and D'Agosta decided to take a brisk turn along the chain-link fence that surrounded the old car yard, just to make sure they hadn't missed any possible points of ingress. As he moved out of the illuminated area, there was still plenty of ambient light to see, but he flicked on his flashlight anyway and moved along, probing this way and that. Coming around a building toward the back of the yard, picking his way past a stack of cubed cars, he saw a crouching figure just inside the fence—*inside*. It was no cop or anyone on his team: the figure was dressed in a ridiculously puffy down jacket, with a hood way too large for his head that stuck out like a horizontal piece of stovepipe.

"Hey! You!" D'Agosta hustled toward the figure, one hand on the butt of his service piece, the other hand holding the flashlight. "Police officer! Stand up, hands in sight!"

The figure rose, hands raised, face completely obscured in the shadow of the fur-fringed hood, turning toward him. He could see nothing but two gleaming eyes in the blackness of the hood.

Creeped out, D'Agosta pulled his piece. "What the hell are you doing here? Didn't you see the police tape? Identify yourself!"

"My dear Vincent, you may put away your weapon."

D'Agosta recognized the voice immediately. He lowered the gun and holstered it. "Jesus, Pendergast, what the hell are you doing? You know you're supposed to present your credentials before poking around."

"If I must be here, why miss out on a dramatic entrance? And how fortunate it was you who happened upon me."

"Yeah, right: lucky you. I might have busted a cap in your ass."

"How dreadful: a cap in my ass. You continue to amaze me with your colorful expressions."

They stood looking at each other for a moment, and then D'Agosta pulled off a glove and stuck out his hand. Pendergast slipped off his own black leather gloves and they shook, D'Agosta gripping his arm. The man's hand was as cool as a piece of marble, but he pulled back his hood and exposed his pale face, white-blond hair slicked back, silver eyes unnaturally bright in the dim light.

"You say you have to be here?" D'Agosta asked. "You on assignment?"

"For my sins, yes. I'm afraid my stock in the Bureau has declined rather sharply for the moment. I am—what is that colorful term of yours?—temporarily in shit's creek."

"Up shit creek? Or do you mean you're in deep shit?"

"That's it. Deep shit. Without the paddle."

D'Agosta shook his head. "Why are the feds involved in this?"

"A superior of mine, Executive Associate Director Longstreet, hypothesizes the body may have been brought here from New Jersey. Crossing state lines. He thinks organized crime could be involved."

"Organized crime? We haven't even collected the evidence. New Jersey? What's this bullshit?"

"Yes, Vincent, I'm afraid it's all fantasy. And for one purpose: I am being taught a lesson. But now I feel rather like Br'er Rabbit being thrown into the briar patch, because I have found you here, in charge. Just like when we first met, back at the Natural History Museum."

D'Agosta grunted. While he was glad to see Pendergast, he was not at all glad the FBI was involved. And despite the uncharacteristically light banter—which felt forced—Pendergast didn't look good...not at all. He was thin, almost skeletal, and his face was hollow, dark circles under his eyes.

"I realize this is not a welcome development," Pendergast said. "I shall do my utmost to keep out of your way."

"No problem, you know how it is with the NYPD and the FBI. Let me bring you over to the crime scene and introduce you around. You want to examine it yourself?"

"When the EGT is finished, I'd be delighted."

Delighted. He didn't sound delighted. He'd be even less so when he saw the three-day-old body without a head.

"Ingress and egress?" Pendergast asked as they walked back.

"Seems pretty evident. The guy had a key to the back gate, drove in, dumped the body, left."

They arrived back at the area before the open garage and entered the glare of the light. The EGT was almost finished, packing up their stuff.

"Where did all the leaves come from?" Pendergast asked, without much interest.

"We think the body was hidden in the bed of a pickup truck under a big pile of leaves, tied down beneath a tarp. The tarp was left in a corner, leaves and body dumped against the back wall. We're working on interviewing the neighbors, trying to determine if anyone saw a truck or car in here. No luck so far. There's a lot of traffic in this area, day and night."

D'Agosta introduced Special Agent Pendergast to his detectives and Caruso, none of whom made much effort to hide their displeasure at the arrival of the FBI. Pendergast's appearance didn't help any, looking like he'd just returned from an Antarctic expedition.

"Okay, clear," said Caruso, not even looking at Pendergast.

D'Agosta followed Pendergast into the garage as he strolled over to the body. The leaves had been swept away and the body lay on its back, a very prominent exit wound between the collarbones, caused no doubt by an expanding, high-powered round. The heart was obliterated; death instantaneous. Even after years of investigating murders, D'Agosta was not so hardened as to find this comforting—little comfort of any kind could be found in the death of so young a person.

He stepped back to let Pendergast do his thing, but he was surprised to see the agent not going through his usual rigmarole, with the test tubes and tweezers and loupes appearing out of nowhere and interminable fussing around. Instead, Pendergast merely walked around the body, almost listlessly, examining it from different angles, cocking his long pale head. Two times around the body, then three. By the fourth round, he didn't even try to conceal a look of boredom.

He came back up to D'Agosta.

"Anything?" D'Agosta asked.

"Vincent, this is truly punishment. Save for the beheading itself, I don't see anything that would mark this homicide as in the slightest degree interesting."

They stood side by side, gazing at the corpse. And then D'Agosta heard a slight intake of breath. Pendergast suddenly knelt; the loupe finally made an appearance; and he bent over to examine the concrete floor about two feet from the corpse.

"What is it?"

The special agent didn't answer, scrutinizing the dirty patch of cement as studiously as if it were the Mona Lisa's smile. Now he moved to the corpse itself and took out a pair of tweezers. Bending over the severed neck, his face less than an inch from the wound, he maneuvered his tweezers under the loupe, dug them into the neck—D'Agosta almost had to turn away—and stretched out what looked like a rubber band but was obviously a large vein. He snipped off a short piece and dropped it in a test tube, dug around some more, pulled out another vein, snipped and stored it, as well. And then he spent another several minutes examining the massive wound, the tweezers and test tubes in almost constant employment.

Finally he straightened up. The bored, distant look had faded somewhat.

"What?"

"Vincent, it appears we have an authentic problem on our hands."

"Which is?"

"The head was severed from the body right here." He pointed downward. "You see that tiny nick in the floor?"

"There are a lot of nicks in the floor."

"Yes, but *that* one has a small fragment of tissue in it. Our killer took great pains in severing the head without leaving any sign, but it is difficult work and he slipped at one point and made that tiny nick."

"So where's the blood? I mean, if the head was cut off here, there'd be at least some blood."

"Ah! There was no blood because the head was cut off many, many hours or perhaps even days after the victim was shot. She had already bled out elsewhere. Look at that wound!"

"After? How long after?"

"Judging from the retraction of those veins in the neck, I should say at least twenty-four hours."

"You mean the killer came back and cut off the head *twenty-four hours later?*"

"Possibly. Or else we are dealing with two individuals—who may or may not be connected."

"*Two* perps? What do you mean?"

"The first individual, who killed and dumped her; and the second...who found her and took her head."

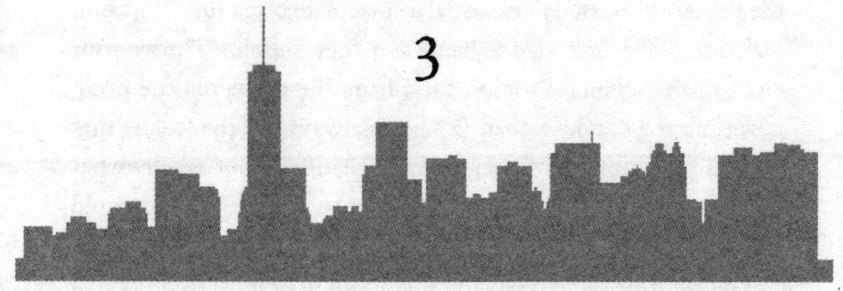

3

Lieutenant D'Agosta paused at the front door of the mansion at 891 Riverside Drive. Unlike the buildings surrounding it, which were gaily hung with Christmas lights, the Pendergast mansion, although in fine shape given its age, was dark and seemingly abandoned. A weak winter sun struggled through a thin cloud cover, casting a watery morning light over the Hudson River, beyond the screen of trees along the West Side Highway. It was a cold, depressing winter's day.

With a deep breath he walked under the porte cochere, stepped up to the front door, and knocked. The door was opened with surprising speed by Proctor, Pendergast's mysterious chauffeur and general factotum. D'Agosta was a bit taken aback by how thin Proctor seemed to have grown since the last time he'd seen him: normally he was a robust, even massive, presence. But his face was as expressionless as usual, and his dress—a Lacoste shirt and dark slacks—characteristically casual for a man supposedly in service.

"Hello, ah, Mr. Proctor—" D'Agosta never knew quite how to address the man. "I'm here to see Agent Pendergast?"

"He's in the library; follow me."

But he wasn't in the library. The agent appeared, suddenly, in the refectory, dressed in his usual immaculate black suit. "Vincent, welcome." He extended a hand and they shook. "Throw your coat on that chair." Proctor, for all that he answered the door, never offered to take a coat. D'Agosta always had the feeling that he was a lot more than a servant and chauffeur, but exactly what he did, and what his relationship was to Pendergast, he could never figure out.

Vincent took off his coat and was about to drape it over his arm when, to his surprise, Proctor whisked it away. As they walked through the refectory and into the reception hall, his eye couldn't help but fall on the vacant marble pedestal, where once a vase had stood.

"Yes, I owe you an explanation," Pendergast said, gesturing to the pedestal. "I'm very sorry Constance gave you a blow to the head with that Ming vase."

"Me, too," said D'Agosta.

"You have my apologies for not providing a reason sooner. She did it to save your life."

"Right. Okay." The story still made no sense. Like so much connected with that crazy series of events. He glanced around. "Where is she?"

A severe look gathered on Pendergast's face. "Away." His icy tone discouraged any further questions.

There was an awkward silence, and then Pendergast softened and extended an arm. "Come into the library and tell me what you've learned."

D'Agosta followed him across the reception hall and into a warm and beautifully appointed room, with a fire on the grate, dark-green walls, oak wainscoting, and endless shelves of old books. Pendergast indicated a wing chair on one side of the fire and took the opposite one himself. "Can I offer you a drink? I'm having green tea."

"Um, a coffee would be great, if you have any. Regular, two sugars."

Proctor, who had been hovering in the entrance to the library, now disappeared. Pendergast leaned back in his chair. "I understand you've identified the body."

D'Agosta shifted. "Yes."

"And?"

"Well, to my surprise we got a fingerprint match. Popped up almost right away, I presume because she'd been digitally printed when she applied for the Global Entry system—you know, the TSA's Trusted Traveler Program? Her name's Grace Ozmian, twenty-three years old, daughter of Anton Ozmian, the tech billionaire."

"The name is familiar."

"He invented part of the technology used in streaming music and video over the Internet. Founded a company called DigiFlood. Hardscrabble childhood, but he rose fast. Now he's rich as hell. Anytime streaming software is loaded on a device, his company gets a piece of it."

"And you say this was his daughter."

"Right. He's second-generation Lebanese, went to MIT on a merit scholarship. Grace was born in Boston, mother died in a plane crash when she was five. She was raised on the Upper East Side, went to private schools, bad grades, never had a job, and sort of lived a jet-setting lifestyle with her father's money. Went to Ibiza a few years ago, then Mallorca, but about a year ago came back to New York to live with her father in the Time Warner Center. He's got an eight-bedroom apartment there—two apartments joined together, actually. Her father reported her missing four days ago. He's been raising holy hell with the NYPD and probably doing the same with the FBI. The guy's got connections up the wazoo and he's been calling in all his chips, trying to find his daughter."

"Undoubtedly." Pendergast raised the teacup to his lips and took a sip. "Was she involved in drugs?"

"Possible. So many of them are—rich as well as poor. No record, but she was picked up intoxicated and disorderly a couple of times, most recently six months ago. A blood test showed the presence of cocaine in her system. Never charged. We're putting together a list of everyone she associated with—she had a pretty big crowd of hangers-on. Mostly Upper East Side trust-funders and Eurotrash. As soon as the father's notified, we'll be going after her 'friends' hammer and tongs. Of course, you'll be in on all of it."

Proctor brought in the cup of coffee.

"You mean he doesn't know yet?" Pendergast asked.

"Ah, no...the ID came in only an hour ago. And that's partly why I'm here."

Pendergast's eyebrows rose, and a look of displeasure gathered on his face. "Surely you don't expect me to make a sympathy call."

"It's not a sympathy call. You've done this before, right? It's part of the investigation."

"To break the news to this billionaire that his daughter has been murdered and decapitated? No, thank you."

"Look, it's not optional. You've *got* to go. You're FBI. We need to show him we're all over this case and so is the Bureau. If you're not there, believe me, this superior of yours is going to hear about it—and you don't want that."

"I can weather Howard Longstreet's displeasure. I'm in no mood to leave my library at present on a bereavement mission."

"You need to see his reaction."

"You think he's a suspect?"

"No, but it's possible the murder could be something involving his business dealings. I mean, the guy *is* supposed to be a world-class prick. He's ruined many a career, seized lots of companies in hostile takeovers. Maybe he pissed off the wrong people and they killed his daughter to get even."

"My dear Vincent, this sort of thing is not my forte."

D'Agosta felt exasperated. He could feel his face burning. Normally he let Pendergast have his way—but this time the man was dead wrong. He was usually so adept at sizing up situations—what the hell was up with him? "Look, Pendergast. If not for the case, do it for me. I'm asking you as a friend. Please. I can't go in there alone; I just can't."

He felt Pendergast's silvery gaze on him for a long moment. And then the agent picked up his teacup, drained it, and placed it back in its saucer with a sigh. "I can hardly say no to an appeal like that."

"All right. Good." D'Agosta stood up, coffee untouched. "But we've got to move. That frigging reporter Bryce Harriman is sniffing around like a hound dog. The news could break at any second. We can't let Ozmian learn about his daughter from a tabloid headline."

"Very well." Pendergast turned and there, as if by magic, was Proctor once again, standing in the library doorway.

"Proctor?" Pendergast said. "Bring the car around, if you please."

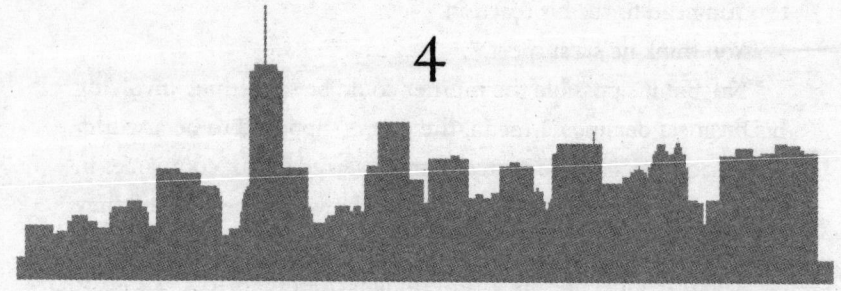

4

THE VINTAGE ROLLS-ROYCE Silver Wraith with Proctor at the wheel—so incongruous in the cramped, pedestrian-clogged labyrinth of Lower Manhattan—squeezed through a traffic jam on West Street and approached the headquarters of DigiFlood, in the heart of Silicon Alley. The DigiFlood campus comprised two large buildings occupying an entire city block among West, North Moore, and Greenwich. One was a massive former printing plant dating back to the nineteenth century, and the other a brand-new skyscraper rising fifty stories. Both, D'Agosta mused, must have killer views of the Hudson River and, in the other direction, the skyline of Lower Manhattan.

D'Agosta had called ahead to say they were coming to see Anton Ozmian, and that they had information about his daughter. Now, as they entered the underground parking garage below the DigiFlood tower, the parking attendant who spoke to Proctor indicated a space directly next to the booth, marked OZMIAN 1. Even before they were out of the car, a man in a dark-gray suit appeared.

"Gentlemen?" He came forward, not shaking hands, all business. "May I please see your credentials?"

Pendergast removed his shield and flipped it open, and D'Agosta did the same. The man scrutinized each one without touching them.

"My driver will stay with the car," said Pendergast.

"Very well. This way, gentlemen."

D'Agosta mused that, if the man was surprised to see a cop and an FBI agent arrive in a Rolls, he gave no sign of it.

They followed him into a private elevator adjacent to the parking space, which their escort operated with a key. With a whoosh of cushioned air the elevator rose precipitously, and within a minute it had reached the top floor. The doors whispered open, and they stepped into what was obviously the executive suite. The decorating scheme, D'Agosta saw, was frosted glass, honed black granite, and brushed titanium. The space was Zen-like in its emptiness. The man walked briskly and they followed him across a large waiting area, curved like the bridge of a spaceship, that led to a central pair of birchwood doors that slipped open noiselessly as they approached. Beyond lay a set of outer offices, staffed by men and women dressed in what D'Agosta took to be Silicon Valley casual chic—the black T-shirts and linen jackets with skinny jeans and those Spanish shoes that were all the rage—what were they called? Pikolinos.

Finally they arrived at what D'Agosta guessed was the entrepreneur's lair itself: another pair of soaring birchwood doors, these so large that a smaller door had been set into one of them for normal comings and goings.

"Gentlemen, please wait here a moment." The man slipped through the smaller door and closed it behind him.

D'Agosta glanced at Pendergast. They could hear, beyond the door, a muffled voice raised in controlled anger. D'Agosta couldn't catch the words but the meaning was pretty clear—some poor bastard was getting his ass reamed out. The voice rose and fell, as if cataloging a list of grievances. Then there was a sudden silence.

A moment later the door opened. A man emerged—silver-haired, tall, handsome, impeccably dressed—blubbering like a baby, his face wet with tears.

"Remember, I'm holding you responsible!" a voice called after him from the office beyond. "We're bleeding proprietary code all over the Internet, thanks to this goddamned insider leak. You find the bastard responsible, or it's your ass!"

The man stumbled blindly past and disappeared into the waiting area.

D'Agosta gave another glance at Pendergast to see his reaction, but there was none; his face was as blank as usual. He was glad to see the agent back in form, at least superficially, his finely chiseled face so pale that it might have been crafted from marble, his eyes especially bright in the cool wash of natural light that filled the space. He was, however, as thin as a damn scarecrow.

The sight of a man reduced to such misery made D'Agosta a little nervous, and he gave himself a quick mental once-over. Since his marriage, his wife, Laura Hayward, had made sure he bought double-breasted suits from only the better Italian clothiers—Brioni, Ravazzolo, Zegna—along with shirts of cotton lawn from Brooks Brothers. The only nod to a uniform was a single lieutenant's bar pinned to his lapel. Laura, it had to be said, had really straightened up his act regarding clothing, throwing out all his brown polyester suits. He found that dressing like a million bucks made him feel secure, even if his colleagues joked with him that the double-breasted look gave him the air of a Mafioso. That sort of pleased him, actually. He just had to be careful not to show up his boss, Captain Glen Singleton, who was known throughout the NYPD as a natty dresser.

Their escort reappeared. "Mr. Ozmian will see you now."

They followed him through the door into a large—yet not cavernous—corner office, looking south and west. The cool, elegant flanks of the Freedom Tower filled one of the windows, seemingly so close D'Agosta could almost touch it. A man came around from behind a black granite desk, which looked like slabs of stone stacked as if for a tomb. He was thin, tall, and ascetic, very handsome, with black hair graying at the temples, a close-cropped salt-and-pepper beard, and steel-rimmed glasses. He wore a white cable-knit turtleneck of thick cashmere, black jeans, and black shoes. The monochromatic effect was dramatic. He didn't look like a man who had just handed someone his ass on a platter. But he didn't look all that friendly, either.

"About time," he said, pointing to a sitting area to one side of the desk, not as a gesture of offering but as an order. "My daughter has been gone for four days. And *finally* I'm graced with a visit from the authorities. Sit down and tell me what's going on."

D'Agosta glanced at Pendergast and saw he was not going to sit down.

"Mr. Ozmian," Pendergast said. "When did you last see your daughter?"

"I'm not going over all this yet again. I've told the story over the phone half a dozen—"

"Just two questions, please. When did you last see your daughter?"

"At dinner. Four nights ago. She went out afterward with friends. Never came home."

"And you called the police when, exactly?"

Ozmian sighed. "The following morning, around ten."

"Weren't you accustomed to her coming in late?"

"Not *that* late. What exactly..."

The man's expression changed. He must, D'Agosta thought, have seen something in their faces. This guy was sharp as a tack. "What is it? You've found her?"

D'Agosta took a deep breath and was about to speak when Pendergast, to his great surprise, beat him to it.

"Mr. Ozmian," said Pendergast, in his quietest, smoothest voice, "we have bad news: your daughter is dead."

The man looked as if he'd just been shot. He actually staggered and had to grip the side of a chair in order to keep himself upright. His face instantly drained of all color; his lips moved, but only an unintelligible whisper came out. He was like a dead man standing.

He swayed again and D'Agosta took a step over to him, grasping his arm and shoulder. "Sir, let's sit down."

The man nodded mutely and allowed himself to be steered into a chair. He felt as light as a feather in D'Agosta's grasp.

Ozmian's lips formed the word *how*, but with only a rush of air coming out.

"She was murdered," said Pendergast, his voice still very quiet. "Her body was found last night in an abandoned garage in Queens. We were able to make an identification this morning. We are here now because we wanted you to hear officially before the newspapers break the story—as they will at any moment." Despite the baldness of his words, Pendergast's voice managed to convey a depth of compassion and sorrow.

Again, the man's lips moved. "Murdered?" came the single strangled word.

"Yes."

"How?"

"She was shot through the heart. Death was instantaneous."

"Shot? *Shot?*" The color was starting to come back into his face.

"We will know more in a few days. I'm afraid you have the task of identifying the body. We will of course be glad to escort you there."

The man's face was full of confusion and horror. "But...*murdered*? Why?"

"The investigation is only a few hours old. It appears she was killed four days ago and her body left in the garage."

Now Ozmian grasped the sides of his chair and rose again to his feet. His face had gone from white to pink and was now turning a fiery red. He stood there for a moment, looking from Pendergast to D'Agosta and back again. D'Agosta could see he was recovering his wits; he sensed the guy was about to explode.

"You," he began. "You bastards."

Silence.

"Where was the FBI these past four days? This was your fault—*your fault!*" His voice, starting out in a whisper, crescendoed by the end into a roar, spittle flecking his lips.

Pendergast interrupted him very quietly. "Mr. Ozmian, she was probably already dead when you reported her missing. But I can assure you that everything was done to find her. Everything."

"Oh, you bungling dickheads always say that, you lying sons of—" His voice choked up, and it was almost as if he'd swallowed too large a piece of food; he coughed and spluttered, face turning purple. With a roar of fury he took a step forward, seized a heavy sculpture from a nearby glass table, raised it, and slammed it onto the floor. Swaying, he shambled to a whiteboard and knocked it aside, kicked over a lamp, and grabbed some kind of award made of ceramic from his own desk and heaved it down on the glass table; both shattered with a terrific crash, sending up a spray of glass splinters and clay chips that fell back like rain onto the granite floor.

At this, their escort in the dark-gray suit came running in. "What's going on?" he asked wildly, stunned to see the ruin strewn across the office and his boss so unmanned. He looked frantically at Ozmian, then at Pendergast and D'Agosta.

His entrance seemed to trigger something in Ozmian and he halted his rampage, standing in the middle of the room, breathing hard. His forehead had been nicked by a piece of flying glass, and a dot of blood oozed from the wound.

"Mr. Ozmian—?"

Ozmian turned to the man and spoke, his voice hoarse but calm. "Get out. Lock the door. Find Isabel. Nobody comes in but her."

"Yes, sir." He almost ran out.

Ozmian suddenly burst into tears, racked by hysterical sobs. D'Agosta, after hesitating, finally stepped forward and grasped his arm, again helping him to sit down in the chair, where he crumpled up, hugging himself and rocking back and forth, sobbing and gasping.

A minute or two later, he began to pull out of it. He jerked a handkerchief from his pocket, carefully wiped his face, and collected himself for a long moment, sitting in silence.

In a flat voice, he spoke. "Tell me everything."

D'Agosta cleared his throat and took over. He explained how two kids had found the body in the garage, hidden in leaves, and how the homicide division jumped on it. He had put on a full CSU team, headed by the best in the business, and he described how more than forty detectives were now working the case. The entire homicide division was giving this its highest priority, with the full cooperation of the FBI. He laid it on as thick as he dared as the man listened, face bowed.

"Do you have any theories about who did it?" he asked when D'Agosta was done.

"Not yet, but we will. We're going to find the person who did this; you have my word." He faltered, wondering how he was going to tell him about the decapitation. He couldn't quite seem to work in that detail, but before this meeting was over he knew that he had to; the newspapers would be full of it. And, most awful of all, the man would be asked to identify a headless body—the body of his daughter. They knew it was her from the fingerprints, but the physical ID process was still the law, even if, in this case, it seemed unnecessary and cruel.

"After you identify the body," D'Agosta went on, "if you feel able, we would like to interview you—the sooner the better. We'll need to learn about her acquaintances that you know of, names and contact info; we'll want to hear about any difficulties in her life, or in your business or personal life—anything that might possibly connect to the killing. As unpleasant as all these questions will be, I'm sure you understand why we have to ask them. The more we know, the sooner we'll catch the person or persons responsible. Naturally you may have an attorney present if you wish, but it's not necessary."

Ozmian hesitated. "Now?"

"We'd prefer to interview you up at Police Plaza, if you don't mind. After you've…made the identification. Perhaps later this afternoon, if you feel capable?"

"Look, I…I'm ready to help. Murdered…Oh, God help me…"

"There's one other thing," said Pendergast in a low voice that instantly caused Ozmian to pause. The tycoon raised his face from his hands and looked at Pendergast, fear in his eyes.

"What?" he asked.

"You should be prepared to identify your daughter by bodily

markings—dermatological peculiarities, tattoos, surgical scars. Or by means other than her body. Her clothing and possessions, for example."

Ozmian blinked. "I don't understand."

"Your daughter was found decapitated. We...have not yet recovered the head."

Ozmian stared at Pendergast for a long moment. Then his eyes swiveled over, seeking out D'Agosta.

"*Why?*" he whispered.

"That is a question we would like very much to answer," said Pendergast.

Ozmian remained sunken in the chair. Finally he said: "Give the address of the morgue to my assistant on the way out and the location where you wish to question me. I'll be there at two PM."

"Very well," said Pendergast.

"Now leave me."

5

Marc Cantucci jerked awake just as the airplane in his dream was about to plunge into the ocean. He lay there in the dark, his racing heart slowing as the familiar and comfortable surroundings of his bedroom took shape around him. He was damn tired of this same dream, in which he was in a jet hijacked by terrorists. They had invaded the cockpit and locked the door, and moments later the plane violently nosed down and went into a sickening plunge under full power toward the distant stormy sea, while out of his window he watched the black water rushing closer and closer, knowing the end was inevitable.

He lay in bed, wondering if he should turn on the light and read for a bit, or try to go back to sleep. What time was it? The room was very dark and the steel shutters on the windows were down, making it impossible to get a sense of the hour. He reached for his cell phone, which he kept on his bedside table. Where the hell was it? He couldn't have forgotten to leave it there; his habits were as regular as a clock. But maybe he had, because it sure as hell wasn't at hand.

Now too irritated to sleep, he sat up and turned on the bedside light, looking around for the phone. He threw off the covers, got out of bed, examined the floor around the table where it might have fallen, and finally went over to the wooden valet rack where he had hung his pants and jacket. A quick check showed it wasn't there, either. This was becoming more than annoying.

He didn't keep a bedside clock, but the alarm system had an LCD clock on it, so he went over and slid open the panel. And now he had a most unpleasant surprise: the panel was dark, the LCD screen blank, the alarm-activated light off. And yet the power in the house was on and the CCTV system, beside the alarm panel, was still working. Very strange.

For the first time, Cantucci felt a twinge of fear. The alarm system was the latest and best money could buy; it not only was hardwired into the house but had its own power supply and no less than two backups in case of power failures or technical problems, along with landline, cellular, and satphone connections to the off-site alarm company.

But here it was—not working.

Cantucci, the former New Jersey AG who had brought down the Otranto crime family before turning mob lawyer himself for the rival Bonifacci family, and who had received more blood-oaths of vengeance than he could count, was naturally concerned about his security.

The CCTV screen was working just fine, doing its usual thing, automatically cycling through all the cameras in the building. There were twenty-five of them, five for each floor of the brownstone in which he lived in, by himself, on East Sixty-Sixth Street. He had a bodyguard who stayed in the house with him during the day, but the man left when the steel shutters automatically descended at seven every evening, turning the house into an impregnable mini-fortress.

As he watched the cameras cycle through each floor, he suddenly saw something bizarre. Punching a key to stop the cycling, he looked at the image with horror. The camera in question covered the main front hallway of the house—and it revealed an intruder. It was a man, dressed in a black leotard, with a black mask over his face. He was carrying a compound bow with four feathered arrows racked in it. A fifth arrow was fitted into the bow and he carried it ahead of him, as if ready to shoot. The bastard looked as if he thought he was Batman and Robin Hood rolled into one.

This was just fucking crazy. How did the guy get past the steel shutters? And how did he get in without setting off the alarm?

Cantucci punched the instant-alarm panic button, but of course it didn't work. And his cell phone was gone—a coincidence? He reached for a nearby landline phone and put the receiver to his ear. Dead.

As the man moved out of the camera's field of view, Cantucci quickly punched in the next camera. At least the CCTV was working.

Now that he thought of it, he wondered why the man hadn't disabled that, as well.

The figure was heading for the elevator. As Cantucci watched, the figure paused before it, then reached out a black-gloved hand and pushed a button. Cantucci heard the mechanism hum as the elevator descended from its position on the fifth floor, where his bedroom was, to the first.

Cantucci immediately mastered his fright. Six attempts had been made on his life; all had failed. This one was the craziest yet, and it would fail, too. The electricity was still on; he could freeze the elevator with the push of a button, leaving the man trapped—but no. *No.*

Moving fast, Cantucci whipped on a bathrobe, opened his bed-side drawer, and took out a Beretta M9 and an extra fifteen-round magazine, which he dropped into the pocket of the robe. The gun already had a full magazine with a round in the chamber—he kept it that way—but he checked anyway. All good.

He quietly but swiftly passed out of the bedroom into the nar-row hall beyond and positioned himself in front of the elevator. It was now rising again. He could hear the clinking and humming of the machinery, and the elevator numbers lit up, showing what floor it was on: three...four...five...

He waited, in firing-ready position, until he heard the elevator shudder to a stop. And then, before the doors could open, he fired into them, the heavy 9mm Parabellum rounds punching through the thin steel with plenty of killing power left on the other side, the noise deafening in the enclosed space. He counted the rounds as he fired, rapidly but accurately—one, two, three, four, five, six—moving in a pattern across and down that would be sure to hit anyone inside. He had plenty of rounds left to finish the job once the doors opened.

The doors slid open. To Cantucci's great shock, the elevator was empty. He ducked inside, firing a couple of rounds upward through the elevator ceiling just to make sure the man wasn't hid-ing up there, and then he punched the STOP button, holding the elevator on that floor so it could no longer be used.

Son of a bitch. The only other way for the killer to get up to his floor was by the stairs. The man had a bow and arrow. Cantucci, on the other hand, had a handgun—and he was an expert in its use. He made a quick decision: *Don't wait, go on the attack.* The stairs were narrow, with a landing between each floor—a poor en-vironment to get off an arrow shot, but ideal for handgun use at close quarters.

Of course it was possible the intruder had a gun, as well, but he sure as hell seemed intent on using his bow. In any case, Cantucci would take no chances.

Firearm at the ready, he raced down the stairs in his bare feet, making almost no noise, ready to fire. But by the time he'd descended as far as the second floor, he realized the man wasn't on the stairs at all. He must've come up, then exited onto one of the lower floors. But which one? Where the fuck was he?

Cantucci exited the stairwell at the second floor and, covering the corners, went into the hall. It was clear. One end opened through an archway to the living room; the other ended in a closed bathroom door.

He quickly checked the CCTV screen in the hall, fast-forwarding through the cameras. There he was! On the third floor, one above, sneaking down the hallway toward the music room. What was he doing? Cantucci would have thought he was dealing with a madman, except this intruder was moving deliberately—as if he had some sort of plan. But what? Was he going to steal the Strad?

Christ, that was it. *That must be it.*

His most prized possession: the 1696 *L'Amoroso* Stradivarius violin that had once been owned by the Duke of Wellington. That, and his life, were the two reasons Cantucci had installed such an elaborate security system in his brownstone.

He watched as the figure moved into the music room and shut the door behind him. Punching the button for the camera inside the room, Cantucci watched the figure move toward the safe that held the Strad. How was he planning to get into the safe? The damn thing was supposedly unbreakable. But of course the bastard had already overcome a sophisticated alarm system; Cantucci knew better than to assume anything.

Obviously the intruder had heard the shots: he must know Cantucci was armed and looking for him. So what was he thinking? None of this made any sense. He watched him stop at the safe, reach out, and punch in some numbers on the keypad. The wrong numbers, evidently. Now he took out a little silver box—some sort of electronic device—and affixed it to the front of the safe. In doing so, he laid down the bow and arrow.

Now was his chance. Cantucci knew where the man was and where he would be for at least the next few minutes, and he knew the bow and arrow were not in his hands. The man would be busy with that metal device and the safe.

Moving silently, Cantucci climbed the stairs to the third floor, peered around the corner, and saw that the door to the music room was still shut, the intruder inside. Sneaking along the carpeted hallway in his bare feet, he paused at the closed door. He could throw it open and gun the man down long before the would-be thief could pick up that ridiculous bow and arrow and let one loose at him.

In one smooth, purposeful motion he grasped the knob with his left hand, threw open the door, and burst inside, gun up and aimed at the safe.

Nobody. Room empty.

Cantucci froze, realizing instantly that he had fallen into some sort of trap, then pivoted around, firing madly into the room behind him, even as the arrow came flashing through the air, striking his chest and slamming him into the wall. A second and third arrow, fired in rapid sequence, pinned his body firmly to the wall—three arrows spaced in a triangular pattern piercing the heart.

The intruder, who had been positioned in the open door of the room across the hall, walked forward and stopped two feet from the victim, held upright by the three arrows, his head flopped forward, arms drooped. The killer reached out and turned on the light in the hall. He leaned the bow up against the wall and looked the victim over, slowly and with deliberation, from head to foot. Then he grasped the victim's sagging head in both hands. He raised it and looked into the staring—but unseeing—eyes. With one thumb he pushed up the victim's top lip, turned the head slightly, briefly examining the teeth, which were white and straight and free of cavities. The haircut was expensive, the skin of the face smooth and tight. For a sixty-five-year-old man, Cantucci had taken very good care of himself.

The intruder released the head, letting it fall forward. He was well satisfied.

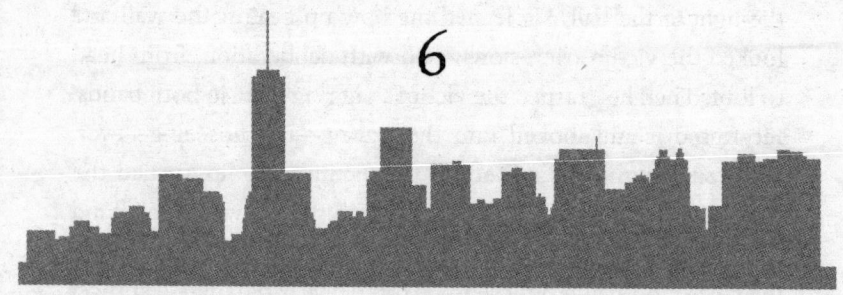

6

AT FOUR O'CLOCK the following afternoon, Lieutenant CDS Vincent D'Agosta sat in Video Room B205 at One Police Plaza, sipping a cup of burnt, sludgy, stone-cold coffee and watching a blurry video recording from a security camera that overlooked the industrial lot in Queens where the body was found. It was the last of three lousy security camera feeds he had spent two hours going through, with no results. He should have assigned this one to a subordinate, but a part of him hated to inflict scut work on his people.

He heard a tapping on the open door and turned to see the tall, athletic figure of his superior, Captain Singleton, dressed in a sleek blue suit, his prominent ears sticking out, silhouetted in the dim light of the corridor. He was holding two cans of beer.

"Vinnie, who you trying to impress?" he asked, coming in.

D'Agosta paused the video and sat back, rubbing his face.

Singleton slid into a nearby seat and set one of the cans down in front of D'Agosta. "That coffee should be arrested and searched. Try this instead."

D'Agosta grasped the ice-cold can of beer, pulled the tab, which

made a welcoming hiss, and raised it. "Much obliged, Captain."
He took a long, grateful pull.

Singleton sat down and opened his own beer. "So what you
got?"

"As far as the security videos, nada. There's a major dead zone
between these three cameras and I'm pretty sure that's where the
action took place."

"Got any footage on the surrounding neighborhood?"

"This is it. Mostly residential—the closest store was a block
away."

Singleton nodded. "Anything to connect this killing with last
night's? The mob lawyer, Cantucci?"

"Other than the decapitation, nothing. The MOs in the two
cases are totally different. Different weapons, different mode of
ingress and egress. Nothing to connect the victims. And in the
Ozmian case, the head was taken twenty-four hours after the victim was killed, while with Cantucci it was cut off immediately
after the victim expired."

"So you don't think they're related?"

"Probably not, but two decapitations back-to-back are a weird
coincidence. I'm not ruling anything out."

"How about the security feeds from Cantucci's place?"

"Nothing. They weren't just erased—the hard disks were
taken. Cameras outside the house and on both corners of Third
Avenue were disabled ahead of time. The guy who did Cantucci
was a pro."

"A pro using a bow and arrow?"

"Yeah. Could be a mob hit, meant to send some kind of message. This Cantucci was a real scumbag. Here's a guy who
brought down one family as AG and then went to work for a
rival. He's dirtier than the wiseguys he defended, twice as rich,

and three times smarter. He had more than his share of enemies. We're working on that."

"And the Ozmian victim?"

"A wild kid. We had the CSU go over her room in her father's place, just as a precaution—nothing useful. And we're checking on her fast-living friends, but no leads so far. We're still probing."

Singleton grunted.

"Autopsy confirmed she was shot through the heart from behind, remained in an unknown location long enough to bleed out, and was then moved to the garage, where the head was taken about twenty-four hours later. We've got a ton of hair, fiber, and latents we're working through, but I have a feeling none are going to pan out."

"And the father?"

"Supersmart. Vindictive. Total asshole. He's got a crazy temper, screams and yells and smashes stuff, then suddenly goes quiet—scary." The man had been so quiet when he'd come to identify the body the previous afternoon—from a mole on her left arm—it had creeped D'Agosta out. "I wouldn't be surprised if he's got his people out there, quietly looking for the killer. I sure hope we get the guy first. Because if Ozmian's people find him before we do, I fear the perp might disappear and we'll never clear the case."

"Isn't he grieving?"

"Sure. In his own way. If his personal life is anything like his business life, seems to me his way of grieving would be to find the perp, whittle him alive, then make a bow tie out of his junk and hang him with it."

Singleton winced, took another sip. "A billionaire vigilante. God save us." He glanced at D'Agosta. "Any connection to the father's business interests? You know, kill the daughter to get revenge on the father?"

"We're looking into that. He's been involved in a bunch of law-suits, gotten his share of death threats. These dot-com people are like Vikings."

Singleton grunted and they sat in silence for a few moments, thinking. This was Singleton's way of managing a case, to sit down late at night when the place was quiet and they could just shoot the breeze. It was why he was such a good cop and a great guy to work for. At last, he shifted in his seat. "You know this guy Harriman from the *Post* who's been poking around, asking questions, harassing my guys? Is he any good?"

"He's a prick, but he gets the story."

"That's too bad. Because this is already big and it's only going to get bigger."

"Yeah."

"And the FBI? What's their agenda—and how'd they decide it was a federal case?"

"I can work with them—don't worry."

"Glad to hear it." Singleton rose. "Vinnie, you're doing a fine job. Keep it up. Any support I can give, anyone you think needs a swift kick in the ass, you let me know."

"Sure thing, Captain."

Singleton left. D'Agosta tossed his empty beer can into the trash with regret and went back to the endlessly boring video feed.

7

LIEUTENANT D'AGOSTA PARKED his squad car in the taped-off area in front of the town house. He got out of the car, his associate Sergeant Curry emerging from the other side. D'Agosta took a moment to look up at the town house, built in pink granite, occupying the middle of a quiet block between Second and Third Avenues, lined with leafless ginkgo trees. The victim, Cantucci, had been the worst kind of mob lawyer there was, slippery as an eel. He'd been in their crosshairs for two decades, subjected to several grand jury proceedings—and they'd never even been able to take away his license to practice at the bar. He was one of the untouchables.

Except he'd gotten touched now—big time. And D'Agosta wondered just how the hell the killer had penetrated the town house's formidable security.

He shook his head and walked through the darkness of the December evening and up to the front door. Curry held the door open and D'Agosta entered the foyer, looking around. It was some house, filled with rare antiques, paintings, and Persian rugs. He caught the faint scent of the various chemicals and solvents used by the CSU team. But their work was now complete, and he wouldn't have to put on the usual booties, hair covering, and gown, for which D'Agosta was grateful as he breathed in the stifling air, the town house's metal shutters still closed.

"All ready for the walk-through, sir?" asked Curry.

"Where's the security consultant? He was supposed to meet me here."

A man materialized from the shadows, African American, small, white hair, wearing a blue suit and carrying himself in a gravely dignified manner. He was said to be one of the top experts in electronic security in the city, and D'Agosta was surprised to see he looked at least seventy years old.

He offered a cool hand. "Jack Marvin," he said, his voice deep, like a preacher's.

"Lieutenant D'Agosta. So tell me, Mr. Marvin—how'd the son of a bitch get through this million-dollar security system?"

Marvin chuckled ghoulishly. "Very cleverly. Would you care for a tour?"

"Sure."

Marvin set off, moving briskly down the central corridor, D'Agosta and Curry following. D'Agosta wondered why the hell Pendergast hadn't shown up here in response to his request. This was just the kind of case that would fascinate him, and given the rivalry between the NYPD and the FBI, D'Agosta thought he'd been doing the agent a favor by extending him an invitation. But then, on the other hand, Pendergast had shown little interest in the case so far—just look at how reluctant he'd been to visit Ozmian.

"What we have in this house," Marvin said, his hands moving constantly, "is a Sharps and Gund security system. Sharps and Gund is beyond state-of-the-art, the best there is. Favored by Persian Gulf oil tycoons and Russian oligarchs." He paused. "There are twenty-five cameras distributed through the house. One there—" he pointed to an upper corner— "there, there, and there." His finger moved swiftly. "Every square inch covered."

He stopped and turned, sweeping his hands to one side and then the other, like a tour guide in some historic mansion. "And here we've got an IR break-beam fence, with motion detectors in the corners, up there and there."

His gesture swept around to the elevator door, and he pressed the button. "The heart of the system is in the attic, in a reinforced locker."

The elevator door—riddled with bullet holes—slid open, and they crowded in.

The elevator hummed its way up to the fifth floor and the doors reopened. Marvin stepped out. "Cameras here, here, and over there. More IR break-beams, motion detectors, pressure-plate sensors in the floor. Bedroom's through that door."

He pirouetted. "The front door and all windows are alarmed, and at sunset the place is sealed with steel shutters. The system has multiple redundancies. It's normally powered by household current, with two independent sources of backup, a generator and a bank of deep-cycle marine batteries. It has three independent reporting methods to live operators standing by: via phone through the household landline, again through a cellular connection, and again through a satphone. Even if nothing happens, the system is designed to report a fair-weather signal every hour."

D'Agosta gave a low whistle. He couldn't wait to hear how this system was defeated.

"The system reports all anomalies. If a battery gets low, it reports. Power failure, it reports. Cellular interference, it reports.

Lightning strike, power surge, spider building a web on an IR detector, it reports. Sharps and Gund has its own security teams that it dispatches, in case the police are slow or tied up."

"Looks impregnable."

"Doesn't it, now? But like everything else ever designed by man, it just so happens to have an Achilles' heel."

D'Agosta was getting tired standing on his feet in the dark hall. An elegant sitting room with comfortable chairs beckoned at the end of the hall, and he'd been up for hours after less than ninety minutes' sleep. "Shall we?" He motioned with his hand.

"I was planning on taking you to the attic. Here are the stairs."

D'Agosta and Curry followed the spry man to a set of narrow stairs, which led into a half-height attic. When Marvin switched on the light, D'Agosta saw a space filled with dust and smelling of mildew. The air was stifling, and they had to crouch low.

"Over here," Marvin said, pointing to a large, new metal cabinet, with the door open. "This is the central control of the security system. It's essentially a large safe. No way to get in unless you have the code—and our perp did not have the code."

"So how'd he get in?"

"Trojan horse."

"Meaning?"

"The Sharps and Gund system is famous for being impervious to computer hacking. They accomplish this by partially isolating each security system from the Internet. You can't transmit data into the system, ever. Not even the Sharps and Gund main office can transmit data to a security system. The security system is designed to send data only one way: *out*. Hackers cannot get in remotely."

"So what if the system needs to be updated or reset?"

"A service technician has to physically go to the location,

open the safe with a code that not even the owner has—that not even the *technician* has, it's generated by a randomizer at the main office and orally transmitted to the tech when he's on-site—and download new data into the system with a direct connection."

D'Agosta shifted, trying not to bump his head against the ceiling. He could see a pair of rat's eyes gleaming in a corner, peering at them. Even in a twenty-million-dollar house, you got rats. He wished Marvin would hurry up and get to the point.

"All right, so how'd the perp get around all this?"

"The first thing he did a few days ago. Out on the street in front of the house, he used a blocking device to interrupt the hourly fair-weather reports of the cellular. He could do this from a parked car, with a fairly inexpensive electromagnetic jammer. Just a couple of random bursts of interference that blocked the cellular signal a few times. It fooled Sharps and Gund into thinking the unit was going bad and needed to be replaced. So they sent two guys—always two guys—out with a new unit. Normally they double-park and one guy stays with the van. But your perp used a couple of traffic cones to snag a really convenient parking space for the van. Just down the street. Very tempting. So they park there and both guys go to the house, leaving the van unprotected for about three minutes."

"You worked this all out?"

"Sure did."

D'Agosta nodded, impressed.

"Your intruder breaks into the truck, gets his hands on the cellular device, swaps out the SD card for one with malware on it, and puts it back. The repairmen return, collect their stuff, go into the house, open the impregnable safe with the code given them from the home office, install the new cellular device, and leave. Then the malware downloads itself into the system and hijacks it. *Totally*. That damn malware unlocked the front door for your killer, then locked it behind him. It turned off the phones. It shut down the IR beams and motion detectors and pressure-plate sensors while leaving the CCTV cameras functioning. It even unlocked the safe so the perp could take the hard drives when he left."

"How could some anonymous perp possibly know enough about the system to create this malware?" D'Agosta asked.

"He couldn't."

"You mean, inside job?"

"Absolutely no question. The intruder must have decompiled the firm's system software in order to write this malware. He knew exactly what he was doing—and he knew the company's proprietary way of doing business. There's no doubt in my mind that an S and G employee or ex-employee was involved. And not just anyone, but someone with a deep familiarity with the installation process—of *this* particular system."

This was a damn good lead. But this attic was getting to D'Agosta. He was bathed in sweat and the air was stifling. He couldn't wait to get back out into the December cold. "Say, are we done up here?"

"I think so." But instead of moving toward the stairs, Marvin lowered his voice. "Got to tell you, though, Lieutenant, when I tried to get a list of present and past S and G employees, I hit a stone wall. The CEO, Jonathan Ingmar, is a first-class obstructionist—"

"Let us handle that, Mr. Marvin." D'Agosta fairly guided him by the shoulders to the staircase. They descended into the cooler air.

"It's all going in my report," said Marvin. "The technical details, the specs of the system, the works. I'll have it for you tomorrow."

"Thank you, Mr. Marvin. You've done an excellent job."

When they emerged onto the fifth floor, D'Agosta took a number of deep, grateful breaths.

8

Mᴀʀᴛɪɴɪ?"

In the apartment on Fifth Avenue, with its living room over-looking Central Park and the Onassis Reservoir, its surface gleaming in the late-afternoon sun, Bryce Harriman eased himself back on the Louis Quatorze sofa, maintaining a cool demeanor, reporter's notebook resting on his knee. The notebook was, of course, for show only: everything was being recorded on his cell phone, tucked into the breast pocket of his suit.

It was eleven o'clock in the morning. Harriman was used to people breaking out the cocktails before noon—he had grown up with that sort of crowd—but in this case he was working and wanted to keep his wits about him. On the other hand, he could see that Izolda Ozmian, sitting opposite him on a chaise longue, really wanted a drink herself…and that would be something he should encourage.

"I'd love one," Harriman said. "A double, straight up, with a twist. Hendricks, if you have it."

He could already see her face brightening. "I'll have the same."

The tall, stooped, lugubrious butler who'd been waiting for

their order responded with a grave nod and a "Yes, Mrs. Ozmian," before rotating with a distinct creaking noise and disappearing into the recesses of the fantastically vulgar and overfurnished apartment.

Harriman felt a distinct advantage over this woman, and he was going to press it for all it was worth. She was a type he understood, someone pretending to be a member of the upper classes and making a hilarious mess of it. Everything about her, from her dyed hair, to her excessive makeup, to her very real diamond jewelry—in which the diamonds were too large to be elegant—made him want to shake his head. These people never would get it. They never would understand that vulgar diamonds, stretch limos, Botoxed faces, English butlers, and giant houses in the Hamptons were the social equivalent of wearing a sandwich board on which was written:

I AM A NOUVEAU RICHE
TRYING TO APE MY BETTERS
AND I DON'T
HAVE A CLUE

Bryce himself was not nouveau riche. He didn't need diamonds, cars, houses, and butlers to announce that fact. All he needed was his last name: Harriman. Those who knew, knew; and those who didn't weren't worth bothering about.

He had started his journalism career at the *New York Times*, where he worked his way up through sheer talent from the copy desk to the city desk; but a small contretemps involving his reporting of an incident that came to be known as the subway massacre, along with being outreported and outmaneuvered on the story by the late, great, and insufferable William Smithback, had led to his unceremonious dismissal from the *Times*. That had been the most painful period in his life. Tail between his legs, he had slunk over to the *New York Post*. In the end, the move proved to be the best thing to happen to him. The ever-vigilant, ever-restraining editorial hand that had muzzled him at the *Times* was far more relaxed at the *Post*. No longer was someone always looking over his shoulder, cramping his style. There was a sort of a slumming chicness attached to the *Post*'s brand of journalism that, he found, had not hurt him with his people. During his ten years at the paper, he'd risen through the ranks to being a star reporter at the city desk.

But ten years was a long time in the newspaper business, and his career had been sputtering of late. For all his feelings of condescension as he looked at this woman, he was still aware of a certain frisson of desperation. He hadn't broken a big story in a long time, and he was starting to feel the hot breath of his younger colleagues on his neck. He needed something big—and he needed it now. And this, he felt, might just be it. He had the knack of sniffing out a certain kind of story, talking his way into seeing a certain kind of people. And that included the woman sitting across from him: Izolda Ozmian, former "fashion" model, social clawer-upper, gold digger par excellence, ex-trophy-wife to the great Anton Ozmian, who in her nine months of connubial bliss had earned herself ninety million dollars in a famous divorce trial. That, Bryce noted privately, came out to $10 million a month, or $333,000 a fuck, assuming they made the beast with two backs once daily, which was a generous estimate, considering Ozmian was one of those dot-com workaholics who practically slept in the office.

Bryce knew his instincts for a story were sharp, and this had all the makings of a good one. But these days he had to worry about his compatriots at the *Post*, those hungry young Turks who would like nothing more than to see him dethroned. He'd had no luck getting in to see Ozmian—which he'd expected—and the cops were being unusually tight-lipped. But he'd had no trouble getting in to see Izolda. Ozmian's second wife was famously bitter and vindictive, and he had a strong sense that here was the mother lode, all tied up in a vicious and beautiful package, waiting to unload a bargeful of trash.

"Well, Mr. Harriman," said Izolda, with a coquettish smile, "how can I help you?"

Harriman started off slow and easy. "I'm looking for a little background on Mr. Ozmian and his daughter. You know, just to help paint a picture of them as human beings—after the tragic murder, I mean."

"Human beings?" Izolda repeated, an edge to her voice.

Oh, this is going to be good.

"Yes."

A pause. "Well, I wouldn't exactly characterize them that way."

"I'm sorry?" Bryce asked, feigning dumb ignorance. "What way?"

"As human beings."

Bryce pretended to take a note, giving her time to go on.

"I was such a naive little girl, an innocent model from Ukraine, when I met Ozmian." Her voice had taken on a whiny, self-pitying note. "He swept me off my feet, boy did he ever, with dinners, private jets, five-star hotels, the works." She gave a snort. Her accent had a pleasing susurrus of Slavic overlain with an ugly Queens drawl.

Harriman knew she hadn't just been a fashion model: her graphically nude pictures were still circulating on the web and probably would be until the end of time.

"Oh what a fool I was!" she said, her voice trembling.

At that moment the butler arrived carrying two immense martinis on a silver tray, placing one in front of her and one by Harriman. She seized hers like someone dying of thirst and sucked down half a swimming pool's worth before placing the glass daintily down.

Bryce feigned a sip. He wondered what Ozmian had seen in her. She was, of course, drop-dead gorgeous, thin, athletic, stacked, her body now curled up on the chaise longue like a cat, but there were a lot of beautiful women in the world he could have picked. Why her? Of course, there might have been reasons that only became apparent in the bedroom. As she talked, his mind drifted over various possibilities in that arena.

"I was taken advantage of," she was saying. "I had no idea what I was getting into. He took a sweet foreign girl and crushed her, like that." She picked up a frilly pillow, twisted it in the most alarming way, then tossed it aside. "Just like that!"

"What was the marriage like, exactly?"

"I'm sure you read all about it in the papers."

Indeed he had, and in fact had written quite a bit about it himself. As she well knew. The *Post* had taken her side—everybody hated Anton Ozmian. The man went out of his way to be detested.

"It's always good to hear it directly from the source."

"He had a temper. Oh my gawd, *what* a temper! A week into our marriage—a *week*—he trashed our living room, broke my Swarovski Kris Bear collection, every single one, crunch crunch crunch, just like that. It broke my heart. He was *horribly* abusive."

Bryce remembered the story. That was when Ozmian had discovered she'd been sleeping with her CrossFit trainer as well as an old boyfriend from Ukraine all along, and there was even a suggestion she had done both of them the morning of the wedding. So far, nothing new. She'd tried to claim he beat her up, but that was disproved in court. In the end she sued for divorce and pried ninety million out of his pocket, which was no mean feat, even if he was a decabillionaire.

Bryce leaned forward, his voice full of sympathy. "How terrible that must have been for you."

"Right from the start I should have guessed, when my little Poufie bit him the first time she met him. And then—"

"I wonder," he continued gently, steering the conversation, "if you could tell me something about his relationship with his daughter, Grace."

"Well, you know she was from the first wife. She wasn't mine, *that's* for sure. *Grace*—what a name!" She gave a poisonous laugh. "She and Ozmian had a close relationship. They were both cut from the same cloth."

"How close?"

"He spoiled her rotten! She partied all the way through college, only graduating when her father gave a new library to the school. Then she did a two-year Grand Tour of the Continent, sleeping her way from one Eurotrash bedroom to the next. Spent a year clubbing in Ibiza. Then she was back in America, burning through Daddy's money, supporting half of Colombia's gross national product, I'm sure."

This was new. During the divorce, the daughter had been more or less off limits to the press. Even the *Post* wouldn't drag a kid into a divorce like that. But she was dead now, and Harriman could feel his reportorial radar starting to ping big time.

"Are you saying she had drug issues?"

"Issues? She was an addict!"

"Just a user, or a genuine addict?"

"Two times in rehab, that celebrity place in Rancho Santa Fe, what was it called? 'The Road Less Traveled.'" She gave another derisive snort of laughter.

The martini was gone and the butler brought her another unasked, whisking away the empty glass.

"And what drug was at issue here? Cocaine?"

"Everything! And Ozmian just let her do it! Enabler of the worst kind. Terrible father."

Now Harriman came to the crux of the matter. "Do you know, Ms. Ozmian, of anything in Grace's past that might have led to her murder?"

"A girl like that *always* comes to a bad end. I worked my butt off in Ukraine, I got myself to New York, no drugs, no alcohol, ate healthy salads without dressing, worked out two hours a day, slept ten hours a night—"

"Was there anything she might have done, such as buying or selling drugs, getting involved with organized crime, or anything else that might have led to her murder?"

"Well, as far as drug dealing, I don't know. But there *was* something in her past. Awful." She hesitated. "I probably shouldn't say—Ozmian made me sign a nondisclosure agreement as part of the divorce settlement..."

Her voice trailed off.

Harriman felt like a prospector whose pick had just glanced off a vein of pure gold. All he had to do was poke around and brush away some dirt. But he played it cool; he had learned that instead of following up with a probing question, the best way to let something like this come out was silence. People felt compelled to talk into a silence. He pretended to look over his notes, waiting for the second double martini to do its work.

"I might as well tell you. *Might as well.* Now that she's gone, I'm sure the NDA is no longer valid, don't you think?"

More silence. Bryce knew enough not to answer a question like that.

"Right at the end of our marriage..." She took a deep breath. "Drunk *and* high, Grace ran over an eight-year-old boy. Put him in a coma. He died two weeks later. Just awful. His parents had to remove him from life support."

"Oh no," said Harriman, genuinely horrified.

"Oh *yes.*"

"And what happened then?"

"Daddy got her off."

"How?"

"Slick lawyer. Money."

"And where did this occur?"

"Beverly Hills. Where else? Had all the records sealed." She paused, finishing her second drink and plunking it down in triumph. "Not that sealing records matters anymore—not for her. Looks like that girl's luck finally ran out."

9

HOWARD LONGSTREET'S OFFICE in the big FBI building on Federal Plaza was exactly as Pendergast remembered it: sparely decorated, lined with books on every imaginable subject—and computerless. A clock on one wall told anyone who was interested that the time was ten minutes to five. With the two dusty wing chairs and small tea table arranged on a hand-knotted Kashan rug in the middle of the room, the space looked more like the parlor of some ancient English gentlemen's club than a law enforcement office.

Longstreet was sitting in one of the wing chairs, the omnipresent Arnold Palmer on a coaster on the table. Shifting his large frame, he ran a hand through his long gray hair, then used the same hand to silently gesture Pendergast to the other seat.

Pendergast sat down. Longstreet took a sip of his drink and replaced the glass on its coaster. He pointedly did not offer one to Pendergast.

The silence stretched on and on before the FBI's executive associate director for intelligence spoke. "Agent Pendergast," he said in a clipped tone, "I'll have your report now. I want to know your opinion, in particular, if the two murders were done by the same person."

"I'm afraid I have nothing to add to the case report you already have on the first homicide."

"And the second?"

"I haven't involved myself with it."

A look of surprise crossed Longstreet's face. "You haven't *involved* yourself? Why the hell not?"

"I didn't receive an order to investigate it. It doesn't appear to be a federal case, sir, unless the two killings are linked."

"Son of a bitch," Longstreet muttered, frowning at Pendergast. "But you're *aware* of the second murder."

"Yes."

"And you don't think they're linked?"

"I prefer not to speculate."

"*Speculate*, damn it! Are we dealing with one killer—or two?"

Pendergast crossed one leg over another. "I will review the options. One, the same killer did both; a third would define him as a serial killer. Two, the killer of the first victim dumped the body, and the head was removed by an unrelated party who then went on to try his own hand at a murder-decapitation. Three, the second murder was a simple copycat effort imitating the first. Fourth, the killings are entirely unrelated, the two decapitations coincidental. Fifth—"

"That's enough!" Longstreet said, raising his voice.

"My apologies, sir."

Longstreet took a sip of his drink, put it down, and sighed. "Look, Pendergast—Aloysius—I'd be lying if I told you I didn't assign you that first murder as a form of punishment for your rogue performance on the Halcyon Key case last month. But I'm willing to bury the hatchet. Because, frankly, I need your peculiar talents on this case. It's already blowing up, as you surely know from the papers."

Pendergast did not reply.

"It's vital we find out the connection between these two homicides—if there is one—or conversely prove there's no link. If we're dealing with a serial killer, this could be the start of something really terrible. And serial killers are your specialty. The problem is, despite the noise we made about the first body being brought in from Jersey and dumped in Queens, there's really no proof it was an interstate crime—making our investigation delicate in terms of protocol. I can't officially involve anybody else from our office—not until the NYPD asks for help, and you know that won't happen unless terrorism is involved. So I need you to get in there and take a close, hard look at the second homicide. If this is the work of a nascent serial killer, I want to know. If it's two separate killers, then we can back off and let the NYPD handle it."

"I understand, sir."

"Will you please quit with the 'sir' business?"

"Very well."

"I know Captain Singleton, he's a stand-up guy, but he's not going to tolerate our involvement for long without a clear federal mandate. I also know you have a long history with the commanding lieutenant...what's his name? D'Agosta."

Pendergast nodded.

Longstreet gave him a long, appraising gaze. "Get to the scene of that second murder. Figure out if it's the same guy or not—and report back to me."

"Very well." Pendergast prepared to rise.

Longstreet lifted a hand to stop him. "I can see you're not your usual self. Aloysius, I need you operating at 100 percent of your game. If there's anything that won't allow you to do that, I have to know. Because something about these homicides feels...I don't know... *strange* to me."

"In what way?"

"I can't put my finger on it, but my radar is rarely wrong."

"Understood. You can be assured of my best."

Longstreet sat back, using the raised hand to make a dismissive gesture. Pendergast stood, nodded dispassionately, then turned and left the office.

10

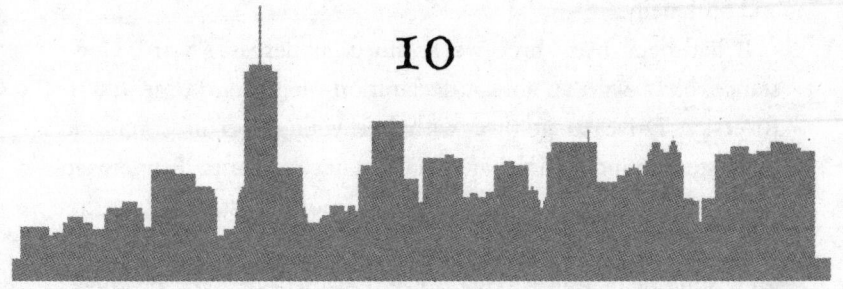

A_N HOUR LATER, Pendergast was back in his set of three adjoining apartments in the Dakota, overlooking Central Park West and West Seventy-Second Street. For several minutes he moved restlessly through the many rooms, picking up an objet d'art and then putting it down, pouring himself a glass of sherry but leaving it forgotten on a sideboard. It was curious, these days, how he found so little pleasure in the diversions that had once offered him interest and reward. The meeting with Longstreet had put him out of sorts—although it was not the meeting, exactly, so much as the probing and irritating comments with which it had ended.

I can see you're not your usual self.

He frowned at the memory. He knew from his Chongg Ran training that the thoughts you most try to banish are the ones that most persistently push themselves back in. The best way to not think of something is to possess it fully, and then cultivate indifference.

Moving from the more public spaces of the apartment to the private, he wandered into the kitchen, where he had a brief discussion in ASL with his deaf housekeeper, Miss Ishimura, about that evening's dinner menu. After some back and forth they ultimately agreed on *okonomiyaki* pancakes with yam batter, octopus, and pork belly.

It had been over three weeks since Pendergast's ward, Constance, had—with an abrupt declaration—left their home at 891 Riverside Drive to go live with her young son in a remote monastery in India. In the aftermath of her departure, Pendergast had fallen into a most uncharacteristic emotional state. But as the days and weeks went on, and the voices that sounded in his head grew still one by one, a single voice remained—a voice, he knew, that was at the heart of his strange disquiet.

Can you love me the way I wish you to? The way I need you to?

He pushed this voice away with sudden violence. "I *will* master this," he murmured to himself.

Moving out of the kitchen, he made his way down the hall to a tiny, windowless, ascetic room not unlike a monk's chamber. It contained only a plain wooden desk, unvarnished, and a straight-backed chair. Taking a seat, Pendergast opened the desk's single drawer and, one at a time, carefully took out the three items it contained and placed them on the tabletop: a hardbound notebook; a cameo; and a comb. He sat a moment, looking at each in turn.

And I—I love you. But you made it very clear that you don't return my love.

The notebook was of French make, with an orange cover of Italian leatherette, containing blank sheets of vellum Clairefontaine paper ideal for fountain pens. It was the kind Constance had used exclusively for the last dozen years, ever since the venerable English purveyor of leather-bound journals she always preferred had gone out of business. Pendergast had taken it from her private rooms in the sub-basement below the mansion: it was her most recent journal, left incomplete on her sudden departure for India.

He had not yet opened it.

Next he turned to the antique tortoiseshell comb and the old, elegant cameo in a frame of eighteen-karat yellow gold. The latter had been carved, he knew, from the prized sardonyx of *Cassis madagascariensis*.

Both items had been among Constance's most favored possessions.

Knowing what I know, having said what we've said—continued living under this roof would be intolerable...

Plucking all three from the tabletop, Pendergast exited the room, went down the hall, and opened the unprepossessing door that led into the third and most private of his apartments. Beyond the door was a small room that ended in a *shoji*, a sliding wood-and-rice-paper partition. And beyond the *shoji* was—hidden deep within the massive walls of the old and elegant apartment building—a tea garden, recreated by Pendergast to the most exacting specifications.

He slowly closed the partition behind him, then paused, listening to the soft cooing of doves and inhaling the scent of eucalyptus and sandalwood. Everything—the path of flat stones meandering before him, the dwarf pines, the waterfall, the *chashitsu* or tea-house that lay half-hidden in the greenery ahead—was dappled in hazy, indirect light.

Now he made his way down the path, past the stone lanterns, to the teahouse. Bending low, he entered the dim confines of the *chashitsu*. He closed its *sadouguchi*, carefully set the three items he'd been carrying down to one side, then glanced around, making sure that everything necessary for the tea ceremony—the *mizusashi*, whisks, scoops, brazier, *kama* iron kettle—was in readiness. He set the tea bowl and container of matcha powder in their proper places, then took a seat on the tatami mat. Over the next thirty minutes, he immersed himself completely in the ceremony: ritually cleaning the various utensils; heating the water; warming the *chawan* tea bowl and, after at last scooping hot water into it, whisking in the proper proportion of matcha. Only then, once every last preparation had been completed with almost reverential exactitude, did he taste the tea, taking it in with barely perceptible sips. And as he did so, he allowed himself—for the first time in almost a month—to let the weight of grief and guilt fully occupy his mind, and in so doing, slowly fall away.

At long last, equanimity restored, he carefully and deliberately went through the final steps of the ceremony, re-cleaning the implements and returning them to their proper places. Now he again glanced at the three items he had brought with him. After a moment, he reached for the notebook and—for the first time—opened it at random and allowed himself to read a single paragraph. Instantly, Constance's personality leapt out through her written words: her mordant tone, her cool intelligence, her slightly cynical, slightly macabre world view—all filtered through a nineteenth-century perspective.

He found it a great relief he could now read the journal with a degree of detachment.

He put the journal carefully back beside the comb and the cameo: the simple, spare walls and floor of this *chashitsu* seemed for the time their best home, and perhaps he would return to contemplate them, and their owner, again in the not-too-distant future. But now there were other matters to deal with.

He left the teahouse, walked down the path, exited the garden, and made his way—with a brisk, firm step—down a long series of passages toward the front door of the apartment. As he did so, he slipped his cell phone out of his suit jacket and speed-dialed a number.

"Vincent?" he said. "Meet me at the Cantucci town house, if you please. I'm ready for that walk-through you spoke of."

And then, replacing the phone, he shrugged into a vicuña overcoat and left the apartment.

11

D'AGOSTA WASN'T ALL that thrilled to be back at the Cantucci crime scene in what was practically the middle of the night, even if it was to meet Pendergast, who had finally agreed to examine the place. Sergeant Curry let him in the front door, and a moment later D'Agosta saw Pendergast's huge vintage Rolls glide up to the curb, Proctor at the wheel. The special agent got out.

Pendergast glided past Curry. "Good evening, my dear Vincent."

They started down the hall. "See all these cameras?" D'Agosta asked. "The perp hacked into the security system, bypassed all the alarms."

"I should like to see the report."

"I've got a complete set for you," D'Agosta said. "Forensics, hair and fiber, latents, you name it. Sergeant Curry will give them to you on the way out."

"Excellent."

"Ingress was through the front door," D'Agosta continued. "The hacked security system let him in. The perp moved extensively through the house. Here's the way it played out, as best we understand it. It seems that while the killer was in the entryway, Cantucci wakes up. We think Cantucci goes to the CCTV and sees the guy downstairs. He puts on his bathrobe and gets his gun, a Beretta 9mm. He thinks the guy is coming up on the elevator, so he fires a bunch of rounds through the door when the elevator arrives—but the killer faked him out, sent the elevator up empty. So now Cantucci, probably checking the CCTV again, goes down to the third floor, where the guy is messing around with a safe holding his Stradivarius violin. And that's where Cantucci is ambushed, killed by three arrows fired in quick succession, all three going through the heart. And then the perp decapitates him—practically as the heart stops beating, if the M.E. is to be believed."

"Must have been a rather sanguinary process."

D'Agosta wasn't sure what Pendergast meant by that and let it go. "The perp then goes to the attic, where the safe holding the security system is located, opens it using the hacked code, takes out the hard drives, and leaves. Egress again out the front door. According to our expert, only an employee, or ex-employee, of the company that installed the security system could have pulled this off. It's all in the report."

"Very good. Let us proceed, then. One floor at a time, every room on each floor, please, even those in which nothing occurred."

D'Agosta led Pendergast through the kitchen, then the downstairs sitting room, opening all the closet doors at his request. They climbed the stairs to the second floor, toured that, and then the third. This was where most of the action had taken place. There were two rooms in the back of the narrow town house, and one large sitting room in front.

"The killing occurred at the doorway to the music room," said D'Agosta, indicating the wall where the arrows had struck. There was a broad, thick shower of blood descending from three splintered marks in the paneled wall, and a huge pool of dried blood in the carpet below. Here Pendergast paused, kneeling. Using a penlight, he probed about, once in a while slipping a small test tube out of his suit pocket, plucking something up with tweezers, putting it in, and stoppering the tube. He then examined the rug and the arrow marks with a loupe fixed to one eye. D'Agosta didn't bother to remind him that the CSU team had already fine-combed everything; he had seen Pendergast turn up fresh clues in even the most thoroughly scrubbed crime scene.

Once he had finished going over the immediate area of the murder, Pendergast continued on in silence, making a slow and painstaking exploration of the music room, the safe, and the two other rooms on that floor of the town house. Next, they proceeded to the upper floors, then climbed into the attic. Again, Pendergast got down on his hands and knees among the dust in front of and inside the security safe, plucking and storing evidence in test tubes.

He half rose beneath the low ceiling. "Curious," he murmured, "very curious indeed."

D'Agosta had no idea what he found curious but he knew if he asked, he wouldn't get an answer. "As I said, it had to be someone who worked for Sharps and Gund. The perp knew exactly how the system worked. I mean *exactly*."

"An excellent line of inquiry to follow up. Ah—regarding the other murder, do you have any further revelations about the daughter?"

"Yeah. We managed to get copies of some sealed files from the Beverly Hills PD. She killed a boy while driving under the influence about eighteen months back—hit and run. Ozmian got her off with some mighty fine lawyering. The boy's family took it pretty hard—threats were made."

"Another obvious line for follow-up."

"Of course. The boy's mother committed suicide, the father supposedly moved back east. We're trying to figure out just where he is so we can talk to him."

"You consider him a suspect?"

"He's got a strong motive."

"When did he come east?"

"About six months ago. We're keeping it all under the radar, for obvious reasons, until we locate him."

They descended once again to the first floor, where Pendergast turned to Curry and the small group of police who stood with him. "I'll have a look at those files now, if you please."

Curry pulled an accordion folder out of his briefcase and handed it to Pendergast. The agent promptly sat down in a chair, opened it, and began leafing through it, pulling out files, eye-balling them, putting them back in rapid succession.

D'Agosta glanced covertly at his watch. Ten minutes after twelve. "Um," he said, "that's a pretty big file. Maybe you'd like to take it home with you? It's all yours."

Pendergast looked up, his silvery eyes glittering with annoy-ance. "I wish to make sure I've overlooked nothing before I leave the premises."

"Right, right."

He fell into silence as Pendergast continued shuffling through the papers. Everyone waited with increasing impatience as the minutes ticked by.

Suddenly Pendergast looked up: "Where's Mr. Cantucci's cell phone?"

"It says right there in the report that they didn't find it. Calls roll over to voice mail. The phone is turned off. We don't know where the hell it is."

"It should have been on his bedside table, where the charger was."

"He probably left it somewhere."

"You searched his office?"

"Yes."

"Our Mr. Cantucci has survived two grand jury hearings and he's been subjected to over a dozen search warrants—not to mention countless death threats. He would not let his cell phone out of his sight. Ever."

"Okay. So what're you getting at?"

"The killer took his phone. *Before* he was murdered."

"How do you figure that?"

"The killer came upstairs, took his cell phone from his bedside table while Cantucci was sleeping, then went back downstairs to the first floor."

"That's crazy. If he did that, why the hell didn't he just kill Cantucci right there, in bed?"

"A most excellent question."

"Maybe he took the cell phone off Cantucci *after* he killed him."

"Impossible. Mr. Cantucci would have called nine-one-one on the cell phone when he realized there was an intruder in the house. The conclusion is inescapable that he did not have his phone when he woke and pursued the intruder."

D'Agosta shook his head.

"And there's a second unaddressed mystery here, Vincent."

"Which is?"

"Why did the killer go to great lengths to disable the alarm system, yet fail to shut down the CCTV system?"

"That one's easy," said D'Agosta. "He used the system to locate his victim—to see where Cantucci was in the house."

"But having retrieved the phone, he already knew where his victim was: in bed, sleeping."

That assumed Pendergast was right in his crazy assertion that the killer took the cell phone and then went back downstairs without killing Cantucci immediately. "Sorry—don't buy it."

"Consider what our Mr. Cantucci did when he woke up. He did not call nine-one-one—because he couldn't find his phone. He realized the alarm system had been deactivated, but the CCTV was still operating. He immediately retrieved his gun and used the CCTV system to locate the intruder. He found him—and saw that he was armed with a hunting bow. Our Mr. Cantucci, on the other hand, had a handgun with a fifteen-round magazine, and he was an expert in its use. Your own files indicate he was a champion small-arms competitor. He assumed his gun and his skills far outmatched the intruder's hunting bow. That encouraged him to stalk the intruder, and I would submit to you that this is exactly what the intruder wanted. It was a setup. The victim was then surprised and killed."

"How can you know all this?"

"My dear Vincent, there's no other way it could have occurred! This entire scenario was expertly choreographed by an individual who remained calm, methodical, and unrushed throughout. This was not a professional hit man. This was someone far more sophisticated."

D'Agosta shrugged. If Pendergast wanted to go off on a tangent, that was his prerogative—it wouldn't be the first time. "So let me ask you again: if you're right about the cell phone, then why not just kill the guy in bed?"

"Because his goal wasn't merely to kill."

"So what was it?"

"That, my dear Vincent, is the very question we must answer."

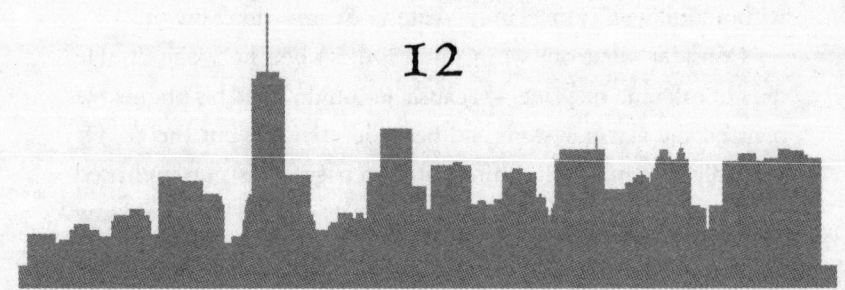

12

Anton Ozmian took his breakfast at 6 AM in his office—a pot of organic pu-erh tea, the scrambled egg whites from two free-range Indian Runner ducks, and a one-ounce piece of bitter 100 percent cacao chocolate. This breakfast had not varied in ten years. Ozmian had to make many difficult business decisions in the course of a day, and to compensate he organized the rest of his life to be as decision-free as possible—starting with breakfast.

He ate alone, in his large office overlooking the watery expanse of the Hudson River, rolling along in the reddish predawn light like a sheet of liquid steel. A soft knock came at the door, and an assistant carried in a stack of the morning's newspapers, which he laid down on the granite desk, and then soundlessly vanished. Ozmian sorted through them, glancing over the headlines in the usual order: the *Wall Street Journal*, the *Financial Times*, the *New York Times*, and the *New York Post*.

The *Post* was the last on his list, and he read it not for its news value but as a matter of anthropological interest. As his eye fell on the cover page and its usual seventy-two-point headline, he froze.

ROAD KILL

Drunk Ozmian girl in past hit-and-run

BY BRYCE HARRIMAN

Grace Ozmian, the recently murdered and decapitated daughter of dot-com mogul Anton Ozmian, struck an eight-year-old boy with her BMW X6 Typhoon in Beverly Hills in June of last year. She fled the scene of the accident, leaving the boy dying in the street. A witness obtained the license plate number, and local police stopped and arrested her two miles from the scene. A blood test determined she had a blood-alcohol content of .16, twice the legal limit.

Her father, billionaire CEO of DigiFlood, subsequently hired a team of lawyers from one of LA's most expensive law firms, Crosbie, Whelan & Poole, to defend his daughter. She was sentenced to a mere 100 hours of community service, and the case records were sealed. Her community service consisted of buttering toast and serving pancakes at a homeless shelter in downtown Los Angeles two mornings a week . . .

Ozmian's hands began to shake as he read the story, first word to last. Soon the shaking was so violent he had to lay the paper down on the desk and let go of it to finish. When he was done, he rose and, with a scream of inchoate rage, picked up the glass mug of tea and hurled it across the room, directly at a Jasper Johns painting of an American flag. The glass shattered, cutting through the canvas and leaving a brown splash across it.

An urgent knock came at the door. "Stay the fuck out!" he

screamed, while at the same time casting about, snatching up a two-pound nickel-iron meteorite, and heaving it at the Johns, where it ripped through the image, splitting it in half and knocking the painting from the wall. Finally, he seized a small bronze Brancusi sculpture and gave the broken picture, now lying on the floor, a few shredding blows, thus completing its destruction.

He stopped, chest heaving, and let the Brancusi drop to the carpet. The obliteration of the painting he had bought for twenty-one million dollars at Christie's had the effect of helping him master his anger. He stood motionless, controlling his breathing, letting the fight-or-flight hormones subside, waiting for his heart rate to come back down. When he felt he had returned to a physiologically stable state, he went back over to the granite desk and examined the *Post* article again. There was an essential detail he had overlooked on the first reading: the byline.

And there it was: Bryce Harriman. *Bryce Harriman.*

He punched the intercom button. "Joyce, I want Isabel in my office immediately."

He went over to the Johns and looked down at it. A total loss. Twenty-one million dollars, and of course there was no way he could collect the insurance, having destroyed it himself. But he found a strange satisfaction in having done so. Twenty-one million dollars didn't even begin to plumb the ocean of his anger. This Bryce Harriman was going to understand, very soon, just how deep that ocean was—because, if necessary, he would drown the bastard in it.

13

D'AGOSTA HAD CATEGORICALLY refused a ride in Pendergast's Rolls-Royce while on duty—how would *that* look?—and as a result Pendergast rode with him in his squad car, silent and displeased. He hadn't worked with Pendergast this closely in a while, and he'd forgotten what a pain in the ass the FBI agent could be.

As Sergeant Curry drove them through stop-and-go traffic on the Long Island Expressway, D'Agosta unrolled the copy of the *Post* he'd picked up that morning and looked at the screaming headline yet again. Singleton had reamed him out that morning for not getting to Izolda Ozmian before Harriman did and putting the fear of God into her about talking to the press. The story had been craftily designed to capture the public's attention, raise the level of hysteria, and ensure Harriman a steady stream of "exclusive" stories to come. It had put D'Agosta in a ferocious mood that morning, which had only deepened as the day progressed. He told himself there was nothing he could do about the piece and that he should just move forward and solve the case as quickly as possible. They'd already tracked down the location where the dead boy's father had settled—Piermont,

New York, where he worked as a bartender. After they finished with this interview in Long Island, Piermont would be D'Agosta's very next stop.

As they pulled into the half-empty mall in Jericho that contained the offices of Sharps & Gund, D'Agosta felt surprise that a big-time security outfit would have its headquarters in such a place. It seemed they had taken over the far end of the mall, occupying a space that was once an anchor store, and he could even see the faint SEARS outline on the now-blank exterior wall. There was nothing to indicate it was even occupied, save a row of reserved parking spaces full of cars—nice cars. *Very* nice cars. It appeared that not only was Sharps & Gund discreet—it was downright invisible.

Sergeant Curry pulled into a visitor space and they got out. It was a cold, gray day, and a bitter wind scraped an old plastic bag across the pavement before them as they approached the double glass doors. Here, finally, was a small Sharps & Gund logo. Discreet, tasteful.

The doors weren't locked. D'Agosta pushed through, Pendergast and Curry following, and he found himself in an elegant, understated reception area, done up in polished hardwoods, with a reception counter twenty feet long, occupied by three receptionists who seemed to be doing nothing but waiting with their hands folded.

"NYPD and FBI here to see Jonathan Ingmar," said D'Agosta, leaning on the counter and removing his shield. "We have an appointment."

"Of course, gentlemen," said one of the receptionists. "Please have a seat."

D'Agosta didn't sit and neither did Pendergast or Curry. They waited at the counter as the receptionist made a call.

"Someone will be out shortly," she said, with a bright-red lipstick smile. "It might be a few minutes."

On hearing this, Pendergast wandered over to the seating area, sat down, crossed his legs, picked up a magazine, and began flipping the pages. Somehow the nonchalance of it irritated D'Agosta. He stood at the counter for a few minutes, then finally took a seat opposite the agent. "He'd better not keep us waiting."

"Of course he will. I predict thirty minutes at the very least."

"Bullshit. I'm just going to go in there, then."

"You won't get past the layers of locked doors and pit-bull assistants."

"Then we'll get a subpoena and drag his ass down to the station and question him there."

"A man like the Sharps and Gund CEO will have lawyers who will make that proposition lengthy and difficult." Pendergast flipped another page of the only magazine in the waiting area. D'Agosta noted it was *People*, and he seemed to be looking through an article on the Kardashians.

With a sigh, D'Agosta rolled the *Post* back up and shoved it into his pocket, crossed his arms, and sat back. Sergeant Curry remained standing, impassive.

It wasn't thirty minutes; it was forty-five. Finally a small, skinny Brooklyn type with a beard, hipster hat, and black silk shirt came to get them. They wound through several layers of ever more elegant and understated offices before being ushered into the presence of Jonathan Ingmar. His office was white and spare, and did not seem to contain any electronic devices beyond an old-fashioned phone sitting on a hectare-size desk. Ingmar was a slender man of about fifty with a boyish face and an untidy mess of blond hair. He had an offensively cheerful look on his face.

By this time, D'Agosta was fighting mad and making a serious effort to control it. It annoyed him that Pendergast seemed so nonchalant, so unbothered, by the extended wait.

"My apologies, gentlemen," said the Sharps & Gund CEO, waving about a beautifully manicured hand, "but it's been a busy day." He glanced at his watch. "I can give you five minutes."

D'Agosta turned on a handheld recorder and set it on the table, then took out his notebook, flipped it open. "We need a list of all past and present employees who worked on or had anything to do with the Cantucci account."

"I'm sorry, Lieutenant, but our personnel records are confidential."

"Then we'll get a court order."

Ingmar spread his hands. "If you can get such an order, naturally we'll obey the law."

"Look, Mr. Ingmar, it's clear that the Cantucci murder was an inside job—planned and executed by someone who worked for your company and had access to your source code. We're not going to be happy if you obstruct us."

"That's pure speculation, Lieutenant. I run a tight ship here. My employees are vetted as much as any CIA recruit, if not more. I can assure you you're barking up the wrong tree. Surely you understand that a security company such as ours must be careful with our employee information?"

D'Agosta didn't like the tone of this man's voice at all. "Okay, Ingmar, you want to do this the hard way? If you don't cooperate right now, we're going to get a court order, we're going to subpoena your personnel records going back to the birth of George Washington—and we're going to haul your ass down to One Police Plaza for questioning."

He halted, breathing hard. Ingmar returned a cool gaze. "Be

my guest. Your five minutes are up, gentlemen. Mr. Blount will show you out."

The eager hipster reappeared but now Pendergast, who had said nothing and hadn't even shown any interest in the conversation, turned to D'Agosta. "May I see that copy of the *Post*?"

D'Agosta handed it to him, wondering what the hell Pendergast was up to. The FBI agent unrolled the newspaper before Ingmar and held it up in front of his face. "Surely you read the *Post* today?"

Ingmar snatched the paper with disdain, glanced at it, tossed it aside.

"But you didn't read Bryce Harriman's front-page article!"

"Not interested. Blount, show them out."

"You should, because tomorrow's front page will feature your company—and you."

There was a chill silence. After a moment, Ingmar spoke. "Are you threatening to leak information to the press?"

"Leak? Not at all. The word is *release*. The public is clamoring for information on the Cantucci murder. Mayor DeLillo is concerned. Law enforcement has a responsibility to the public to keep them abreast of our progress. You and your company will be the poster boys of that progress."

"What do you mean?"

"The leading theory of the crime is that the killer was employed by your company. *Your* company. That makes you a person of interest yourself. Don't you love that phrase, *a person of interest*? So rich with dark suggestion, so full of murky hints—without actually saying anything at all."

D'Agosta saw a most remarkable and satisfying change take place on the face of Jonathan Ingmar, the cool, arrogant look vanishing in a swelling of veins and a flushing of skin. "This is sheer defamation. I'll sue you to within an inch of your life."

"It's only defamation if it isn't true. And it is, in fact, true: you are indeed a person of interest in this case, especially after your petulant refusal to cooperate. Not to mention keeping us waiting for forty-five minutes in your reception area with only the Kardashians for company!"

"Are you *threatening* me?"

Pendergast chuckled in the most grating way. "How clever of you."

"I'm calling my attorney."

But before Ingmar could act, Pendergast had removed his cell phone and was punching in a number. "Is this the city desk? I should like to speak to Mr. Harriman, please."

"Wait! That's enough. Hang up."

Pendergast clicked off the phone. "Now, Mr. Ingmar, do you think we could perhaps impose on you just a few minutes—or perhaps a few *hours*—longer? Let's start with the employees who installed the Cantucci system. I'm so glad to hear about your CIA-level vetting process. Please fetch the vetting files for those individuals. Oh, and we'll also need to have your own file, as well."

"I'm going to raise hell about this. You mark my words."

D'Agosta spoke up. His dark mood had begun to lift. "Let's see, Ingmar. What was it you said again? *Be my guest.* Thank you; we will. So get those files—and get them right now."

14

Curry dropped Pendergast off at the Dakota—the FBI agent had some vague excuse as for why he couldn't accompany them to talk to the dead boy's father in Piermont—while D'Agosta and Curry proceeded to the West Side Highway, over the George Washington Bridge, and up the Palisades Parkway. The town of Piermont, New York, sat beside Route 9W on the west side of the Hudson River, not far from the New Jersey line. Curry was the most taciturn of sergeants, for which D'Agosta was grateful. While Curry drove, D'Agosta glanced through the files they had copied from Sharps & Gund.

Two techs had installed the Cantucci system. One was still with the company and looked pretty straight; the other had left four months earlier. Been fired, actually. The guy's name was Lasher and his personnel file had started out clean when he joined the firm five years back, but in the past year things seemed to have gone downhill. The file was peppered with warning letters regarding lateness; an occasional non-politically-correct observation; and two off-color comments made to female co-workers, both of which they'd reported. The file ended with a report documenting an outburst by Lasher, the specifics left unclear save to say it had been a "furious rant" that had resulted in his immediate dismissal.

Leaning back in the seat as Curry negotiated a traffic slow-down, D'Agosta's mood improved still further. This guy Lasher looked like a prime suspect for the Cantucci murder. He seemed just the kind of disgruntled prick who'd retaliate against the company that fired him. Maybe Lasher killed Cantucci himself; or maybe he partnered with the killer, lending his necessary inside expertise. Either way, this was a damn good lead, and he would make sure the guy was interviewed as soon as possible.

D'Agosta was more than ever convinced the two murders were not at all connected and should be treated as separate cases. As proof of this, totally separate leads were developing nicely on both fronts. The father of the dead kid, Jory Baugh—whom they were on their way to see—was clearly a person of interest in the Ozmian killing. This could be a double win for him, clearing two big cases at the same time. If this didn't earn him a promotion, nothing would.

He turned to Curry. "Let me fill you in on this guy in Piermont, Baugh. The dead kid was his only child. Grace Ozmian, the hit-and-run driver whose death we're investigating, got off practically scot-free. After the boy's death, the family fell apart. The mother became an alcoholic and eventually committed suicide. The father spent time in a mental clinic and lost his Beverly Hills land-scaping business. He moved east six months ago. Works in a bar."

"Why move east?" asked Curry. "He got family here?"

"Not that I know of."

Curry nodded again. He was a big guy with a round head and a reddish crew cut. He didn't look smart, and he didn't talk smart, but D'Agosta had eventually figured out he *was* smart—

damn smart. He just didn't open his mouth until he had something to say.

They left the Palisades Parkway for 9W north. It was four o'clock and rush hour was not yet in full swing. In a few minutes they came into the town of Piermont. It was a charming little spot, nestled on the river, with a marina alongside a gigantic pier that gave the town its name, cute wooden houses perched on the hills above the Hudson, and a dramatic view of the Tappan Zee Bridge. D'Agosta pulled out his cell phone and called up Google Maps.

"The bar's called The Fountainhead. Right on Piermont Avenue." He gave Curry directions and moments later they were pulling up to an attractive watering hole. A blustery wind off the Hudson battered them as they exited the car and entered the bar. At quarter past four it was still almost deserted, with a lone bartender behind the bar. He was a big guy, built like a longshoreman, wearing a wifebeater, his muscled arms covered with tats.

D'Agosta went up to the bar, removed his shield, laid it down. "Lieutenant D'Agosta, NYPD homicide. This is Sergeant Curry. We're looking for Jory Baugh."

The big guy stared at them with cold blue eyes. "You've found him."

While this surprised D'Agosta, he didn't show it. He had managed to get a couple of blurry pictures of Baugh from the Internet, but they didn't look much like this pumped-up bastard. The guy was hard to read: his face was a blank.

"May we ask you a few questions, Mr. Baugh?"

"What about?"

"We're investigating the murder of Grace Ozmian."

Baugh laid down his bar towel, crossed his massive arms, and leaned on the bar. "Shoot."

"I just want you to understand that you're not at present a suspect and this interview is voluntary. If you do become a suspect, we'll stop the interview and explain your rights to you and give you the opportunity to have a lawyer present. Do you understand?"

Baugh nodded.

"Can you recall your movements on Wednesday, December 14?"

The man reached under the bar, pulled out a calendar, glanced at it. "I was working here at the bar from three to midnight. I go to the gym every morning, eight to ten. In between I was at home." He shoved the calendar back. "Okay?"

"Is there anyone who can verify your movements?"

"At the gym. And here at the bar. In between, no."

The M.E. had narrowed the time of death to around 10 PM December 14, give or take four hours. To get into the city from here, kill someone, give the victim time to bleed out, shift the body to the garage in Queens, maybe come back a day later to cut off the head...D'Agosta would have to work this one out on paper.

"You satisfied?" Baugh asked, a note of belligerence creeping into his voice. D'Agosta looked at him. He could feel the man's anger seething just beneath his skin. A muscle in one of his crossed arms was jumping.

"Mr. Baugh, why did you move east? Did you have friends or family here in Piermont?"

Baugh leaned forward on the counter and pushed his face toward D'Agosta. "I threw a dart at a fucking map of the United States."

"And it hit Piermont?"

"Yeah."

"Funny how close the dart landed to where your son's killer was residing."

"Hey, listen, pal—you said your name's D'Agosta, right?"

"Right."

"Listen, Officer *D'Agosta*. For over a year I've been fantasizing about killing the rich bitch who ran over my son and left him bleeding to death in the middle of the street. Oh *yeah*. I thought of killing her in so many ways you can't even count them—setting her on fire, breaking every bone in her body with a baseball bat, whittling her into little pieces with a knife. So, yes, it's funny how close the dart landed. Isn't it? If you think I killed her, good for you. Arrest me. When my boy died, my life ended anyway. Arrest me and finish the job that you cops and lawyers and judges started last year—the job of destroying my family."

This little speech was delivered in a low, menacing tone without the least trace of sarcasm. D'Agosta wondered if the guy had crossed over the line to being a suspect, and decided he had.

"Mr. Baugh, I'd like to inform you of your rights at this time. You have the right to remain silent and refuse to answer questions, and anything you say may be used against you in a court of law. You have the right to have an attorney present and may call one now, before we ask you anything further. If you decide to continue answering our questions, you can stop at any time and call an attorney. If you can't afford one, an attorney will be provided to you. Now, Mr. Baugh, do you understand your rights as I've explained them to you?"

At this Baugh began to laugh: a low rumble that finally emerged as a deep dog-like bark. "Just like on TV."

D'Agosta waited.

"You want to hear that I understand?"

"Yes."

"Well then, here's what I understand: when my kid was hit and left to die, and they found out the driver was Grace Ozmian, the concern of everyone shifted. Like *that*." Baugh snapped his fingers so hard D'Agosta had to fight not to flinch. "The cops, the lawyers, the insurance people, their concern was suddenly for her and all the money, power, and influence her daddy began throwing around. Nothing for me and my family—oh, he's just a fucking gardener. Ozmian gets sentenced to two months flipping pancakes and the records are deep-sixed, while I'm sentenced to losing my family forever. So you want to know what I understand? What I *understand* is that the criminal justice system in this country is fucked. It's for the rich. The rest of us poor bastards get nothing. And so if you're here to arrest me, then arrest me. Nothing I can do about it."

D'Agosta asked calmly: "Did you kill Grace Ozmian?"

"I think I need that free lawyer you promised me now."

D'Agosta stared at the guy. At this point he didn't have enough evidence to take him into custody. "Mr. Baugh, you can call legal services—" he wrote down the number—"anytime. I'm going to verify your alibi for the evening of December fourteenth, which means we'll be speaking to your employer, interviewing patrons of the bar, and consulting the tapes from that security camera up in the corner there." He pointed. They had already put in a subpoena for the security tapes with the bar's owner and he knew they were safe; D'Agosta hoped Baugh would do something stupid and try to destroy them.

Baugh laughed harshly. "Sure, do whatever the fuck you want."

15

AT TWO O'CLOCK in the morning, the mansion in East Hampton, New York, was quiet. The eighteen-thousand-square-foot house occupied a twelve-acre lot between Further Lane and the Atlantic Ocean, set amid a park-like expanse of lawns, a putting green, an artificial pond, and a "folly" designed to resemble a miniature Egyptian temple. The house itself was a three-story modernist construction in cement, glass, steel, and chrome that looked like an upscale dentist's office. Its large plate-glass windows glowed quietly in the night air, casting a warm light across the gigantic lawns surrounding it.

The man stood on the empty December beach, in the shadow of a stone breakwater, and examined the house with a pair of night-vision binoculars. The wintry Atlantic thundered and rolled at his back. The moon had set, and the faint river of light that was the Milky Way rose from the sea horizon and arched over his head. The estate gave every appearance of quiet and repose.

The man with the binoculars was keenly aware this was only an illusion.

He scanned the grounds, the levels of the house, and the windows, committing every detail to memory. From his vantage point he could not see the first floor, but he was intimately familiar with the layout of the house, which he had been able to obtain from the absurdly open and unprotected central computer system of Cutter Byquist, the celebrity architect who had designed the house. These included CAD-CAM diagrams of construction drawings, mechanical and electrical plans, security systems, plumbing, even the music system. The electronic security system was relatively basic. The owner was an old-fashioned individual who placed his trust not in electronics but in trained, well-paid human beings, many of whom were former South African special forces soldiers of the notorious and now-disbanded 8 Reconnaissance Commando regiment.

In his fifty-five-year life span, the target who owned this fortress-estate had made many, many formidable enemies. There were a number of individuals and organizations that would very much like to kill him, either for revenge, for silence, or merely to send a message. As a result, his estate would be well prepared against any kind of intrusion.

After a few minutes of recon, the man felt a faint, quick vibration from the cell phone in his pocket. That was the first of what would be many such timed reminders.

The op would now begin.

He had mapped out the details with military precision, down to the very second. He expected the unexpected, of course—and he was prepared for that, as well—but he always liked to start off following a timetable in which every step he took, every action, had been choreographed.

He lowered his binoculars and tucked them into his backpack. He checked his Glock; his SOG knife; his GPS device. He was not yet in a hurry. The plan for this initial phase was slow and methodical. Later, at the end, there would be a rush. That was due to the one weakness in his plan: the target had a panic room built in between his bedroom and his wife's. If there was a premature alarm raised, the target would have time to take refuge within it—and the op would need to be aborted. The panic room appeared to be impregnable. It was the one hardened technological element of an otherwise simple system. In addition to sophisticated electronic locks, it had multiple sets of dead bolts. Again, the old-fashioned approach—you couldn't hack a dead bolt.

The man now moved up the beach, slowly, keeping to the shadows, and was soon among the dunes. He was dressed in an outfit of tight black silk, his exposed skin darkened with black greasepaint. He had selected for the operation a late-December weekday night with no moon. The beach and the town were utterly dead.

He moved soundlessly among the dunes, keeping to the low areas, until he came to the rise of land that led to the estate. A slope of brush terminated at a nine-foot stone wall that marked the property boundary, with a row of iron spikes atop it. On the far side was a thick boxwood hedge surrounding a long, smooth, open lawn that led to the front porticoes of the mansion.

He ran his hand over the face of the wall. The stone was rough, and afforded enough hand- and footholds for an experienced rock climber like himself to scramble up it. He waited for the second vibration signal, and when it came he swarmed up the wall in a few simple moves. He knew that the iron spikes were more for show than protection, and that an invisible IR break-beam ran along the top, serving as a perimeter alarm.

On his way over the wall, he made sure to interrupt that beam.

He dropped down the other side, into the hidden space between the hedge and the inside of the wall. There he crouched, in a dark corner, invisible in the deep shadow, waiting. He could just see, through gaps in the hedge, the vast sweep of lawn and the façade of the house. The indirect glow from the house's windows, along with some tastefully arranged spotlights, threw out enough ambient light to cast a glow across the greensward. The illumination was both a blessing and a curse.

Soon he heard two security men with a dog coming across the lawn on the far side. Another vibration from his phone marked his estimate of their arrival time. They were, so to speak, right on schedule. He was reassured in the soundness of his planning. He knew that outdoor IR break-beams like this one experienced frequent false alarms from animals and birds. That would probably be assumed to be the case with this beam. But to make sure, for the past several nights, at irregular intervals, he had tossed a small, weighted piece of canvas onto the wall and then pulled it back as a way to interrupt the beam at this very spot, triggering the same routine investigation that he had timed for the present moment.

He could hear the panting of the dog as the group approached the hedge, and the irritable murmuring of the two men. Special forces soldiers were normally trained not to talk and to use hand signals only. Not only that, he could smell cigarette smoke.

These men had become soft.

"I hope Scout gets the critter this time," one of the men said.

"Yeah, fucking squirrel probably."

The dog suddenly whined. It had scented him.

One of them spoke to the dog. "Scout, go get it. *Go get it, boy.*"

They released the dog and it shot through a gap in the hedge—coming straight at him, no barking, no warning: a dog trained to kill. He braced himself and met the dog straight on as it leapt at him, delivering a single swipe with his SOG knife to the animal's throat, severing its windpipe. With a gurgling cough the animal struck him a glancing blow as it fell, tumbling to rest at his feet.

"Hey—did you hear that?" one of the men asked, his voice low. "Scout? Scout? Return, Scout. *Return*."

Silence.

"What the fuck?"

"Scout, *return*." A little louder now.

"Should we call for backup?"

"Not yet, for chrissakes. He's probably off chasing the squirrel. Let me go in and see."

He heard the first man noisily pushing his way into the hedge. This, he began to think, was proving too damn easy. But it would get harder; he was confident of that.

He set himself into a crouching position, ready to spring, still cloaked in darkness. As the blundering noise grew close, he sprang up and drove the SOG into the man's throat, jerking it sideways, again cutting the windpipe before his victim could make a sound. Even as the man fell facedown the intruder shouldered him aside and rushed forward, driving through the hedge like a linebacker, bursting out and leaping straight at the second man, standing in the open about ten feet away, still smoking a cigarette. With a shout, the man reached for his sidearm and managed to get it partway out of its holster before the intruder, airborne, slashed him through the neck with the SOG. The guard fell backward and the man landed on top of him, taking a faceful of arterial blood. The firearm bounced away on the lawn, unfired.

The man lay on the body as it jerked about for a few seconds before going still. He waited, unmoving, listening. The action had taken place about three hundred yards from the house, and they were far enough away to be obscured by darkness. He doubted the man's aborted shout had reached the ears of anyone else. There were klieg lights that would go on in a general alarm or intruder emergency, but nothing happened.

When the intruder was assured that the alarm had not been raised, he rose up from the dead guard. Kneeling, he searched the body, removing a radio, two magnetic key cards, a flashlight, and the man's hat. He turned on the radio and saw it was set to broadcast at channel 15 in the VHF range. He left it on in reception mode and tucked it in his belt, left the gun where it was, put the hat on his head, and tucked the magnetic key cards into his shirt pocket.

He grabbed the feet of the body and dragged it back into the hedge, hiding it near where the man's partner lay. Then he proceeded westward, walking in the gap between the hedge and the wall. When he came to the property corner, he turned and walked north, a distance—according to his GPS—of five hundred yards. He was now on the opposite side of the house and had only to cross a 150-yard expanse of lawn.

There he waited for the faint vibration of his cell phone's timer to signal the next phase.

When it came, he snugged the dead guard's hat tighter onto his head and proceeded across the grass, walking purposefully, flashlight on, moving it back and forth. While the hat wouldn't fool anyone close up, he would look all right from a distance.

The intruder was almost completely soaked in blood, and he knew if the other dogs scented him, they would freak out. But that would not happen unless the wind, which was coming from the east, shifted: and it would not shift in the weather pattern at this time of night.

He made it across the space unseen, and merged into the bushes along the side of the house just as a man on patrol with a dog came around from the front, walking along the grass. The movement of air was still in his favor. He waited in the dark until they had passed around the corner, and then he moved between bushes and house to the beginning of the flagstone patio, which surrounded the pool. A long pergola ran alongside the patio, and he used that as cover to reach a small cabana containing the pool pump and filters. The door was locked, but it was standard hardware that came with the shed and therefore rudimentary. He jimmied it and stepped into the cramped, darkened space, closing the door only partway.

Again he waited for the vibration.

He now raised the radio and held it to his lips, while taking out a small magnet. He depressed the BROADCAST button while holding the magnet near the mike.

"I'm at the pool," he whispered. "Got a big snake here, need backup." His voice, muffled in static thanks to the magnet, was almost unintelligible.

"What's that about a snake?" came the reply. "Didn't copy, repeat."

He repeated the message, easing up slightly on the magnet to reduce the static.

"Copy, who's this?" came the reply.

Now he broadcast just static.

"All right, I'm on my way over."

He knew it would be the closest responder: the man with the dog who had recently passed him. As expected, the man came around the corner again with the dog on a leash, and he paused, sweeping his light this way and that. "Hey, where are you? Is that Pretorious?"

He remained in the dark, waiting.

"Son of a bitch," the guard muttered, and then did exactly as expected—he released the dog and said: "Go find the snake. Go find it."

The dog, scenting the man in the cabana, naturally made a bee-line for him and charged through the door, where he was met with the flashing point of the SOG. The dog fell forward silently.

"Sadie? Sadie? What the hell?" The guard pulled his sidearm and, gripping it, ran into the cabana, only to be met with the same knife to the throat. The pistol fired as the man went down.

Now, this was an unfortunate development. The alarm would be raised prematurely. But knowing the psychology of his target—the man's macho instincts, his brutal toughness, his loathing of cowardly behavior—he felt sure that one gunshot wouldn't be enough to send him into the panic room. No: the man would arm himself, call his guards, figure out what was going on, and stay put—for the time being.

He was well along on his plan, with three men and two dogs down, which was exactly half the security complement. But he now had to move much faster, before the remainder could discover the extent of their losses, organize themselves, and close ranks in defense of the target.

All this consideration took less than a second in the intruder's mind. He snatched up the dying guard's radio and jumped over the body, still flopping and gurgling. Removing another magnet from his pocket and a piece of sticky tape, he taped down the TRANSMIT button of the man's radio, slapped the magnet on, and dropped them onto the lawn. The sound of the gunshot had of course alerted the other security guards, and his radio had burst into overlapping queries as the guards tried to check in with each other, figure out where each was, and determine who if anyone might be missing. With the magnet and tape, he had at least rendered their main channel useless with loud static, and with the other guard's radio he did the same to the emergency backup channel. That would sow confusion for at least a few minutes until the remaining guards found and agreed on a clear channel.

A few minutes were all he needed.

The klieg lights were snapping on. A siren sounded. He had to move very fast. There was no longer any point in stealth: he heaved a piece of porch furniture through the sliding glass doors, setting off another alarm, and then he leapt through the breach and raced across the living room to the stairs, taking them three at a time to the second floor.

"Hey!" He heard a guard running behind him.

He stopped, whirled about, dropped to one knee, and fired his Glock, taking off the top of the guard's head and then dropping a second guard who came tearing around the corner after him.

Five guards, two dogs.

Sprinting along the second-floor corridor, he reached the target's bedroom door. It was made of solid steel and was, as expected, locked. Reaching into his backpack, he slapped a preprepared packet of C-4 with detonator and sticky pad onto the lock, ran around the corner, and entered the wife's room. They had recently divorced, and the steel door to her empty room was wide open, as he'd expected. The panic room stood between the target and his wife's room, and each had their own door into it. The panic room's door lay behind a panel on the wall, which he yanked open. The door beyond was shut, but it wasn't yet in full lockdown mode and could be opened—unlike the target's huge steel bedroom door—with a single charge of C-4. He slapped a second charge on the wife's panic room door, retreated to a safe distance, and then, with a remote detonator, blew both charges simultaneously—the target's bedroom door and the wife's panic room door—so they sounded like one charge. The charge on the steel bedroom door wasn't strong enough to blow it open—it was merely intended to scare the shit out of the owner.

But the charge on the panic room door was heavier, and it did indeed knock the unsecured but locked door open. The intruder slipped inside the panic room, where the air was filled with smoke and dust. The lights were off. He quickly took up a position just next to the door in the far wall of the little room: that is, the door leading into the target's bedroom. Almost immediately he heard the target opening the door and stumbling inside, in terror and confusion due to the ineffectual explosion he'd just heard outside his bedroom door. The man turned, pulled shut the door, and slammed home the bolts. Then he scrabbled along the wall, found the switch, and turned on the lights.

And then he stared at the intruder already inside the panic room, his eyes widening. Yes, indeed, the target had just locked himself inside the panic room with his about-to-be killer. The intruder deeply enjoyed this moment of irony. The target was dressed only in boxer shorts, his comb-over askew, eyes bloodshot and bulging, slack jowls quivering, belly protruding. He still carried the sour reek of vodka.

"Mr. Viktor Alexeievich Bogachyov, I presume?"

The victim stared at him in abject terror. "What…who…are you…and for God's sake—*why*?"

"Why not?" said the intruder, raising the SOG knife.

Two minutes and fifteen seconds later, the intruder slipped over the stone wall and dropped down onto the other side. He could hear, from the compound, the sounds of multiple alarms and, beyond that, in the distance, approaching police sirens. He had killed the last guard on the way out, but in his kindness had spared the dog, who proved to be more intelligent than the humans and had fallen quivering and whining at his feet, urinating on himself—and thereby saving his own life.

He sprinted across the beach to the stone breakwater and ran along it to a small speedboat, sheltered between two big boulders in the lee of the breakwater, its quiet four-stroke engine still idling in neutral. He tossed his now-heavy backpack into the boat, jumped in after it, gently depressed the throttle, and headed into the black, heaving Atlantic Ocean. As he sped into the night, pleasant thoughts went through his head of the mise-en-scène the police were just now discovering as they entered the estate and began to search the grounds.

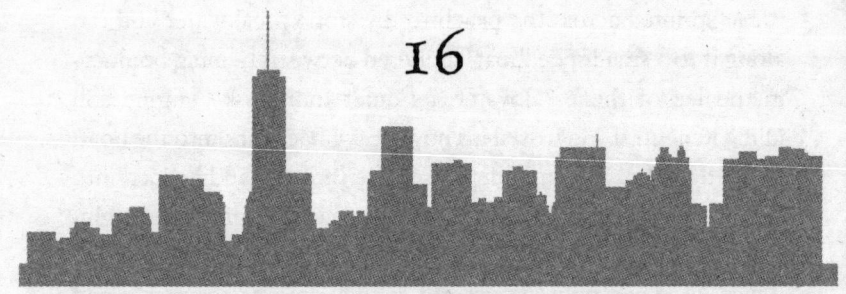

16

THIS TIME PENDERGAST insisted on taking Proctor and the Rolls, and D'Agosta was too weary to protest. It was December 22, Christmas was only three days away, and over the last week he had barely found time to catch a few hours of sleep, much less think about what he was going to buy his wife, Laura, for a present.

Proctor had driven them out to East Hampton on a morning that was gray and bitterly cold. D'Agosta found he was grateful for the extra space the rear compartment of the big vehicle provided, not to mention the fold-down desk of brilliantly polished wood that allowed him to catch up on his paperwork. As the car eased onto Further Lane, the estate and the activity surrounding it came into view. Police barricades had been set up across the road, there were ribbons of crime scene tape vibrating in a cold December wind, and the roadside was lined with parked CSU and M.E. vans. A bunch of uniforms were walking around, some with clipboards, trying to keep from freezing to death.

"Christ," said D'Agosta. "Too many damn people on-site."

As they pulled into the improvised parking area, outlined on a patch of grass with crime scene tape and signs, he saw everyone turn and gape at Pendergast's Silver Wraith.

He got out one side and Pendergast got out the other. Pulling his coat tight against the frigid wind coming off the Atlantic, D'Agosta headed toward the command and control van, Pendergast following.

Inside the small space he found the East Hampton chief of police. D'Agosta had spoken to him on the phone earlier and was relieved at the man's professional attitude, and now he was even more pleased to see him in person: a rugged older man with iron-gray hair and mustache, and an easygoing manner.

"You must be Lieutenant CDS D'Agosta," he said, rising and grasping his hand firmly. "Chief Al Denton."

A lot of small-town cops couldn't stand working with the NYPD, maybe for good reason, but this time D'Agosta sensed he was going to get the cooperation he needed. He turned to give space for Pendergast to introduce himself and was surprised to see the agent had vanished.

"Show you around?" Denton asked.

"Uh, sure. Thanks." *Typical of Pendergast.*

Denton threw on a coat, and D'Agosta followed the chief back out into the blustery morning. They crossed Further Lane and came to the main gates into the compound, a vast, partially gilded affair involving many tons of wrought iron. The gates stood open and were guarded by two cops, one holding a clipboard. There was a rack with Tyvek suits, masks, gloves, and booties, but the chief waved him past. "The CSU team's completed the house," he said, "and most of the grounds."

"That was fast."

"Out here, with the winter weather, we've got to move fast or the evidence will deteriorate. So we called in SOC assets from all across the East End. Say, where's the FBI guy you said was coming with you?"

"He's around here somewhere."

The chief frowned, and D'Agosta didn't blame him: it was considered rude not to liaise with local law enforcement. They passed between the gates, walked through a staging area set up under a tent, and headed down the graveled drive leading toward the mansion. It was a gigantic cement eyesore of a house, looking like a bunch of slabs piled together, propped up by glass, about as warm and cozy as the Kremlin.

"So this Russian guy, what's his name—?"

"Bogachyov."

"Bogachyov. How long's he been in East Hampton?"

"He bought the land a few years ago, took a couple of years to build the house, moved in six months ago."

"He give you any problems?"

Denton shook his head. "Nothing *but* problems. Right from the beginning. When he bought the place, the seller said he was cheated and sued. That case is still in court. In the middle of the night, Bogachyov tore down a historic shingle house. Claimed he didn't know it was landmarked. Lawsuit over that. Then he built this monstrosity, which violated a whole bunch of town ordinances, all without the right permits. More lawsuits over that. And then he stiffed the contractors; stiffed his help; even stiffed the guys who mow his lawn. Lawsuits up the wazoo. He's the kind of jackass who just does whatever the hell he wants. It wouldn't be an exaggeration to say he's maybe the most hated man in this town. Was, I should say."

"Where'd he get his money?"

"He's one of these Russian oligarchs. International arms broker or something equally unpleasant. The house, the land, all owned by a shell company, or at least that's what's on the tax rolls."

"So there are plenty of people who'd want to see him dead."

"Hell, yes. Half the town. And that's not even counting the people he's stepped on, or killed, in his own business dealings."

As they came up to the house, D'Agosta spied Pendergast, walking rapidly around the far corner.

Denton saw him, too. "Hey, that guy shouldn't be in here."

"He's—"

"Hey, you!" Denton called out, breaking into a jog, D'Agosta following. Pendergast stopped and pivoted. His long black coat and gaunt, ivory face made him look uncannily like the Grim Reaper.

"Mister—!"

"Ah, Chief Denton," said Pendergast, striding forward, slipping a black leather glove off a pale hand, grasping the chief's hand with a quick bow. "Special Agent Pendergast." He then swiveled back around and continued on his way, striding at high speed across the lawn toward the tall hedge at the ocean end of the property.

"Um, if there's anything you need—?" called the chief at his retreating back.

Pendergast waved a hand behind him. "I need Vincent. Are you coming?"

D'Agosta set off after him, struggling to keep up, the chief right behind. "Don't you want to examine the house?" D'Agosta managed to ask.

"No." Pendergast quickened his pace still further, coat flapping behind him, bent slightly forward as if bracing himself against the stiff wind.

"Where are you going?" D'Agosta asked, not receiving an answer.

They finally reached the hedge, which D'Agosta could see hid a tall stone wall. Here Pendergast whirled. "Chief Denton, has your CSU team gone over this area yet?"

"Not yet. There's a lot of ground to cover, and this is pretty far from the scene of the crime—" But before he finished his sentence Pendergast had turned away and was walking alongside the hedge, looking this way and that, placing his feet carefully, like a cat. Suddenly he halted, dropped to his knees.

"Blood," he said.

"Okay," said Denton. "Nice catch. We should back away from here, get the CSU team out before we disturb anything—"

But Pendergast was up and moving again, head bowed, following the stains, which led into the hedge—and that was when D'Agosta saw something white inside the tangle of green. They peered into the depths, where D'Agosta could make out a gruesome sight.

"Two bodies and a dead dog," said Pendergast, turning to Denton and slowly backing away. "Yes, please do get your CSU team out here. In the meantime, I'm going over the wall."

"But—"

"I'll move a little farther down so as not to disturb this area. Vincent, come with me, please. I'll need a hand."

Chief Denton stood near the scene of carnage, calling for the CSU team on his radio, while D'Agosta followed Pendergast down the hedge line for a hundred feet.

"This looks like a good spot." Pendergast pushed into the hedge, D'Agosta following. They emerged into the gap between hedge and wall.

Pendergast pressed against the wall, as if testing it. "In this bulky coat, I'll need a hand up."

D'Agosta didn't argue; he helped him up.

The agent scrambled like a spider to the top, slipped over the short iron spikes, then stood up and looked around with a pair of binoculars. Then he called down to D'Agosta.

"Go back to the car, have Proctor drive around and out on the beach. I'll meet you there."

"Right."

Pendergast disappeared over the wall and D'Agosta turned away. As he emerged from the hedge, he could see a team of CSU guys running across the lawn, all dressed, masked, and bootied up, with Denton pointing to the area where the bodies had been found. Denton joined him as he was walking back across the lawn.

"How the hell did he do that so quickly?" he asked. "I mean, we would have found it eventually, but he just walked straight out there like it was attached to a neon sign."

D'Agosta shook his head. "I don't ask, and he doesn't tell."

Sitting once again in the back of the Rolls, D'Agosta watched as Proctor drove into a public parking area adjacent to the beach about half a mile south of the victim's house. The man got out, released a precise amount of air from the tires, then got back in, gunning the engine and shooting down a sandy lane that provided vehicle access to the beach. Soon the Rolls was flying north along the strand, the booming Atlantic on their right, the mansions of the rich on their left. In a moment D'Agosta could see Pendergast's slender figure standing on the end of a rocky breakwater. As Proctor slewed to a stop, Pendergast came back along the breakwater, strode up the beach, and slid into the backseat.

"He came and went by small craft, which he hid next to that breakwater," Pendergast said, pointing. Then he pulled open his own folding desk, which held a slim MacBook, which he opened and used to call up Google Earth. "The assassin, leaving the scene of the crime, was extremely vulnerable and exposed out on the water, even at night. He would have disposed of his boat at the earliest opportunity. And it all would have been planned ahead of time."

He peered at the Google Earth image, moving it around their current location. "Vincent, look—there's an inlet right here, just six miles away, leading into Sagaponack Pond. And just inside the inlet is a marshland with a public parking area immediately adjacent." He leaned toward the front seat. "Proctor, please drive there posthaste. Sagaponack Pond. Don't bother with the road—take the beach."

"Yes, sir."

D'Agosta gripped his seat as the Rolls accelerated, performed a slewing U-turn in a fountain of sand, and then roared down the beach at high speed, just within the high-tide area where the sand was harder. As they picked up speed, rocking from side to side, the car was buffeted by wind and sea spray from the ocean and occasionally plowed through a skimming of water from a retreating wave, throwing up a curtain of spray. They passed an elderly couple walking hand in hand, who stared at them slack-jawed as the 1959 Silver Wraith boomed past at close to sixty miles an hour.

In less than ten minutes they had arrived at the inlet, where the beach stopped and another breakwater led out into the gray and foaming Atlantic. Proctor brought the Rolls to a shuddering halt, fishtailing in another great spray of sand. Before it had even come to rest, Pendergast was out the door and striding up the beach, D'Agosta once again running to keep up. He was astonished at Pendergast's energy after the previous days of apathy and apparent sloth. It seemed this set of murders had finally hooked him.

They hopped over a beach fence, crossed an area of scrubby

dunes, and soon a sheet of slate-colored water came into view, surrounded by a broad marshland. Pendergast plunged into the marsh grass, his handmade John Lobb shoes sinking into the mucky ground. With little enthusiasm D'Agosta followed, feeling the icy mud and water invade his own Bostonians. A few times Pendergast paused to look around, his nose in the air almost like a bloodhound's, before moving ahead in a different direction, following soggy and almost invisible animal pathways.

Suddenly they reached the edge of the marsh—and there, not twenty feet along the verge, just emerging from the brown water, was the prow of a sunken skiff.

Pendergast glanced back, his silver eyes glittering. "And now, my dear Vincent, I think we have found our first actual piece of evidence left by the killer."

D'Agosta edged over and looked at the boat. "I'll say."

"No, Vincent." Pendergast was pointing at something on the ground. "This: a clear foot impression from the killer."

"Not the boat?"

Pendergast waved his hand impatiently. "I have no doubt it was stolen and has been thoroughly scrubbed of evidence." He crouched in the marsh grass. "But this! A size thirteen shoe, at least."

17

THE CONFERENCE ROOM at One Police Plaza was a big blond space on the third floor. D'Agosta had arrived early with Singleton, the deputy commissioner for public information, Mayor DeLillo, and a row of uniformed officers, so that when the press arrived they would see an impressive, solid wall of blue and gold, backed by suits and the mayor himself. The idea was to create a reassuring visual for the evening news. In his years at the NYPD, D'Agosta had seen the department move from inept, ad hoc responses to the press to this: professional, well staged, and quick to react to the latest events.

He wished he felt the same confidence in himself. The fact was that, with the rise of bloggers and digital bloviators, there was far more media now in a typical press conference, and they were less well behaved. Most of them were outright pricks, truth be told, especially among the social media crowd, and these were the people whose questions D'Agosta had to answer—with a self-assurance he didn't feel.

As the press crowded in, the television cameras rising in the back like black insects, NBC and ABC and CNN and the rest of the alphabet soup, the print press along the front, and the digital jackasses just about everywhere, it looked like this was going to be a doozy. He was glad Singleton was leading off the briefing, but even so, D'Agosta began to sweat when he thought of his turn at the podium.

Minor arguments broke out as everyone jockeyed for the best seats. The room had been warm before the crowd arrived and it was fast heating up. In the wintertime, a crazy New York City regulation forbade them from turning on the A/C despite the fact that the ventilation in the room was abysmal.

As the sweep of the second hand on the big wall clock moved toward the hour, the mayor stepped to the podium. The television lights were on and the photographers crowded forward, elbowing each other and muttering expletives, the fluttering sound of their shutters like countless locust wings.

Mayor DeLillo gripped the sides of the podium with his big bony hands and gave the room a sweeping look of competence, resolve, and gravitas. He was a large man in every way—tall, broad, with a head of thick white hair, enormous hands, a jowly face, and large eyes glittering under bushy brows.

"Ladies and gentlemen of the press and the people of the great city of New York," he boomed out in his legendary deep voice. "It is the policy of our police department to keep the community informed on matters of public interest. That is why we are here today. I can assure you that the entire resources of the city have been put in service of this investigation. And now Captain Singleton will speak to you about the particulars of the case."

He yielded the podium. There was no shaking of hands; this was all serious business.

Singleton took his place at the podium, waiting for the sound level to drop toward a rustling silence.

"At two fourteen this morning," he began, "East Hampton police responded to multiple alarms at a residence on Further Lane.
They arrived to find seven bodies on the grounds and in the house
of a large estate. These were the victims of a multiple homicide—
six security guards and the owner of the estate, a Russian national
by the name of Viktor Bogachyov. In addition, Mr. Bogachyov was
found decapitated, the head gone."

This occasioned a flurry of activity in the audience. Singleton
plowed ahead. "The East Hampton police requested the assistance of the NYPD in determining whether this homicide was
connected to the recent killing and decapitation of Mr. Marc Cantucci on the Upper East Side..."

Singleton droned on about the case in general terms, consulting a binder of notes that D'Agosta had put together for him.
In contrast with the mayor, Singleton spoke in a monotonous,
police-jargony deadpan voice—a just-the-facts-ma'am sort of
tone—turning each page with a deliberate movement. He spoke
for about ten minutes, outlining the bare facts of the three
killings, starting with the latest and working back to the girl.
As he reeled off information that almost everyone already knew,
D'Agosta could feel the impatience of the crowd begin to rise. He
knew his turn would be next.

Finally, Singleton halted. "I will now turn the briefing over
to Lieutenant D'Agosta, Commander Detective Squad, who will
speak more specifically and answer questions about the homicides, the possible connections among them, and some of the
leads his team has been developing."

He stepped away and D'Agosta took to the podium, trying to
project the same gravitas that the mayor and Singleton had. He
glanced over the assembled press, his eyes watering in the bright
lights. He looked down at his notes, but they were a wavering

mass of gray. He knew, from prior experience, that he was not very good at this. He had tried to tell Singleton as much and beg off, but the captain hadn't been sympathetic. "Get out there and do it. If you want my advice, strive to be as boring as possible. Give them only the information you have to. And for God's sake don't let any of the bastards take control of the room. You're the alpha male in there—don't forget it." This retrograde advice was delivered with a manly slap on the back.

And here he was. "Thank you, Captain Singleton. And thank you, Mayor DeLillo. The homicide division is following up on several promising investigative threads." He allowed for a pause. "I wish I could go into detail, but most of what we have so far falls into the category of 'non-releasable information,' which the department defines as: One: Information posing an undue risk to the personal safety of members of the department, victims, or others. Two: Information that may interfere with police operations. And three: Information that adversely affects the rights of an accused or the investigation or prosecution of a crime."

He paused and heard what sounded like a collective groan from the crowd. Well, Singleton had told him to be boring.

"Since you have most of the details of the first two homicides, I will focus on what we've learned so far about last night's homicide in East Hampton." D'Agosta went on, describing the third killing in much more detail than Singleton. He spoke of the six dead bodyguards, the discovery of the boat and other evidence, but he held back mention of the size thirteen foot—that crucial detail he wanted to keep in reserve. He spoke of Bogachyov's many lawsuits and shady business dealings. It was alleged, for example, that Bogachyov had been brokering decommissioned nuclear equipment and missile parts through Chinese shell companies connected to the North Korean regime.

And then he returned to the crime, praising the fine work of the East Hampton Police Department—until a voice shouted out in interruption: "But are the killings *connected*?"

D'Agosta halted, losing his place. Was that that son of a bitch Harriman? It sure sounded like him. After a moment of scanning his notes he went on, talking about his department's work liaising with East Hampton, when the voice interrupted again.

"Connected, or not? Can we have an answer?"

It *was* that damn Harriman. D'Agosta looked up from his papers. "We are for the time being treating the three homicides as separate cases, but this doesn't mean we don't believe they may be connected."

"Which means what?" Harriman shouted.

"It means we haven't decided."

"Three decapitations in a week—and you're saying they're *not* connected? And this new murder—it's just like the second, right?"

"The third homicide does bear some similarities to the second one, yes," said D'Agosta.

"But *not* to the first murder? Is that what you're saying?"

"We're still looking into that…" D'Agosta suddenly realized he was allowing Harriman to do exactly what Singleton had warned him about: hijack the room. "I'd like to finish what I was saying earlier, please. According to East Hampton PD, the investigative threads include—"

"So you're implying there are *two* murderers? The first who killed Grace Ozmian, and another murderer who did two and three? In other words, the first killing inspired a serial killer to commit the others? And it's actually not just two and three—counting the dead guards you mentioned, it's technically nine."

This was going south fast. "Mr. Harriman, save your questions for the Q and A."

But the discipline of the crowd was breaking down, and several other questions were being shouted at the podium. Singleton stepped forward, held up his hand, and the crowd shushed. D'Agosta felt his face flush.

"I think we're ready for questions," said Singleton, turning back to D'Agosta.

There was an uproar of questions all shouted at once.

"Ms. Levitas of *Slate*," said D'Agosta, pointing at a woman in the rear, as far from Harriman as possible.

"Just to follow up on the previous question, how can these killings *not* be connected?"

Damn that Harriman—even when he wasn't asking questions he was still orchestrating the press conference. "We're considering all possibilities," said D'Agosta stolidly.

"Is it a serial killer?"

This shouted question came from Harriman again. How the hell did he get into the front row? Next time D'Agosta would see that he was buried in the back of the room, or preferably out in the hall. "As I've said repeatedly, we are working on all possibilities—"

"Possibility?" Harriman shouted. "You mean a serial killer is actually a *possibility*?"

Singleton spoke firmly: "Mr. Harriman, there are other reporters in the room. We call on Mr. Goudreau of the *Daily News*."

"Why is the FBI involved?"

"We're marshaling all law enforcement assets," said Singleton.

"But what's the federal angle?" Goudreau followed up.

"In the first homicide there was a suggestion of possible interstate transportation of the body. And the third homicide, with its potential international ramifications, has reinforced federal involvement. We are grateful to the FBI for giving us the benefit of their expertise."

A roar of shouted questions came from the audience.

"One more question!" said Singleton, looking around. This was followed by another eruption.

He pointed. "Ms. Anders of Fox."

The Fox anchor was trying to speak but was drowned out by her peers, who kept shouting questions.

"Quiet, please!" Singleton boomed out. It worked. A hush fell.

"My question is for the mayor: What steps are you taking to keep the city safe?"

The mayor strode forward with a heavy step. "Aside from putting forty detectives and another hundred uniformed officers on the case, we're pulling over two thousand officers into over-time patrol, and we're taking many, *many* other steps I cannot enumerate for security reasons. I can assure you that every possible action is being taken to keep our citizens safe."

"Lieutenant, *where are the heads?*"

Harriman again—the fucker.

"You heard the man," said D'Agosta. "No more questions!"

"No!" came another shout. "Answer the question!"

The sound level went up as more took up the refrain. *Where are the heads? What about the heads? Answer the question!*

"We're working on that," said D'Agosta. "Now—"

"You mean you don't know, do you?"

"As I said—"

But they wouldn't let him finish. "Any idea *why* the killer's taking the heads?" someone else yelled.

"Not yet, but—"

Singleton broke in smoothly. "We've asked the FBI Behavioral Science Unit in Quantico to help us with that very question."

This was news to D'Agosta, and he realized it was something Singleton must have just pulled out of his hat—a damn good idea.

"When will you—?"

"Thank you ladies and gentlemen, this press conference is over!" Singleton said, and turned off the mike. As the room broke up, Singleton passed by him, speaking in an undertone: "In my office, please."

As D'Agosta turned to gather his papers, he glanced in the direction of the mayor and found the man staring at him, a dark look in his big glistening eyes.

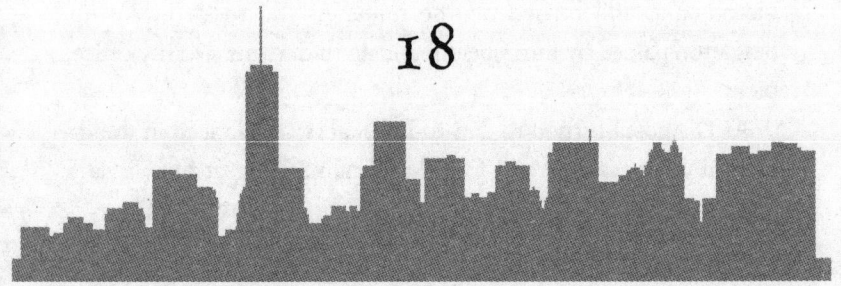

18

SITTING IN THE passenger seat of a squad car driven by Sergeant Curry, D'Agosta had a rare moment of peace and quiet to think. This time, the chewing-out in Singleton's office actually hadn't been as bad as D'Agosta feared. The captain had pointed out, more in a paternal way than as a reprimand, that D'Agosta had let Harriman dominate the conference in exactly the way he had warned him against, but that all in all it could have been worse and he was sure D'Agosta had learned a valuable lesson.

"Just get us something, *anything*," said Singleton, "by the end of the day tomorrow that we can get in the paper. We've *got* to show progress. You bring me something good and all will be forgiven." He clapped D'Agosta on the back in another fatherly way as he was on his way out, then gave his shoulder a warning squeeze.

That had been the previous afternoon. D'Agosta had twelve hours left to come up with something.

Hard on the heels of Singleton's command—like a curse—the results came back from the security camera in Piermont's Fountainhead bar. They confirmed beyond all doubt that Baugh had indeed been in the bar, mixing drinks, from three in the afternoon until after twelve on the night Grace Ozmian was killed. When D'Agosta mapped out the time necessary to get from Piermont to Queens and back, and matched it against the window of uncertainty as to when the girl's killing occurred, he realized there was no possible way Baugh could have murdered the girl. So that lead—which had seemed so promising—was DOA. Unless Baugh hired a killer...but that, in D'Agosta's judgment, seemed highly unlikely: Baugh was the type who'd want to do it himself.

Curry braked and muttered a curse when a black stretch limo cut him off as he navigated the congestion leading into the Holland Tunnel. D'Agosta's best hope for some sort of newsworthy breakthrough was the interview he was headed to now, a very promising lead in the Cantucci murder. He knew the killer was, almost beyond doubt, someone connected to the security company Sharps & Gund—an employee, or ex-employee. He was on the way to interview a certain William Paine, one of the two Sharps & Gund technicians who had installed the security system in the Cantucci house. While D'Agosta already knew Paine himself was not a suspect—D'Agosta had verified the man had been in Dubai for the past three weeks on a big system install—he felt sure that Paine would be able to point him to other possible suspects. More important, Paine could verify that this had been an inside job. What he needed more than anything was hard information connecting Sharps & Gund to the Cantucci murder, not mere speculation but something solid enough to go public with.

They emerged from the Holland Tunnel and made their way through Hudson County and across Newark Bay and the wasteland of Port Newark, finally reaching the enclave of Maplewood. One turn, another, and a third and they had arrived at their destination. There, parked along the curb, was Pendergast's Rolls, the dark form of Proctor inside, waiting behind the wheel.

The house was a modest two-story Colonial of white clap-board, a brown lawn, and a garden withered by the early-winter cold. It must have snowed in Jersey last week, D'Agosta thought, given the icy crusts remaining in spots on the lawn.

Curry pulled up behind the Rolls and they got out and walked up the front steps, rang the doorbell. A big lumbering man an-swered, introduced himself as Paine. "FBI's already here," he said sourly as they followed him into the living room.

Pendergast was sitting on the sofa, as gaunt and white as ever. D'Agosta removed his iPad, on which he sometimes took notes, while Curry took out his steno notebook. Pendergast never took notes or even seemed to carry paper and pen with him.

"Lieutenant," said Pendergast, "I've been waiting for you and I've resisted the urge to ask questions."

D'Agosta nodded his appreciation. He and Curry took seats, along with Paine.

"Let me open by saying you're not a suspect," said D'Agosta. "Understood?"

Paine nodded, hands clasped. He looked a little ragged, eyes bloodshot, clothes rumpled, hair mussed. Jet lag, maybe? "I want to be as helpful as I can," he said, in a tone that implied just the opposite.

D'Agosta led him through the preliminary questions about age, residence, how long he'd worked at Sharps & Gund, and so forth, receiving short, uninformative answers. Finally D'Agosta got to the meat of the interview.

"I'd like you to describe for us the Cantucci security system: how it worked, how it was set up, and especially how it was cir-cumvented."

At this Paine crossed his arms and began to describe the system in general terms, much as Marvin had done earlier. D'Agosta listened, taking a few notes, getting the strong impression as he did so that the guy was holding back. He asked a few probing questions about system details, and got in return more vague answers and evasion, until Paine finally said: "I really can't answer any more questions of a technical nature."

"Why not?"

"You must know I've signed NDAs about all this and I'm not supposed to talk about it. I could be fired—even sued."

"Has Ingmar threatened you with retaliation if you talk to us?" D'Agosta asked.

"Not in any specific way, but the general message was clear."

"Mr. Paine, do you wish to terminate the interview? I want you to understand that if you do, we will get a subpoena, take you down to the station, and you'll be compelled to answer questions under oath."

"I realize that."

"Is that what you want us to do?"

"Yes, in fact. Because then my ass will be covered."

Son of a bitch. The guy was calling his bluff. D'Agosta leaned forward. "Believe me, we're going to remember just how *helpful* you were, and we're going to return the favor."

Paine looked back at him, eyes blinking behind large glasses. "So be it. The harder you ride me, the better it'll look to Ingmar. Look, Lieutenant, I *need* my job."

At this Pendergast spoke, his voice mild and honeyed. "So what you require, Mr. Paine, is to be coerced?"

"That's about it."

"Since we are short on time, and getting a subpoena will take several days, I wonder if there isn't a way we can *coerce* you right here and now."

Paine stared. "Like how? Is that a threat?"

"Heavens, no! I'm just thinking of creating a little drama. Sergeant Curry, I assume you carry a battering ram in that squad car of yours?"

"Always."

"Excellent! Here's what we'll all do. We'll leave the house, drive away, then return shortly with sirens blaring. Mr. Paine, you will refuse to open the door. Sergeant Curry, you will enter stage center and batter down the door in a suitably spectacular and destructive fashion, so that all the neighbors will hear. We shall lead Mr. Paine out of the house in handcuffs—after suitably disarranging his clothing and hair and perhaps tearing a few buttons off his shirt in the process—and take him to the station where we can finish the interview. All this without need of a subpoena, because, Mr. Paine, you will agree on video—for the legal purposes of law enforcement, you understand, and it won't ever get back to your employer—that this was entirely voluntary and you understand your rights and all the rest."

A silence. Paine looked at D'Agosta, then back at Pendergast. "Who's going to pay for my door?"

Pendergast smiled. "Consider which will cost more: a new door, or the four-hundred-dollar-an-hour attorney you will need to hire if the lieutenant serves you with a subpoena and takes you downtown for what will be *at least* a twelve-hour interview, possibly stretching over several days—unless of course you want to take your chances with one of the pro bono hacks supplied by the state."

A long silence. "Okay," said Paine, actually breaking into a sort of cynical smile. "This is going to be interesting."

"Excellent," said Pendergast rising. "We shall be back. In, say, an hour?"

19

AFTER THE BIG hullabaloo in Maplewood—all the neighbors, D'Agosta had noticed with a certain gratification, had been plastered to their windows—they had taken Paine down to 1PP and he was now comfortably ensconced in a small conference room, where he had become a most cooperative and friendly witness. The official setting seemed to loosen his tongue, and he had gone into great technical detail about the Cantucci system. They were now moving on to Sharps & Gund itself.

"I was the senior man on the Cantucci install," Paine was saying. "A lot of the people I have to deal with are difficult, but Cantucci was a royal pain in the ass. There was a lot of stuff he didn't like—cosmetic stuff, mostly, such as the placement of cameras or the color of the CCTV monitors—and he just about nitpicked us to death. He was the kind of guy who didn't want to sully himself by dealing with the low-level people like myself. He always took his complaints right to Mr. Ingmar, every little thing. It drove Ingmar crazy that Cantucci would only talk to him, calling him up at all hours of the day and night and treating him like his lapdog. Ingmar really came to hate him, and even talked about firing him as a client, except that the man owed us a lot of money. They had a shouting match once, on the phone."

"What about?" D'Agosta asked.

"Money. Cantucci wasn't paying the bills. Said he wouldn't pay a dime until the install was completed to his satisfaction."

"And did he pay in the end?"

"Not totally. He chiseled Ingmar over the final bill, finding fault with every little thing and deducting for it. I think we got about eighty cents on the dollar. I'm pretty sure Ingmar took a loss on the job."

"What was the total?"

Paine thought for a moment. "I'd guess around two hundred. Plus a monthly fee of two grand."

D'Agosta shifted position, consulted his notes. He was now getting to the heart of his questions. "Would Ingmar have been capable—did he personally have the knowledge—to bypass the security system the way the killer did?"

"Yes. Absolutely."

"Who else at Sharps and Gund would have sufficient skills to do what the killer did, in circumventing the system?"

"My install partner, Lasher. Possibly the guy who heads the IT department, maybe the chief of programming and design. But I really don't think either of them knew how the Cantucci system itself was laid out or had access to the technical lockbox." He paused, considering. "Really, Ingmar and Lasher are probably the only two, other than me of course."

This is good, D'Agosta thought. *Really good.* "You and Lasher were the techs who responded to and performed the repair that had apparently been rigged, staged for by the killer?"

"I was the guy, but Lasher had been fired by that time, so I went with another techie."

"Which is?"

"Hallie Iyer. She still works for the company."

"Would this Ms. Iyer have enough knowledge to circumvent the system?"

"No. No way. She's pretty junior in the firm, hasn't been with it more than a couple of months."

"Tell us about your ex-partner, Lasher," said D'Agosta. "The one who helped you with the original install. What kind of guy was he?"

"He was a strange one. Man, he gave me the creeps—not from day one, though. It came on kind of gradually. At first he was really closemouthed, didn't say a word, but as we worked together more he sort of let down his guard. Oh, I can see why Ingmar hired him—he knew his stuff, no doubt about that—but he talked some strange shit."

"Such as?"

"That the Apollo moon landings were faked, that the jet contrails you see in the sky are actually chemical trails the government is spraying on people to brainwash them, that global warming is a Chinese hoax. Unbelievable crap."

Pendergast, who had been silent, broke in. "How did a fellow with these views pass Sharps and Gund's allegedly CIA-level vetting system?"

Paine laughed. "CIA-level? Is that what Ingmar told you?" He shook his head. "Ingmar hires on the cheap, no benefits, long hours, no overtime, a ton of travel. The only vetting he does is to make sure you don't have a criminal record, and even then he'd probably hire you because you'd come cheaper. Lasher seemed normal at first, but then he got weirder and weirder."

"Anything in particular?" D'Agosta asked.

"It was mostly about women. A total creep. No social skills, asked them out on dates right in front of the whole office. Always angry, too, making disparaging comments, telling stupid jokes, bragging. Lot of talk about big tits—you know the kind."

D'Agosta nodded. He knew the kind.

"He should've been fired the first time it happened. Ingmar tried to ignore it but eventually had to do something about it. He would have lost some of his valuable female employees otherwise. But it was probably Cantucci's constant complaints that actually got Lasher the ax."

This Lasher was looking better and better. And they still had a decent window before Singleton's thirty-six-hour deadline passed.

"You know where Lasher lives?" asked D'Agosta.

"Yeah. West Fourteenth Street. At least, he lived there when he was fired."

Time to wrap up this interview. "Agent Pendergast, you got any more questions?"

"No, thank you, Lieutenant."

D'Agosta rose. "Thank you, Mr. Paine, a squad car will take you home." He walked out of the room with Pendergast. Once the door was shut, D'Agosta said: "So what do you think? We've got two suspects, in my view: Lasher and Ingmar himself."

Pendergast did not respond, and D'Agosta couldn't read his face. "I mean, this guy Ingmar, he's got the means, the motive, and the ability."

"Oh, Ingmar was never a suspect."

"What do you mean? You called him a 'person of interest' right to his face."

"Only to intimidate him. He wasn't behind the killing."

"How can you be so sure?"

"For one thing, he would not have needed to break into the van to exchange the cell phone circuit board—he could have substituted the board in the office. Breaking into a van on a city street is a risky business, and there was no guarantee the two men would have both left it unguarded."

"Lasher could have done it in the office, too."

"No. Lasher had been fired prior to the service call."

"Right, right, but I still think Ingmar is a suspect."

"My dear Vincent, if Ingmar wanted to kill Cantucci, why would he do it in a way that would damage his own company? If Ingmar wanted Cantucci dead, he would have done it *outside* his home."

D'Agosta grunted. He had to admit that made sense. "So that leaves Lasher as the only suspect? Is that what you think?"

"I think nothing. And I would advise you to think nothing, either—at least, not until we have more evidence."

D'Agosta didn't agree, but he sure as hell wasn't going to argue with Pendergast. In the ensuing silence Curry, looking up from his phone, said: "Lasher still lives on West Fourteenth Street."

"Good, let's send a team over there right away for a voluntary prelim. Nothing in-depth, just see if he's a viable suspect, if he has an alibi." He turned to Pendergast. "You want to go? I can't, got a ton of paperwork."

"I, unfortunately, have a previous engagement."

D'Agosta watched his black-clad frame leave the office. He hoped to God his guys would come back with just enough to get the media break that Singleton and the mayor so desperately wanted by the end of the day—otherwise he'd never hear the end of it.

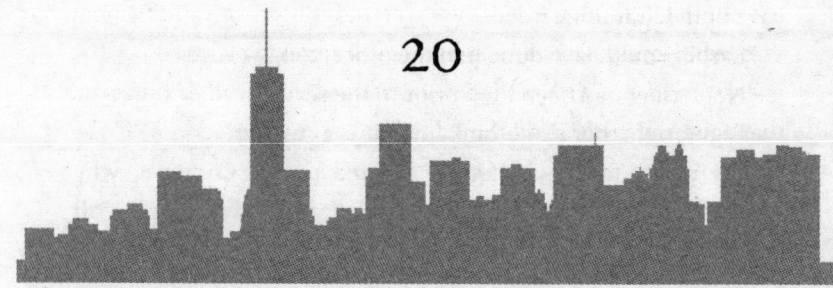

20

When Pendergast entered the office this time, Howard Longstreet—who was sitting in a cracked and comfortable leather wing chair, reading a report with a red-stamped classified jacket—motioned him wordlessly to the sister chair. Pendergast took the proffered seat.

Longstreet spent another minute or two looking over the document, then slipped the papers into an open safe by his desk, closed and turned the lock. He looked up. "I understand you've become more active in investigating these decapitation killings."

Pendergast nodded.

"Perhaps you can fill me in on the most recent one."

"The third killing was, like the second, carefully planned and executed. The security assets were neutralized in what appears to have been a precise and orderly sequence. The challenge of the victim's having a safe room was dealt with in a most clever manner. It would appear the entire sequence was choreographed down to the last step."

"You make it sound like a ballet."

"It was."

"Any fresh evidence?"

"We have the make and model of the getaway boat, along with the engine VIN. However, those were not illuminating. The boat was reported stolen that night from a nearby marina in Amagansett, and no physical evidence remained. We did, however, manage to retrieve a single, remarkably clear footprint near the scene—size thirteen."

Longstreet grunted. "Planted?"

A smile. "Perhaps."

"The police still cooperating?"

"The East Hampton chief was unhappy about a certain drive I took along their beach. But he and the NYPD are officially grateful for our assistance."

Longstreet took a sip from his Arnold Palmer, sitting on a coaster on the nearby table. "The last time we spoke, Aloysius, we were dealing with two murders in which both victims were beheaded. I asked you to determine whether there was a connection between the homicides; if both were the work of a single killer. Now we have three such murders, in addition to six others that could best be described as collateral damage, and the question is even more pressing. Are we dealing with a serial killer?" He raised his eyebrows quizzically.

"I take it you're aware of the NYPD's theory?"

"You mean, that one individual killed Grace Ozmian, and that killing in turn inspired a second and third killing by somebody else. Is that what you think, too?"

Pendergast paused a moment before speaking. "The similarities in the M.O. between victims two and three are striking. In both cases the killer was methodical, calm, deliberate, and exceptionally well prepared. It's likely they were the work of a single individual."

"And the first one?"

"Highly anomalous."

"What about motive?"

"Unclear. We focused on two suspects with strong motives in the first two killings. The suspect in the Ozmian killing was cleared. The second suspect, an ex-employee of Sharps and Gund, will soon be questioned. He looks promising, so far."

Longstreet shook his head. "That's the strangest thing. The victims seem so unconnected that it's hard to imagine a linking motive. What does a mob lawyer have to do with a Russian arms dealer with an irresponsible socialite?"

"I would submit to you that the *apparent* lack of motive might, in fact, be motive itself."

"There you go again, Aloysius, talking riddles."

Instead of responding, Pendergast waved a hand.

"You're still avoiding my question: Do you or do you not agree with the theory that the first murder was committed by a different person than murders two and three?"

"It all revolves around the anomaly of the first beheading—why wait twenty-four hours? The other two happened almost before the victims were dead."

"You're still evading my question."

"Another item I find interesting. No matter how violent or messy the murders may be, the beheadings were done with great fastidiousness. This would argue against the first murder being done by a different killer. On top of that, the first body appears to have been—unlike the others—deliberately concealed."

Longstreet grunted. "Interesting, as you say—but on its own, inconclusive."

"We're in a logical bind. It could, as the police are assuming, be a copycat situation, especially since murders two and three have numerous points of congruency not found in the first. However, equally logically, the coincidence of three beheadings in the space of a week would strongly suggest a single killer. We suffer from a paucity of evidence."

"You and your 'paucities' and 'logical binds,'" Longstreet growled. "It almost got us killed by that recon party of Ugandan mercenaries—remember?"

"And yet we're sitting here today, are we not?"

"True—that we are." He reached over and pressed a buzzer on a nearby intercom. "Katharine? Please bring an Arnold Palmer for Agent Pendergast."

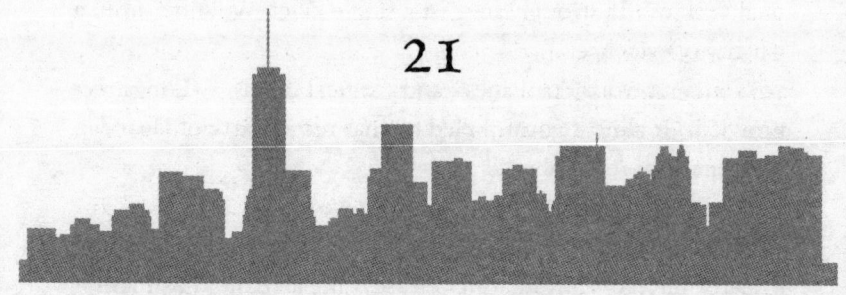

21

ANTON OZMIAN SAT behind his vast desk of black granite, staring out the south-facing windows in his corner office, his gaze taking in the myriad lights of Lower Manhattan reflected in an overcast winter sky.

He looked past the bulk of the Freedom Tower, past the buildings of the Battery, and over New York Harbor toward the dark outline of Ellis Island. His grandparents, coming by ship from Lebanon, had been processed there. Ozmian was glad that some self-important, xenophobic bureaucrat had not tried to Americanize the name to Oswald or some such nonsense.

His grandfather had been a watchmaker and repairer of clocks, as had his father. But as the twentieth century drew to a close, it became a dying profession. As a child, Ozmian had spent hours in his father's workshop, fascinated by the mechanical movements of fine watches—the fantastically tiny systems of springs, gears, and rotors that made visible that ineffable mystery called "time." But as he grew, his interests turned to complex systems of another sort: the instruction registers, accumulators, program counters, stack pointers, and other elements that made up computers—and the assembly language that governed them all. This system was not unlike a fine Swiss watch, in which the ultimate goal was to make the greatest use of the least amount of energy. That was how assembly language coding worked—if you were a true programming acolyte, you constantly strove to shrink the size of your programs and make each line of code do double or triple duty.

A young man who'd grown up in the outskirts of Boston, after college Ozmian had passionately immersed himself in a number of unusual hobbies—composing, cryptography, fly fishing, and even, for a time, big-game hunting. But his hobbies fell by the wayside when he discovered a way to blend his interest in music and ciphers with his fanaticism for tight code. It was this marriage of interests that helped him develop the streaming and encoding technologies that would become the backbone of DigiFlood.

DigiFlood. He flushed at the thought of his company, whose stock price had soared for years, now being hammered because of the unauthorized leak of its most valuable proprietary algorithms onto the Internet.

But now—as happened so often—his thoughts returned to the killing of his only daughter...and the filth about her that had been exposed by that motherless ass-fucker of a reporter, Bryce Harriman.

A distinctive triple rap on the door of his office interrupted these free-flowing thoughts.

"Come in," Ozmian called out without turning his gaze from the window.

He heard the door open; the soft tread of someone entering; the door closing again. He did not look around; he knew very well who had just stepped inside. It was his most unusual and enigmatic employee with the noble, ancient, and unusually long name of Maria Isabel Duarte Alves-Vettoretto. Over the years Alves-Vettoretto had worked for Ozmian in many capacities: aide-de-camp, confidante, expediter—and enforcer. He sensed her presence come to rest a respectful distance from his desk and he turned to face her. She was compact, athletic, and quiet, with a tumbling mane of rich mahogany hair, dressed in tight-fitting jeans and an open silk blouse with pearls. In all his years, he had never found anyone quite so remorselessly efficient. She was Portuguese, it seemed, with antique notions of honor, vengeance, and loyalty, whose ancestors had been involved in Machiavellian intrigue for eight hundred years. In her, the art had been honed to perfection.

"Go ahead," Ozmian said, turning his gaze away from her intense face to stare out the window as she spoke.

"Our private investigators have submitted a preliminary report on Harriman."

"Give me the short version."

"All reporters are of questionable character, so I'll leave out the minor sins and peccadillos. Aside from being a muckraking, ambulance-chasing, rumormongering, backstabbing journalist, the man is a straight arrow. A preparatory school product who comes from old, old money—money that is petering out with his generation. The bottom line is that he's clean. No prior convictions. No drugs. He used to be a reporter for the *Times*, but then—for reasons that aren't relevant—he made a lateral move to the *Post*. While that might seem like a career killer, he did very well for himself at the *Post*. There isn't anything in there that will give us traction." A pause. "But…there is one piece of information worthy of special note."

"Go on."

"His girlfriend—they had been dating since college—died of cancer about three years ago. He was very active in trying to help her fight it. And after her death, it became a crusade for him. He wrote articles about cancer awareness and possible new cures, and he gave a lot of visibility to various nonprofit cancer prevention groups. Also, even though he doesn't make much money as a reporter, he made a variety of donations to various cancer causes, some of his own money and some from family trusts, over the years: especially the American Cancer Society. He also set up a small charitable foundation himself in the name of his deceased girlfriend."

Ozmian waved his hand dismissively. Harriman's good works held no interest for him. "Why do you say of special note?"

"Only that this interest suggests a point of entry for . . . extreme leverage. Should the need arise."

"Has he written anything else about my daughter?"

"No. All his most recent articles have focused on the subsequent killings. He's milking them for all they're worth."

There was a pause while Ozmian contemplated the cityscape beyond his windows.

"How would you like me to proceed?" Alves-Vettoretto asked.

For a long moment, Ozmian remained silent. Then he fetched a deep sigh.

"Nothing yet," he said. "If these new murders are working him into a lather, maybe he won't publish any more shit about my Grace. That's my concern. Fighting this rogue release of our proprietary code is consuming all my time—if he's no longer a problem, I'd rather not get distracted if I don't have to."

"Understood."

And now, for the first time, Ozmian wheeled around in his chair. "But keep an eye on him—and on what he writes. If necessary, we'll squash him like the roach that he is: but only if necessary."

Alves-Vettoretto nodded. "Of course."

Ozmian turned back around, giving another wave with one hand as he did so. The door opened softly; closed again. But Ozmian barely heard it. He was looking out over the harbor, his mind already far away.

22

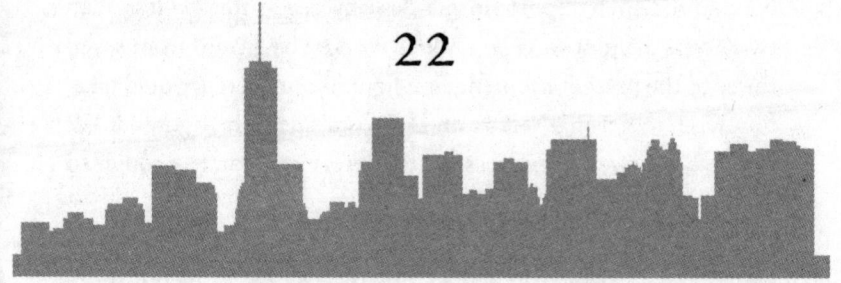

Eᴅᴅʏ Lᴏᴘᴇᴢ ᴅᴏᴜʙʟᴇ-ᴘᴀʀᴋᴇᴅ the squad car on Fourteenth Street, reported their arrival to the dispatcher, then got out with his partner, Jared Hammer. The two homicide detectives took a moment to check their surroundings. The place, 355 West Fourteenth Street, was an unremarkable five-story brick apartment building next to a funeral home. It was one of those neighborhoods that had suddenly gotten expensive with the rise of the Meatpacking District, but was still dotted here and there with crappy old buildings and rent-controlled apartments filled with sad-sack tenants.

As Lopez contemplated the façade, a cold wind scraped an old piece of newspaper along the street in front of them. The sun had already set, and not even a trace of afterglow stained the western sky. He shivered.

"Getting colder by the minute," said Hammer.

"Let's get this over with." Lopez patted the pocket of his suit jacket, checking for his shield, his weapon, and his cuffs. Then he glanced at his watch and said, out loud: "Arrival five forty-six ᴘᴍ."

"Copy."

Lopez knew that D'Agosta was a stickler for paperwork and got pissed off when times were rounded off and details left out. He wanted their report on his desk by seven thirty—less than two hours from now. When Lopez worked backward from seven thirty to the present moment, and figured out what it would take, timewise, to get that report on D'Agosta's desk, he figured it left them about twenty minutes for the interview. Barely enough to get someone talking.

Maybe the guy, Lasher, wouldn't be home. At five forty-six on December 23, two days before Christmas, he might be out shopping. He hoped that was the case, because it meant he could get home on time for once, and maybe even do a little Christmas shopping himself.

He went over to the intercom. The apartments were labeled and, sure enough, the one next to 5B said LASHER.

He pressed the buzzer and they waited.

"Who is it?" came a faint voice.

So he was home. Too bad. "Mr. Terence Lasher?"

"Yes?"

"Detectives Lopez and Hammer of the New York City Police Department. We'd like to come up and ask you a few questions."

Without a response, the door buzzed open. Lopez looked at Hammer and shrugged. This was unusual: normally, there would be a whole bunch of questions after they identified themselves.

They started up the dingy staircase. "Why is it always the top floor of a walk-up?" wheezed Hammer. "Why can't they ever live in the basement?"

Lopez didn't say anything. Hammer was overweight and didn't work out, while Lopez was lean and fit and got up at five thirty every other morning to hit the gym. While he liked Hammer— the guy was easygoing—he was a little sorry to have drawn him as a partner, because the guy slowed him down. And he always wanted to stop for doughnuts. As a cop, Lopez wouldn't be caught dead in a doughnut shop.

They trudged up the stairs. There were two apartments per floor, one in the front and one in the back. Apartment 5B was in the rear of the building. They arrived on the landing, and Lopez gave Hammer a few minutes to recover his breath.

"Ready?" Lopez asked.

"Yeah."

Lopez knocked on the door. "Mr. Lasher? Police."

Silence.

Lopez gave it a harder rap. "Mr. Lasher, may we come in? It's the police. We just have a few questions, no big deal."

"Police," came the whispery voice from behind the door. "Why?"

"We just want to ask you a few questions about your former position with Sharps and Gund."

No reply.

"If you wouldn't mind opening up," Lopez continued, "this won't take long at all. Totally routine—"

Lopez heard the faint, metallic click of a break-action shotgun being closed and he screamed "Gun!" and hit the floor just before a massive blast tore a hole in the door. But Hammer was not so fast and took the charge squarely in the gut, the force of it punching him backward into the opposite wall, where he slumped down.

Scrambling to his partner, Lopez heard a second blast, hitting the wall above him. He grabbed Hammer under the arms and dragged him to safety out of the line of fire, around the corner to the landing, while at the same time unholstering his radio.

"Officer down!" he screamed. "Shots fired, officer down!"

"Oh *fuck*," said Hammer, gasping, holding his hands over the wound.

The blood was just pouring out from between the man's fingers. Lopez, crouching over his supine partner, pulled out his Glock and aimed it at the door. He almost pulled the trigger but stopped himself; firing blindly through a closed door into an unknown apartment was a violation of departmental rules of engagement. But if the motherfucker opened the door or fired again, he would take him down.

Nothing more happened; there was silence on the other side of the two dark ragged holes in the door.

Already he could hear sirens.

"Oh Jesus," groaned Hammer, gripping his abdomen, crimson blossoming across his white shirt.

"Hang in there, partner," Lopez said, pressing down on the wound. "Just hang in there. Help is coming."

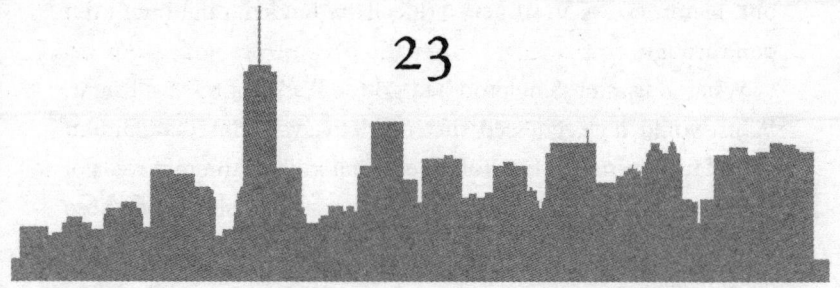

23

Vincent D'Agosta stood on the corner of Ninth Avenue, looking down Fourteenth Street. It was a madhouse. The entire neighborhood had gone into lockdown, the target building evacuated; they had the ESU team and had deployed two negotiators, an armored cherry-picker, a robot, a K-9 unit, and a bunch of snipers, with a chopper circling above. Beyond the police barricades was practically the entire press contingent of the city—network television, cable, print media, bloggers—everyone. The shooter was still holed up in the apartment. So far they hadn't been able to get a peep out of him, or even a glimpse. The armored cherry-picker was maneuvering into position and would soon have a clear shot, and four guys were on the roof, laying down Kevlar mats and punching holes through the membrane to lower cameras inside.

D'Agosta was coordinating the assault by radio, choreographing it like a ballet, with multiple lines of action, each one of which could resolve the standoff. The rational part of him wanted to take Lasher alive. He had gone from a person of interest to suspect number one in the Cantucci killing, and dead he'd be a lot less useful. On the other hand, the motherfucker had shot a cop. The primitive part of D'Agosta's brain wanted to take the bastard out. Hammer was in surgery, critically wounded, might not even pull through.

What a disaster. Singleton had gotten his "progress," all right. Who would have guessed that a relatively routine assignment would turn into this? He wondered what kind of shit rain was going to come down on him now; but he quickly shook off those thoughts. *Just get through this with a successful outcome—then worry about fallout.*

The sun had set hours before and a brutal wind was howling off the Hudson and blasting down Fourteenth Street, the temperature plunging. His radio crackled to life. It was Curry. "The negotiator has made contact. Channel forty-two."

D'Agosta adjusted his headset to channel 42 and listened. The negotiator, speaking from behind a bulletproof shield, was talking to the shooter through the door. It was hard to pick up what Lasher was saying, but as the negotiation continued D'Agosta gathered pretty quickly that Lasher was one of those anti-government types who believed that 9/11 was perpetrated by the Bushes, that the Newtown massacre was a hoax, and that the Federal Reserve and a cabal of international bankers secretly ran the world and were in a conspiracy to take away his guns. For these reasons he didn't recognize the authority of the police.

The negotiator was speaking in a calm voice, going through the usual routine, trying to get him to give up and come out, nobody was going to hurt him. Thank God the guy was alone in the apartment and didn't have a hostage. Snipers were in place but D'Agosta had resisted his impulse to give them the order to shoot on sight. He could feel the pressure all around him to put into motion the string of events that would result in Lasher being killed. That would be easy enough, and no one would second-guess him.

Another ten minutes passed. The negotiator was getting nowhere: this guy Lasher had drunk the anti-establishment Kool-Aid, and he was convinced that if he surrendered they would kill him. They wouldn't let him live, he told the negotiator—he knew too much. He alone knew what they were up to, he knew their evil plans, and for that they would execute him.

There was no reasoning with the son of a bitch. D'Agosta was getting colder and more impatient by the minute. The longer this went on the worse he would look as commander.

"All right," he said. "Retire the negotiator. Get ready to drop a flash-bang through the roof and go in through the door and the wall simultaneously. On my orders. I'm coming up."

He wanted to be on-site; he didn't want to coordinate this from afar. He walked down the block and went into the shabby building, passing the ESU, the K-9 team, the heavy trucks and armored cherry-picker. They really liked their toys, he thought with a certain affection, and brought them out at every opportunity.

He climbed the stairs to the fourth floor, one below the action. He confirmed that the four men on the roof had carefully and silently opened a hole right down to the drywall ceiling of the apartment, and that it was ready to be punched through and a flash-bang dropped. The two A-Team units on the fifth floor both confirmed they were in position and ready to roll.

"Okay," said D'Agosta into the radio. "Proceed."

A moment later he heard the sharp *crack-boom* of the stun grenade, followed by the double crash of the A-Team units simultaneously breaching the door and wall and storming the apartment. A shot rang out from inside, followed by another and another—and then it was over.

"Disarmed and apprehended," came the announcement over the channel.

D'Agosta ran up the stairs, taking them two at a time, and entered the apartment. Here was Lasher, on the floor, cuffed, with two cops on him, in the middle of a tiny, messy, and malodorous hole of an apartment. They hauled him to his feet, whimpering. He was about five foot three, skinny, with acne and a wisp of a goatee. He was bleeding profusely from both the shoulder and the abdomen.

This is Lasher?

"He fired at us, sir," one of the officers said, "justifying return fire to disarm him."

"Good." D'Agosta stepped aside as a medic came in to treat the gunshot wounds.

"You hurt me!" Lasher blubbered, and D'Agosta saw he was pissing himself.

D'Agosta scanned the room. There were posters for death-metal groups on the walls, a disorganized scatter of guns in a corner, half a dozen disassembled computers and heaps of other electronic devices of unknown function. The whole place was comico-absurd-frightening, like a dystopian movie set. This level of weirdness wasn't what he'd been expecting. Looking at Lasher, his hair full of plaster dust, blood ponding across the littered floor, his skinny body shaking—well, was this really the guy who stalked and killed Cantucci with such ruthless precision? He just couldn't see it. Then again, there was no denying the little prick had just shot a cop with a sawed-off shotgun . . . and then tried to kill some more.

"It hurts," Lasher said more faintly, then slipped out of consciousness.

"Get him to Bellevue." With a deep sigh, D'Agosta turned away. He would question the bastard once he was stabilized—his wounds were severe, but maybe not fatal. But not tonight. He needed to get some sleep—and the paperwork just kept piling up.

Christ, what a headache he had.

24

AT FIVE O'CLOCK in the morning of December 24, about an hour before dawn, Special Agent Pendergast appeared at the door of apartment 5B in the building at 355 West 14th Street. He found the lone cop guarding the scene of the crime—the CSU had already finished—who was almost, but not quite, dozing in his chair.

"I'm so sorry to trouble you," Pendergast began as the man leapt to his feet, the cell phone he'd been holding in his hand dropping to the floor.

"I'm sorry, sir, I'm—"

"Please," said Pendergast in a soothing voice, sliding out his FBI shield and letting it fall open. "Just going to have a peek—if that's all right with you, of course."

"Oh sure," said the cop, "of course, but do you have the authorization . . . ?" His face fell slightly as Pendergast shook his head gravely.

"At five in the morning, my good friend, it is hard to get a signature. However, if you think you should call Lieutenant D'Agosta, naturally I'd understand."

"No, no, that's not necessary," he said hastily. "But you *are* already authorized on the case—?"

"Of course."

"Well, then, I guess you can go ahead."

"Good man." Pendergast sliced the crime scene tape from the door, broke the seal, and slipped into the apartment, turning on his light and easing the door shut behind him. He did not want to be disturbed.

He shone the light around the miserable space, pivoting as he did so, taking everything in. The light lingered on each poster, then moved to the scatter of guns on a piece of dirty carpet on the floor, the heap of computer equipment, circuit boards and old CRTs, now spattered with blood. His gaze roved over a crude workbench hammered together out of deal lumber, its top scarred and burned; the wall behind it hung with tools. It moved to the rumpled bed, across the kitchen nook, unexpectedly tidy—and all the way back around to where it had started.

Now he moved toward the workbench. This was his focus of interest. He inspected it from left to right, examining every last thing with the flashlight and occasionally a loupe, now and then picking up something with a pair of jeweler's tweezers and slipping it into a test tube. His pale visage, illuminated by the reflected flashlight, floated like a disembodied face, silvery eyes glittering in the darkness.

For fifteen minutes he performed his examinations until suddenly he froze. In the corner where the rough deal table had been pushed up against the wall, his light had illuminated what appeared to be two grains of yellowish salt. The first one he picked up in his fingers; he rubbed it, examined the resulting whitish dust on his fingertips, sniffed at it, and finally tasted it with the tip of his tongue. The second grain he picked up with the tweezers and dropped into a tiny ziplock bag, sealing it and slipping it back into his jacket pocket.

He turned and left the apartment. The policeman on duty, waiting with rigid attention, rose. Pendergast took his hand warmly. "I thank you, Officer, for your help and attention to duty. I shall certainly mention it to the lieutenant when I see him next."

And then he slipped down the stairs as silently and smoothly as a cat.

25

ALMOST EXACTLY TWELVE hours after Pendergast left Lasher's apartment, Bryce Harriman was pacing restlessly through his one-bedroom apartment on Seventy-Second and Madison. The apartment was in a converted prewar building, and the conversion had given the apartment a bizarre layout that allowed for a true circuit: from the living room, through the kitchen, into one door of the bathroom, out the other door into the bedroom, and then from the bedroom through a short, closet-lined hallway that led back to the living room.

The building had high ceilings, a posh lobby, and twenty-four-hour doormen, but the apartment was rent-stabilized and held under the name of Harriman's aunt. When she passed away, which would probably be fairly soon, he'd have to leave and find someplace more in keeping with his salary. Just one more example of the fading fortunes of the Harriman family.

It was furnished in an eclectic style of cast-off pieces left to him by elderly relations, now departed. Many of them were valuable, and all were old. The only new thing in the entire apartment, outside of the kitchen appliances, was the laptop that sat on a Queen

Anne table of figured Brazilian maple with cabriole legs—once in the possession of Great-Uncle Davidson, now these ten years under the earth.

Harriman paused in his pacing to approach the table. Besides the laptop with its glowing screen, there were three piles of paper, one for each murder, the sheets covered with notes, scrawls, doodles, rough diagrams, and the occasional question mark. He shuffled through them restlessly for a moment, then resumed his pacing.

That nagging frisson of professional anxiety, which had subsided somewhat after his coup with the Izolda Ozmian interview, had surfaced once again. He knew, he *knew*, what great stories these murders could be—but he was having his share of problems covering them. One difficulty was that his police sources weren't that good, and they were not eager to help him out. His old archrival Smithback had been a master at cozying up to cops, buying them drinks, buttering them up, and cadging stories out of them. But, although he hated to admit it, Harriman just didn't have the knack. Maybe it was his WASPy upbringing, the years at Choate and Dartmouth, growing up with the yacht-club-and-cocktail set—but whatever the reason, he just couldn't relax with cops, couldn't talk their talk. And they knew it. His stories suffered as a result.

But there was an even bigger problem here. Even if he was buddy-buddy with all the cops on the force, Harriman wasn't sure it would help him this time around. Because they seemed as confused by these killings as he was. A dozen different theories were circulating: one killer, two killers, three killers, a copycat killer, a lone killer pretending to be a copycat. The theory *du jour* was that the Ozmian girl had been killed by one murderer, then decapitated later by somebody who had gone on to do more copycat killings. The cops wouldn't say exactly why they thought the second and third killings were connected, but from what Harriman had been able to dig up it looked pretty clear the modus operandi was similar in both cases.

So in the wake of the Izolda Ozmian interview, he'd dutifully banged on all the doors, shown up at all the scenes, and coughed up the best stories he could. He'd made himself as visible during the press conference two days before as he possibly could without holding up a neon sign. But he wasn't fooling himself: visibility alone didn't sell papers, and these new stories of his were long on innuendo but short on facts and evidence.

He made two more perambulations of the apartment and stopped once again in the living room. The laptop sat there, word processor open, cursor blinking at him like a taunting middle finger. He looked around. Three walls of the room were covered with half-decent oils, watercolors, and sketches he'd inherited; the fourth wall was devoted to pictures of his deceased girlfriend, Shannon, as well as to a few plaques and awards he'd received for his work on spotlighting cancer research. The most prominent plaque was for the Shannon Croix Foundation, a fund he had set up in her name to gather money for medical research into uterine cancer. He had accomplished this with the help of the *Post*, which from time to time did charity drives in coordination with a series of articles. The foundation had become modestly successful, having brought in several million dollars. Harriman was on the board. There was nothing he could do to bring Shannon back— but at least he could do his best to ensure her death had not been entirely in vain.

With a sigh, he forced himself to take a seat at the table and shuffle through the three piles again. It was strange as hell—three beheadings, all in the same area, all within less than two weeks—

but with no clear connection between them. Here were three people from different backgrounds, of different social strata, of different ages, professions, and proclivities. Different everything. It was crazy.

If only there was a commonality, he thought. Now, wouldn't that be something? Not three stories, but one. One huge story. If he could find some common thread running through these murders, these three piles of paper...It could be the story of a lifetime.

He leaned back in his chair. Maybe he ought to head down to the precinct again, try to get some more info about the shootout the night before. They'd really called out the cavalry for that one. He knew it involved a person of interest in the Cantucci murder. But that's all he could find out.

He just didn't buy into these complex theories of copycats and multiple killers and conflicting motivations. His gut told him it was one killer. And if so, the killings *had* to have something in common besides the decapitations—a common motivation. But what? After all, here were three disgustingly rich scumbags who had never even met one another, and yet...

At this, he paused. *Three disgustingly rich scumbags.* Could that be it? Could that *possibly* be it?

Maybe not everything about the three victims *was* different, after all. It seemed so simple. So clean. Three rich scumbags who—in the killer's mind—deserved to die. The more he thought about it, the more it made sense. Perfect sense.

In fact, it was the *only* theory that made sense.

He felt that tingling sensation running up his spine that only occurred when he was on to something big.

But he had to be careful here—very careful. It was a theory, after all. He didn't want a repeat of that Von Menck story from a few years back, the crazy old scientist predicting New York's imminent destruction by fire. That particular piece had landed him in hot water. No: if he really was on to something here, it had to be a theory that was backed up by solid reporting, facts, and evidence.

Slowly, deliberately, he paged through first one pile of sheets, then the second, and then the third, thinking carefully as he did so, looking for holes in his theory. Here were three people of overtly bad character. Ozmian, rich party girl; Cantucci, mob lawyer; Bogachyov, arms dealer and all-around asshole. But...it turned out Grace Ozmian had a terrible secret. And he would bet that the other two also had some grotesque evil hidden in their past. *Of course they did.* They weren't just low-grade scumbags: each one must have done a horrible deed, like Grace Ozmian, that had never been adequately punished—the very nature of their professions made it almost inevitable. The longer he thought, the more he examined the evidence, the more certain he became. It was so simple, so obvious, it had been staring him in the face all the time.

He began pacing the apartment again, but now the pacing was different: excited, animated. Nobody had figured it out. The police didn't have a clue. But the more he examined his discovery from every possible angle, the more he became confident...no, *convinced*...that he was right.

He strode back into the living room, sat down at the Queen Anne table, and pulled the laptop toward him. For a minute he sat motionless, composing his thoughts. And then he began to type: slowly at first, then faster and faster, the keys clacking deep into the snowy night. This would be a Christmas Day story that nobody would soon forget.

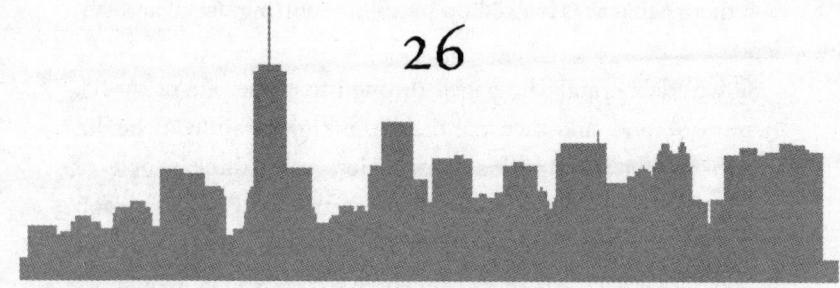

26

THE DECAPITATOR REVEALED

Headless Killings Linked

Bryce Harriman, New York Post — December 25

For almost two weeks, New York has been gripped by fear of a murderer. Three people have been brutally killed, their heads removed and spirited away, by an unknown perpetrator or perpetrators. Six others, security guards who apparently got in the way, were also murdered.

The NYPD are stymied. They have admitted they do not know if it is one murderer, or two—or even three. They don't have a motive. They don't have solid leads. The investigation has been desperately seeking a connection among the chief victims—*any* connection—without success.

But is this a classic case of not seeing the forest for the trees? An exclusive *Post* review of the evidence does suggest a connection, and the very motive, that the police have been floundering to find.

The *Post* analysis of the evidence lays out certain facts about the primary victims.

Victim one: Grace Ozmian, 23-year-old party girl with no greater aspiration in life than to spend Daddy's cash, indulge in illegal drug use, and lead a parasitic lifestyle when she's not in court getting slapped on the wrist for the hit-and-run killing of an eight-year-old boy while driving drunk.

Victim two: Marc Cantucci, AG turned mob lawyer, 65, who's raked in millions protecting New Jersey's most notorious crime bosses, a man who's beaten every grand jury investigation of his activities from embezzlement and extortion to racketeering and murder.

Victim three: Viktor Bogachyov, Russian oligarch, 51, who made his living by brokering decommissioned nuclear weapons via China, who then left his native country to take up residence in a massive Hamptons estate, where he promptly embroiled himself in lawsuits for nonpayment of taxes, stiffing employees, and riding roughshod over town regulations.

Can anyone look at these three "victims" and claim there is no connection among them? The *Post* analysis shows the glaring commonality: all three are utterly lacking in human decency.

These three "victims" are exceedingly rich, fla-

grantly corrupt, and entirely reprehensible. You
don't have to be an expert in criminal profiling to
find the thread that unites them: they have no redeeming value. The world would be better off if they
were dead. They are the very embodiment of the worst
of the ultra-rich.

So what is the motive to murder three such people?
That now seems obvious. These killings may well be
the work of a person who has taken upon himself the
role of judge, jury, and executioner; a killer who
is certainly a lunatic, perhaps also a religious or
moral absolutist, who chooses his victims *precisely*
because they embody the most depraved and dissolute
aspects of our contemporary world. And what better
place to find such icons of excess than among the one
percenters in New York City? And what better place to
sow vengeance—to, quite literally, turn Gotham into
a City of Endless Night?

While the three victims were murdered by various
means, all were then decapitated. Decapitation is the
most ancient and pure of punishments. The Decapitator
smites his victims with the sword of righteousness,
the scythe of God's wrath, and sends their souls to
perdition.

What, then, is New York to learn from these
killings? Perhaps the Decapitator is preaching to
the city. The killings are a warning to New York
and the country. That warning has two parts. The
first is made clear by the lifestyles of the victims, and it says: ye one percenters, mend your
ways before it's too late. The second part of

the warning is evident in the way the Decapitator selects his victims from the most invulnerable, protected, and bodyguarded in our midst. And that warning is:

No one is safe.

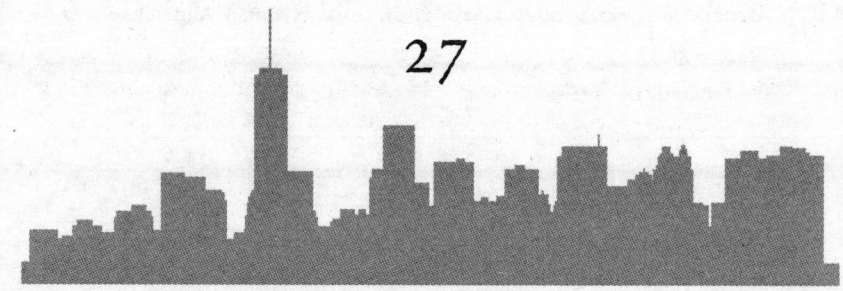

27

D'AGOSTA NEVER LIKED hospitals. It was more than a dislike; as soon as he entered one, with all the bright surfaces and fluorescent lights and bustle and beeping and the air laden with the smell of rubbing alcohol and bad food—he started to feel physically sick himself.

It was especially annoying to have to come in on Christmas Day at 5 AM in order to question a crazy cop-shooting motherfucker. As much as Laura understood—she was an NYPD captain, after all—it didn't stop her from getting resentful that he was out half the night again and again and could do nothing but crash when he got home, then get up and go off yet again—on Christmas morning, no less, not even lingering for coffee—and with only a few hastily purchased presents for her, to boot.

He had found Lasher in a room in a special lockdown wing of Bellevue, with four cops guarding him and a nurse hovering around. The wacko's gunshot wounds had been severe, and the doctors had taken more than twenty-four hours to stabilize him sufficiently to be questioned. He'd be fine. On the other hand,

D'Agosta's own man Hammer was in the ICU, still struggling for his very life.

Lasher was weak, but the injuries hadn't taken the bullshit out of him. For the past fifteen minutes, for every question D'Agosta had asked, no matter how mundane, the answer had quickly veered off into chemtrails, the JFK assassination, Project MKUltra. The guy was fucking nuts. On the other hand, he had no alibi for Cantucci's murder. He'd contradicted himself several times as he tried to explain his whereabouts and activities on the night of the murder and the day preceding. D'Agosta was almost sure he was lying, but at the same time the man was so crazy that it was hard to imagine him pulling off a slick murder like Cantucci's, techie or not.

On top of that, Pendergast had pulled another one of his disappearing acts, not answering texts, emails, or phone calls.

"Let's go over this again," said D'Agosta. "You say that on December eighteenth, you spent the day in the apartment, online, and that your Internet records will prove that."

"I told you, man, I—"

Overriding him, D'Agosta said: "Well, we looked at your Internet records for that day and the computer was scrubbed clean. Now, why would you erase those records?"

Lasher coughed, grimaced. "I go to great lengths to keep my browsing history secret, because you government people—"

"But you said the Internet records would, quote, 'prove I was online all day and night.'"

"And they would! They would, if I wasn't *forced* by government drones, digital wiretaps, and brain-wave transmitters to take extreme measures for my own protection—"

"Lieutenant," the nurse said, "I warned you about exciting this man. He's still very weak. If you press him, I'll be forced to end the interrogation."

D'Agosta heard some murmuring behind him and turned to see Pendergast at the door, being logged in to enter. *Finally.* Ignoring the nurse, he turned back to Lasher. "So your proof is no proof at all. Now, is there anyone in the building who could confirm you were there all day?"

"Of course."

Pendergast had now entered the room.

"Who?"

"You people."

"How's that?"

"You've been shadowing me for months, monitoring my every move. You *know* I didn't kill Cantucci!"

D'Agosta shook his head and turned to Pendergast. "You got anything you want to ask this asshole?"

"Not directly. But allow me to ask you, Vincent: did you get the results of the blood work on Mr. Lasher?"

"Sure."

"And did he test positive for methamphetamine hydrochloride?"

"Hell, yes. High as a kite."

"I thought so. Shall we step out into the hall?"

D'Agosta followed him out of the room.

"I don't need to ask any questions," Pendergast said, "because I know this fellow is innocent in the matter of the Cantucci killing."

"And how would you know that?"

"I found a sample of methamphetamine in his apartment. The large, yellowish salt-like grains I recognized immediately as a special 'brand,' if you will, of meth, known by its crystal shape, color, and consistency. A quick bit of research revealed the DEA had the meth cook of this particular variety under observation, in preparation for making an arrest, and that the product was sold out of a particular nightclub. So a certain colleague of mine arranged for me to view the surveillance videos the DEA had been taking of the nightclub's entrances and exits. And sure enough: Lasher was seen entering the nightclub, and then exiting it forty-five minutes later, no doubt making a buy...precisely during the period when Cantucci was killed."

D'Agosta stared at him, then finally laughed and shook his head. "Fucking A. It isn't Baugh, it isn't Ingmar, it isn't Lasher—every single decent lead has gone to hell. I feel like I'm rolling a ball of shit up an endless mountain."

"My dear Vincent, Sisyphus would be proud."

As they left Bellevue, a big New York *Post* truck making an early morning delivery had parked in the crosswalk, and as they went around it, the driver dropped a fat bundle of papers on the sidewalk beside them. The headline screamed:

THE DECAPITATOR REVEALED!!

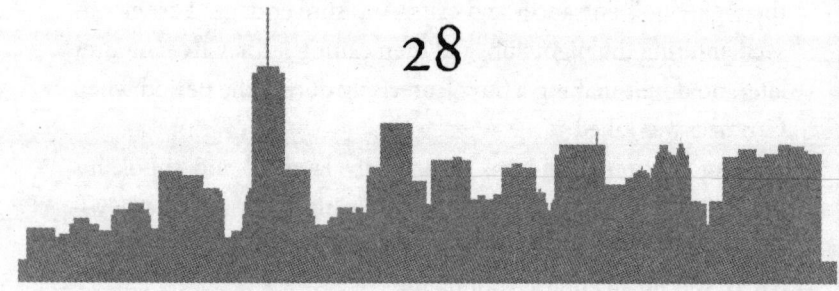

28

This is a first," said Singleton, as D'Agosta and the captain emerged from the Municipal Building for the short walk from One Police Plaza to City Hall. It was a sunny, brutally cold morning, with the temperature hovering at ten degrees. As yet there had been no snow, and the streets were like halls of frosty sunlight.

D'Agosta was filled with dread. He had never been called to the mayor's office before, let alone with his captain. "Any idea what we're going to face?" he asked.

Singleton said, "Look, it's not good. It's not even bad. It's horrendous. Normally, the mayor makes his views known through the commissioner. As I said, this is a first. Did you see that look he gave after the press conference?"

Without further discussion they turned into City Hall Park and entered the opulent neoclassical rotunda of City Hall itself. A gray-suited lackey, waiting for their arrival, routed them around security and took them up the stairs, down a vast and intimidating marble hall lined with dark paintings, to a set of double doors. They were ushered through an outer office and directly into the mayor's private office. No waiting.

No waiting. To D'Agosta, that seemed the worst omen of all.

The mayor stood behind his desk. Lying upon it were two neatly squared copies of the *Post*: yesterday's, with the big Harriman story, and beside it that morning's edition, with a follow-up piece by Harriman.

The mayor did not offer them a seat or sit down himself, nor did he offer his hand.

"All right," he said, his deep voice booming, "I'm getting pressure from all sides. You said you were developing leads. I need to know where we're at. I want to know the latest details."

Singleton had previously made it clear that D'Agosta, as the CDS on the case, was going to do the talking. *All* the talking. Unless the mayor directly addressed Singleton.

"Mayor DeLillo, thank you for your concern—" D'Agosta began.

"Cut the bullshit and tell me what I need to know."

D'Agosta took a deep breath. "It's..." He decided not to spin it. "Honestly, it's not good. We had a number of leads in the beginning, several of which seemed promising, but none of them panned out. It's been frustrating."

"*Finally* some straight talk. Keep going."

"In the first killing, we had reasons to suspect the father of the child the victim had killed in a hit-and-run. But he has an ironclad alibi. In the second killing, we were certain it was someone connected with the victim's security system. In fact, we're still sure of it—but the three most likely suspects did not pan out."

"What about that guy, Lasher, who shot one of your cops?"

"He has an alibi."

"Which is?"

"Caught on videotape by the DEA in a drug deal at the exact time of the killing."

"Christ. And the third killing?"

"The labs are still developing the evidence. We found the boat that the killer used—stolen, of course. But it looks like a dead end. There was no evidence in the boat and no evidence at the marina from which it was taken. We did, however, get a clear footprint of the killer. Size thirteen."

"What else?"

D'Agosta hesitated. "As for solid leads, that's it so far."

"That's *it*? *One* bloody footprint? Is that what you're telling me?"

"Yes, sir."

"And the FBI? Have they got anything? Are they holding out on you?"

"No. We have excellent rapport with the FBI. They would appear to be as stumped as we are."

"What about the FBI Behavioral Science Unit, the shrinks that are supposed to look into motivation and provide a profile. Any results?"

"Not yet. We've routed all relevant material to them, of course, but normally it takes a couple of weeks to get results. We've escalated our request, however, and we hope to have something in two days."

"Two days? Jesus."

"I'll do everything I can to hurry it up."

The mayor swept up yesterday's copy of the *Post* and waved it at them. "What about this? This Harriman story? Why didn't you see this possibility yourselves? Why does it take a goddamn reporter to come up with a viable theory?"

"We're absolutely looking into it."

"Looking into it. Looking *into* it! I got three bodies. Three headless bodies. Three rich, *notorious*, headless bodies. And I have a cop on life support. I don't need to tell you the kind of heat I'm getting."

"Mr. Mayor, there isn't any hard evidence yet backing up Harriman's idea it's a vigilante, but we're investigating that possibility—just as we're looking at many others."

The mayor dropped the paper back on the desk in disgust. "This theory that we've got some kind of crusading psycho out there, raining down judgment on the wicked, has really struck a chord. You know that, right? A lot of people in this town—important people—are getting nervous. And there are others cheering the killer on like some kind of serial-killer Robin Hood. We can't have this threat to the social fabric. This is not Keokuk or Pocatello: this is New York, where we have everyone under the sun finally living in harmony, enjoying the lowest crime rate of any big city in America. I am not going let that come apart on my watch. You got that? *Not on my watch.*"

"Yes, sir."

"It's a joke. Forty detectives, hundreds of beat cops—one footprint! If I don't see immediate progress, there will be hell to pay, Lieutenant. *And* Captain." He thumped the desk with a massive, veined hand, looking from one to the other. "*Hell* to pay."

"Mr. Mayor, we're pulling out all the stops, I promise you."

The mayor took a deep breath, his massive frame swelling, and then exhaled with a dramatic rush of air. "Now get out there and bring me something better than a damned footprint."

29

WHEN ALVES-VETTORETTO entered her boss's eyrie on the top floor of the DigiFlood tower, Anton Ozmian was sitting behind his desk, typing furiously at a laptop computer. He glanced up without stopping, eyed her through his steel-rimmed glasses, and nodded almost imperceptibly. She took a seat in one of the chrome-and-leather chairs and settled in to wait. The typing went on—sometimes fast, sometimes slow—for another five minutes. Then Ozmian pushed the laptop away, put his elbows on the black granite, and stared at his aide-de-camp.

"The SecureSQL takeover?" Alves-Vettoretto asked.

Ozmian nodded, massaging the graying hair at his temples. "Just had to make sure the poison pill was in place."

She nodded. Ozmian enjoyed hostile takeovers almost as much as he enjoyed firing his own employees.

Now Ozmian came out from behind the desk and took a seat in one of the other chrome-and-leather chairs. His tall, thin frame seemed strung tight as a bowstring, and she could guess why.

Ozmian gestured at a tabloid that sat on the table between

them: a copy of the Christmas edition of the *Post*. "I assume you saw this," he said.

"I did."

The entrepreneur picked it up, face contorting into a grimace as if he were handling dogshit, and turned to page three. "'Grace Ozmian,'" he quoted, his voice full of barely controlled rage. "'Twenty-three-year-old party girl with no greater aspiration in life than to spend Daddy's cash, indulge in illegal drug use, and lead a parasitic lifestyle when she's not in court getting slapped on the wrist for the hit-and-run killing of an eight-year-old boy while driving drunk.'" With a sudden violent gesture, he tore the tabloid in two, then into four, and then threw it dismissively on the floor. "That Harriman just won't let it rest. I gave him a chance to shut up and move on. But the shit-eating bastard keeps rubbing my face in it, tarnishing my daughter's good name. Well, his chance has come and gone."

"Very good."

"You know what I'm saying, right? The time has come to swat him—swat him flat as a mosquito. I want this to be the last filth the scumbag will ever write about my daughter."

"Understood."

Ozmian eyed his deputy. "Do you? I'm not just talking about putting a scare into him. I want him neutralized."

"I will make sure of that."

A twitch of the lips that might have been a smile passed quickly across Ozmian's narrow face. "I presume that, since we last talked about this issue, you've been considering an appropriate response."

"Of course."

"And?"

"I have something rather exquisite. Not only will it accomplish the desired task, but it will do so with an irony I think you'll appreciate."

"I knew I could count on you, Isabel. Tell me about it."

Alves-Vettoretto began to explain, Ozmian leaned back in his chair, listening to her cool, precise voice lay out the most delicious plan. As she continued, the smile returned to his face; only this time it was genuine, and it lingered for a long time.

30

BRYCE HARRIMAN BEGAN to ascend the steps to the main entrance of the *New York Post* building, then stopped. He'd climbed these steps a thousand times over the last few years. This morning, however, was different. This morning, Boxing Day, he'd been summoned to the office of his editor, Paul Petowski, for an unscheduled meeting.

Such a thing was very unusual. Petowski didn't like meetings—he preferred to stand in the middle of the newsroom and yell out his commands, rapid-fire, scattering assignments and follow-ups and research jobs like confetti over the surrounding staff. In Harriman's experience, people were summoned to Petowski's office for one of only two reasons: to get either chewed out—or fired.

He climbed the final steps and went through the revolving door into the lobby. Not for the first time since the day before, he felt plagued with self-doubt about his article—and the theory behind it. Oh, naturally, it had been vetted and okayed before publication, as had its follow-up, but he'd heard through the grapevine that it had caused quite a reaction. But what kind of reaction? Had it backfired? Was there blowback? He stepped into the elevator, swallowing painfully, and pressed the button for the ninth floor.

When he stepped out into the newsroom, the place seemed unusually quiet. To Harriman, the quiet had an ominous undertone: a watching, listening quality, as if the very walls were waiting for something bad to happen. Christ, was it really possible he had screwed up big time? His theory had seemed so sound—but he'd been wrong before. If he got booted from the *Post*, he'd have to leave town if he was going to find another job in the newspaper business. And with papers everywhere losing circulation and cutting costs, it would be a bitch to land another position, even with his reputation. He'd be lucky to get a job covering the dog races in Dubuque.

Petowski's office was in the back of the huge room. The door was closed, the shade pulled down over the window—another bad sign. As he threaded his way between the desks, passing people who were making a show of being busy, he could nevertheless feel every eye swiveling toward him. He glanced at his watch: ten o'clock. It was time.

He approached the door, knocked diffidently.

"Yeah?" came Petowski's gruff voice.

"It's Bryce," Harriman said, working hard to keep his voice from squeaking.

"Come in."

Harriman turned the knob, pushed the door open. He took a step in, then stopped. It took him a moment to process just what he was looking at. The small office was crowded with people: not just Petowski, but Petowski's boss, the deputy managing editor; her boss, the executive editor; even Willis Beaverton, the crusty old publisher himself. Seeing Harriman, they all broke out into applause.

As if in a dream, he heard the ovation; he felt his hand being pumped; felt hands slapping his back. "Brilliant piece of work, son!" Beaverton, the publisher, told him in a blast of cigar breath. "Absolutely brilliant!"

"You doubled our newsstand circulation, single-handedly," said Petowski, his usual scowl replaced by an avaricious smile. "That was the biggest Christmas issue we've had in almost twenty years."

Despite the early hour, somebody broke out a bottle of champagne. There were toasts; there were plaudits and laudations; Beaverton made a short speech. And then they all filed out again, each congratulating Harriman in turn as they went past. In a minute, the office was empty save for him and Petowski.

"Bryce, you've stumbled on something big," Petowski said, moving back behind his desk and pouring the last of the champagne into a plastic cup. "Reporters search their entire lives for a story like this." He drained the cup, let it drop into the wastebasket. "You stay on this Decapitator story, hear me? Stay on it hard."

"I intend to."

"I have a suggestion, though."

"Yes?" Harriman asked, suddenly cautious.

"This one percenter versus ninety-nine percenter angle. That really touched a nerve. Play it up. Focus on those one percenter predatory bastards and what they're doing to this city. Guys like Ozmian in their glass towers lording it above the rest. Is this city going to become a playground for the uber-rich while the rest barely scrape together a living in the darkness below? You get what I mean?"

"I sure do."

"And this phrase you used in the last piece, *City of Endless Night.*

That was good. *Damn* good. Turn it into a kind of mantra, work it into every piece."

"Absolutely."

"Oh, and by the way: as of now, I'm giving you a hundred-dollar-a-week raise." He leaned over the desk and—with a final slap to the back—ushered Harriman out of his office.

Harriman stepped through the door and into the big newsroom. His shoulders stung from Petowski's hearty blow. As he glanced slowly around at the sea of faces staring back at him—and, in particular, took in the sour expressions of his young rivals—he began to sense, with a kind of golden inner glow, the upwelling of a feeling quite unlike any he'd ever experienced before: intense, total, and consummate vindication.

31

BALDWIN DAY DETACHED the five-terabyte external hard drive from the desktop computer and slipped it into his briefcase for the short journey to the top floor of the Seaside Financial Center building near Battery Park. He made the same trip once a day, carrying the precious data that kept the company, LFX Financial, speeding along the highway of profit and yet more profit. On that drive were the names and personal information of many thousands of people his data-marketing team's research had turned up as leads, or, as they called them in the maze of call center cube farms that occupied three floors of the Seaside complex, "colonels." The leads were mostly retired vets and the spouses of soldiers on active duty. Most precious of all the "colonels" were the widows of vets who owned homes with paid-off mortgages. Every day at 4 PM sharp, Day delivered this hard drive to the executive office suite on the top floor, where the founders and co-CEOs of the firm, Gwen and Rod Burch, had their offices. The Burches would peruse the lists of leads, and they had a nose for sniffing out the best from the extraordinary masses of data. They would pass along their edited and annotated list to the massive boiler room operation of LFX Financial, which would go to work on it, calling thousands of "colonels," trying to land them as "clients," although the more appropriate word, Day thought, might be *suckers*. Every boiler room caller had to sign up at least eight clients a day, forty a week—or be fired.

Day had been looking for another job almost from the moment he discovered what the company actually did. He was desperate to get out of LFX, not because he was underpaid or overworked—he had no complaints there—but because of the kind of rip-off scam they were engaged in. When he first joined LFX as team leader in the high-sounding Department of Analytics and realized what was going on, he was sickened. It just wasn't right.

And of course, on top of that there was always a chance the government might take a stronger interest in the LFX shenanigans. After all, it *was* the Burches he was working for.

These thoughts went through his mind as he got on the crowded elevator, tapped his security card against the reader, and pressed the button for the top floor. Security was super tight at the company ever since a discharged soldier, suffering from traumatic brain injury caused by an IED in Iraq, barged into the lobby with a handgun, shooting and wounding three people before turning the gun on himself. His name had been on one of those lists Day had sent upstairs about three months before the incident. That was how long it took LFX to take away the guy's house—three short months. After the shooting, nothing changed at LFX Financial regarding company practices and incentives, except that a fanatical security regime had been implemented and a sense of paranoia had thickened the air. Part of that security regime was the isolation and compartmentalization of computer networks, which was the reason why he now had to transfer data to the executive suite the old-fashioned way: by carrying it up on foot.

The elevator doors opened into the elegant lobby of the Seaside building's top floor. The Burches went in for over-the-top opulence, lots of dark wood paneling, gold leaf, faux marble, plush carpeting, and fake Old Masters on the walls. Day passed through the lobby, nodding to the receptionists, and again tapped his card on the reader next to the door. At the prompt he pressed his finger on a fingerprint scanner; the wooden door swung open to reveal the outer executive suite of offices, bustling with the comings and goings of secretaries and assistants. This was the busiest time of day at LFX Financial, just as the contracts were pouring in from the boiler room.

Day smiled and nodded to the various secretaries and assistants as he passed by on his way to the Burches' private suite.

He checked in with Iris, the head office honcho, just outside the door. Iris was a tough old bird, no nonsense, "good people" as they say. Anyone who could survive working this close to the Burches had to be both capable and tough.

"I think the Burches are in conference," she told him. "At least, Roland just came out a few minutes ago."

"You know I have to deliver this in person."

"Just warning you, that's all." She looked at him over her glasses and gave him a brief smile.

"Thanks, Iris."

He crossed the plush carpet to the set of double doors that led into the inner sanctum and placed his hand on the cold brass knob. He always felt a twinge at this moment, just before entering. Beyond lay a gilded monstrosity of a space, done up in gold and black and occupied by two truly horrible trolls. Nine times out of ten they never even looked at him when he dropped off the drive, but once in a while they'd throw out a random disparaging comment, and a few times they had dressed him down for some perceived infraction.

When he went to turn the door, the handle was locked. This was unusual.

"Iris?" He turned. "The door's locked."

The secretary leaned over the intercom on her desk and pressed a button. "Mr. Burch? Mr. Day is here to drop off the data."

She waited, but there was no answer.

"Mr. and Mrs. Burch?" she asked again.

Still no answer.

"Perhaps it's out of order." She rose and strode briskly to the door, giving it a firm double rap.

A wait.

Another double rap, done twice.

More waiting.

"How odd. I *know* they're in there." She tried the handle, tried it again. Then she took the electronic card dangling from her neck, tapped it on the reader, and pressed her thumb.

With a click the door released.

Day followed Iris into the grand and vulgar space. For a split second he thought there'd been a new decorating scheme that had done over the room in red. Then he realized he was staring at blood, more blood than he had ever seen in his life, more blood than he thought possible could exist in the two headless corpses that lay on the soaked carpet before his feet.

Day heard a sigh and turned just in time to catch Iris as she folded and sank toward the floor. He dragged her back out of the room, his feet squishing along the wet carpet. The door closed automatically behind him as he laid her on a sofa in the reception area, to the sudden consternation of everyone in the outer office space. Then he sought out a seat for himself and eased down in it, head in his shaking hands.

"What is it?" a secretary asked sharply. "What's happened?"

Day's mind was not clear enough to speak. But it was already evident what had happened.

"What's *happened*?" she demanded again as he tried to clear his head enough to answer while people gathered around, and others approached the closed door to the inner office, hesitatingly.

"For God's sake, tell us what happened!"

Others in the room now rushed to the door of the inner office and tried to open it, but the door had relocked automatically when it shut.

"Vengeance," Day managed to say. "Vengeance is what's happened."

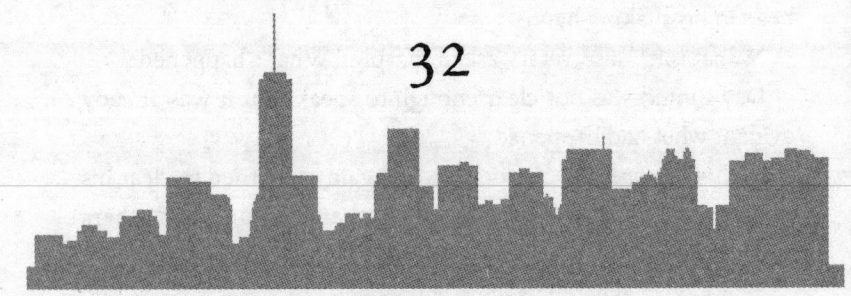

32

Aт тне entrance to the top floor, next to the elevator, the Crime Scene Unit had set up a gowning station, with racks of Tyvek suits, masks, gloves, and booties. Lieutenant D'Agosta donned the full array, as did Pendergast. D'Agosta couldn't help but notice that the agent did not look good in the suit; not good at all. The baggy outfit looked more like a burial shroud when coupled with his pale skin and gaunt frame.

They signed in at the makeshift entrance, where Sergeant Curry, already gowned, was waiting for them. The entire floor had been segregated as a crime scene, and the forensic teams were in full collection mode, many on their hands and knees, going over everything with tweezers and test tubes and ziplock evidence bags. Once dressed, D'Agosta paused to watch. They looked good, damn good. Of course, with him and the FBI on-site now, everyone was putting on a show for their benefit, but these were the best the NYPD had to offer and their professionalism was on display for all to see. He wished to hell they would find something solid he could take to the mayor—and fast. This new double homicide probably meant the case would be taken away from him if his team didn't show serious progress. With luck they'd learn something important from the two who'd discovered the body.

As D'Agosta looked around, he said, "This is a crazy place to commit a murder."

Pendergast inclined his head. "Perhaps it isn't, strictly speaking, a murder."

D'Agosta let this one pass, as he did so many of Pendergast's other cryptic remarks.

"You want to walk the whole floor or just see the murder scene?" Curry asked.

D'Agosta looked at Pendergast, who shrugged almost with indifference. "As you wish, Vincent."

"Let's just have a look at the scene," D'Agosta told Curry.

"Yes, sir." Curry led them across the reception area. The place had the hushed feeling of a sickroom, or a hospital ward for terminal patients, and it smelled strongly of forensic chemicals.

"There are cameras everywhere," said D'Agosta. "Were they disabled?"

"No," said Curry. "We're downloading the video from the data drives now. But it looks like they captured everything."

"They recorded the killer coming and going?"

"We'll know as soon as we take a look. We'll go down to the security office after this, if you want."

"I want." He added: "Wonder how the perp walked out of here with two heads under his arms."

At the far end of the outer offices, D'Agosta spied a man, also in a CSU suit, taking pictures with a cell phone in a ziplock bag. He was clearly not a cop or crime scene investigator, and he looked a bit green around the gills. "Who's that guy?" he asked.

"He's with the SEC," said Curry.

"SEC? What for? How'd he get clearance?"

Curry shrugged.

"Bring him over."

Curry went and fetched him. The man was large and bald with horn-rimmed glasses, wearing a gray suit under his gown, and he was sweating something fierce.

"I'm Lieutenant D'Agosta," he said, "Commander Detective Squad, and this is Special Agent Pendergast, FBI."

"Supervising Agent Meldrum, SEC Division of Enforcement. Glad to make your acquaintance." He stuck out his hand.

"Sorry, no handshaking at a crime scene," said D'Agosta. "You know—might exchange DNA."

"Right, they did mention that, sorry." The man pulled his hand back sheepishly.

"If you don't mind me asking," D'Agosta said, "what's the SEC's interest and who authorized you on the crime scene?"

"Authorization from U.S. Attorney's Office, Southern District. We've been after these two for a long time."

"That right?" D'Agosta asked. "What'd they do?"

"Plenty."

"When we finish the walk-through," said D'Agosta, "and get rid of these damn suits, I'd like you to fill us in."

"Glad to."

They walked across the open space toward a pair of ornate wooden doors, which were wedged open. Light streamed out from the interior of the inner office, and the primary color D'Agosta could see beyond was a deep crimson. There was a team inside, moving with exquisite care on mats laid down over a blood-soaked rug.

"Oh, Jesus. Did the perp leave them arranged like that?"

"The bodies haven't been moved, sir."

The two bodies lay stretched out on the floor, side by side, arms folded over their chests, carefully arranged by the killer or killers. In the intense lights set up by the CSU team it looked fake, like a movie set. But the smell of blood was real, a mingling of damp iron and meat starting to go bad. While the sight was awful enough, D'Agosta could never get used to the smell. Never. He felt his gorge rise and struggled to calm the spastic reaction that had abruptly seized his stomach. The blood was *everywhere*. This was crazy. Where was the blood spatter guy? There he was.

"Hey, Martinelli? A word?"

Martinelli rose and came over.

"What's the story with this blood? This some kind of deliberate paint job?"

"I've still got a lot of analysis to do."

"Prelim?"

"Well, seems both the victims were beheaded standing up."

"How do you know?"

"The blood on the ceiling. That's sixteen feet. It shot straight up, arterial jetting. In order for it to reach that height, their heart rate and blood pressure must've been sky-high."

"What would cause that? The high blood pressure, I mean."

"I'd say these two knew what was coming, at least during the last few moments. They were made to stand up and knew they were about to be decapitated, and that produced an extremity of terror that would have resulted in spikes in both blood pressure and heart rate. Again, that's my first impression only."

D'Agosta tried to wrap his head around it. "Chopped off with what?"

Martinelli nodded. "Right over there."

D'Agosta turned and there it was: a medieval weapon of some kind, lying on the floor, its blade completely covered in blood.

"It's called a bearded ax. Viking. Replica, of course. Razor-sharp."

D'Agosta glanced at Pendergast, but he was even more opaque than usual inside the Tyvek suit.

"Why didn't they scream? Nobody heard anything."

"We're pretty sure a secondary weapon was involved. Probably a firearm. Used in a threatening way to keep them quiet. On top of that, those doors are extremely thick, and the entire suite is heavily soundproofed."

D'Agosta shook his head. It was the craziest thing, killing the twin CEOs of a major company right in their own offices at the busiest time of day, with cameras running and a thousand people around. He looked again at Pendergast. In contrast to his usual poking and prying about with tweezers and test tubes, this time he was silent, and as calm as if he were out for a stroll in the park. "So, Pendergast, *you* got any questions? Anything you want to look at? Evidence?"

"Not at present, thank you."

"I'm just the blood spatter guy," Martinelli said, "but it would seem to me the killer's sending some kind of message. The *Post* is saying that—"

D'Agosta cut him off with a gesture. "I know what the *Post* is saying."

"Right, sorry."

Pendergast now spoke at last. "Mr. Martinelli, wouldn't the perpetrator be covered in blood after decapitating two standing people?"

"You'd think so. But the handle is unusually long on that ax, and if he stood at some distance, decapitated each of them with one clean swipe, and if he were agile enough to jump aside to avoid the jetting arterial blood as the bodies fell, he might just get away without being splattered."

"Would you say he was proficient in the use of that ax?"

"If you look at it that way, yes. It's not easy to decapitate some-one with a single blow, especially if they're standing up. And to do it without getting covered in blood—yeah, I would say that takes serious practice."

D'Agosta shuddered.

"Thank you, that is all," said Pendergast.

They met up with the SEC guy in the security office in the base-ment. On their way down, passing through the lobby, they had seen a crowd in front of the building. At first D'Agosta thought it was the usual unruly press, and it was that, of course, but more. The waving signs and muffled chanting indicated it was some sort of demonstration against the one percent. *Damn New Yorkers, any excuse to protest.*

"Chat over there?" he said, indicating a seating area in the wait-ing room. The NYPD techies were downloading and preparing the last of the security footage.

"As good as any."

The three of them took their seats, the SEC guy, Pendergast, and D'Agosta.

"So, Agent Meldrum," D'Agosta said. "Brief us on the SEC in-vestigation."

"Of course." Meldrum handed over a card. "I'll have copies of our files sent over to you."

"Thank you."

"The Burches are, or rather were, a married couple—twenty-two years. Back during the financial crisis they set up an invest-ment scheme that took advantage of people with distressed mort-gages. It collapsed in 2012 and they were arrested."

"And they didn't go to jail?"

Meldrum engaged in a mirthless stretching of the lips. "Jail? I'm sorry, Lieutenant, where have you been these past ten years? I can't tell you how many cases I've worked on where, instead of prosecuting, we negotiated a settlement and levied a fine. These two swindlers got slapped on the wrist and quickly opened a new rip-off shop—LFX Financial."

"Which does what?"

"Targets the spouses of soldiers and retired vets. Two basic swindling schemes. You got a soldier overseas. The spouse—usually a wife—is stateside, having a tough time economically. So you get the wife to take out a balloon mortgage on the house. Small initial payments, then the rate resets to what they can't afford. LFX takes the house, flips it, rakes in the bucks."

"Legal?"

"Mostly. Except there are special rules about foreclosing on a soldier on active duty that they didn't follow. That's where I come in."

"And the second scheme?"

"LFX would identify the widow of a vet who's living in a nice house, fully paid off. They'd persuade her to take out a small reverse mortgage. No big deal, done all the time. But then LFX would force a default on the reverse mortgage for some bogus reason: nonpayment of homeowner's insurance or some other trumped-up or trivial violation of terms. Just enough of an excuse to take the house, sell it, and keep an obscene amount of the proceeds as late fees, fines, interest, penalties, and other jacked-up charges."

"In other words, these two were the scum of the earth," said D'Agosta.

"You bet."

"Must have had a lot of enemies."

"Yes. In fact, some time back there was a mass shooting in this very building—a soldier who lost his home came in and aired out the place before committing suicide."

"Oh yeah," said D'Agosta. "I remember that. So you think the two were killed by a victim seeking revenge?"

"It's a reasonable hypothesis, and that's what I thought when I first got the call."

"But you don't think so now."

"No. It seems pretty clear to me it's the same psycho who did those other three headless people: a vigilante type punishing rich dirtbags. You know, like what the articles in the *Post* are saying."

D'Agosta shook his head. As much as he couldn't stand that bastard Harriman, his theory was looking more and more likely. He glanced at Pendergast and couldn't help but ask: "What do you think?"

"A great deal."

D'Agosta waited, but it was soon clear that would be the extent of his comment. "It's insane. You got two people decapitated in the middle of the day in a busy office building. How'd the killer get past security, how'd he get into the office, how'd he kill them, cut their heads off, and get out—with nobody seeing anything? Seems impossible, like one of those locked-room mysteries by—what's his name?—Dickson Carr."

Pendergast nodded. "In my opinion, the important questions are not so much *who* the victims were, *why* they were selected, or *how* the murder was done."

"What else is there to a murder than the who, why, and how?"

"My dear Vincent, there's the *where*."

33

THE SOUND ENGINEER clipped the lavalier mike to Harriman's shirt, adjusted it, and then retreated to his station. "Speak a few words, please," he called over. "In a normal voice."

"This is Bryce Harriman," Harriman said. *"Let us go then, you and I, when the evening is spread out against the sky..."*

"Okay, we've got good levels." The engineer gave the producer a thumbs-up.

Harriman looked around the studio stage. A television studio always amused him: 10 percent of it was done up to look like somebody's living room, or an anchor's desk, and the rest of the space was always a huge mess, all concrete floor and hanging lights and green screens and cameras and cable runs and people standing around watching.

This was the third show he'd done this week, and each had been bigger than the one before. It was like a barometer of how successful his article, and its follow-ups, had been. First, there was the local New York station—taped, not live—that had given him a two-minute spot. Next had been an appearance on *The Melissa Mason Show*, one of the most popular talk shows in the tristate area. But then the news of the double murders had broken—murders that fit his predictions to a T. And now he was appearing on the big kahuna: *America's Morning with Kathee Durant*, one of the biggest nationally televised morning shows in the country. And there was Kathee herself, sitting not two feet away from him, getting her face touched up during the commercial break. The *Morning* set was done up to look like an upscale breakfast nook, with American naive paintings on the fake walls and two wing chairs with doily antimacassars facing each other, a large-screen monitor in between.

"Ten seconds," said somebody from the dim recesses of the stage. The makeup person ducked away, and Kathee turned toward Harriman. "It's great to have you here," she said, flashing her million-dollar smile at him. "It's such an awesome story. I mean, *awe*some."

"Thanks." Harriman smiled back. He watched as a number counted down on a digital screen, then a red light appeared on one of the three cameras pointed at them.

Kathee turned her dazzling smile toward the camera. "This morning we're lucky to have with us Bryce Harriman, the *Post* reporter who—people are saying—has done what the NYPD could not: figure out the motivation of the killer who's been dubbed 'the Decapitator.' And in the wake of the recent double murder—which fits exactly with Mr. Harriman's theory, first described in an article he published Christmas Day—the story really seems to have touched a nerve. Celebrities, millionaires, rock stars, even mob bosses have begun fleeing the city."

As she spoke, the monitor between them—which had been displaying the *America's Morning* logo—came alive with brief video clips of people getting into limousines; private planes taxiing on runways; familiar faces rushing past paparazzi, surrounded by security entourages. The clips were familiar: Bryce had seen them all before. He'd seen it happening in person, as well. People, powerful people, were deserting Manhattan like rats fleeing a sinking ship. And all because of him. Meanwhile, Joe Q. Public was watching it all unfold with the sick thrill of at last seeing the one percenters get theirs.

Kathee turned to Bryce. "Bryce, welcome to *America's Morning*. Thanks for coming."

"Thanks for having me, Kathee," Harriman said. He shifted slightly, presenting his best profile to the camera.

"Bryce, your story is the talk of the town," Kathee told him. "How did you happen to figure out what has been eluding the best minds of New York's finest for what seems like weeks?"

Harriman felt a thrill course through him as he remembered Petowski's words: *Reporters search their entire lives for a story like this.* "Oh, I can't take all the credit," he said with fake modesty. "Really, I was just building on the groundwork that the police had already laid."

"But what was the, how can I put it, the lightbulb moment?" With her perky nose and blond wave, she looked just like a Barbie.

"Well, there were a lot of theories flying through the air at the time, you'll recall," Bryce said. "I just didn't buy into the notion that there was more than one murderer at work. Once I'd made that realization, it was just a question of looking for what all the victims had in common."

She glanced over at a teleprompter, which was scrolling lines from Harriman's first article. "You said that the victims were all 'utterly lacking in human decency.' That 'the world would be better off if they were dead.'"

Harriman nodded.

"And cutting off their heads is, you believe, a symbolic gesture?"

"That's right."

"But I mean, beheading...any chance this is the work of jihadists?"

"No. That doesn't fit the pattern. This is the work of one man, and he's using decapitation for reasons that are very much his own. True: this is an ancient punishment, a manifestation of God's wrath at the sin and depravity so rampant in today's society. Even the term *capital punishment* comes from *caput*, the Latin word for 'head.' But this killer is preaching, Kathee: he's warning New York, and by extension the whole country, that greed, selfishness, and gross materialism will no longer be tolerated. He's targeting the most predatory of the one percenters who seem to be taking over our city these past few years."

Kathee nodded vigorously, eyes shining, drinking in his every word. Bryce realized something: with this one story, he had become a celebrity. He'd taken the most high-profile series of murders in many years and, single-handedly, *owned* it. His follow-up articles, carefully scripted for maximum sensation and to polish his own image, were just icing on the cake. Everyone in New York was hanging on his every word. They wanted, *needed* him to explain the Decapitator to them.

And he would be only too happy to oblige. This interview was a golden opportunity to fan the flames—and that was just what he would do.

"But what is he preaching, exactly?" Kathee asked. "And who is he preaching to?"

Bryce tugged self-importantly at his tie, careful not to disturb the mike. "It's quite simple, really. Look what's happened to our city, the corrupt wealth pouring in from overseas, the fifty- and hundred-million-dollar apartments, the billionaires walling themselves off in their gilded palaces. New York City used to be a place where everyone, rich and poor, rubbed shoulders and got along. Now the uber-rich are taking over our city, stomping on the rest of us. I think the killer's message to them is: *Mend your ways*." He gave these last words an ominous spin.

Kathee's eyes grew wider. "Are you saying that the Decapitator's going to keep killing the super-rich?"

Harriman let a long, pregnant moment pass. Then he nodded. *Time to fan those flames.* "I do. But let's not become complacent. He may be starting with the rich and powerful," he intoned. "But if we don't heed his warning...that may not be where he stops. We're *all* at risk, Kathee—every last one of us."

34

THE SECURITY OFFICES for the Seaside Financial building, and LFX Financial in particular, were located in a windowless basement suite of painted cinder block and functional metal furniture. But the actual surveillance system, D'Agosta realized as soon as they entered, was state-of-the-art, brand-new, and run by a more-than-competent group. The head of the security team, a guy named Hradsky, had sequestered all the video from the entire building and had organized and copied it onto hard drives for the NYPD tech team, who had carted it away. But D'Agosta didn't want to wait to see it at 1PP, which would take hours, if not a day, to set up. He wanted to see it immediately. And so Hradsky had obligingly organized it and had everything ready to roll when D'Agosta and Pendergast arrived with Sergeant Curry in tow.

"Gentlemen, come on in." Hradsky was a small guy with black hair, a rack of dazzling white teeth, pink gums, and a big smile that was, apparently, continuously on display. He looked more like a barber than a security tech, but as D'Agosta watched the man bustle about the viewing room, switching on this, plugging in that, and tapping on this and that keyboard, he realized they were damn lucky. Most security directors were unhelpful, if not downright hostile. This guy aimed to please and clearly knew what he was doing.

"So what, exactly, would you fellows like to see?" Hradsky said. "We have a lot of cams and over a thousand hours of video created in just the last day. We sent it all back with your people."

"What I want is simple. There's a cam right outside those inner office doors. I want you to go to that feed and start at the moment the bodies were discovered—and run the tape backward at double speed."

"Very well."

It took Hradsky only a moment to set things up and darken the room. A surprisingly clear image popped up on the screen, a wide-angle view of the inner double doors and the area surrounding them, with desks on either side. It started out with the guy who found the bodies sitting with his head in his hands, while a secretary was laid out on a couch next to him. Then they staggered up, the guy dragging the lady backward into the inner office. A few moments later they came back out, walking backward, and here was the guy trying the locked door handle with the lady, and then the lady walked backward to her desk and the guy walked backward out of view and the doors remained closed while people swarmed this way and that in the outer office.

They waited as the seconds continued to run backward. And then the doors opened and a man with a large instrument case appeared on stage left, walking backward, and entered the office doors, backward, the door shutting.

"Freeze!" D'Agosta said.

Hradsky froze it.

"Play forward in slo mo."

He played it forward, and now the doors opened and the man walked out.

"Freeze frame." D'Agosta got up and stared. It was a remarkably clear shot. "That's our guy, right? He was the last one out of the office before the bodies were found. That's *gotta* be him." He looked at Pendergast, half expecting a contradiction.

But no, Pendergast said: "Your logic is airtight."

"Look at the thing he's carrying. Big enough for either a sword *or* two heads! And the timestamp is just when the M.E. put the time of death. Holy shit, that's him!"

"It would seem without a doubt," said Pendergast.

"So who is he?" D'Agosta turned to Hradsky. "You seen him before?"

Hradsky moved the frame forward and backward, isolated the guy's face, expanded it, and worked a few software controls to sharpen it. "He looks familiar. I think he works here. Shit, it's McMurphy!"

"Who's that?"

He pressed a button and a digital personnel file sprang on the screen. There was a picture of the man beside his name: Roland McMurphy, assistant vice president, with all his personal data: phone, address on Columbus Avenue, everything.

"That's our guy." *At last.* D'Agosta had difficulty keeping the exultation from his voice.

"Um," Hradsky said, "I don't think so."

"What do you mean?"

"*McMurphy?* I can't even begin to imagine him doing this. He's one of those slope-shouldered guys, you know, with the double chin, a hypochondriac, butterfly collector, cello player, scurries around like he's about to get whipped."

"It's sometimes the guys you least suspect," said D'Agosta. "They explode."

"We can verify his presence. We keep digital records of everyone who comes in and out of the building." Hradsky was paging through some on-screen records. "Says here he didn't come in to work—called in sick, it seems."

"So he called in sick and then sneaked in." D'Agosta turned to Curry. "Send two squad cars to his place with a backup and SWAT team alert. Do it now."

"Yes, Lieutenant." He moved away and got on the phone, making calls.

Hradsky cleared his throat. "I'd like to think that what you suggest, him sneaking in, would be difficult if not impossible. We've got state-of-the-art security here."

Pendergast said quietly, "May I make a request?"

D'Agosta glanced at him. "Yeah, go ahead."

"The killer left the office at four oh one PM. How long does it take to get from there to the main entrance?"

"I'd say about six to eight minutes," said Hradsky.

"Excellent. Let us check the lobby camera at four oh seven to see whether he left."

Hradsky set it up and a moment later, sure enough, they watched the man with the cello case walk out of the lobby at four oh eight.

"Now," said Pendergast, "continue running the original office cam in reverse until we see him *entering*."

They watched as the video ran backward, and then they saw the man emerge from the door and walk backward out of view.

"Three fifty PM," said Pendergast. "Now we know the murder took place over the course of eleven minutes, between three fifty and four oh one. Excellent. Mr. Hradsky, take us to the lobby cam eight minutes before to see if he enters the building."

D'Agosta watched as Hradsky did so—and there was the man, coming in the door at 3:42 PM. They watched as the man entered the revolving door, went straight to the electronic gate, and slid in his security card, which promptly opened the gate.

"What's the timestamp on swiping the card?" asked Pendergast.

"Three forty-three and two seconds," said Hradsky.

"Please check your security logs for whoever logged in at that precise moment."

"Yes. Smart." Hradsky tapped some more, then frowned at the image on his screen. He stared a long time, lips pursed. He tried it again.

"So?" D'Agosta asked. "Who was it?"

"Nobody. Nobody signed in at that time."

At that moment Curry emerged from a far corner, after having made a series of phone calls. "Lieutenant?"

"What is it?"

"Roland McMurphy was in the hospital the entire day having a colostomy bag installed."

They emerged from the lobby into the plaza in front of the Seaside Financial building, where a noisy crowd had formed, shouting and waving placards.

"Not another demonstration," D'Agosta said. "What the fuck do they want now?"

"No idea," said Curry.

As D'Agosta searched the seething mass for a path through, he began to get an inkling of what was going on. There were, in fact, two very different groups protesting. One was waving signs and shouting slogans like *Down with the One Percenters!* and *Decapitate Corporate Greedsters!* They were at the young, scruffy end of the spectrum, pretty much the same crowd D'Agosta remembered from the Occupy Wall Street protests of a few years before. The other group was quite different; many of them were young, too, but dressed in coats and ties, looking more like Mormon missionaries than radical leftists. They were not shouting anything, just silently carrying signs with various slogans, such as WHO OWNS YOU?... WELCOME TO THE NEW BONFIRE OF THE VANITIES... THE BEST THINGS IN LIFE AREN'T "THINGS"... and CONSUMERISM IS A FATAL ILLNESS.

Even though the two sides seemed to agree on the wickedness of money, there were shouted insults and scuffles where they were crowding together as more and more people arrived from various side streets to join in. As D'Agosta watched, he saw that one man seemed to be the leader of the quieter group—a thin, gray-haired man wearing a dirty down coat over what looked like monk's robes. He was holding a sign that said

VANITIES

With crudely painted fire underneath the word.

"Hey, see that guy? What do you make of him?"

Pendergast glanced over. "An ex-Jesuit, by the looks of the threadbare cassock underneath his jacket. And the sign is evidently an allusion to Savonarola's 'bonfire of the vanities.' That's a rather interesting twist on the current situation, wouldn't you say, Vincent? New Yorkers never cease to surprise me."

D'Agosta had a vague recollection of hearing something about a madman named Savonarola in Italian history but he couldn't quite pull it up. "Those quiet ones—they scare me more than the rabble. They look like they mean it."

"Indeed," said Pendergast. "It appears that we are not just dealing with a serial killer, but with a social protest movement—or even two."

"Yeah. And if we don't solve this soon, New York's going to have a frigging civil war."

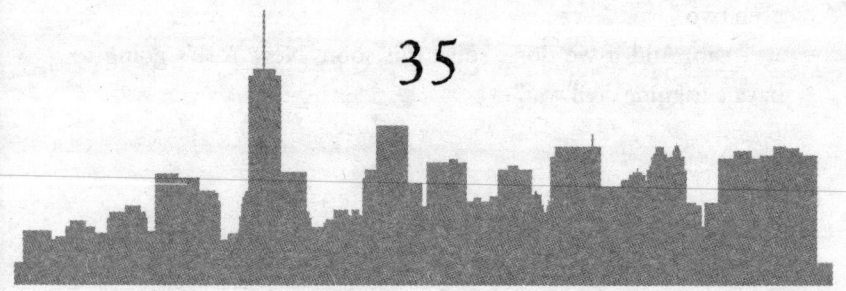

35

Marsden Swope emerged into the December chill in front of his East 125th Street apartment and breathed deeply, trying to rid his lungs of the dead air of his basement studio. Following the protest of the previous afternoon, he felt energized. Ever since— for eighteen hours straight—Swope had been sitting at his old Gateway computer, blogging, tweeting, Facebooking, Instagramming, and emailing. It was astonishing, he thought, how one modest idea could snowball into something so big in such a short period of time. The world was hungry for what he had to offer. How strange this felt—after all his years of laboring in obscurity and poverty.

He took several more deep breaths. He felt light-headed, not just from staring at a computer screen for so long, but also because he hadn't eaten in two days. He felt no hunger, but he knew he had to eat something to keep going; while his spirit was nourished, his body was running on empty.

Out on the sidewalk, in the bright, cold winter light, cars rushed by, heedless people going about their meaningless business. He walked down to Broadway and crossed it, passing under the elevated tracks as a train rumbled overhead, clacking and thundering on its way northward, then he angled toward the McDonald's on the corner of 125th and Broadway.

The place was occupied with the usual derelicts trying to escape the cold by nursing a cup of coffee and the inevitable group of Asian guys playing cards. He paused: here were the very invisibles, the poor, who had been trodden upon, crushed, and ground into the dirt by the rich and powerful of this fallen city. Soon, very soon, their lives would change...thanks to him.

But not quite yet. He went to the counter and ordered two dozen Chicken McNuggets and a chocolate milk jug, collected his order, and took it to a table. He might as well have been invisible: nobody knew him, nobody looked at him. And to be sure, there wasn't much to look at—a small man in his fifties with thinning gray hair, a close-cropped beard, skinny and undernourished, dressed in a brown Salvation Army down jacket, slacks, and secondhand shoes.

Formerly a Jesuit priest, Swope had left the Society of Jesus ten years earlier. This was to avoid being expelled, mostly due to his highly vocal disgust with the hypocrisy of the Catholic Church regarding all the money and property it had accumulated over the centuries, in direct contradiction to Jesus's teachings on poverty. As a Jesuit he had taken a vow of poverty, but what a contrast that was with the obscene riches of the church. "It is easier for a camel to go through the eye of a needle than for a rich person to enter the kingdom of God" was, in his mind, the clearest statement Jesus ever made in his time on earth, and yet—as he had expressed many times to his superiors, much to their displeasure—it was the one universally ignored by many so-called Christians.

But not now. No longer were the downtrodden going to take this. The answer wasn't an outer revolution, the kind espoused by so many others who had suddenly begun protesting. Nothing would ever change humanity's greed. No, what Swope was calling for was an *internal* revolution. You couldn't change the greed of the world but you could change yourself, make a commitment to poverty and simplicity and rejecting the vanities.

And so he had left under a cloud and continued his lonely crusade online, railing against money, wealth, and privilege. He had been a voice in the wilderness—until he joined that demonstration, on a whim. And as he talked to folks, and marched, and talked some more, he realized he had finally found his people and his calling.

Only two days ago, while reading about the Decapitator killings in the *New York Post*, he had an idea. He would organize a bonfire. A symbolic bonfire, like the one put on by the monk Savonarola in the central square of Florence on February 7, 1497. On that date, thousands of Florentine citizens had answered Savonarola's call to bring into the great piazza items of vanity and greed, pile them up, and burn them in a symbolic cleansing of their souls. And the citizenry had responded with enormous enthusiasm, flinging on cosmetics, mirrors, obscene books, playing cards, rich clothes, frivolous paintings, and other manifestations of worldly greed, then setting them alight in a gigantic "bonfire of the vanities."

And then, as if on cue, he had heard about the demonstration on social media, joined it, and it had crystallized all his previous thoughts and ideas around that one idea: a twenty-first-century bonfire of the vanities. And what better place to do it than New York City, the Florence of the modern world, the city of billionaires and bums, the richest and the poorest, the midnight playground of the rich and the midnight pit of despair of the poor.

And so the ex-Jesuit, Marsden Swope, had put out a modest

appeal on social media to everyone out there fed up with the materialism, narcissism, greed, selfishness, inequality, and spiritual emptiness of our modern society. He had invited them to attend this new bonfire of the vanities, to take place somewhere in New York City. So as to confuse and confound the authorities, the actual place and date of the bonfire, he wrote, would be kept secret until the very last minute. But it would take place in a public arena, a *very* public area, and it would happen so quickly the authorities would not have time to stop it. His readers, *followers*, should prepare themselves and await his instructions.

The idea, Swope wrote, came from the brutal killings of the Decapitator. Here was a person who pretended to recognize the evil in our modern world. If you believed in Satan (and there was much evidence to support that belief), you understood that the Decapitator was actually Satan's servant. He was capitalizing on the predatory evil of the one percenters and their corporate henchmen to spread more evil. The Decapitator had set himself up in judgment as God himself, the ultimate blasphemy. He was an agent that would deflect the faithful from their real duty, which was to ask forgiveness, seek to purify themselves, to take the beam out of their own eye before trying to remove the mote from their brother's. Those other protestors, the ones calling for the destruction of the rich, were as much Satan's servants as the rich themselves. No, you don't destroy the rich—you do as Jesus did, and *convert* them.

To that end, Swope was offering a bonfire of expiation. He asked everyone who wished to attend to bring something symbolic to be burned, something that represented to them the evil they wished to expunge in themselves. It should be an emblem of the purification each wished to undergo, the atonement they hoped to achieve, the penance they wanted to earn.

His modest postings had hit a nerve. At first, there was almost no response. And then there were a few retweets and a scattering of Facebook shares. Suddenly, like a rocket, it took off. Boy, oh boy, had the message gone viral. For eighteen hours straight, his computer had been pinging nonstop with posts and likes and responses to his appeal: hundreds of thousands. People were captivated. They yearned to purify themselves, to shed the dreck of materialism and greed. Thousands and thousands had posted pictures of the things they'd chosen for his bonfire of the vanities. It was astonishing, truly, how people in the tristate area had responded. They were all awaiting his announcement of *where* and *when*.

The last Chicken McNugget disappeared into his mouth and he chewed slowly and thoughtfully, barely tasting it. He drained the chocolate milk jug. His bodily needs taken care of, he cleared his table, dumped the refuse, and headed out the door and into the bitter December cold, back down 125th Street to his basement studio and his ancient PC.

There, he would continue rallying the city to his cause.

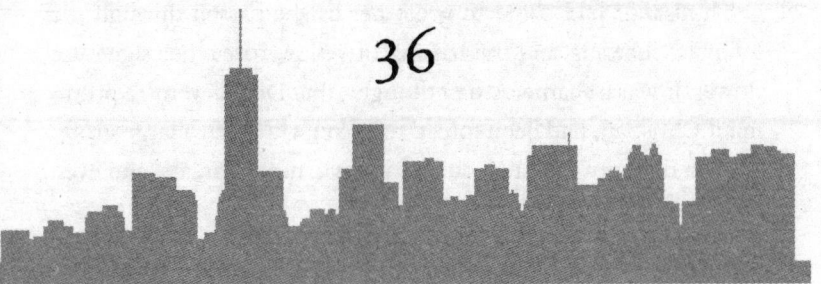

36

Dr. Wansie Adeyemi was a most impressive-looking woman when she arrived at the United Nations to deliver a 10 AM speech to the General Assembly, Charles Attiah thought. He had been called in for a time-and-a-half shift for the UN Department of Safety and Security, where he was posted in the soaring lobby of the General Assembly building. He joined eighty other DSS guards whose job was to manage the dignitaries and delegations arriving for the speech, along with crowds surging to see Dr. Adeyemi, who had won the Nobel Peace Prize earlier that year. Attiah was especially anxious to see her and had in fact requested this overtime detail, due to the fact that he was of Nigerian descent—and was proud of Adeyemi, now Nigeria's ambassador and most famous citizen, and wanted to hear her speech to the UN.

Adeyemi had arrived about an hour before, with a large entourage and her own security detail, dressed in spectacular Nigerian *kitenge* dress, printed in a stunning black-and-white geometric pattern with bright-colored borders, and wearing a shimmering orange silk scarf wound around her head. She was tall, stately, dignified, and remarkably young given all her achievements, and Attiah was thrilled by her charisma.

Thousands had come to greet her as she passed through the lobby to cheering and the tossing of yellow roses, her signature flower. It was a shame, Attiah thought, that Dr. Adeyemi, a prominent Christian, had been forced to travel with such a large group of armed security guards, due to a fatwa, death threats, and even an assassination attempt.

Attiah had helped keep the respectful crowd in check behind velvet ropes as Dr. Adeyemi had passed through. She had been inside the hall now for an hour, giving a speech on HIV/AIDS and pleading for more funding from world governments for the string of HIV clinics she had established across West Africa. He couldn't see her, but the speech was being broadcast live into the lobby for the general public to listen. Adeyemi spoke eloquently in English about the work of her clinics and the remarkable decline in new HIV infections due to her organization's efforts. Thousands of lives had been spared because of her clinics, which provided not just lifesaving drugs but also educational programs. All this, however, had made her a target of Boko Haram, who claimed that her clinics were a Western plot to sterilize Muslim women, and who had bombed several of them.

The General Assembly loved the speech, interrupting many times to applaud. Here was something purely good, Attiah thought; something every nation could agree on.

Attiah could hear the speech winding up. Now Dr. Adeyemi's vibrant voice was reaching a crescendo of expression, calling on the world to pledge to eradicate HIV/AIDS as it had smallpox. It was possible. It would take money, dedication, and education on the part of the governments of the world—but it was within reach.

More cheering, and she concluded to a rousing standing ovation. Attiah braced himself for the surge about to enter the lobby. Soon the doors opened and the foreign delegations, dignitaries, press, and guests streamed out, followed by Adeyemi and her entourage of Nigerian politicians, doctors, and social workers. The group was surrounded by her security contingent. What a world this was, Attiah thought, that even a saint such as her had enemies. But that was the way it was, and the security around her was tight as a drum, even on top of the United Nations' highly trained DSS.

The crowd continued pouring out, excited, talking, still full of the inspiring speech. They streamed along the velvet ropes, all very orderly, surging as Dr. Adeyemi, her entourage, security guards, and fans moved through the lobby. The place was as full of people as Attiah had ever seen it, all centered on Adeyemi like bees clustering around a queen. The press was there, of course—bristling with television cameras.

Suddenly Attiah heard a series of rapid reports: *bang, bang-bang-bang, bang!* Well trained in firearms, he recognized instantly that the sounds were not, in fact, gunfire, but firecrackers. But the crowd had no such revelation, and the effect was electric: sudden, overwhelming panic. Shrieks and screams filled the lobby as people ran for cover, any cover, dashing madly about in all directions, colliding, falling, trampling each other. It was as if their brains had been shut off and pure instinct had taken over.

Attiah and his fellow guards tried to bring order and implement the carefully rehearsed anti-terrorist drill, but it was hopeless. Nobody was listening; nobody *could* listen; and the velvet ropes, the stanchions, the barricades all went down like a house of cards.

Fifteen seconds after the firecrackers, there were two hollow *booms!* one after the other, and in the blink of an eye the vast lobby filled with blinding thick smoke, which raised the level of terror to a pitch he hardly believed possible. People were crawling along the ground, screaming, grasping and tearing at each other like drowning souls. Attiah tried to help, did everything in his power to calm people down and lead them to the established safety zones, but they all seemed to have become crazed, mindless animals. He heard sirens through the murk as the police and fire and anti-terrorist teams arrived at the plaza outside, invisible in the smoke. The blind panic went on, and on, and on...And then the atmosphere began to clear, first just a thinning of the darkness, then a dirty-brown light, and then it cleared to a haze. The lobby doors were open, the forced-air systems roaring full-tilt, the NYPD cops were charging in, along with a slew of anti-terror units. As the smoke cleared, Attiah could see that almost everyone was still lying on the ground, having done what they could to take cover after the smoke bombs went off by dropping flat and crawling to safety.

And then Attiah saw a sight that struck such horror into his heart that he would never forget it as long as he lived. Lying on the floor, on her back, was the body of Dr. Wansie Adeyemi. He knew it was her because of the distinctive *kitenge* robe. But she had no head. Two security guards, whom Attiah assumed had been sheltering her, also lay dead next to her.

A huge pool of blood was still spreading from this scene of carnage, and as the full dimensions of the murderous situation dawned on the people around her corpse, a shrieking wail of grief rose up as her security guards charged about in confusion and fury, looking for the killer, even as the NYPD was mobilizing, organizing, directing, shouting, and clearing the mass of terrorized people.

Staring across the lobby, with its dark, drifting smoke, the cries of the frightened, the suited and helmeted figures rushing through the gloom with their loudspeakers blaring directions, the dense mass of flashing lights and sirens outside—Attiah felt like he had descended into Hell itself.

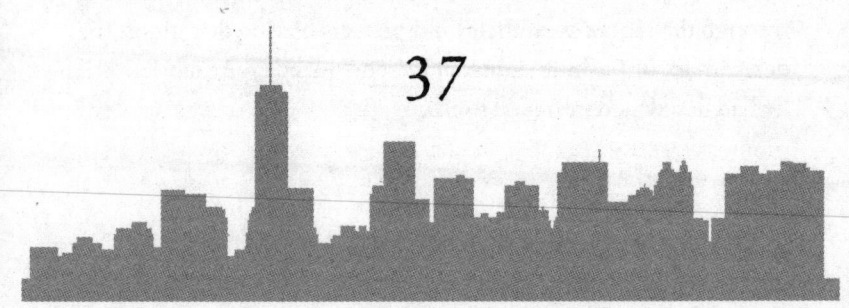

37

Bʀʏᴄᴇ Hᴀʀʀɪᴍᴀɴ ᴍᴀᴅᴇ the long ascent of the DigiFlood building, the glass elevator showing the lobby dwindling to a speck
beneath him. Anton Ozmian himself had requested a meeting,
and that of course was enough to make Harriman curious indeed—but at the moment he had other things on his mind, as
well.

First and foremost was the murder of Dr. Wansie Adeyemi.
Ever since his interview on *America's Morning* the day before, Harriman had been the toast of the town, his every prognostication
taken as gospel. It had been a wonderfully heady feeling. And so
this new murder, tragic as it was, had been like a sucker punch to
his gut. On the face of it, the beheading—and in particular the nature of the victim—seemed to have nothing in common with the
earlier deaths. And therein lay the rub. Harriman realized that his
command of the Decapitator story depended on the upholding of
his theory. He'd already gotten three calls from his editor that day,
asking if he'd dug up the dirt yet.

The dirt. That dirt was precisely what he needed—the skeletons
in the closet of this saintly woman, this Mother Teresa, who had

just won a Nobel Peace Prize. There *had* to be skeletons, he reasoned—nothing else made sense. And so in the hours that followed news of Adeyemi's death, he'd launched on a desperate search for that sordid but well-hidden past: doing deep background, talking to everyone he could find who knew anything about her, pressuring people, demanding they reveal what he was certain they were hiding. And as he did so—aware that he was making a terrific nuisance of himself—he was acutely aware that if he couldn't dig up anything on the woman, then his theory, his credibility, and his command of the story would be in jeopardy.

In the middle of this frantic search, he'd received a cryptic note from Ozmian, asking him to drop by his office that afternoon at three. "I have important information regarding your effort," the note had read—nothing more.

Harriman was well aware of Ozmian's reputation as a ruthless entrepreneur. Ozmian was probably pissed off he had interviewed his ex-wife, Izolda, and surely he was angry about all the shit about his daughter Harriman had published in the *Post*. Well, he'd dealt with angry people before. He expected this meeting with Ozmian to be similar, one long screaming session. So much the better—everything was on the record unless it was specifically excluded. Most people didn't realize that when dealing with the press, and in fury they often made outrageous—and highly quotable—statements. But if on the other hand Ozmian did have "important information"—perhaps regarding his search for Adeyemi's dark past—he dared not pass up the chance to get it.

He stepped out as the elevator doors opened onto the top floor of the DigiFlood tower, announced himself to the waiting secretary, then allowed himself to be led by a flunky through one soaring space after another until he at last reached a pair of massive birchwood doors, with a smaller door set into one of them.

The flunky knocked; a "come in" was heard from beyond; the door was opened; Harriman entered; and the flunky retreated backward as one might when in the presence of a monarch, closing the door behind him.

Harriman found himself in a severely decorated corner office, with a magnificent view overlooking the Battery and One World Trade Center. A figure was sitting behind a vast, tomb-like desk of black granite. He recognized the thin, ascetic features of Anton Ozmian. The man looked back at him, expressionless, his eyes barely blinking, like a hawk's.

Several chairs were arranged in front of the desk. In one of them sat a woman. She didn't look corporate to him—she was a little too casually, if stylishly, dressed—and he wondered what she was doing in his office. Girlfriend? But the faint smile playing about her lips seemed to suggest something else.

Ozmian motioned Harriman to one of the other chairs, and the reporter took a seat.

The room fell into silence. The two kept their eyes trained on Harriman in a way that quickly became unsettling. When it seemed apparent neither one planned on saying anything, Harriman spoke up.

"Mr. Ozmian," he said, "I received your note, and I understand you have information that is relevant to my current investigation—"

"Your 'current investigation,'" Ozmian said. His tone was flat, emotionless, like his eyes. "Let's not waste time. Your *current investigation* has subjected my daughter to the vilest slanders. Not only that, but you have sullied her character in a manner by which she—from beyond the grave—cannot defend herself. I, therefore, will defend her myself."

This was about what Harriman had expected to hear, only in a more controlled fashion. "Mr. Ozmian," he said, "I reported the facts. Simple as that."

"Facts can and should be reported in a fair and impartial way," Ozmian said. "Calling my daughter a person 'of no redeeming value' and saying 'the world would be better off if she were dead' is not reporting. It is character assassination."

Harriman was about to respond when the entrepreneur abruptly rose from his desk, stepped around it, and took a seat in a chair next to him, sandwiching the reporter between Ozmian and the woman.

"Mr. Harriman, I'd like to think I'm a reasonable man," Ozmian went on. "If you will guarantee not to say or write another word against my daughter—if you will simply pen a few positive things about her to mitigate the harm you've caused—then we need say no more about it. I won't even ask you to directly recant the scurrilous lies you've already bandied about."

This was surprisingly mild, thought Harriman, even if he was offended at the implication he could be influenced like this. "I'm sorry, but I have to report the news as I see it, and I can't play favorites because somebody's feelings might be hurt. I know it's not pleasant to hear, but there's nothing I reported about your late daughter that wasn't true."

There was a brief silence. "I see," said Ozmian. "In that case, let me introduce my colleague here, Ms. Alves-Vettoretto. She will explain what is going to happen if you print one more word—just one—that defames my daughter."

Ozmian sat back just as the woman whose name he didn't quite catch sat forward. "Mr. Harriman," she said in a quiet, almost silky voice, "I understand that you are the founder and motivating force behind the Shannon Croix Foundation, a charitable fund for cancer research named after your late girlfriend, who died of uterine cancer." She had a faint accent, hard to place, that gave her words a certain preciseness.

Harriman nodded.

"I further understand that the fund—with the support of the *Post*—has been quite successful, having brought in several million dollars, and that you are on its board."

"That's right." Harriman had no idea where this was going.

"Yesterday, the fund had just over a million dollars in its account—a business account that, by the way, is held in the name of the foundation, with you having fiduciary responsibility over it."

"What of it?"

"Today, the account is empty." The woman sat back again.

Harriman blinked in surprise. "What—?"

"You can check for yourself. It's quite simple: all the money from that account has been transferred to a numbered bank account in the Cayman Islands, established by you, with your signatures and videotaped presence and clerks who can all testify as to your presence there."

"I've never even been to the Cayman Islands!"

"But of course you have. All the flights, your passport number, a beautiful electronic trail has been created especially for you."

"Who's going to believe that?"

The woman went on patiently. "All the money has been transferred from the foundation's account to your personal, offshore account. Here is a record of the transaction." She reached into a slender crocodile briefcase lying on an adjacent table, removed a piece of paper, and held it in front of Harriman for several seconds before returning it.

"No way. That's crap. That's not going to hold up!"

"Indeed it will. As you might imagine, our company has many fine programmers, and they created a most lovely digital theft leading back to you. You have one week to publish a positive story about Grace Ozmian. We'll even furnish you with a 'fact sheet' containing all the necessary information to make your job easier. If you do that—and if you promise not to write about her anymore after that, ever—we'll put the money back and erase the financial trail."

"And if I don't?" Harriman asked in a strangled voice.

"Then we'll simply leave the money where it is. Soon, it will be noted the money is missing; and then, a reasonably astute investigation will find the trail and uncover the owner of that numbered bank account. Of course, if the investigators have any trouble, we'll be glad to give them a little anonymous help."

"This..." Harriman paused to catch his breath. "This is blackmail."

"And you simply do not have the knowledge, or the resources, to undo it. The clock is ticking. At any moment the missing money will be noted. You'd better hurry up."

Ozmian shifted in his chair. "As Ms. Alves-Vettoretto says, it's really quite simple. All you have to do is agree to our two conditions—neither of which is onerous. If you do, everyone stays happy—and out of prison."

Harriman could barely believe what he was hearing. Five minutes ago, he'd been a lionized reporter. Now he was being framed as an embezzler, at the expense of his own deceased girlfriend. As he sat there, barely able to move, a dozen scenarios—none of them good—paraded before his mind. With a shudder that racked his entire frame, he realized that he had no choice.

Silently, he nodded.

"Excellent," said Ozmian, still without allowing any expression to form on his face. "Ms. Alves-Vettoretto here will give you the bullet points for the article about Grace."

The woman on Harriman's other side reached into her briefcase again, pulled out a piece of paper, and handed it over.

"And now that concludes our business." Ozmian stood up and walked back behind his desk. "Ms. Alves-Vettoretto, would you please escort Mr. Harriman to the elevator?"

Two hours later, back in his apartment, Harriman lay on the living room sofa, from which he had not moved since returning from the DigiFlood tower and checking online to discover that the account was, indeed, empty. His beautiful career lay hanging in the balance, victim of a slick and heinous blackmail scheme. And his beautiful theory lay in ruins. Of the two, the former was the worse: as much as he hated the idea of losing the story of his career, he hated the thought of the disgrace more—the shame and infamy of everyone believing he had embezzled from his own dead girlfriend's memorial fund. That humiliation and scandal was almost worse than the stiff prison term that surely would result.

But what could he do? How was he going to frame this Grace Ozmian story her father was insisting on, this sudden about-face, and make it look credible? Maybe he could write some human-interest piece, pointing out the good things in Grace's life, trying to position it as attempting a laudable balance after all the bad press she'd gotten, the moral being that even the worst villains had a good side. But that wouldn't go down well with his editor at the *Post*, a newspaper that so loved their villains. He likely wouldn't even be able to get it past his editor. And the thought of succumbing to blackmail made him feel sick; his whole being revolted at knuckling under to that arrogant billionaire bastard.

The longer he thought about it, the more Bryce Harriman, the newly minted celebrity, the darling of the papers and the airwaves, began to reassert himself. *Scurrilous lies*, Ozmian had said. *Character assassination*. Well, two could play that game. This blackmail of Ozmian's—perhaps it could be a story in itself. He, Harriman, had the backing of the entire might of the *Post* behind him, from Paul Petowski all the way up to Beaverton, the publisher. More than that—he had the backing of the people of New York as well.

He was not going to take this shit. It was time, he realized, to do some more digging—this time into Anton Ozmian. And in short order, Harriman felt sure, he'd dig up enough dirt from Ozmian's own past to turn the tables and neutralize this frame job. And who knew? The story might just deflect attention from his problems with the late Saint of the United Nations.

He leapt up from the couch and headed for his laptop, filled with sudden new purpose.

38

Wʜᴇɴ D'Aɢᴏꜱᴛᴀ sᴛᴇᴘᴘᴇᴅ through the Second Avenue entrance to the Nigerian Mission to the United Nations, he was instantly aware of a heavy pallor hanging in the lobby air. It had nothing to do with the barricades outside, or with the heavy NYPD presence, supplemented by Nigerian security. Instead, it had everything to do with the black armbands that were worn by practically everyone in sight; with the lost-looking, downcast faces of the people he passed; with the small knots of people who spoke together in mournful tones. The mission had the feeling of a building whose heart had been ripped from it. As was indeed the case; Nigeria had just lost Dr. Wansie Adeyemi, its most promising stateswoman and recent Nobel Prize winner, to the Decapitator.

And yet, D'Agosta knew, Dr. Adeyemi couldn't be the saint she was cracked up to be. It just didn't fit the theory he believed, also enthusiastically endorsed by the NYPD task force. Somewhere in that lady's background he would find a cruel and sordid past, which the killer knew about. Earlier in the afternoon, he'd called Pendergast and run by him various ways to uncover the smoking gun D'Agosta knew must be hidden somewhere in the woman's history. Pendergast had finally suggested that they arrange an interview at the Nigerian Mission with someone who'd known Dr. Adeyemi intimately, and he offered to set it up.

D'Agosta and Pendergast passed through several layers of security, showing their badges numerous times, until at last they found themselves in the office of the Nigerian chargé d'affaires. He knew of their coming and, despite the people milling about and the heavy cloak of tragedy that lay over everything, he escorted them personally down the hall to a nondescript door labeled OBAJE, F. He opened it to reveal a small, neat office, with an equally neat man sitting behind a spotless desk. He was short and wiry, with close-cropped white hair.

"Mr. Obaje," the chargé d'affaires said in a stony voice, "these are the men I told you to expect. Special Agent Pendergast of the FBI and Lieutenant D'Agosta of the NYPD."

The man rose from behind the desk. "Of course."

"Thank you," said the chargé d'affaires. He nodded at Pendergast and D'Agosta in turn, then left the office with the air of a man who had just lost one of his own family.

The man behind the desk looked at his two guests. "I am Fenuku Obaje," he said. "Administrative assistant to the permanent UN mission."

"We greatly appreciate your taking a moment to speak with us in this tragic time," Pendergast said.

Obaje nodded. "Please, take a seat."

Pendergast did so, and D'Agosta followed suit. *Administrative assistant?* It looked like they were going to get the royal brush-off with some low-level functionary. *Is this the best Pendergast could do?* He decided to withhold judgment until they'd spoken with the diplomat.

"First," Pendergast said, "let me extend to you our deepest

sympathies. This is a terrible loss, not just for Nigeria, but for all peace-loving people."

Obaje made a gesture of thanks.

"It's my understanding that you knew Dr. Adeyemi well," Pendergast continued.

Obaje nodded again. "We practically grew up together."

"Excellent. My colleague, Lieutenant D'Agosta, has just a few questions he'd like to ask you." With this, Pendergast turned pointedly toward D'Agosta.

D'Agosta understood immediately. He was champing at the bit to peel off the veneer of holiness and get the dirt on Adeyemi; Pendergast was kindly giving him the lead to do so. The ball was in his court. He shifted in his chair.

"Mr. Obaje," he said. "You just told us you and Dr. Adeyemi practically grew up together."

"A figure of speech. We went to university together. Benue State University, in Makurdi—we were both part of its first graduating class in 1996." A smile of pride briefly broke through the pained expression that was practically graven onto his face.

D'Agosta had taken out his notebook and was jotting this down. "I'm sorry. Benue?"

"One of the newer Nairobi states, created in 1976. 'Food Basket of the Nation'—"

"I see." D'Agosta continued his scribbling. "And you knew her well at the university?"

"We were reasonably well acquainted, both at school and in the years that followed immediately after."

Immediately after. Good. "Mr. Obaje, I realize this is a very difficult time for you, but I must ask you to be as candid with us as possible. We are trying to solve a series of murders here—not just that of Dr. Adeyemi, but several others as well. Now, everything

I've heard about Dr. Adeyemi has been laudatory in the extreme. People are practically calling her a saint."

"In Nigeria, that is, in effect, what she's considered."

"Why is that, exactly?"

Obaje spread his hands as if the reasons were too numerous to list. "All this is a matter of record. She herself became the youngest governor of Benue State, where she instituted numerous measures aimed at reducing poverty and improving education, before ultimately moving to Lagos. She went on to establish a series of HIV clinics across West Africa. In addition, she almost single-handedly instituted a wide range of educational programs. Despite constant threats of violence, and without thought to her own safety, she courageously pursued a message of peace across our neighboring countries. All these initiatives have saved many thousands of lives."

"That sounds impressive." D'Agosta continued to scribble. "But I've often noted, Mr. Obaje, that when somebody rises particularly fast in life, they do so by stepping on somebody else's toes. I hope you'll excuse the question, but did Dr. Adeyemi achieve her success at the expense of others?"

Obaje frowned, as if he didn't understand the question. "I'm sorry?"

"Did she walk over other people in order to secure her personal successes?"

Obaje shook his head vigorously. "No. No, of course not. That was not her way."

"What about her past? Her family? Did you ever hear any rumors about them? You know—misdeeds of one sort or another? Perhaps her father made his fortune through unscrupulous business dealings, for example?"

"Her father died when she was twelve. Not long afterward, her mother entered a convent and her only brother enrolled in a seminary, eventually becoming a priest. Wansie made her own way in the world—and she made it honestly."

"Left on her own at such a young age—that's hard no matter where you live. Did she perhaps cut corners in order to get ahead, or—you're a man of the world, Mr. Obaje—find that she had to supplement her income via certain, ah, time-honored ways?"

The look of sorrow on Obaje's face turned to one of surprise and affront. "Of course not, Lieutenant. Frankly, I'm disturbed and shocked by this line of questioning."

"My apologies." *Better back off just a little.* "I'm just trying to establish if she had any enemies who might have wished her ill."

"She certainly did have enemies. Jihadist groups were violently opposed to the HIV clinics and her educational efforts with women. It seems to me that is a lead you should be following up."

"Was Dr. Adeyemi married?"

"No."

"Were there any men—or, perhaps, women—that she had any relationships with? I mean of an especially close nature."

Obaje answered with a peremptory "No."

It did not take D'Agosta long to write down this response, but he made a show of taking additional copious notes. At last he looked up again. "You said you knew the ambassador both during university and afterward."

Obaje gave a clipped nod. "For a time, yes."

"Then—once again, please forgive my bluntness, but it's our duty to ask difficult questions—during that time did you ever hear gossip about her; anything that might reflect badly?"

At this, Obaje stood up. "No, and frankly, once again I'm taken aback at the tenor of your questions. You've come into my office with the obvious intent of tarnishing her reputation. Let me tell you, Lieutenant—her reputation is above reproach, and you will find nothing, anywhere, that will lead you to a different conclusion. I don't know what lies behind this crusade of yours, but I will not entertain it or you any longer. This meeting is at an end. Now, sir: kindly leave this office and this building."

Out on the street, D'Agosta angrily shoved his notebook into his coat pocket. "I should have expected that," he growled. "Frigging whitewash. Turning the lady into a martyr." He shook his head. "Administrative assistant. Christ."

"My dear Vincent," Pendergast said as he wrapped his overcoat more tightly around his narrow person, "let me tell you a little bit about Mr. Obaje. You heard him tell you that Dr. Adeyemi was the youngest governor of Benue State."

"Yeah. So?"

"What he did not tell you was that he was also a candidate for that same governorship. At the time, Obaje's political star was on the rise. Great things were expected of him. But he lost the election—by a landslide. After that, Obaje's star continued to fall. And now you find him here, an administrative assistant in the Nigerian mission, his career eclipsed, thanks to Dr. Adeyemi—through no fault of her own, of course."

"What's your point?"

"Simply this: I singled him out for an interview because he had the greatest reason to disparage and denigrate her."

"You mean, to trash her?"

"In your vernacular, precisely."

D'Agosta's jaw worked for a moment. "Why the hell didn't you tell me that going in?"

"If I had, you wouldn't have pressed him as hard as you did. I did this to spare you countless additional hours of fruitless research and interrogatory. You could spend a month hunting for skeletons, but I fear you won't find any. The truth is as simple as it looks: the woman *is* a saint."

"But that can't be! It knocks the hell out of our motive."

"Ah, but it is not 'our' motive."

"You don't buy it?"

Pendergast hesitated. "There is indeed a *motive* for these murders. But it is not the motive that you, the NYPD, and all of New York seem to believe."

"I..." D'Agosta began, then stopped. He felt deflated, manipulated, kept in the dark. It was typical Pendergast, but in this instance he felt dissed—and it made him irritated. More than irritated. "Oh, I get it—you've got a better theory. One that you've been keeping, *as usual*, from everyone."

"I am never arbitrary. There is always a method to my mystifications."

"So let's hear this dazzling theory of yours."

"I didn't say I had a theory; I only said yours was wrong."

At this D'Agosta laughed harshly. "Well, shit, then go knock yourself out chasing your theories. I know what *I've* got to do!"

If Pendergast was surprised by this outburst, it manifested itself only in a slight widening of his pale eyes. He said nothing, but after a second or two merely nodded, turned silently on his handmade English shoes, and began making his way down Second Avenue.

39

THIS TIME, WHEN Pendergast arrived for a visit to the DigiFlood campus, his Rolls-Royce was not ushered into Anton Ozmian's personal parking space, or even into the corporate garage at all; rather, Proctor was forced to double-park in the maze of streets of Lower Manhattan. Nor was Pendergast whisked heavenward in a private elevator; rather, he was obliged to slip in with the rest of the masses at the building's main entrance and present himself at security. His FBI credentials were sufficient to get him past the three guards at the checkpoint and onto an elevator to the top floor, but there, at the entrance to the Zen-like executive suite, he was met by two hulking men, squeezed into dark suits, who both appeared able to crack Brazil nuts between their knuckles.

"Special Agent Pendergast?" said one in a gruff voice, looking at a text message on his cell phone as he spoke.

"Indeed."

"You don't have an appointment to see Mr. Ozmian."

"I have tried several times to make just such an appointment, but, alas, without success. I thought perhaps appearing here in person might precipitate a more favorable result."

This volley, delivered in a buttery drawl, bounced off the two men without perceptible effect. "Mr. Ozmian doesn't see visitors without an appointment."

Pendergast hesitated a moment for effect. Then, once again, he slipped a pale white hand into his black suit and removed the wallet containing his FBI shield and ID. Letting it drop open, he showed it to first one, then the other, allowing it to remain before each face a good ten seconds. As he did so, he made a show of examining their nameplates and, apparently, committing them to memory.

"An appointment was merely a courtesy," he said, allowing a little iron to mingle with the butter. "As a special agent of the Federal Bureau of Investigation, looking into an active homicide, I go where I please, when I please, as long as I have reasonable suspicion to do so. Now, I suggest you speak to your minders and arrange an audience with Mr. Ozmian without delay. Otherwise, there might be unpleasantness in store for each of you, personally."

The two men absorbed this a moment, then looked at each other with uncertainty. "Wait here," one of them said, and he turned and walked across the large waiting area, disappearing through the pair of birchwood doors, while the other stood guard.

It was fifteen minutes before he returned. "Follow us, please."

They passed through the set of doors into the complex of offices that lay beyond. But instead of making their way through the labyrinth to the final, massive doors that led into Ozmian's private office, the men steered Pendergast in another direction, toward a side corridor, with every door closed. Stopping at one, the men knocked.

"Come in," came a voice.

The men opened the door and motioned Pendergast inside,

and then, without entering themselves, closed the door behind him. Pendergast found himself inside a well-appointed office with a view of the Woolworth Building and one wall covered floor-to-ceiling with legal tomes. Behind the neat desk sat a thin, balding man with round glasses who looked very much like an owl. He gazed back at Pendergast with a neutral expression. Something like a smile passed briefly across his thin lips before disappearing again.

"Special Agent Pendergast," the man said in a high, reedy voice. He indicated a few chairs arranged on the far side of the desk. "Please sit down."

Pendergast did so. From three security staffers, to two bodyguards, to one lawyer—an interesting progression.

"My name is Weilman," the man said from across the desk. "Counsel to Mr. Ozmian."

Pendergast inclined his head.

"I'm told you informed Mr. Ozmian's, ah, staffers that, in pursuing your job as a special agent of the FBI, you have the right to come and go as you please and to interview whoever you are in the mood to speak with. Mr. Pendergast, you and I both know that is not the case. I have no doubt that Mr. Ozmian would be happy to speak to you—assuming that you have a court order on your person."

"I do not."

"I'm so sorry, then."

"Given the fact that I am investigating the death of his daughter, *I* would have thought that Mr. Ozmian would be eager to help further that investigation."

"And he is! But it's my understanding, Mr. Pendergast, that you have already spoken with Mr. Ozmian. He agreed to an interview—an exceedingly painful one. He further aided your investigation by identifying his daughter's body—an even more painful undertaking. In turn, he has been repaid for this cooperation by a total lack of progress, and a shocking silence from investigators. As a result, he sees no reason why he should subject himself to additional painful interviews—especially when he has no faith in you or the NYPD to solve this case. Mr. Ozmian has given you all possible relevant information on his daughter already. I would advise you to stop going over old ground and instead *focus* on *solving* the case."

"Cases," Pendergast corrected. "A total of fourteen people are dead."

"Mr. Ozmian could not care less about the other thirteen, except insofar as those deaths might help solve his daughter's."

Pendergast sank back slowly into his chair. "It occurs to me that the public might be interested to learn that Mr. Ozmian is not co-operating with the investigation."

Now it was Weilman's turn to sink back into his chair, and a bloodless smile curdled on his pale face. "Mr. Ozmian's name has for years been put before the public in, shall we say, a less-than-flattering light." The lawyer paused. "Let me put it to you directly, and forgive the vulgarity: Mr. Ozmian does not give a rat's turd what the public thinks. At present, he has only two concerns: running his company and bringing the murderer of his daughter to justice."

As Pendergast considered this, he realized it was true: like King Mithridates, who had taken increasing doses of poison until he was no longer susceptible to its effects, Ozmian no longer cared a whit about his reputation. This rendered his usual method of threats and implied blackmail ineffective.

Pity.

But he was not going to let it go just yet. He tapped the breast of his suit coat—whose inner pocket contained nothing—with a look of complacency. "As it happens, we've recently made a not inconsiderable breakthrough—one that the FBI wanted to share with Mr. Ozmian. Not only will he find it interesting, but he may be able to supply information of his own that will help us pursue it further. This discovery is confidential for the time being, which was why I did not mention it before. I would thus ask you to keep any mention of its existence to yourself when you now ask Mr. Ozmian to give me a private audience."

For a moment, the two men simply looked at each other. And then the faint smile appeared once again on the lawyer's face. "A promising development indeed, Agent Pendergast! If you'll just give me a summary of what you have hidden in your pocket, I'll convey it to Mr. Ozmian right away. And I have no doubt that, if it is really as big a breakthrough as you suggest, he'll be delighted to see you."

"Protocol requires that I hand him the information personally," Pendergast said.

"Of course, of course—after I give him the summary."

A silence fell over the room. After a moment, Pendergast let his hand fall away from the breast of his jacket. He stood up. "I'm sorry, but this information is restricted to Mr. Ozmian himself."

At this, the lawyer's smile—or was it a smirk?—grew a little wider. "Of course," he said, rising as well. "*When* you have the subpoena, you may show it to him. And now, may I escort you to the elevator?"

Without another word Pendergast followed the man out of his office and through the tall, echoing spaces to the elevator bank.

40

LES TUILERIES, THE three-star Michelin restaurant located on a quiet residential block in the East Sixties just off Madison Avenue, was doing a brisk if discreet business on this, the evening before New Year's Eve. Les Tuileries was that rarest of things in modern New York, a French restaurant of the old style, all dark wood and patinaed leather, comprising half a dozen rooms like elegant cubbyholes, full of banquettes tucked away in nooks beneath oil paintings in heavy gilt frames. Waiters and under-waiters, as numerous as doctors in an ICU surgical bay, were fawning over the patrons. Here, half a dozen men in starched white, at a cue from the maître d', simultaneously whisked away silver domes from plates arranged around a large table with the precision of well-drilled soldiers on a parade ground, revealing the delectables hidden beneath. There, a senior waiter was expertly deboning tableside a fillet of Dover sole—flown in from England that morning, naturally. Elsewhere, another waiter was folding anchovies, capers, and a raw egg into a bowl of *Salade Niçoise à la Cap Ferrat* under the discerning eye of his patrons.

In a far corner of one of the rear rooms of Les Tuileries, almost hidden within a rich crimson banquette, Executive Associate Director Longstreet and Special Agent Pendergast had just finished their appetizers—*Escargots à la Bourguignonne* for Longstreet, and a terrine of morels and foie gras for Pendergast. The sommelier returned with a second six-hundred-dollar bottle of Mouton Rothschild, vintage 1996—Longstreet had tasted the first and sent it away, pronouncing it corked—and as the man opened it, Longstreet gave Pendergast a sidelong glance. He had always fancied himself a gastronome, and had dined in as many of the finest Parisian restaurants as his time and independent means allowed. He was as much at home here as in his own kitchen. He saw that Pendergast was equally comfortable, perusing the menu and asking probing questions of the waiter. A love of French cuisine and wine was something they had long shared, but Longstreet had to admit that outside of gastronomy, and despite all the time they had spent together in close quarters during their tour in the special forces, the man was, and would always remain, a cipher.

He accepted the small pour of the rather young first-growth wine the sommelier offered him, swirling it around, examining its color and viscosity, then finally sipping it, aerating it over his tongue as he did so. He took a second, more critical sip. Finally, he put down the glass and nodded to the sommelier, who went off to decant the bottle. After the sommelier had returned to fill their glasses, their waiter crept forward. Longstreet ordered calves' brains sautéed in a Calvados sauce; Pendergast in turn requested the *Pigeon et Légumes Grillés Rabasse au Provençal*. The waiter thanked them, then disappeared into the dim, cozy space beyond the table.

Longstreet nodded his approval. "Excellent choice."

"I can never resist truffles. An expensive habit, but one I find impossible to break."

Longstreet now took a deeper, more contemplative sip of Bordeaux. "These murders are generating a tremendous furor—on all sides of society. The rich, because they see themselves being targeted, and the rest because of the vicarious thrill of seeing the ultra-wealthy get theirs."

"Indeed."

"I wouldn't want to be your pal D'Agosta these days. The NYPD is catching holy hell. And we've not escaped embarrassment, either."

"You're referring to the behavioral profile."

"Yes. Or, more precisely, the lack of one." At the request of the NYPD, Longstreet had submitted the Decapitator case to the FBI's Behavioral Sciences Unit in Quantico and asked for a psychological profile. Serial killers, no matter how bizarre, fell into types, and the BSU had developed a database of every known type in the world. When a new killer appeared on the scene, the BSU was able to slot him into one of the existing patterns in order to create a psychological profile—his motivations, methods, patterns, work habits, even such things as his socioeconomic background and whether or not he had a car. This time, however, the BSU had been unable to profile the Decapitator; the killer fit no previously known pattern. Instead of a profile, Longstreet had gotten back a long, defensive report that boiled down to one fact: for this killer, the Quantico databases were useless.

Longstreet sighed. "You're our serial-killer expert," he said. "What do you make of this one? Is he as unique as the BSU claims?"

Pendergast inclined his head. "I'm still struggling to understand. To be honest, I'm not sure we're dealing with a serial killer at all."

"How can that be? He's killed fourteen people! Or thirteen, if you don't count the first."

Pendergast shook his head. "All serial killers have at base a pathological or psychotic motivation. In this case, maybe the motivation is...relatively *normal*."

"Normal? Killing and decapitating half a dozen people? Have you lost your mind?" Longstreet almost laughed out loud. This was classic Pendergast, never failing to astonish, taking delight in confounding everyone around him with some outrageous statement.

"Take Adeyemi. I'm quite sure she has no skeletons in her closet, no sordid history. Nor was she exceptionally rich."

"Then the current theory about the Decapitator's motivation is worthless."

"Or perhaps..." Pendergast paused as their dinners were served.

"Perhaps what?" Longstreet asked as he tucked into his calves' brains.

Pendergast waved a hand. "Many theories come to mind. Perhaps Adeyemi, or one of the other victims, was the real target all along, and the other murders are nothing more than a smokescreen."

Longstreet tasted his dish and was disappointed: the pale pink calves' brains were overdone. Laying his silverware on the plate with a clatter, he summoned the waiter and sent the dish back for another. He turned to Pendergast again. "Do you really think that's likely?"

"Not likely. In fact, barely possible." Pendergast paused a moment before continuing. "I've never encountered a case so resistant to analysis. Obviously, the heads are missing and the primary victims were surrounded by heavy security. Those are the only commonalities we have so far. That's not nearly enough to build a case on. It leaves open a wide variety of possible motivations."

"So what now?" Although he'd never admit it to the man, Longstreet enjoyed watching Pendergast's mind at work.

"We must go back to the beginning, to the first murder, and work our way forward from there. It's the key to everything that's happened since, for the very reason that it enjoys the debut position. It is also the most curious of the killings—and we must understand the anomalies before we can understand the patterns in what followed. Why, for example, did somebody take the head twenty-four hours after the girl was murdered? Nobody seems troubled by this anymore, except for me."

"You really think it's important?"

"I think it's vital. In fact, earlier today I dropped in on Anton Ozmian to get more information. Unfortunately, my usual bag of tricks didn't get me past his retinue of toadies, lawyers, lickspittles, bodyguards, lackeys, and other impedimenta. It was with some embarrassment I was forced to withdraw."

Longstreet suppressed a smile. He would have loved to have witnessed Pendergast obstructed like that; it happened so rarely. "Why do I feel this is leading up to a request?"

"I need the power of your title, H. I need the full weight of the FBI behind me in order to beard the lion in his den."

"I see." Longstreet let a pregnant silence build. "Aloysius, you know that you're still on my shit list, right? You maneuvered me into dishonoring an oath that I swore to with my life."

"I'm acutely aware of that."

"Good. I'll do what I can to get you inside the door, then—but after that, it's your show. I'll come along, but only as an observer."

"Thank you. That will be entirely acceptable."

Their waiter returned with a fresh, steaming plate of calves' brains. He slipped the plate before Longstreet, then took a step back, looking on tremulously, waiting for his patron's opinion. The executive associate director cut a slice off one edge with a stroke of his knife, speared it with his fork, raised the jiggling mass to his mouth.

"Perfection," he pronounced, chewing with half-closed eyes.

At this, the waiter bowed with mingled pleasure and relief, then turned and disappeared into the gaslit gloom.

41

Bryce Harriman stepped out onto the front porch of the small, neat-looking Colonial on a residential street of Dedham, Massachusetts, then turned back to shake the hand of the owner—a physically feeble but clearheaded man of about eighty, with a thin cap of white hair plastered to his head with brilliantine.

"Thank you very much for your time and your candor, Mr. Sanderton," Harriman said. "And you're sure about the affidavit?"

"If you think it's necessary. It was a damned awful thing—I was sorry I had to witness it."

"I'll see that a notary brings you a copy for signing by dinnertime, along with an overnight pouch to send it back to me."

With another thanks, and another warm handshake, Harriman went down the steps and walked toward the Uber that idled at the curb. It was already late afternoon on New Year's Eve, and with holiday traffic it would be a bitch getting back to New York and his Upper East Side apartment. But Harriman didn't care about that. In fact, at the moment he didn't care much about anything except the triumph he was about to unleash.

Harriman subscribed to the old maxim that, if one were to

write to any six upstanding pillars of the community with the message *All is discovered—flee at once*, every last one of them would head for the hills. Dirt was what was needed here; and—save for his late journalistic nemesis Bill Smithback—nobody was better at digging up dirt than Bryce Harriman.

His big break had occurred just after breakfast, as he was online perusing old newspapers from the Boston suburbs in which Ozmian had grown up. And, in the *Dedham Townsman*, he'd found what he was looking for. Nearly thirty years ago, Ozmian had been arrested for destruction of property at Our Lady of Mercy Catholic Church on Bryant Street. That was all there was, a single item buried in an old newspaper—but it was all Harriman needed. A call to Massachusetts revealed that Ozmian had been quickly released and the misdemeanor charge dropped, but that didn't deter him. By eleven, he was on the shuttle to Boston. By two, he had been to Our Lady of Mercy and obtained a list of people, with addresses, who had been church members at the time of the incident. And it had taken knocks on only three doors before he found someone—Giles Sanderton—who not only recalled the event but had been an eyewitness.

And the story he had to tell was a doozy.

As the cab made its way to Logan Airport, Harriman reclined in the backseat, going over his notes. Sanderton had been at the noon mass some three decades back—being celebrated by a Father Anselm, one of the church's more venerable priests—when in the middle of the homily the church door opened and a teenage Anton Ozmian appeared. Without a word he walked to the front of the church, knocked over the altar table, plucked up a crucifix, swung it like a baseball bat at Father Anselm, knocked him to the floor, and then proceeded to beat the living shit out of him. Leaving the priest bleeding and unconscious at the base of the pulpit, Ozmian had dropped the bloody crucifix onto his prostrate form and, turning, strode out of the church as calmly as he had come in. There had been no sign of anger in his face—just cool deliberation. It had been months before Father Anselm could talk or walk normally again, and shortly afterward he moved into a home for retired priests, and died not long thereafter.

Harriman rubbed his hands together with ill-concealed glee. It had all come together so fast it was almost like magic. At breakfast, he'd had nothing—and now, by midafternoon, he had proof of a story about Ozmian that was so ugly and brutal—beating a priest almost to death with a crucifix!—that it would be what he needed to force his will on Ozmian. While the man claimed to be indifferent to the world's opinion, this horrific revelation would almost certainly provoke the board to relieve him of his position. DigiFlood had initially been backed by several top venture capital firms and hedge funds, not to mention a sizable investment from Microsoft. These companies had reputations to protect, and they held more than 50 percent of DigiFlood's stock; yes, Harriman was sure Ozmian would be pushed out if his revelations were published.

It was odd there had been no assault-and-battery charges, until Harriman discovered that a sizable sum of money had been "donated" by Ozmian's family to the local parish. That was the final piece of the puzzle.

It was perfect. Better than perfect. First, it gave him something to write about besides Adeyemi, whose enduring saintliness was proving most inconvenient. Second, this was a story that Ozmian could not afford to ignore. As the cab pulled into the airport, Harriman found himself confronted by just one question. Should he publish the story first and neutralize Ozmian that way? Or should he first take it to Ozmian and threaten to publish it, in order to force him to cancel his own blackmail scheme?

As he mulled this over, he recalled Ozmian's sneering words, and they still smarted as much as when he'd first heard them. *It's really quite simple. All you have to do is agree to our two conditions— neither of which is onerous. If you do, everyone stays happy—and out of prison.* That settled it: he would take the story to Ozmian in person and threaten to ruin him with it. That would be poetic justice. In fact, he couldn't wait to see Ozmian's face when he dangled the piece under his nose.

Harriman found himself pleased afresh with how brilliantly he had found the means to take on this captain of industry—and beaten him at his own game.

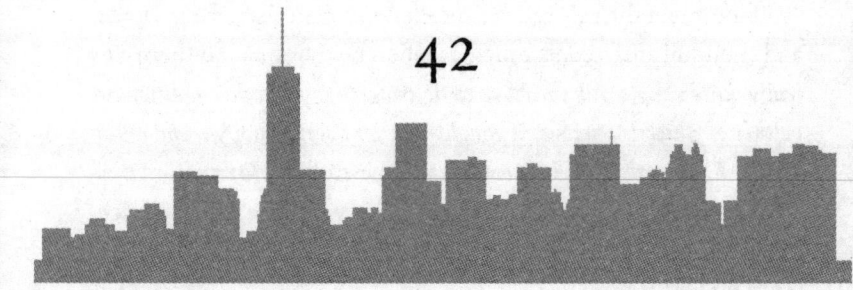

42

Wнат а дау it had been for Marsden Swope. The anti-one-percenter demonstrations had really taken off, the Twitterverse, Facebook, and Instagram seething with calls for demonstrations. The biggest one had gathered around the towering new structure at 432 Park Avenue, the tallest residential building in the world, where apartments were selling for up to a hundred million dollars each. Somehow, that building—even though it was unconnected with the murders—seemed to have become for the demonstrators the very symbol of greed, excess, and ostentation, the perfect example of how the ultra-rich were taking over the city.

So he went down to observe. And it was quite a scene: rank after rank of protestors chanting, blocking the entrances, creating gridlock all around. And then a tweet had gone out calling for eggs, instantly viral, and within minutes the protestors had emptied the neighborhood stores of eggs and were hurling them at the façade from all sides, coating the snow-white marble and lustrous glass with a dripping, slippery mess of yellow goo. The police had moved in, the area was barricaded, and Swope had barely escaped by ditching his jacket and passing himself off as a priest in his cassock and dingy clerical collar.

More than ever, the melee had convinced Swope that violence was not the answer: that the one percenters and the anti-one-percenters were all part of the same conspiracy of hatred, evil, and violence. Swope now understood that he could wait no longer—he must act to stop the madness rising on all sides.

It was a few minutes past one in the morning when Swope crossed Grand Army Plaza and headed into the winter fastness of Central Park. As he'd walked up Fifth Avenue, he had been forced to thread his way through knots of laughing, drunken New Year's revelers, but now as he moved deeper into the park, past the zoo and Wollman Rink, their numbers thinned until he was left blessedly alone.

He had a lot on his mind. With this latest murder, the city seemed to boil over. It was not just the protest at 432 Park. There were more stories of the super-rich fleeing. Some guy had started a blog that cataloged the private jets taking off from Teterboro Airport, with photos taken with a massive telephoto lens showing individual billionaires and their families climbing into their Gulfstreams and Learjets and modified B727s—hedge fund managers, captains of finance, Russian oligarchs, and Saudi princes. The demonstrations favoring the Decapitator, the "down with the one percenters" rabble, had also intensified, with one demonstration blocking Wall Street for four hours until the police finally broke it up.

The responses to his call for a bonfire of the vanities had also swelled enormously—so many, in fact, that he had decided the time was ripe to put his plans into action. It was a true miracle—well over a hundred thousand people had responded and claimed to be on their way to New York City, or already there, awaiting his announcement of where and when. The papers were calling New York the City of Endless Night. Well, and so it was, but with God's help he would turn it into the City of Endless Righteousness. He would show everyone, rich and poor alike, that *all* wealth and luxury were anathema to eternal life.

When he reached the Sheep Meadow, he paused. Crossing it, he continued to the Mall, walked north, passed Bethesda Fountain, then skirted the mazy byways of the Ramble, deep in thought. Savonarola had held his original bonfire in the central square of Florence. That had been the heart of the city, an ideal place to broadcast his message. But today's New York was different. You couldn't stage a bonfire in Times Square—not only was it overrun with tourists, but the police presence was so heavy it would be over before it started. No—his ideal spot would be large, open, and easy to get to from any number of directions. His followers, carrying their luxuries to be burned in the fire, would need to have time to gather, start the bonfire, and throw in their "vanities." It was imperative that they not be stopped too quickly.

Stopped. Swope noticed that his own feet had stopped, as if of their own accord. He glanced around. There were only a few distant revelers visible now, hurrying out of the park and heading for home. To his left rose the dark bulk of Belvedere Castle, its battlements illuminated by the glow of Manhattan. Beyond lay the monolithic wall of Central Park West apartment buildings, marching northward in an endless procession, broken by the façade of the Museum of Natural History. And directly before him, spread out in all its glory, stretching on almost as far as the eye could see until it terminated at the dark wall of trees surrounding the reservoir, lay the Great Lawn.

The Great Lawn. Even the name resonated deeply within Swope. This, indeed, was a spot capable of holding the multitudes that would respond to his call. This, indeed, was a central location, easily accessible by all. This, indeed, was an ideal place for a bonfire—and a place that the police would not be able to lock down and clear out.

A great conviction rose up in his mind: as if of their own accord, guided by heaven, his feet had led him to the perfect spot.

He took a step forward, then another; and then, charged with a sudden onrushing of emotion, he planted his feet in the grass and spoke the first words he had said aloud in more than two days:

"Here shall be the bonfire of the vanities!"

43

It HAD TAKEN Longstreet some time to make the phone calls and apply the necessary pressure, especially over a holiday, but by 1 PM on New Year's Day, Pendergast's Rolls was once more creeping into the underground parking garage of the DigiFlood complex in Lower Manhattan. The guards meeting their car led them to what seemed the farthest spot from the elevators, necessitating a five-minute walk back to the entrance, where they were denied access to the private elevators, and instead were required to take the concrete stairs up to street level and enter the building through the main lobby. And here they were selected for extra vetting by security. Howard Longstreet felt his annoyance rising, but he kept his mouth shut. This was Pendergast's deal, and the special agent seemed to take it in stride, unperturbed, not remarking on the treatment that could only, Longstreet felt, be aimed at humiliating them.

At last they cleared security and rode an elevator to the top floor. Now they were ushered into a small, windowless room, where they were seated and made to wait, watched over by an impassive young drone in an expensive suit.

After an hour in the room, with no visible sign of annoyance from Pendergast, Longstreet finally lost his temper. "This is outrageous!" he said to the drone. "Two senior FBI agents on an active investigation, being obstructed! We're doing Ozmian a favor by trying to solve the case of his murdered daughter—and we're forced to sit here like this?"

The drone only nodded. "I'm sorry—orders."

Longstreet turned to Pendergast. "I'd just as soon go back to Federal Plaza, get a court order ourselves—and a SWAT team for good measure—and beat down the man's door with a battering ram."

"*Du calme*, H; *du calme*. All this is obviously calculated to create a particular effect—as was the case with my visit here two days ago. Mr. Ozmian wishes to demonstrate total control of the situation. Let us allow him to believe he has that. Remember what you told me earlier: this is my show; you're just along to observe. Even in the waiting, we've been shown valuable information."

Longstreet swallowed and sat back, determined to let Pendergast handle it his way. The two sat in the room for another half an hour before the door opened once again and they were at last ushered into Ozmian's private eyrie. As they approached the huge double doors through soaring spaces, Longstreet was surprised at the number of people busily working all around them on what was a major holiday. Things such as holidays probably meant very little to Anton Ozmian.

The man himself was sitting behind his massive desk, arms folded and fingers interlaced on the surface of black granite. He regarded them impassively. A woman sat in one of the chrome-and-leather chairs arrayed before the desk. She seemed more interested in the view of New York Harbor through the floor-to-ceiling windows than she was in the new arrivals.

After an insolently lengthy interval of silence, Ozmian gestured for Pendergast and Longstreet to take seats. "Special Agent Pendergast," he said laconically. "How nice to see you again." He turned to Longstreet. "And you are—?"

"Howard Longstreet, executive associate director for intelligence."

"Ah, of course. You're the person responsible for expediting this meeting."

Longstreet began to speak, but Pendergast restrained him with a gentle hand on his arm.

Ozmian smirked at Longstreet. "Well, I'm pleased you're here. Because this investigation could certainly use some intelligence." The CEO turned his attention back to Pendergast. "No doubt you've come to fill me in on the blitzkrieg swiftness and rapier-like brilliance with which you've been advancing the case."

"No," Pendergast said. He was still, Longstreet noted, adopting the deferential posture he'd assumed while waiting at security.

At this, Ozmian affected surprise. He sat back in his chair, fixing Pendergast with his ascetic stare. "Very well, then. Why are you here?"

"Mr. Ozmian, in your line of work, you buy out, take over, or otherwise absorb other companies and their technologies."

"It's been known to happen."

"Is it fair to say that not all of these companies are eager to be so acquired?"

A look of amusement came over Ozmian's face. "That's right. It's called a hostile takeover."

"Forgive my ignorance. In matters of business, I am but a child. Is this the case with most of your takeovers? That they are *hostile*?"

"In many cases, the CEOs and shareholders were happy to be made rich."

"I see." Pendergast appeared to consider this for a moment, as if such a thing had not occurred to him before. "But there are some who aren't so happy?"

Ozmian shrugged, as if the observation was so obvious as not to merit reply.

"Again, you'll pardon my ignorance," Pendergast continued in the same deferential tone. "And if these people were unhappy—extremely unhappy—they may well have come to hate you, personally?"

There was a brief silence during which Pendergast sat forward, almost imperceptibly, in his chair.

"What are you getting at?"

"Allow me to rephrase. The question is too vague, admittedly, because I'm sure that many people hate you. Mr. Ozmian, who hates you the most?"

"That's a ridiculous question. Takeovers are the bread and butter of corporate life, and I don't pay attention to whiners whose companies I've acquired."

"Perhaps then you've made a serious miscalculation—one that has landed you in your current unfortunate circumstance."

"Unfortunate circumstance? Are you referring to my daughter's death?" His face darkened; Longstreet could see he was enraged.

As Longstreet watched, Pendergast sat forward a little more. "Consider my question very carefully, Mr. Ozmian, as I ask you once again: who hates you *most of all*?"

A look Longstreet could not quite read passed across Ozmian's face before it mastered its anger and once again assumed its remote, faintly supercilious expression.

"Think carefully," Pendergast pressed, a faint iciness now lacing his voice. "Who hates you so much that he would kill your daughter, and not even leave it at that, but come back and take her head?"

Ozmian did not reply. His face had grown very dark.

Pendergast straightened up and pointed a white finger at the chairman of DigiFlood. "Who hates you that much, Mr. Ozmian? I know that you must have a name in your head. And, by not telling me that name, *you're indirectly aiding the person who, perhaps, killed your daughter.*"

A strangled, poisonous atmosphere filled the room. Both Ozmian and his unnamed associate were now staring at Pendergast with undivided attention. Ozmian's expression once again became studiously neutral, but behind that face Longstreet could sense wheels turning furiously. A minute passed, then two, before he spoke again.

"Robert Hightower," Ozmian said at last, in a neutral voice.

"Again," Pendergast said. It was an order, not a request.

"Robert Hightower. Ex-chairman of Bisynchrony."

"And why does he hate you?"

Ozmian shifted in his chair. "His father was a beat cop from a long line of NYPD beat cops. Grew up poor in Brooklyn. But he was a mathematical whiz. He devised an algorithm for simultaneously compressing files while streaming them in real time. He kept improving it, maximizing bandwidth use while increasing the binary resolution. When the algorithm was able to process a bit depth of thirty-two, I became interested. He wanted no part of the DigiFlood family. I sweetened my offer several times, but he continued to rebuff me. The algorithm was his pet, he said; his life's work. In the end, I was forced to dilute the value of Bisynchrony's stock—never mind how. He was forced to sell me everything. At the time, he blamed me for what he melodramatically called 'ruining his life.' Brought several lawsuits against me, which did nothing but drain his bank account. Telephoned me again and again, threatening to kill me, ruin my business, and destroy my family, until finally I had a restraining order slapped on him. His wife's car went over a cliff a year after the takeover. She was behind the wheel, intoxicated. Totally unrelated, of course."

"Of course," Pendergast said drolly. "And why did you not share this information with the police earlier?"

"You asked who hates me the most. I answered the question. But there are a hundred others who hate me, too. I can't imagine any of them murdering an innocent girl and cutting off her head."

"But you said Robert Hightower actually threatened to kill you and your family. Did you believe him?"

Ozmian shook his head. He looked defeated. "I don't know. People say stupid things. But Hightower...he went off the deepest end." He looked from Pendergast to Longstreet and back again. "I answered your question. Now get out."

It was clear to Longstreet that he would have no more to say on this or any other subject.

Pendergast rose from his chair. He made a slight bow without offering to shake hands. "Thank you, Mr. Ozmian. And good day."

Ozmian responded with a perfunctory nod.

Minutes later, as the elevator doors whispered open and they stepped out into the main lobby, Longstreet could not restrain a chuckle. "Aloysius," he said, slapping the man's slender back, "that was a tour de force. I don't think I've ever seen anyone turn the tables quite so neatly. Consider yourself officially out of the doghouse."

Pendergast acknowledged the compliment in silence.

Across the expansive lobby, Bryce Harriman—who had just entered from the chilly street via the bank of revolving doors—

stopped in his tracks. He recognized the man exiting one of the elevators: it was Special Agent Pendergast, the elusive fed who had figured, one way or another, in several of the murder cases he'd reported on over the years.

The FBI agent could be doing only one thing here at DigiFlood: following up on the Decapitator case, perhaps even interviewing Ozmian. That would put Ozmian into a foul mood. So much the better. A moment later he was hurrying toward the security station.

44

Lieutenant Vincent D'Agosta sat in the tidy living room of the apartment he shared with Laura Hayward, moodily drinking a Budweiser and listening to the bleat of traffic on the avenue below. From the kitchen came sounds of cooking—the creak of an oven door opening, the whuff of a gas burner being lit. Laura, a superb cook, was in the midst of outdoing herself in the preparation of a New Year's Day feast.

D'Agosta knew why she was working so hard—to cheer him up, make him forget the Decapitator case . . . if only for a little while.

The prospect filled him with guilt. He didn't feel worthy of all this effort—in fact, at the moment, he didn't feel worthy of anything.

He drained his Budweiser, moodily crushed the can in his fist, then placed it on a magazine that sat on the end table. Four similarly crushed cans were there already, lined up like injured sentries.

He was popping the tab on his sixth when Laura emerged from the kitchen. If she noticed all the empties, she said nothing; she merely sat down in an armchair across from him.

"Too hot in there," she said, nodding toward the kitchen. "Anyway, all the heavy lifting is done."

"Sure I can't help?" he asked for the fourth time.

"Thanks, but nothing to do. We'll be eating in half an hour—hope you've got a good appetite."

D'Agosta, who felt more thirsty than hungry, nodded and took another pull.

"What the hell ever happened to Michelob?" he asked suddenly, holding up the can of Bud almost accusatorily. "The *real* Michelob, I mean. Now, there was a premium beer. And that fat-bellied brown bottle with the gold foil at the neck—you really felt you were drinking something special. But today everybody's crazy for craft beers. It's like they've forgotten what a classic American beverage tastes like."

Laura said nothing.

D'Agosta lifted the can to take another pull, then put it aside. "Sorry."

"Don't be."

"I'm sitting around, sulking like a kid, feeling sorry for myself."

"Vinnie, it's not just you. It's everybody who's on the case. I mean, it's tearing apart the whole city. I can't even imagine the pressure you're under."

"I've got a ton of detectives working on this—and they're just going around and around in circles." *They're probably spending miserable New Year's Days, too*, he thought. *And it's my fault. I haven't moved the case forward.*

He sat forward, realized he was a little drunk, sat back again. "It's the goddamnedest thing. This Adeyemi. I've talked to anyone who might have an ax to grind with her. Nothing. Even her enemies say she's a saint. I've had my people digging twenty-four seven. Christ, I've even thought of flying to Nigeria myself. I just *know* there's some deep shit in her background!"

"Vinnie, don't beat yourself up about it. Not today."

And yet he couldn't leave it alone. It was like a sore tooth that your tongue kept returning to, testing and probing despite the pain. The worst of it, he knew, was a feeling he couldn't shake: that the whole case was unraveling, coming apart before his eyes. Like the rest of the NYPD and everyone else in the city, he was sure it was some crazy psycho targeting the worst of the one percenters. God knew when Harriman first published the idea, it made perfect sense to him and everyone else. But no matter what stone he looked under, he couldn't make this latest killing fit the pattern.

Then there was Pendergast. More than once, he'd thought back on what the FBI agent had said: *There is indeed a motive for these murders. But it is not the motive that you, the NYPD, and all of New York seem to believe.* He felt bad that he'd blown his stack. But the man could be so damn infuriating—trashing your theories while withholding his own.

What he had to do, D'Agosta realized, was refocus. After all, Pendergast hadn't come out and said *he* thought Adeyemi was a saint, exactly. He'd just implied they were looking at things the wrong way. Maybe instead of a history of hidden bad behavior, Adeyemi had done one truly horrific thing in her life. That would be a whole lot easier to cover up. Harder to find, admittedly—but once found, bingo.

He was woken from this reverie by the clatter of china; Laura was setting the dining room table. Leaving his beer unfinished, he rose and went over to help her. In the last few minutes, he'd found that his appetite had, in fact, sharpened. He'd forget about the case for a little while, enjoy his wife's company and cooking...and then get back to headquarters and start making a fresh round of calls.

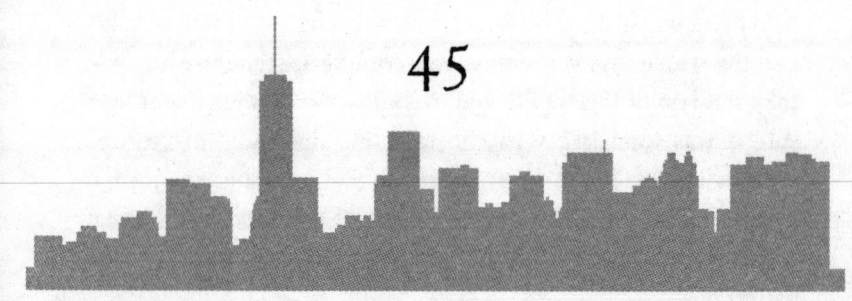

45

From her chair, Isabel Alves-Vettoretto watched her employer read over the three sheets of paper that Bryce Harriman had handed him, then read them over again.

She gave Harriman an appraising glance. Alves-Vettoretto was a dead shot at reading people. She could sense a mix of emotions warring within the reporter: anxiety, moral outrage, pride, defiance.

Now Ozmian finished his second reading and—leaning over his massive desk—handed Harriman's proposed article to Alves-Vettoretto. She read it through with mild interest. *So the reporter had done his homework*, she thought. Alves-Vettoretto had studied accounts of the great conquerors of world history, and now a quotation of Julius Caesar's came to mind: *It's only hubris if I fail.*

She set the papers carefully on the edge of the desk. In the brief period between Pendergast's walking out and Bryce Harriman's being ushered in, Ozmian had been uncharacteristically still, poring over something on his computer, deep in thought. But now his gestures became quick and economical. After Alves-Vettoretto had put down the papers, she caught a silent glance from Ozmian.

Understanding what the glance meant, she stood up and excused herself from the office.

What she had to do had been carefully set up and putting it in motion took five minutes. When she returned, Harriman was placing another piece of paper on Ozmian's desk with an air of triumph—it appeared to be a copy of the affidavit Harriman had said he'd gotten from the eyewitness in Massachusetts.

Now Ozmian was talking and Harriman was listening.

"And so this 'counter-blackmail,' as you call it, consists of three parts," Ozmian was saying, his voice calm, indicating the draft of the article. "You lay out, in detail, the events of thirty years ago, in which, before a crowd of churchgoers, I beat Father Anselm senseless at Our Lady of Mercy church. And you've got the affidavit to prove it."

"That's pretty much it."

Ozmian leaned across the desk. "I couldn't be less concerned with public opinion. However, I must confess—" and here he faltered for a moment. The anger seemed to drain away and a deflated look came over his features. "I must confess that the board of DigiFlood might not welcome this information getting out and casting a shadow over the company. I congratulate you on your investigative skills."

Harriman accepted this compliment with dignity.

Ozmian swiveled in his chair, stared out the vast windows for a moment. Then he turned back to Harriman. "It seems like we're at a Mexican standoff. So here's what's going to happen. I'll take the frame off you, transfer the funds back into the account of the Shannon Croix Foundation, and make it look like a bank error. In exchange, you'll leave me with the original of that affidavit when you leave—and you'll agree not to publish anything on what happened at Our Lady of Mercy."

As Ozmian spoke, Alves-Vettoretto noted that Harriman fairly glowed. He swelled in his chair like a peacock. "And what about my reporting on the murder?"

"I would ask you frankly, man-to-man, not to sully my daughter's name any further than you've already done. There are plenty of murders after hers to occupy your pen."

Harriman absorbed this gravely. When he spoke, his voice was freighted with gravitas. "I'll try. But I have to tell you—if newsworthy information about your daughter comes to light, I'll have to write about it. Surely you understand?"

Ozmian opened his mouth as if to protest, but ultimately said nothing. He slumped slightly in his chair, giving the faintest nod as he did so.

Harriman rose to his feet. "We have a deal. And I hope you've learned something from all this, Mr. Ozmian—despite your money and power, it's never a good idea to take on the press. Especially in the form of a reporter as dedicated and experienced as myself. Truth will out, Mr. Ozmian."

This miniature lecture on ethics accomplished, the reporter swiveled on one heel, and—without offering to shake hands—made for the double doors, trailing an air of injured virtue.

Ozmian waited until the doors had closed behind Harriman. Then he turned to look inquiringly at Alves-Vettoretto, who nodded in response. And as she did so, she noted that Ozmian's equanimity—which had become rather discomposed in the wake of the meeting with Agent Pendergast—now appeared to be fully restored.

Harriman could barely restrain himself from leaping with triumph in the elevator as it shot downward toward the lobby. It had worked—just as he'd known it would work, during that dark night of the soul in his apartment, mere days before. All it had taken was the right kind of reportorial skill. And, truth be told, he had been a little modest just now, in his talk with Ozmian—there were few others who could have uncovered the man's vicious little secrets as quickly and thoroughly as he'd done.

He had won. He had met the great and terrible Ozmian on the battlefield, with weapons of the entrepreneur's own choosing—blackmail—and he had emerged victorious! The way he had caved so completely, even on the tender point about his daughter, spoke volumes.

The elevator doors whisked open and he strode through the lobby, out the revolving doors, and onto West Street. His cell phone—which had vibrated once or twice during the final minutes of his conference with Ozmian—now began to vibrate again. He took it out of his pocket.

"Harriman here."

"Bryce? This is Rosalie Everett."

Rosalie had been one of Shannon Croix's best friends, and she was second in command on the foundation's board of directors. She sounded unaccountably breathless.

"Yes, Rosie. What is it?"

"Bryce, I don't quite know how to say this, and still less what to make of it…but I just now received, in a series of email attachments, a large number of documents—financial documents. It looks like they were sent by accident, not five minutes ago. I'm no accountant, but it appears that all the foundation's assets—just shy of a million and a half dollars—have been transferred from our business account and placed in a private holding in the Cayman Islands, in your own name."

"I—I—" he sputtered, too overcome by shock to articulate anything.

"Bryce, this has to be some kind of mistake. Right? I mean, you loved Shannon....But it's right here in black and white. All the other board members have been getting copies, too. These documents—God, here come more of them—they all imply you emptied the foundation's bank account just before the holiday. This is some kind of forgery, right? Or maybe a bad New Year's joke? Please, Bryce, say something. I'm frightened—"

With a click, her voice was cut off. Harriman realized that, involuntarily, his fingers had curled into fists, ending the call.

A moment later, it rang again. After rolling over to voice mail, it rang again. And then again.

And then came the chirrup of a text message being received. With the slow, strange movements of a bad dream, Harriman looked down at the screen of his phone.

The text was from Anton Ozmian.

Almost against his will, Harriman opened the messages pane of his phone and Ozmian's text sprang onto the screen:

Idiot. Proud pillar of the fourth estate, indeed. In your smug satisfaction at uncovering this story, you never thought to ask yourself the most germane question of all: *why I beat up that priest*. Here's the answer you should have dug up yourself. When I was an altar boy at Our Lady, Father Anselm abused me. I was serially raped. Years later, I returned to that church to make sure he never preyed on his charges again. Here's another good question: why was I charged only with a misdemeanor, which was quickly dropped? Sure, there was a courtesy payment, but the church refused to cooperate with any criminal investigation because they knew what damaging information would come out if they did. Now, ask yourself: if you publish this story, where is the public's sympathy going to lie? With the priest? Or me? Even more germane, what will DigiFlood's board of directors do? What will the world think of you for exposing my youthful abuse and its predictable psychical aftermath, which I overcame to found one of the most successful companies in the world? So go ahead and publish your story.

A. O.

P.S. Enjoy prison.

But even as he read the text with mounting horror, the lines began to shimmer and grow faint. A second later, they were gone, replaced by a black screen. Harriman frantically tried to take a screen shot, but it was too late—Ozmian's message had disappeared as quickly as it had arrived.

He looked up from his phone with a groan of disbelief and panic. This was a nightmare, it had to be. And sure enough—just as would happen in a nightmare—he saw, about half a block down West Street, two uniformed NYPD officers looking in his direction. One of them pointed at him. And then—as he stood rooted to the spot, unable to move—they began running toward him, releasing the thumb breaks on their holsters as they did so.

46

LONGSTREET, WITH PENDERGAST a silent shadow at his side, stood at the door to the garage of Robert Hightower's row house on Gerritsen Avenue in Marine Park, Brooklyn. The door was open, allowing a chill wind to blow in—the short driveway was covered in a dusting of snow that had fallen late the night before—but Hightower seemed not to mind. The space was filled with beat-up worktables; personal computers of varying degrees of obsolescence; circuit boards spewing rivers of cabling; old CRT monitors missing their glass tubes; battered tools hanging from pegboard walls; band saws and compression crimpers and table vises; an assortment of soldering guns; half a dozen small-parts organizers, most of their drawers open, spilling screws and nails and resistors. Hightower, fussing over a worktable, was in his late fifties, solidly built, with short but thick iron-gray hair covering the dome of his skull.

He picked up a tin of soldering flux, pressed the cap onto it, and tossed it toward the back of one of the tables. "So of all the people he screwed, destroyed, ruined, or otherwise fucked over, Ozmian claims I'm the one who hates him the most."

"That's correct," said Longstreet.

Hightower barked a sarcastic, mirthless laugh. "What a distinction."

"Is it true?" Longstreet asked.

"Consider a man who had everything to live for," he said, busying himself at the worktable, "nice home, beautiful wife, great career, happiness, success and prosperity—and then the bastard ripped all that away. So do I win first prize in the hatred category? Yeah, I probably do. Guess I'm your man."

"This algorithm you devised," Longstreet said. "The audio codec for compressing and streaming files simultaneously. I can't pretend to understand it, but according to Ozmian it was original and quite valuable."

"It was my life's work," Hightower said. "I didn't realize just how much of my own self was wrapped up into every line of that code until it was stolen from me." He paused, surveying the benches. "My dad was a beat cop, just like his dad and his dad. Money was tight. But he had enough to buy the parts for a ham radio set. Just the parts. I built it myself. And that's how I learned the basics about electrical engineering, telephony, audio synthesis. Got a college scholarship on the strength of that. And then my interests turned from hardware to software. Same melody, different instrument." Finally, he rose from his fussing and turned toward them, looking from one to the other with eyes that Longstreet could only describe as haunted.

"Ozmian took it away from me. All of it. And here I am." He swept a hand around the garage, laughing bitterly. "No money. No family. Parents dead. And what am I doing? Living in their house. It's like the last decade never happened—except that I'm a dozen years older, with nothing to show for it. And I have one cocksucker to thank for all that."

"It's our understanding," Longstreet said, "that during and after the takeover, you harassed Mr. Ozmian. You sent him threatening messages, said you were going to kill him and his family—to the point where he had to get a restraining order."

"So?" Hightower replied belligerently. "Can you blame me? He lied under oath, cheated, lawyered me to death, stole my company, fired my employees—and you could see he loved every minute of it. If you were half a man, you'd do the same. I could take it, but my wife couldn't. Drove off a cliff, drunk. They said it was an accident. Bullshit." He laughed harshly. "*He* did that, too. Ozmian *killed* her."

"I understand," Pendergast said, speaking for the first time, "that during this difficult period—before your wife's tragic death—the police were called to your house on several occasions, responding to a domestic disturbance?"

Hightower's hands, which had been roaming over the top of the workbench, suddenly went still. "You know as well as I do that she never filed a complaint."

"No."

"I've got nothing to say about it." His hands began to stir once again. "Funny. I keep coming out here, night after night, puttering about. I guess I'm trying to come up with a second brainstorm. But I know it's useless. Lightning never strikes twice."

"Mr. Hightower," Pendergast asked, "may I ask where you were on the evening of December fourteenth? Ten PM, to be precise."

"Here, I suppose. I never go anywhere. What's so special about that evening?"

"That was the night Grace Ozmian was killed."

Hightower wheeled back toward them. Longstreet was surprised at the expression that had suddenly appeared on his face.

The haunted look had been replaced by a ghastly smile; a mask of vengeful triumph.

"Oh, yeah, *that* December fourteenth!" he said. "How could I forget that red-letter night? Such a *crying* shame."

"And your whereabouts the following night?" Longstreet asked. "When her dead body was decapitated?"

As he was asking the question, a shadow appeared in the doorway of the garage. Longstreet glanced over to see a tall man in a leather jacket standing in the snow. His stony expression, the quick and impassive way with which he sized up the situation, told Longstreet the man was in law enforcement.

"Bob," the man said, nodding at Hightower.

"Bill." Hightower indicated his guests. "FBI brass. Here asking questions about the night Ozmian's daughter lost her head."

The man said nothing, betraying no expression.

"This is William Cinergy," Hightower explained to Longstreet and Pendergast. "NYPD, Sixty-Third Precinct. My neighbor."

Longstreet nodded.

"I grew up in a police family," Hightower said. "And this is a police neighborhood. We members of the blue fraternity tend to nest together."

There was a brief silence.

"Now that I think of it," Hightower said—and the unnerving travesty of a smile had not left his face—"Bill and I were out drinking the night Ozmian's kid was killed. Weren't we, Bill?"

"That's right," Bill said.

"We were at O'Herlihey's, around the corner on Avenue R. It's a cop bar. As I recall, a lot of the boys were there—weren't they?"

Bill nodded.

"And they'd all remember me buying them a round—say, at about ten PM?"

"Damn straight."

"There you have it." Hightower slid off the stool, his face becoming an expressionless mask once again. "And now, if that's all, gentlemen," he said, "Bill and I have a football game to catch on ESPN."

They sat in Longstreet's work sedan, idling at the Gerritsen Avenue curb, looking out at the little row house.

"So," Longstreet said, "what do you think about the way that guy practically flung that flimsy alibi in our faces?"

"Whether the alibi is valid or not, I don't think we have much of a chance of breaking it."

"What about your cop friend—D'Agosta? Maybe he can crack the blue wall."

"You know I would never ask him to do that. And there's another consideration."

Longstreet looked at him.

"While Hightower had the motive, it doesn't explain the killings that followed."

"That's already occurred to me," Longstreet said. He continued to look at the house, and the curl of smoke that came drifting up from its chimney. "Maybe he developed a taste for it. I've seen cops go rogue before, start taking justice into their own hands when the courts won't do it for them. One thing's for sure—this merits following up."

"We're going to have to be careful in doing so," Pendergast said. "We must keep this lead quiet for now—with the NYPD *and* FBI. You never know who might pass information along."

"You're right, of course. Let's work on this individually. Compartmentalize. Minimize our communication. Keep in touch by phone or encrypted email only." Longstreet went silent for a moment, staring at the house. The blinds had been pulled tight across the picture window of what he assumed was the living room. "That look he gave us," he said. "When he passed off that alibi. It was almost like a challenge."

At this, Pendergast gave an almost convulsive shudder. "*Challenge*," he repeated. "But of course."

Longstreet frowned. "What are you talking about?"

But Pendergast said nothing more, and after a moment Longstreet put the car in gear and pulled away from the curb.

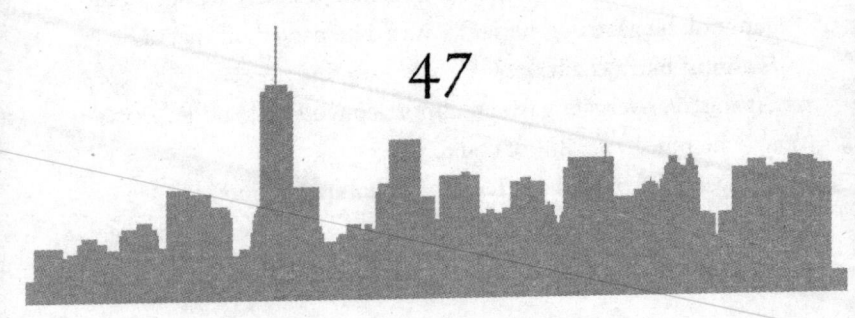

47

MARSDEN SWOPE SAT at the only desk in his tiny apartment. The time was six o'clock in the morning of January 3.

January 3. A date that would initiate the purification of the city.

He had no illusions. It would start small, he knew—if you could call so many pilgrims "small." But he had a tool that prophets before him had not: the Internet. The one thing he had instructed his followers not to dispose of was their cell phones. They were critical for two reasons: first, they allowed him to orchestrate the logistics of the bonfire, and second, they would be able to document it.

What would start as a single act of purification in Manhattan would spread: to big cities and small towns, from America to Europe and beyond. The world, divided more than ever between the haves and have-nots, was hungry for this message. The people would rise up and unite to rid their lives of greed, materialism, and the ugly social divisions caused by money, forsaking wealth for a life of simplicity, purity, and honorable poverty.

But he must not get ahead of himself. He had paved the way, set things in motion—but now his next act was crucial. His followers, he knew, were awaiting his signal. The trick would be to get them to assemble on the Great Lawn at precisely the right moment, without alerting the authorities.

Turning back to his desk, he composed a tweet for his base: short, instructive, and to the point:

TONIGHT. Pray, fast & prepare for what is to come. Final LOCATION & instructions sent at 3 PM.

> —The Passionate Pilgrim (@SavonarolaRedux)
> January 3, 6:08 AM

He read it over once, then again, and then—satisfied—posted it and sent it on its way. At three he would send his final instructions and then it would all be in God's hands.

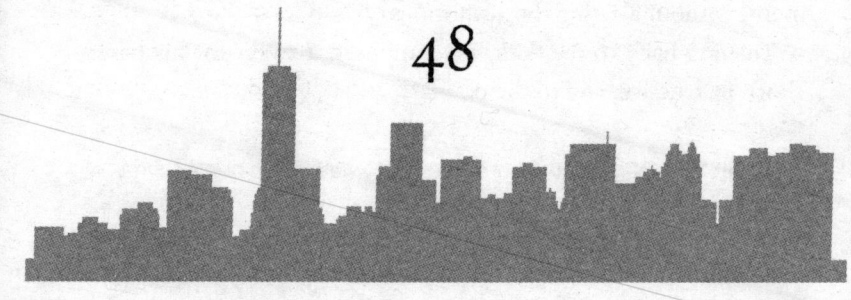

48

HOWARD LONGSTREET'S CELL phone chirruped just after 6 AM.

He sat up with a grunt and glanced at it. It was not his personal cell, but the official mobile phone that the FBI issued to its agents and supervisors. It had the ability to send and receive both cleartext and encrypted mail—and the icon on the screen told him he had just received an encrypted note from S. A. Aloysius Pendergast.

He plucked the phone from the table, ran the email through the decryptor, then read it.

We must speak on a matter of great urgency. Significant breakthrough made. Connections proving far deeper than expected. Secrecy vital. Meet at old King's Park, Building 44, 2 PM to plan apprehension of perps (sic). Any attempted contact in the interim is inadvisable. Backup is vital; bring Lt. D'Agosta, to whom I have also reached out.

P.S. We are being surveilled.

A.

Longstreet cleared the message from his phone, then replaced it thoughtfully on the nightstand. *Perps.* The plural was no typo, as the "sic" indicated. *More than one.* This was indeed deeper than expected. Was it Hightower and others? He tried to parse Pendergast's shorthand. It seemed he had made a critical discovery about the man. But the message also implied that Hightower's connections to law enforcement ran deeper than either of them had suspected. *Perps.* Was Pendergast hinting at a conspiracy within the NYPD? It wasn't beyond the bounds of possibility, given the NYPD's old history of corruption. No wonder secrecy was paramount—especially since Pendergast had enough evidence to use the word *apprehension.*

Pendergast, Longstreet knew, disliked email and rarely sent it. However, in this case the situation was dire enough, the stakes high enough, and the suspected perps well placed enough to make a high degree of caution necessary.

What about this business of being surveilled? Did this mean his work phone was actually at risk? Longstreet found that hard to believe; the FBI had the latest in encryption and protection. Damn that Pendergast and his deliberately inscrutable ways. He found himself tugged with curiosity as to what the agent had uncovered. And also...what was this place, "old King's Park"?

Reaching for his laptop, he turned it on, fired up the secure Tor browser, and used it to access the Dark Web. This was a highly irregular undertaking for a ranking member of the FBI, he knew, but if his email, phone, and texts were vulnerable, as Pendergast implied, so were his browsing habits. At least now he could make an untraceable search.

It took only a few minutes to learn that King's Park was a vast, rambling psychiatric hospital on the North Shore of Long Island, built in the late nineteenth century and now abandoned.

He downloaded a map of the site and quickly familiarized himself with it. Building 44 was a small warehouse, originally used for depoting food supplies for the enormous complex.

Committing the map to memory, Longstreet closed the browser, then quickly shut down the computer. Why King's Park Psychiatric Center? But as he considered the matter further, he realized it was an ideal location for a meeting—outside New York City limits, thus curbing the effectiveness of any dirty NYPD surveillance, yet both isolated and easy to get to. And Building 44 had no doubt been chosen for its access to Old Dock Road, which bisected the grounds of the sanitarium.

There was only one more thing to do: reach out to D'Agosta. He would use his regular cell phone for this, just the one call, and keep it banal. He looked through his log of his associates' contacts, found D'Agosta's number, and dialed.

Although it was not yet six thirty in the morning, the call was answered on the first ring, and the voice on the other end did not sound sleepy. "Yeah?"

Longstreet noticed the voice did not identify itself. "Lieutenant?"

"Yeah."

"Do you know who I am?"

"I'm pretty sure you're the one our mutual acquaintance calls 'H.'"

"Correct. Please keep your answers as brief as possible. Has he contacted you?"

"Yes."

"And suggested a place where the two of us should go?"

"No place. Just told me to expect a call from you—urgent and confidential."

"Fine. I'll meet you outside your, ah, place of business at noon."

"Okay."

"Absolutely confidential."

"Got it."

The line went dead.

Longstreet replaced the phone. Despite a long career in covert operations, he could not help feel a quickening of excitement. After years of commanding large assault teams, a small, tactical operation like this was like going back to his roots. That Pendergast—always full of surprises. He had handled this extremely well. Nevertheless, the lieutenant's involvement would be crucial if this was an NYPD situation.

He lay down in bed, hoping not for sleep—that was now impossible—but for clarity of mind and concentration of purpose. Noon would be at hand soon enough, and the case would enter its final stretch: the takedown. He hoped to God this nightmarish string of serial murders was finally at an end.

He closed his eyes as the breaking dawn light illuminated the bedroom curtains.

49

Bᴙʏᴄᴇ Hᴀʀʀɪᴍᴀɴ ᴡᴀs led by the armed corrections officer down the sterile hallways of the Manhattan Detention Complex, then ushered into a tiny room with a table bolted to the floor, two chairs, a clock, and an overhead light—both fitted with wire screens. There were no windows; he only knew that it was quarter to nine in the morning because of the clock.

"Here you are," the officer said.

Harriman hesitated, looking at two beefy, shaved-head characters already in the holding cell who were eyeing him as if sizing up a cut of rare roast beef.

"Come on, let's go!" The guard gave Harriman a light shove. He entered and the door clanged shut behind him, the bolt shooting into place with a clank.

He shuffled in and took a seat. At least he wasn't wearing leg irons anymore, but the orange prison jumpsuit was stiff and abrasive against his skin. The last many hours had passed in a dreadful kind of blur. The arrest, the trip in a squad car to the local precinct, the waiting, the arraignment and booking for embezzlement, and then the depressingly short ride to the detention complex just a few blocks away—it was over almost before he could process what had happened. It was like a nightmare from which he could not shake himself awake.

As soon as the guard was gone, one of the brawny guys came and stood over him, real close, staring down.

Harriman, not knowing what to do, finally raised his head. "What?"

"*My* seat."

Harriman jumped up with alacrity while the man sat down. Two seats: three men. No cot. This was going to be a long day.

As he sat on the floor, back propped against the wall, listening to the yammer and bluster of fellow prisoners up and down the cell block, the mistakes he'd made paraded themselves before his eyes in dumb show. He'd been blinded by overconfidence, re-inforced by his recent celebrity—and he'd fatally underestimated Anton Ozmian.

His first mistake, as Ozmian had taken pains to point out, had been to overlook the obvious question: Why had Ozmian beaten up the priest in the first place? Why no repercussions? It had been such an outrageous assault, right in front of an entire congregation, that his reportorial alarm bells should have rung, five-alarm.

His second mistake had been tactical: showing the piece to Ozmian before publishing it. That had not only tipped his hand, but also given Ozmian time to react. With bitter self-recrimination, he remembered all too well how Ozmian's lieutenant had slipped out for a few minutes early in their meeting—only to return after setting the frame job in motion, no doubt. And then they'd kept him there in the office, talking, while the trap was being sprung. By the time he walked out of the DigiFlood building, flushed with success, he was already dead meat. He recalled, with a fresh wave of frustration and shame, what Ozmian had told him earlier: *Our company has many fine programmers, and they created a most lovely digital theft leading back to you. And you simply do not have the knowledge, or the resources, to undo it.* That was proving all too true: in one of the few calls he'd been allowed to make, he'd told his editor what had happened to him, how he'd been framed, and how he'd write a hell of a story about Ozmian that would explain it all. Petowski's response had been to call him a liar and hang up.

It seemed an eternity, but it was actually only six hours later when his two cellmates, who had blessedly ignored him, were taken out of the holding cell. And then it was his turn. A guard came, unlocked the door, and ushered him down the hall to a tiny room with chairs and a table. He was told to sit, and a moment later a man arrived, wearing a well-tailored suit and gleaming shoes that squeaked as he walked. He had a cheerful, almost cherubic face. This was Leonard Greenbaum, the lawyer Harriman had retained—not a public defender, but an experienced and lethal defense attorney, the most expensive Harriman could afford... given the fact that most of his assets had now been frozen. The man nodded a greeting, put his heavy leather case on the table, sat down across from Harriman, opened the case, removed a pile of papers, and spread them out before him.

"I'll be brief, Mr. Harriman," he told the reporter as he looked over the papers. "After all, at this point there really isn't much to say. First, the bad news. The district attorney has an airtight case against you. The paper trail has been all too easy to establish. They have the records of your opening the Cayman Islands account, along with a video of you entering the bank, they have records of you secretly transferring all the funds from the foundation, and they have evidence of your intent to flee the country the day after tomorrow, in the form of a one-way plane ticket to Laos."

This last was news to Harriman. "Flee the country? To *Laos*?"

"Yes. Your apartment has been searched by order of the court and all documents and computers seized. It's all in there, Mr. Harriman, as clear as day, along with the electronic ticket."

Greenbaum's voice had taken on a sorrowful, even reproachful tone, as if he wondered why Harriman had been quite so thick-headed.

Harriman groaned, put his head in his hands. "Look, it's all a setup. A frame job for blackmail. Ozmian created all this out of thin air. He's got the best hackers in the world working for him, and they staged this whole thing! I told you about my meetings with Ozmian, how he threatened me. There will be records that I was in the building, not once but twice."

"Mr. Ozmian admits you were in the building, but states you were simply looking for more information on his daughter for a new article."

"He did this to me as pure revenge because of what I wrote about his daughter! The man texted me right as I left the building, telling me what he did and why!"

The lawyer nodded. "You are, I take it, referring to the text that cannot be located on your phone or anywhere else."

"It's got to be somewhere!"

"And I agree. That's the problem. In my experience—and no doubt, that of the prosecution—texts simply don't delete themselves. There's always some trace left somewhere."

Harriman slumped in his chair. "Look, Mr. Greenbaum, I hired you to defend me. Not catalog all this phony evidence of guilt!"

"First of all, please call me Lenny. I'm afraid we're going to be working together for a long time." He put his elbows on the table and leaned forward, his voice sympathetic. "Bryce, I will defend you to the utmost. I'm the best in the business and that's why you hired me. But we have to face facts: the DA has an overwhelming case. If we insist on going to court, you'll be convicted and they will throw the book at you. The only chance you have—the *only* chance—is to plead."

"Plead? You think I'm guilty, don't you?"

"Let me finish." Greenbaum took a deep breath. "I've spoken with the DA, and under the right circumstances he's inclined to be lenient. You've got no priors, and you've led an upstanding, law-abiding life so far. In addition, you're a well-known reporter who has provided a public service to the city with this recent case. As a result, he might be willing to think of this as a onetime aberration, albeit egregious. After all, stealing funds from a charitable foundation for cancer patients, established under the pretext of memorializing a deceased friend..." His voice trailed off.

Harriman swallowed. "Lenient? Lenient how?"

"That's to be decided—if you give me authority to negotiate. The fact is, none of the extradited money was actually spent, and you did not flee the country. I could get you off with intent. If you were to plead guilty to that, with luck I'd say you'd have to do no more than—oh, two years, three, tops."

With another groan, Harriman let his head sink back into his hands. There was no other word for it, this was in fact a living nightmare—a nightmare that, it now seemed, he would not wake from for at least a couple of years.

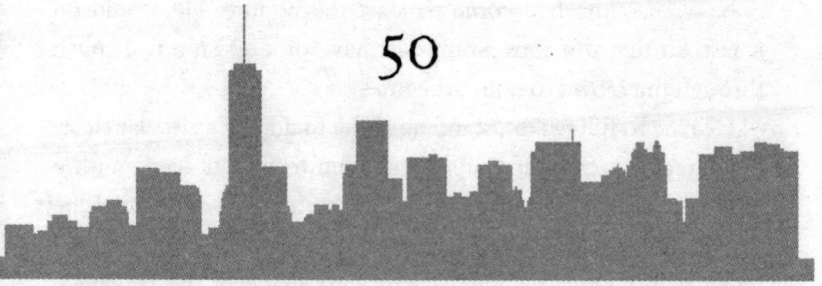

50

SEVERAL MILES TO the north of the Manhattan Detention Center, Marsden Swope stood next to a tarp spread in the center of the Great Lawn. He waited with a thrill of satisfaction mingled with a sense of humility as people began emerging from walkways, stands of trees, and nearby avenues and—slowly, haltingly, as if sensing the gravity of the occasion—walking across the vast lawn to gather silently around him. A few passersby, hurrying to their destinations in the cold January air, slowed to stare at this motley and growing assemblage. But so far they had not attracted the attention of the authorities.

Swope knew his message had reached a varied group, a real cross section of America, but he could not have imagined just how diverse it would be. All ages, races, creeds, and income brackets were now quietly surrounding him in a deepening circle. People wearing business suits, headdresses, tuxedos, saris, baseball uniforms, kaftans, Hawaiian shirts, gang colors—it went on and on and on. This was what he had so fervently hoped, that the one percenters and ninety-nine percenters would unite in their rejection of wealth.

"Thanks be to God," Swope whispered to himself. "Thanks be to God."

Now the time had come to start the bonfire. He would do it fast, so that the cops would not have time to stop it or push through the crowd to douse the fire.

He rose to full height, standing in the middle of a circular clearing, already surrounded by pilgrims ten to fifteen deep. With a gesture that was both dramatic and—he hoped—deferential, he threw off his cape to reveal a garment he had woven himself over many painstaking evenings: a hair shirt made of the roughest, coarsest animal hair he'd been able to acquire. Next, he took hold of the tarp and snatched it away, revealing a large white X he had spray-painted on the grass. Beside it were two jerrycans of kerosene.

"People!" he cried out. "Children of the living God! You have gathered here—rich and poor, from all over the country—for a single purpose: to unite in ridding ourselves of the luxuriant and prideful possessions that are so hateful to God, the wealth that Jesus so clearly stated would prevent our entry into heaven. Let us now solemnly swear to divest ourselves of these trappings of greed and purify our hearts. At this place, in this time, let us each make a symbolic offering to the bonfire of the vanities, as our promise to live from this day until the end of our days lives of simplicity!"

Now he backed away from the painted cross, picking up the jerrycans as he did, until he had joined the front line of the circle. Reaching into a pocket of his torn jeans, he plucked out a pen—a gold-filled fountain pen that his father, whom he had not seen or communicated with in a decade, had given him on graduating from the Jesuit seminary. He held the pen up for all to see; its precious metal inlay glinted in the rays of the setting sun. Then he threw it into the open area, where it landed, nib down, in the center of the painted cross.

"Let all who wish to walk in the way of grace," he intoned, "follow my example!"

There was a brief ripple through the crowd, like a shudder of expectation. This was followed by a moment of stasis. And then incredible showers of items were tossed from the surrounding circle, landing on the grass marked by the cross: designer handbags, clothing, jewelry, watches, car keys, sheaves of bearer bonds, ziplock bags of drugs and packets of marijuana, stacks of hundred-dollar bills, books detailing diet and get-rich-quick schemes, along with some surprising items: a jewel-studded dildo, an electric guitar with a beautifully book-matched top, and a Smith & Wesson handgun. Countless other things that beggared description rained down or were dropped onto the quickly growing pile. The heap of glitter and tinsel and empty luxury mounted up, including a perfectly astonishing number of women's shoes—stiletto pumps, mostly.

Now a transcendent glow, a sense of divine inevitability, suffused Swope like the caress of an angel. *This must be how Savonarola felt*, he realized, all those centuries ago in Florence. Taking one of the jerrycans of kerosene, he stepped forward and, unbunging it, poured it in widening circles over the ever-growing litter of vanities. Things thudded around him and fell against his head and shoulders, but he took no notice.

"And now!" he said, throwing aside the empty can and producing a box of wooden safety matches. "Let our new life in purification begin with fire!"

Pulling a match from the box and striking it into life, he threw it onto the pyre—and in the huge, yellow-orange *crump* of fire and heat that rose, he could see—briefly illuminated as if by daylight—the dark images of thousands of additional pilgrims, coming in from all sides of the Great Lawn, to join in this latter-day bonfire of the vanities, even as luxuries continued to rain down into the conflagration.

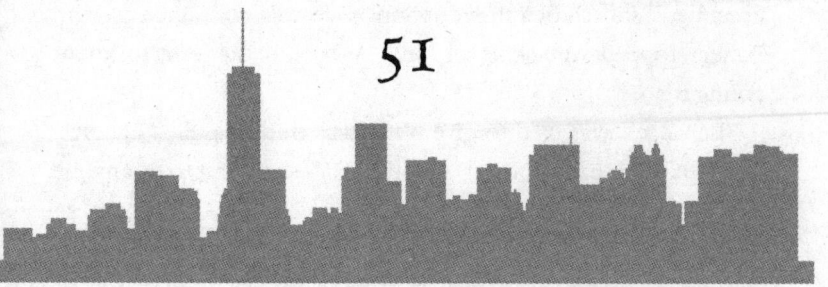

51

Dusk was falling over the city as Mrs. Trask bustled her way northward up Riverside Drive, her string bag full of groceries for the evening's dinner. Normally she didn't wait until such a late hour to do her shopping, but she had gotten preoccupied rearranging and cleaning the third-best set of china, and hadn't realized how late it had become. Proctor had offered to drive her, but these days she preferred to get out for a bit of a walk—an early evening's constitutional did her good, and besides, what with all the gentrification the neighborhood had undergone in recent years, it had become a pleasure to do her own shopping at the local Whole Foods. But as she walked across the circular driveway of 891 Riverside, heading toward the servants' entrance at the back of the house, she was dismayed to see a dark figure hovering in a shadow near the front door.

Her immediate instinct was alarm, and to call for Proctor—until she saw that the figure was no more than a boy. He looked shiftless and dirty—what she would have referred to growing up in London's East End as a street urchin—and as she approached he came out of the shadows.

"Begging your pardon, ma'am," he said, "but is this the residence of Mister, um, Pendergast?" He even had the Bow Bells accent and speech of a street urchin.

She stopped well short of him. "Why do you want to know, young man?"

"Because I was paid to give him this." And he pulled an envelope out of his back pocket. "And there doesn't seem to be anyone as is answering the door."

Mrs. Trask considered a moment. Then she extended her hand. "Very well, I'll see that he gets it. Now scarper."

The youth handed her the letter. Then, with a tug of a forelock, he turned and hurried away down the driveway.

Mrs. Trask watched him vanish into the bustle of the city. Then, shaking her head, she made her way to the back kitchen entrance. Really, one never knew what to expect, working for her employer.

She found him sitting in the library, a cup of green tea untouched on the table beside him, staring into the low fire burning in the grate.

"Mr. Pendergast," she said, standing in the doorway.

The agent did not respond.

"Mr. Pendergast?" she said in a slightly louder tone.

At this, he roused himself. "Yes, Mrs. Trask?" he said, turning toward her.

"I found a young boy waiting outside. He said nobody was answering the door. Did you not hear the bell?"

"I did not."

"He said he'd been paid to bring you this letter." She advanced, bringing with her the dirty, folded envelope on a silver salver. "I wonder why Proctor did not answer the door?" she couldn't help but add—as she slightly disapproved of Proctor and the liberties he sometimes took with the master.

Pendergast looked at the letter with an expression Mrs. Trask could not quite fathom. "I believe he did not answer because the doorbell was never rung. The boy lied to you. Now, if you would please place it on the table."

She put the salver down beside the tea set. "Will there be anything else?"

"Not for the present, thank you, Mrs. Trask."

Pendergast waited until she had exited the library; until her steps had died away down the hallway; until the entire mansion was quiet once again. And still he did not stir, or act, or do anything but regard the envelope the way he might an explosive device. What it was, he could not be sure—and yet he had all too strong a premonition.

At last, he leaned forward, picked it up by one edge, and unfolded it. The envelope was printed with a single word, typed on a manual typewriter: ALOYSIUS. He regarded this for a long moment, his sense of premonition increasing. Then, he gingerly slit the envelope open along its narrow edge with a switchblade he kept nearby for a letter opener. Looking inside, he saw a single sheet of foolscap and a small USB memory stick. He slid the sheet out onto the salver, then used the tip of the switchblade to unfold it.

The typewritten note it contained was not long.

Dear A. Pendergast:

This is the Decapitator writing you. The endgame has arrived. On the USB stick you will find a short video starring Lt. D'Agosta and Associate Director Longstreet. They are my captives. Quite frankly, they are the bait: to bring you to me for a special evening. I am in Building 44 of the abandoned King's

*Park Psychiatric Center on the North Shore of Long Island. Come
to me alone. Do not send in the cavalry. Do not bring Proctor or
anyone else. Tell no one. If you do not arrive by 9:05 PM, which
if my message has been delivered properly should be in approx-
imately fifty-five minutes, you'll never see either of your friends
alive again.*

*While you don't yet know who I am, you certainly know a
great deal about my talent. Since you are an intelligent man
yourself, you will parse out the situation you now find yourself in and realize there is only one thing to do. Naturally you
will view the video, ponder the situation, and consider various
courses of action; but in the end you will understand you have
no choice but to come here, now, alone. So don't dawdle. The
clock is ticking.*

*One other requirement: bring your Les Baer 1911 .45 and an
extra eight-round magazine, both fully loaded, and make sure
there is an extra round in the chamber, for a total of seventeen
rounds in all. This is vitally important.*

Sincerely,
"The Decapitator"

Pendergast read the letter through twice. He took the USB
stick and inserted it into the port on his laptop. There was only
one file on it. He clicked it.

A video sprang to life: D'Agosta and Longstreet, tied, gagged,
and immobilized, each with a single hand free. They were
staring at the camera, sweat beading on their brows, holding
between them with their free hands that morning's *New York
Times*. The video had no sound. The background appeared to
be a derelict, warehouse-like room. The two men were beaten,

bruised, and bloodied—D'Agosta worse than Longstreet. The video lasted only ten seconds and it played again, and again, in an endless loop.

Pendergast viewed the video a few more times and read the note again before putting both back in the envelope and sliding it into his suitcoat pocket. For three minutes he remained very still in the library, his face bathed in flickering firelight, before rising to his feet.

The Decapitator was right: he simply had no choice but to comply.

Pendergast had only a vague knowledge of King's Park, a gigantic decaying psychiatric hospital complex on Long Island not far from the city. A quick Internet search filled in the details: it had been abandoned decades ago, leaving numerous crumbling buildings scattered over expansive grounds sealed up behind chain-link fences; it was infamous for the electroshock treatments it so liberally administered to hopeless cases, before the advent of effective psychiatric drugs. The campus was situated in Sussex County between Oyster Bay and Stony Brook.

He printed out a map of the psychiatric center, folded it into his coat pocket, removed a spare .45 magazine from a drawer, checked to see it was full of rounds and slipped it into his other pocket, then removed his Les Baer to confirm it was fully loaded. He racked a round into the chamber, removed the magazine to insert a fresh round, and pocketed the gun.

As he was putting on his vicuña overcoat in the front hall, Proctor approached silently, like a cat. "May I be of assistance, sir?"

Pendergast glanced at him. Mrs. Trask must have told him of the letter. There was an eagerness in Proctor's face that was both unusual and disturbing. The man, of course, always knew or guessed a great deal more than he let on.

"No, thank you, Proctor."

"No need for a driver?"

"I have a yen to take a night drive by myself." He held out his hands for the keys.

For a moment, Proctor stood immobile, his face a mask. Pendergast was well aware Proctor knew he was lying, but there was no time to prevaricate in a more satisfactory fashion.

Reaching into a pocket, Proctor wordlessly handed Pendergast the keys to the Rolls-Royce.

"Thank you." And with a nod, Pendergast slipped past him and headed toward the garage, buttoning his overcoat as he went.

Just forty-eight minutes later, he turned off Route 25A onto Old Dock Road, which ran through the main campus of King's Park Psychiatric Center. It was now almost nine, and a bitter night had fallen. He guided the big car down the deserted road, dark shapes of buildings, shuttered and forlorn, passing by on both sides.

He slowed, made a U-turn, pulled the Silver Wraith up and over the curb, turned off the headlights, then drove the vehicle over the frozen ground, pulling it in behind a stand of trees where it would not be visible from the road. There he stopped and consulted the map. Across the road stood a cluster of buildings his map identified as GROUP 4, or THE QUAD, which had once housed the geriatric insane. To his right, two hundred yards behind the chain-link fence surrounding the campus, rose a vast, ten-story structure shown on the map as BUILDING 93, its gables and towers rising up against the night sky. The massive façade was bathed in ghostly moonlight and punctuated with empty, inky windows, which stared over the frozen campus like some monstrous, many-eyed beast. As Pendergast contemplated it, he felt a whisper, a shiver, of the memories it retained of the patients who had been shuttered inside, gibbering, weeping, beyond despair, subjected to experimental drug testing, lobotomies, electroshock treatments, and perhaps worse. A bloated moon, veiled by scudding clouds, was rising above its battlements.

Hidden within the building's immense shadow, Pendergast knew from the map, lay the much smaller two-story structure known as Building 44. This was where he would find the Decapitator.

Exiting the vehicle and quietly closing its door, he made sure the street was empty before approaching the fence. A set of wire clippers appeared in one gloved hand, and it was the work of two minutes to cut a flap in the cheap chain-link fence large enough to permit entry without catching and tearing his overcoat, of which he was very fond. Slipping through, he walked silently over the hard ground, his breath flaring in the moonlight, past Building 29—a power plant constructed in the early 1960s, now rusting and deserted like everything else. Beyond, he picked up an abandoned railroad spur line and followed it to where it ended at the loading dock of Building 44.

Pendergast's research indicated Building 44 had been a warehouse for the storage of food for the psychiatric center. The small structure was sealed, its windows covered with plywood and tin, its doors locked and chained. Not a glimmer of light could be seen through the cracks.

He glanced around once again, then lightly sprang up onto the building's loading bay at the end of a railroad trestle. Grasping a handle, he lifted the door slowly, keeping to a minimum the inevitable complaint of rusted metal, until it was just high enough to allow him to slip underneath. He waited, listening. But there was no sound from within.

He found himself in a large loading area, empty of everything except a stack of wooden packing crates piled in one corner, covered in cobwebs. Ahead, across the wide floor of cracked concrete, a door stood open in the far wall. The faintest illumination could be seen beyond. It looked like a trap—which Pendergast had known from the beginning was precisely what it was.

A trap intended for him; but traps sometimes worked both ways.

Pausing, he glanced at his watch. It was nine oh two—three minutes left until the time limit expired.

Silently, he crossed the expanse of the loading area and approached the door. Placing the fingertips of one hand on it, he slowly opened it wider. Beyond lay a narrow corridor, punctuated on both sides by open doors. From one of the right-hand doors, almost closed, leaked the light that faintly illuminated the hallway. Absolute silence reigned.

Pulling his Les Baer, Pendergast slipped through the doorway and moved down the corridor until he reached the lighted door. He waited a few moments to assure himself there was no activity. Then he placed his palm on the door, gave it a sharp shove, stepped forward with the weapon raised, and panned the room.

The light was sufficiently dim as to illuminate only the immediate portion of the space he was standing in. The deeper recesses, going back through rows of empty shelves, were too dark to make out. There was a table in the center of the pool of light, with a figure seated in a chair, his back to Pendergast. He recognized the man instantly: even from the rear, the rumpled suit, powerful frame, and long gray hair could only belong to one man—Howard Longstreet. He was, it seemed, looking into the inky darkness at the rear of the room, head propped on one arm in an attitude of alert repose.

Pendergast paused for a moment, frozen by surprise. The man was not bound—in fact, he seemed to be under no restraint whatsoever.

"H?" he said in a voice barely more than a whisper.

Longstreet did not reply.

Pendergast took a step toward the seated figure. "H?" he said again.

Still Longstreet said nothing. Was he unconscious? Pendergast stepped toward the seated figure and reached out, resting a hand on Longstreet's shoulder and giving him a gentle shake.

With a quiet, slippery kind of sigh, the man's head fell off, hit the table with a dull thud, rolled away, and came to rest, rocking slightly, Longstreet's gray eyes staring up at Pendergast in silent agony.

At the same time, the lights abruptly went off. And from out of the darkness came a low chuckle of triumph.

52

Just as quickly as blackness fell, brilliant light suddenly flooded the room. There—seated in a wooden chair in a far corner—sat Lieutenant D'Agosta. He was hog-tied to the chair, wearing nothing but boxers and a sleeveless coat stuffed with packets of plastic explosive—a suicide vest. A cue-ball gag was in his mouth. He looked at Pendergast, his eyes on fire.

"I arrived within the requisite fifty-five minutes, Mr. Ozmian," Pendergast said. "And yet you killed Howard Longstreet. That was not part of the deal."

A moment passed. And then, Anton Ozmian stepped quietly into the room. He was wearing blacked-out camos, and in one hand he held a 1911 handgun—trained on Pendergast—while the other cupped a remote detonator.

"Place your weapon on the floor, please, Agent Pendergast," he said in a cool voice.

Pendergast complied.

"Now nudge it toward me with your foot."

Pendergast did so.

"Take off your jacket, turn around, place your feet apart, and spread-eagle yourself against the wall."

Pendergast did this as well. The opportunity, he was fairly sure, would come for turning the tables, but for now there were no options except to obey. He heard Ozmian approach; he felt the cold hard muzzle of the gun against the nape of his neck as the man searched him, uncovering the spare magazine along with several knives, lock picks and bump keys, a garrote, two cell phones, money, some test tubes and tweezers, and a single-shot derringer.

"Put one hand behind your back while balancing yourself against the wall with the other."

When Pendergast did this, he felt a pair of plastic zip cuffs slip around his wrist. Then his other hand was pulled back and cuffed as well. He heard Ozmian step back.

"Very good," the entrepreneur said. "Now you may have a seat beside your friend. And we'll have a little talk."

Wordlessly, Pendergast sat down next to the body of Longstreet—which, no longer propped up by the arm, had fallen forward onto the table, next to Longstreet's lolling head. D'Agosta looked on from his chair in the far corner, his own eyes wide and red-rimmed.

Ozmian settled into a chair on the other side of the table and inspected Pendergast's primary weapon. "Very nice. You'll be getting it back soon, by the way." He put it down, paused a moment. "First: I never promised to keep both men alive. My exact words were, 'you'll never see *either* of your friends alive again.' As you can see, Lieutenant D'Agosta is still very much alive—for the time being. Second: congratulations on deducing that I was the Decapitator. How did you do it, exactly?"

"Hightower. You led us to a suspect who was simply too perfect. That was when I sensed a master puppeteer at work, and started to assemble the pieces."

"Very good. Have you also guessed *why* I am killing these particular people?"

"Why don't you tell me?" Pendergast said.

"I'd much rather hear it from you."

"The hobby you supposedly gave up many years ago—big-game hunting. You were desirous of the ultimate thrill: the 'most dangerous game,' so to speak."

Ozmian grinned widely. "I *am* impressed!"

"I am puzzled about one thing: why your daughter was your first victim. Although I suspect it had something to do with your recent company troubles."

"Well, I'll help you with that one, as it's getting late and the game will soon begin. As you've guessed, it was my own daughter, my *dear, devoted* daughter, who leaked our proprietary code onto the Internet—almost capsizing my company in the process."

"I take it, then, that your relationship wasn't quite as close as you pretended."

At this, Ozmian paused for a moment. "When she was a girl, we were quite close. Bosom companions, actually. She worshipped me, and in her alone I found unconditional love. But as puberty approached, she zigged when she should have zagged. She had a brilliant mind when she wanted to use it, not to mention a remarkable facility with computers from a very early age. I'd always expected her to be my partner and eventual replacement. Her betrayal of me when it came was, as you can imagine, all that much keener."

"Why did she betray you?"

"The zig rather than the zag. You know how it goes, Agent Pendergast: a family gone wrong thanks to too much money, too many ex-wives, too much dysfunction." He scoffed. "Oh, we kept up appearances—today it's all about celebrity-watching and paparazzi, isn't it, and we both had skin in that game. But the fact is, my daughter became a drug-addicted, self-destructive, vicious little slut who hated everything about me except my money. And when I cut that off, she used her considerable skills to break into my private computer and do the one thing she knew would hurt me the most. She tried to ruin the company I had built—for *her*."

"And so, in a fit of rage, you killed her."

"Yes. They tell me I have 'anger management issues.'" Ozmian made air quotes. "The only thing is, I never seem to regret my outbursts. It's been quite useful to me in business."

"And once you'd cooled off…I presume you got to thinking. About her head."

"I see you've found the final piece of the puzzle. There was Grace's body, lying in a Queens garage. And there I was, in my freshly cleaned apartment, sipping cognac and thinking. To be honest, I was shocked at what I'd done. I'd been consumed with fury, but after that was gone a depression set in. It wasn't just Grace—it was my whole life. Here I'd achieved everything I ever wanted. Made a fortune. Humiliated my enemies. And still I felt unfulfilled. Restless. My thoughts turned to big-game hunting. You see, I'd given it up after bagging the biggest, baddest game there was—including, by the way, a black rhino, a bull elephant, and a few other critically endangered species, although naturally I kept *those* a closely guarded secret. But in my edginess it occurred to me that I'd become bored with big-game hunting *prematurely*. You see, I'd never hunted the biggest game of all. Man. Not just your average, run-of-the-mill cretin, however. No—my 'big game' would be powerful, affluent men with enemies: men who had surrounded themselves with layers of security; smart men, alert men, men who would be almost impossible to take down. Oh, and lest I be called sexist, women as well. I ask you, as a fellow big-game hunter: what better game to stalk than *Homo sapiens*?"

"And you decided your own daughter would become your first trophy. An honor for her, really. So you went back and cut off her head."

Ozmian nodded again. "You understand me astonishingly well."

"Your choice of targets had nothing to do with them being corrupt. That's why Adeyemi didn't seem to fit the profile. The attraction was that she, like the others, was surrounded by supposedly impenetrable security. She was extremely challenging to 'bag.'"

"And you want to know the true irony? I meant her to be *my final trophy*. But then you and Longstreet here forced your way into my office. And you thought you played me so well. Ha ha! I had such fun telling you about Hightower. I wish I could have seen old Hightower's face when you paid him a visit. I hope you sweated him good! The whole time you were peppering me with questions, I was thinking of one thing: how lovely that pale, fine head of yours would look when mounted on my trophy wall."

His laughter echoed in the shabby space.

A muffled grunt of rage, like a wounded buffalo, came from D'Agosta. Ozmian ignored it.

"After that visit, I was intrigued with you. And what I found only solidified my belief that *you*, not Adeyemi, should be my ultimate trophy. I also realized the best way to lure you in." He nodded toward Longstreet's corpse. "In my office, I sensed that you two had a history. It wasn't hard to learn about your good friend D'Agosta, either."

He reached out, took hold of a lock of Longstreet's hair, and gave the decapitated head a desultory spin. "With *both* of them at my mercy, I knew you would have no choice but to come out here and play my game."

Pendergast said nothing.

Ozmian sat forward in his chair. "And you *do* know the game we are about to play—right?"

"It is all too clear."

"Good!" He paused. "We will both be on totally fair and equal footing." He raised his gun. "We will each have the same weapon, the venerable 1911, and an additional magazine. You might think you have a slight advantage in that Les Baer of yours, but mine is equally fine. We will each also have a knife, watch, flashlight, and our wits. Our hunting ground will be the adjoining structure, Building Ninety-Three. You saw it on your way in, that abandoned hospital?"

"I did."

"I give myself no advantage. This will be a sporting stalk in which we are simultaneously the hunter and the hunted. No fox, no hound; just two experienced hunters each stalking their ultimate prey: each other. The winner will be the one who bags the loser!" He waved the detonator in D'Agosta's direction. "The lieutenant is an insurance policy to make sure you abide by the rules of the hunt. That suicide vest is on a two-hour timer. If you kill me, you can simply take the timer from my pocket and shut it off. But if you cheat—by walking away, or trying to alert the authorities—all I need to do is press the remote and *boom* goes D'Agosta. The detonator also ensures that the hunt is completed within two hours: no dawdling or hiding and running out the clock. In a few minutes, I'll give you back your gun and extra magazine, remove the handcuffs, furnish you with blacked-out clothing... and give you a head start. Make for Building Ninety-

Three. After ten minutes, I'll come after you and the stalk will commence."

"Why?" Pendergast asked.

"Why?" Ozmian laughed. "Didn't I already explain? I've done it all, I'm standing on the summit, and the only view I have is looking down. This will be the most delicious thrill of my life—the ultimate, the *final* thrill. Even if I'm to die, at least I'll go out with a bang, no pun intended—knowing it took the very best to kill me. And if I survive, then I'll have a memory to cherish...no matter what the future brings."

"That wasn't my question. What I meant was, why Building Ninety-Three?"

For a moment, Ozmian looked nonplussed. "You're kidding, right? It is perfect for a hunt like ours. It's over four hundred thousand square feet, a huge, rambling ruin, with ten floors divided into numerous wings, miles of corridors, and over two thousand rooms! Imagine the possibilities for traps, ambushes, and blinds! And we're far, far from any busybody who might hear gunshots and call the cops."

Pendergast stared at Ozmian through narrow eyes, saying nothing.

"I see you're not satisfied. Very well. There *is* a second reason." He gave Longstreet's head another casual spin on the tabletop. "There was a day during my twelfth year when our dearly beloved parish priest, Father Anselm, locked me in the sacristy and raped me repeatedly. He said while he did it that God and Jesus were watching and it was all right with them, and he threatened me with hell and worse if I ever told. I had a mental collapse. I stopped speaking, stopped thinking, stopped everything. My family, having no idea what had happened, assumed I'd gone crazy. A diagnosis was made of catatonic schizophrenia. King's Park back then had a stellar reputation, the one hospital in the country they were sure would cure me. Yes, Agent Pendergast: I became a patient of the main complex in King's Park. One of the last, it turns out. And here, I eventually recovered. Not through anything *they* did, but through my own internal resources."

"King's Park was known for its electroconvulsive treatments."

"Indeed it was—and that was why it was shut down in the end. But the shock treatments—and worse!—were reserved for the gibbering lunatics, incorrigibles, and pathetic wretches. I fortunately escaped that fate."

"And, I'm given to understand, cured yourself."

"Your sarcastic tone is unpleasant, but yes, indeed I did. One day I realized that I had something important to do: revenge. Perhaps the strongest human motivator there is. So I picked myself up, dusted myself off, and convinced the credulous and easily manipulated doctors that they had cured me. I resumed my life. I continued growing up, went to high school, and finally did the thing I had resolved to do—punish Father Anselm. Death was too much of a release for that man: my goal was to make the rest of his life full of misery and pain. And then I went to Stanford, graduated summa cum laude, founded DigiFlood, made billions of dollars, fucked beautiful women, traveled the world, lived a life of unimaginable luxury and privilege—in short, I did all the things that truly gifted human beings like myself do."

"Indeed," Pendergast said drily.

"Anyway, to resume, not long after my discharge, King's Park was abandoned, shut up, and left to rot."

"How fitting for you, then, that this will be the place of the final hunt."

"I see you're getting into the spirit of it already. Surely you understand how this experience will bring things full circle for me.

Of course, I barely knew the building then: just the room where I was drugged and held in restraints day and night, and the therapy room where I told my doctor a bunch of lies that he believed and carefully wrote down. I'm as essentially unfamiliar with the place as you are—there will be no advantage there."

Ozmian placed the Les Baer on the table, along with an extra magazine, while pocketing the detonator. Next to it he laid a watch, a flashlight, and a fixed-blade knife.

"Your gear." He stood up. "And so, Agent Pendergast. Shall we begin?"

53

THE NIGHT WAS bitter, without a breath of wind, a full moon just peeking above the towers of Building 93, throwing a bone-white light over the landscape. Clad in the camos and soft shoes Ozmian had forced on him, Agent Pendergast paused beyond the door of Building 44, the vapor from his breath trailing through the night air. Building 93 lay about a hundred yards away, a great black wedge against the moonlit sky, surrounded by a battered chain-link fence. A swath of open ground lay between him and the fence, covered with stubble and patches of crusty snow, with a scattering of dead trees and hollow stumps. A knoll rose on the right, covered with scrubby weeds.

To see Longstreet so brutally decapitated; to see D'Agosta beaten and trussed up like a pig for slaughter; to realize how utterly Ozmian had deceived him—the horror of it pressed in on Pendergast, threatening to unseat his intellect and overwhelm him with grief, fury, and self-reproach. He breathed deeply, closed his eyes, and centered his mind, thrusting those distractions aside. A minute passed—a precious minute, but he knew that if he did not regain his focus and balance, he would be lost for sure.

Sixty seconds later he opened his eyes. The night remained cold and soundless, the moonlight as clear as water. Now he began assembling various possibilities in his mind, running through the trajectories of potential actions, determining which of the branching sets to consider further and which to discard.

He concluded there was a better option than making a beeline for Building 93—and that was to immediately go on the offensive. He would strike hard at Ozmian the moment he exited Building 44. Moving with cat-like swiftness over the frozen ground, being careful to leave no trail, he circled the building, performing a quick reconnaissance. It was a two-story structure of brick, dilapidated but still sound, with a steeply pitched roof. The windows of both stories had been blocked with plywood covered in tin, and sealed so effectively that no light from inside leaked out. There would be no exit from one of those.

As he rounded the corner at the back of the building he spied a rear door. He gently touched the handle and found it was locked, then ran a finger along the exposed hinges and brought it to his nose. Fresh oil. A further examination revealed the hinges had recently been cleaned, as well.

Completing the reconnoiter, Pendergast understood that Building 44 had only two means of egress—front and back. The roof was too steep and exposed to allow for any escape that way. It was an ideal setup for an ambush.

Perhaps too ideal: it felt almost like a setup. In fact, as he reflected further, it *was* a setup: Ozmian was expecting him to hold back and press an attack the moment the man exited.

But setup or not, even if he chose to cover one of the exits at random, he still had a 50 percent chance of getting the drop on Ozmian. By anticipating Ozmian's strategy, he could improve those odds.

Pendergast ran through the logic. Since Ozmian had previously prepared this rear door, he intended for this to be his exit point while Pendergast was staking out the front loading dock entrance. Given this train of deduction, Pendergast should therefore stake out the rear door.

But that logic, complex as it was, might still be too simple. If Ozmian were truly a clever man, he would anticipate that he, Pendergast, would discover the rear door, observe the freshly oiled hinges, and therefore stake out that exit point.

Therefore, Ozmian will leave by the front door. It was a clear case of double-reverse psychology. This oiled back door, so carefully prepared, was a red herring, a trap, created to lure Pendergast into making this an ambush point.

Four minutes left in his head start.

Pendergast slipped around to the front of the building once again, now convinced that this was where Ozmian would exit. As he scanned the frozen landscape, he saw an excellent point of cover: a dead oak tree still cloaked in the long moon-shadow cast by Building 93. He sprinted over to it, leapt up to grasp a low branch, swung himself up, climbed to a higher limb, and took up a crouching position, hidden behind the trunk. He removed his Les Baer, its cold weight a physical reassurance. Bracing himself against the trunk, he took a bead on the front loading dock.

Thirty seconds.

But then, even as the seconds ticked off, Pendergast once again had misgivings. Was he overthinking the situation, giving Ozmian too much credit? Perhaps the man had a simple plan after all to exit by the rear door. If he did, Pendergast not only would miss his chance but would be highly vulnerable in his position on the tree limb, especially if Ozmian did indeed plan to circle around from the rear and fire at him from the weedy knoll.

Ten seconds.

For better or worse he had made his choice. Iron sights trained on the metal rolling door, his shoulder braced against the trunk, he waited, stilling his breath.

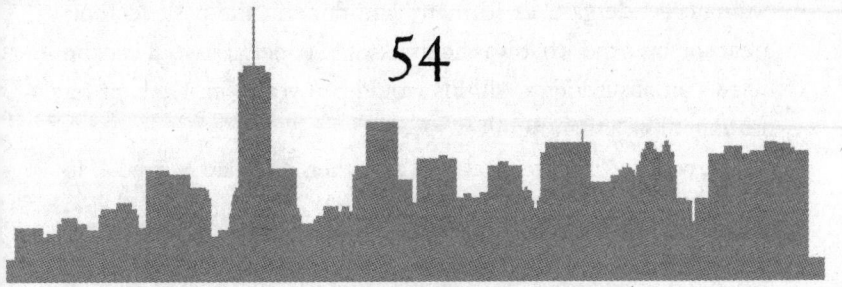

54

VINCENT D'AGOSTA, TRUSSED and gagged, watched as Ozmian sat calmly in the chair opposite him. The man, who had been so shifty and restless before Pendergast's arrival, was now supremely calm, his eyes closed, his hands on his knees, his back straight in the old wooden chair. He appeared to be meditating.

D'Agosta cast his eyes about the large, unheated space. It was so cold that the blood that had drained from Longstreet's head, puddled on the metal table, was already freezing. A harsh fluorescent illumination came from a trio of remotely controlled spotlights hung in the corners of the room.

Once again, his mind began racing. He savagely upbraided himself for his own gullibility: not only for falling into the trap, but for being angry with Pendergast and refusing to try to see things his way. Longstreet was already dead—and a most horrible, agonizing death it had been. And now, because of his stupidity, Pendergast might well be killed, too.

Above all, his hatred of Ozmian and thirst for revenge glowed like a furnace inside him. But even as he considered every one of his options, everything he might do to turn the situation around, he knew that he was helpless to act. It was all in Pendergast's hands. Ozmian would not get away with it. He would underestimate Pendergast, as so many had done in the past, to their great sorrow. And what was he thinking? Pendergast would *not* be killed—an absurd idea. All this would be over soon. He kept repeating it like a mantra: *All over soon.*

A few long minutes passed, and then Ozmian stirred. He opened his eyes, stood up, raised his arms, and went through a series of stretches. Walking over to the table where his equipment was laid out, he tested his flashlight and put it in a pocket, slipped the knife into his belt, checked his pistol, made sure a round was in the chamber, and shoved it into his waistband. The extra magazine went into another pocket. Then he turned to D'Agosta. The look on his face was one of eagerness and focus. D'Agosta found the calm assurance unnerving.

"Let's play a little game, you and I," he said. "Let's see if, in the five minutes remaining before I begin my pursuit, I'm able to anticipate your friend's moves." He took a step, then another, trailing his hand on the metal table. "Shall we?"

A queer smile played about his lips. D'Agosta, of course, could not respond even if he wanted to.

"My first guess is your partner doesn't make a beeline for Building Ninety-Three. He's not a man to run."

Another pensive turn around the table.

"No...Instead, he decides to press the attack immediately. He decides to ambush me as I emerge from this building."

Ozmian made another turn. He was certainly enjoying himself, D'Agosta thought, and he wondered how much the bastard would enjoy taking a round in the brainpan from Pendergast's .45. He was going to be in for the surprise of his life.

"So your partner reconnoiters this building. Lo and behold, he discovers the back entrance. And then he notices the hinges have been cleaned and oiled."

He paused. D'Agosta stared, eyes full of hatred.

"Naturally, he concludes that I have secretly prepared this back door as my exit point. He stakes it out, ready to take me down as soon as I emerge."

How the scumbag was enjoying the sound of his own voice.

"What do you think, Lieutenant? Following me so far?" He put a pensive finger to his chin. "But you know what? I *don't* think he's staking out the back door. Do you know why?"

He resumed his slow pacing. "Being a clever man, and knowing how clever I am, your friend will think further. And he will decide that the oiled hinges are, in fact, a ruse. He will think I oiled the door to *mislead* him into thinking I'd be leaving by that exit."

He took a few more pensive steps. "And so what does he do? He stakes out the front door!"

A low chuckle. "Okay, now he's staking out the front door. But from what vantage point? As every hunter knows, big game don't normally expect an attack from above. The best way to hunt deer, for example, is from a stand in a tree."

Slow steps.

"Humans are like deer. They don't think to look up. And so Agent Pendergast climbs into that big dead oak out front, beautifully positioned and in deep shadow. I predict he is up in that tree as I speak, with his gun aimed at the loading dock door, waiting for me to exit."

No logic, no matter how elaborate, D'Agosta thought, was going to save the ass of this son of a bitch. Pendergast would outmaneuver him at every turn. The man wouldn't last five minutes.

"And therefore my move is this: I will leave by the back door, circle around to a brushy knoll off to the right—and shoot your partner out of that tree."

A mirthless smile.

"If my reasoning is correct, your partner is going to be dead in—" he checked his watch—"two minutes and twenty seconds."

He stopped his pacing and leaned on the table, above the decapitated head and freezing pool of blood. "I hope to God I'm wrong. I hope your friend is smarter than that. If my hunt ends prematurely, it will be a keen disappointment."

He turned, patted himself down, checked everything one last time, then made a curt bow. "And now, I'll take my leave...through the back door. If you hear shots in the back, you'll know he surprised me. If, on the other hand, you hear shots in the front, then you'll know my scenario has come true."

And with that, he turned and walked to the door and disappeared down a hall toward the rear of the building.

D'Agosta turned his attention to the clock Ozmian had placed on the table. The ten-minute waiting period was up. He waited, listening for the shots he was sure would come from the back as Pendergast ambushed Ozmian when he emerged. But there were none. A few minutes passed, and then the silence was broken by two shots—from the front.

55

Running across the frozen ground, Pendergast saw he'd made his first mistake, which had almost cost him his life. Waiting in the tree, when the front door did not open after the ten-minute head start had passed, he immediately realized he had judged wrong and, knowing he was a sitting duck, had stepped off the branch and dropped in free fall—at the very moment two shots from the weedy knoll ripped into the trunk precisely where he had been crouching.

He caught the lower limb just as he fell past it, swung hard with his feet, and landed on the ground at a run. Glancing back, he saw Ozmian burst from the weeds and sprint after him, gun in hand, in hot pursuit. Not only had he made an error, but he had wasted a precious ten-minute head start that would have allowed him to choose his entrance into Building 93. Clearly, Ozmian had anticipated his chain of reasoning and done him one better.

Pendergast sprinted on, heading for the eastern side of Building 93, where there appeared to be a gap in the ragged chain-link fence. The western wing, he could see, had partially burned; streaks of soot from the conflagration rose from black window frames and a massive crack ran up the façade, like a gigantic House of Usher, traversing all ten stories. As he ran, his mind was working, reevaluating the branching possibilities, dismayed and humiliated by the fact that he had underestimated his opponent. The only positive outcome of the skirmish was that his opponent had wasted two rounds: Ozmian now had fifteen to his seventeen.

In the endgame—if it ever got to that—a two-round advantage could be decisive.

The chain-link fence loomed up and Pendergast raced along it to the gap and dove through; rising again, he bulled through a dense stand of brush, clambered over a heap of fallen bricks, and—after a lightning reconnaissance—leapt through an open window frame into the building. He rolled, regained his feet, and went on running, angling into the darkest shadows. Flicking on his light for but an instant, he took one turn, then another, then another; at the third bend of the hallway he halted and crouched, with a clear field of fire back down the hall he had just come. A moment later he heard faint running steps, saw the approaching glow of a flashlight from around the corner; as soon as it appeared Pendergast fired. It was a long shot and he missed, but it had the desired effect: Ozmian ducked back around the corner, taking cover. It had halted the man's headlong pursuit and bought him a minute or two.

Pendergast pulled off his shoes and, tossing them aside, sprinted down the corridor in his socks, turned through a dogleg, and suddenly found himself in a large, open room, dimly illuminated by moonlight.

Moving swiftly to the center, he flattened himself behind a cracked cement pillar where he had a clear field of fire in all directions. There he paused, breathing in the moldy, sour air of the interior. He took a moment to reconnoiter. If Ozmian entered the room through the same archway he had, he would have a clear shot and this time would not miss; but Ozmian was not likely to take that risk. The man was no longer in hot pursuit; he was now in tracking mode.

There was enough moonlight coming in through the shattered window frames for Pendergast to see the general outlines of the room. It was a cafeteria, with tables arrayed among a disorder of chairs, the linoleum coming up in curls. Some of the tables were still set, as if awaiting a seating of the dead. The floor was strewn with cheap flatware, plastic cups and dishes. A row of shattered windows allowed in not only bars of pallid light, but also vines that had crept within and grown up the walls. The air smelled of rat urine, damp concrete, and decaying fungus.

As he continued to take in the dim surroundings, he saw that the many layers of paint that once covered the ceilings and walls had cracked and peeled off, flaking away and raining down like confetti all over the floors. The chips and curls of paint mingled with dust, debris, and trash to form a thick layer, creating an ideal tracking environment. It was like snow: one could not walk through it without leaving footprints, and there wasn't a way to brush out or hide one's tracks, either. On the other hand, as he scanned the floor he noted there were already tracks everywhere, crisscrossing this way and that, laid down by urban archaeologists and those people called "creepers" who made a hobby of exploring dangerous, abandoned buildings.

Pendergast made a snap decision: to gain the commanding heights by heading upstairs. Ozmian would no doubt anticipate this; he had already been outguessed once. But the key nevertheless was gaining a physical advantage—and that meant up. He had to move fast, put additional distance between him and his pursuer. At some point he could then double back, circle around, and with luck come up behind his pursuer, becoming the pursuer himself.

All these thoughts flashed through his mind in the space of no more than ten seconds.

A building like this would have multiple staircases, in the center and at the wings. Pendergast slid away from the pillar, crossed the dining hall, and, making sure it was clear, headed down a corridor deeper into the eastern section of the hospital. As he ran down the darkened hall, he could hear the paint chips crunching underfoot. At the end of the hall, a set of double doors, one detached and leaning, revealed the staircase he'd hoped to find. Pendergast ducked into the space beyond—the stairwell had no windows and was as black as a cave—and paused again to listen. He half expected to hear the footfalls of his pursuer, but even his keen ears could hear nothing. Feeling sure nevertheless that he was being tracked, and by a master, he grasped the iron rail of the staircase and ascended, two steps at a time, into the foul, cold, pitch dark.

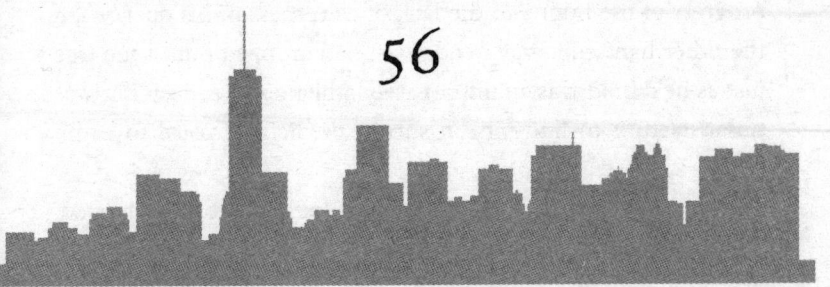

56

Oᴢᴍɪᴀɴ ᴡᴀɪᴛᴇᴅ ɪɴ the blackness at the bottom of the stairwell and listened to the faintly receding steps of his quarry as he ascended, counting each one. The man was evidently taking two steps at a time, given the slight delay between footfalls, and was no doubt heading for "high ground," a wise if predictable decision.

For Ozmian, entering Building 93 after all these years had triggered a surprisingly deep emotional reaction. Even though the memory of those times had dimmed almost to the vanishing point, when he first entered the old cafeteria, the underlying smell of the place was still there, and it had released an unexpected rush of memories from that awful period of his life. So intense was the flood of remembrance—the sadistic aides, the raving fellow patients, the lying, smiling psychiatrists—that he staggered, the past intruding horribly into the present. But only for a moment. With a brutal application of will he shoved those recollections back into the bunker of memory and returned his focus to the stalk. The experience had given him a sudden insight. He had chosen this place as a kind of exorcism, a way to drive out the ghosts of that period once and for all.

In the dark, still listening and counting the receding steps, he ordered his thoughts. So far, he was mildly disappointed in the progress of the hunt and the lack of cleverness of his quarry. On the other hand, the way Pendergast had dropped out of the tree just as he'd fired was an impressively athletic move, even if it was unsatisfactory to find him in such a predictable place to begin with.

Ozmian sensed that the man had resources yet to be tapped, and the thought excited him. He had confidence that his quarry was good enough to give him a decent, perhaps even epic, stalk; one that would repay his effort and trouble.

The extremely faint footfalls finally vanished: the quarry had exited on a floor. Ozmian would not know which floor precisely until he had counted the steps between floors one and two and done a quick mental division.

Now he, too, began to mount the stairs, moving swiftly and silently but not too fast. Upon reaching the second floor he was able to calculate that his quarry, taking two steps at a time, had exited on the ninth floor. The top floor would have been the most obvious, but the ninth made more sense, as it still allowed his prey additional avenues of escape. As he continued climbing the stairs, he realized that he had never felt so alive to the thrill of the chase as he did now. It was an atavistic pleasure that only the true hunter could appreciate, something built into the human genome: this love of the stalk, the pursuit, and the kill.

The kill. He felt a quiver of anticipation. He recalled his first big-game kill. It was a lion, a big black-maned male that he had winged with a bad shot. It had fled, and because he had wounded it he had a responsibility to track and kill it. They followed it into elephant grass, his gun bearer becoming more and more nervous, expecting a charge at any moment. But the lion didn't charge, and the spoor led them into even worse country, deep heavy brush. Here the bearer refused to continue and so Ozmian had taken the gun himself, advancing into a dense stand of mopane. He got that unmistakable tingling sensation and knelt, gun pointed; the lion leapt out, coming at him like an express train; he fired a single slug that went into the lion's left eye and tore off the back of his head as he came down on top of him, all 550 pounds of muscle. He recalled that feeling of ecstasy at the kill even as he lay pinned, with a broken arm, the lion hot with stink and crawling with bugs and flies, his blood flowing over Ozmian's own body.

But that feeling had grown harder and harder to come by—until it returned when, at last, he began hunting human beings. He only hoped the kill of this one would not come too soon.

At the eighth floor he switched on his light briefly and examined the stair treads, noting with satisfaction the spoor of his quarry's passage. And at the ninth floor, another brief examination confirmed what he'd already determined—his quarry had exited the stairwell and headed down the long hall of the east wing.

He paused at the landing, catching his breath and listening. Up here, a cold wind blew, moaning around the building, adding a layer of sound that covered the fainter noises of movement. He crept to the edge of the shattered opening leading into the hallway, where a steel door hung sideways on rusted hinges, and peered through the gap between the door and the frame, which provided a view down the corridor. The main ELOPEMENT RISK door that blocked off the wing, imprisoning its patients at night, had been battered down long ago by urban explorers, and it lay broken on the floor. Faint moonlight filtered into the corridor, providing just enough light to see. The hall stretched the length of the eastern wing, ending in a distant window that framed, grotesquely, the withered claw of a potted plant. A rotten rag of curtain flapped back and forth, like a white waving hand. Doors opened on either side leading into tiny lockdown bedrooms, which he remembered so clearly, really nothing more than prison cells, each with its own closet and bathroom. He remembered that his own cell, like these, had been padded, the pads stained with the dirt, snot, and tears of previous occupants.

He quickly suppressed this new jolt of memory.

Moving with infinite silence and care—in case his quarry had set up another ambush—Ozmian slipped into the shadows, creeping along the dark side of the corridor, his back against the wall. He ventured a split-second flash of light across the floor, where he once again identified his quarry's fresh tracks among the others, heading toward the far end of the wing. Pendergast had gotten rid of his shoes, as had Ozmian, the better to move in silence.

Gun in hand, sliding along the wall, he continued his stalk. Toward the end of the hall he saw that Pendergast's footprints veered into one of the rooms. And the door had been shut. Remarkable he had managed to do it without making a sound.

Interesting. The man had made no move to try to cover his tracks, even though he knew Ozmian was after him. All this meant Pendergast had a plan, most likely another ambush, which the tracks would lead Ozmian into. But what kind of ambush? Probably one that, even if it failed, would flip the tables on Ozmian, turning the pursued into the pursuer.

He paused at the closed door, then took a step back. Made of metal, it had been designed to be strong enough to withstand even the most lunatic assault, though now the hinges were corroded and broken, the screws pulling out of the metal covering. But he knew that you could not lock these doors from the inside; only from the outside.

Grasping the handle, staying well to one side out of the line of fire, he turned it, half expecting a fusillade of shots to come tearing through.

Nothing. He pushed the door open, still keeping to one side, and then, in a single furious movement, handgun at the ready, spun into the room and swept it while moving diagonally across the small space. It was empty, except for a bed with a mattress, a closet, and a ragged teddy bear lying on the floor. The window was gone, leaving an open frame, moonlight pouring in along with an icy wind, the bleak landscape outside rolling away to the distant water of Long Island Sound.

Examining the floor, he saw that Pendergast's tracks headed into the bathroom—with the bathroom door shut but, of course, again not locked.

His own cell-like room had been identical to this. The attached bathroom had a window, but it was too small for a person to fit through. So if Pendergast had gone in there, he was now trapped. Once again he examined the floor. The tracks plainly went in, but didn't come out.

Ozmian smiled and raised his gun.

57

A CHILL WIND moaned and whistled around the corner of the building as Pendergast crouched on the outside ledge, ten stories of empty space below him. The projecting brick coping and the four-inch stone lintels offered a precarious foothold. With his Les Baer in his right hand, he aimed down, bracing himself against the façade for the recoil, waiting for the moment when Ozmian stuck his head out the window to check whether Pendergast had escaped that way, after establishing he was not hiding in the bathroom.

Pendergast had taken the deception as far as he could. He had indeed exited the room by the window, leaping first from the bathroom interior to the bed frame—closing the door with one hand as he did so—and from there to the outer sill, so as not to leave tracks. He'd edged out on the sill, as he hoped Ozmian would ultimately assume. But then he had scaled the decorative brickwork to the tenth floor, taking up an unexpected vantage point. Ozmian would expect him either right or left on the ledge outside the ninth-floor window—not one story above. Or so he hoped. The man would be anticipating an ambush...but from the wrong direction. Still, in mulling over the plan, Pendergast had to admit that so far Ozmian had outplayed him in the game of reverse, double-reverse, and double-double-reverse psychology.

He waited. And waited. But Ozmian did not appear.

Perched on the ledge, in the freezing gusts of wind, Pendergast now understood he had made another error in judgment. Again the man had not responded as expected. Either he had been outmaneuvered again, or Ozmian was engaged in some other strategy of his own. For perhaps the first time in his life, Pendergast felt stymied and anxious. Nothing he had done so far had worked. It was like a nightmare in which, no matter how hard he tried, he couldn't get his legs to move fast enough. And now, he had made himself a perfect target, crouching on the ledge. He had to get back inside the building as soon as possible.

Even as he crept along the ledge, he was thinking. As every hunter knew, the key to a successful stalk was to first understand the behaviors and thought patterns of your prey. You had to "learn" your quarry, as his mentor had once told him. In this case he was now "learning" Ozmian; how he thought, what he wanted, what motivated him. And he had a surprising revelation, one that might allow him ultimately to prevail—if Ozmian acted as he hoped.

He moved along the ledge to a broken window on the tenth floor, paused, and gave a swift glance inside. It was another padded, cell-like room, bathed in a streak of moonlight and empty save for the skeleton bed and chair. Lightly as a cat, he leapt from the sill onto the floor and crouched again, sweeping the room with his gun. Empty. He went to the door, turned the handle.

Locked—from the outside.

This was precisely the situation he had anticipated, spinning around to cover the bathroom door, but he was too late. Ozmian had emerged from it with amazing speed and stealth, and Pendergast felt the icy barrel of Ozmian's 1911 pressed into his ear as the man's other hand seized him by the wrist, giving it a sharp wrench calibrated to jerk the Les Baer free of his grip. It clattered to the floor.

Now was the moment of truth.

After a long, agonizing silence, Pendergast heard a sigh.

"Eighteen minutes?" came Ozmian's voice. "Is that all you could manage?" He released the wrist and took two steps back. "Turn around. Slowly."

Pendergast complied.

"Those misleading footprints into the bathroom. Not bad. I almost wasted a couple of rounds firing through the door. But then I realized that was too easy; of course you'd left by another route—the window. You were waiting on the ledge. That much was clear. But then it occurred to me that you wouldn't be waiting on the ledge one might expect, to the left or right of the window. No—you'd add an additional layer of deception by climbing up a story! So while you were inching up the façade, I took the stairs at my leisure, figured what room you would end up in, and set up my trap. Recall, this is a psychiatric hospital, and the patients were locked *into* their rooms—not the other way around. How convenient for me that you seem to have overlooked that small point."

Pendergast said nothing. Ozmian couldn't resist gloating, toying with him. It led Pendergast to believe that his risky guess was correct: if Ozmian caught him this early in the game, *he would give him a second chance*. Too much of Ozmian's sense of self-worth was riding on this hunt for Ozmian to end it so quickly. But it was more than that; not killing him right now would say something important to Pendergast about the power this place held over Ozmian, and it would give him a deep and revealing glimpse into Ozmian's psyche.

"I expected better from you, Pendergast. What a disappointment." Ozmian aimed the gun at his head, and as Pendergast saw the man's finger tighten on the trigger, he suddenly realized he was wrong: Ozmian wasn't going to give him a second chance. As he closed his eyes, bracing himself for the roar and ensuing oblivion, an image jumped into his mind, utterly unexpectedly—the face of Constance—just before the hot explosion of the shot.

58

Marsden Swope looked on with a kind of passionate, benevolent grace, feeling an almost paternal love for the murmuring, chanting, singing throng that surrounded him.

Although he could not help feel a little disappointment in the actual number of believers that had shown up on the Great Lawn—in the dark it was hard to say how many, but it certainly wasn't the countless thousands he had anticipated. Perhaps that was to be expected. Many had fallen by the wayside, like the rich man who wanted to follow Jesus and went away saddened when Jesus told him to give away all he owned first.

But there was another problem. The pile had grown so quickly, and with so many non-burnable items, that it had overwhelmed the fire that was meant to consume it. Swope had exhausted his supply of jerrycans and now the massive heap was simply smoldering, sending up coils of foul-smelling black smoke. Swope had sent one of his disciples—no, that was wrong, one of his *brethren*—out to get more fuel, and he hoped he would return soon.

The crowd around him was now swaying gently back and

forth, singing "Peace in the Valley" in low, earnest voices. Swope joined in with a glad heart.

The one thing that really surprised him was the lack of police presence. Granted, the initial blaze had died down, but even so a crowd of this size, massing on the Great Lawn late at night with no permit, would surely have attracted the quick attention of law enforcement. But there had been no sign of them. Oddly, this was a disappointment to Swope, because it was his intention to confront the powers of the state and prevent—with his very life, if necessary—any interruption of the bonfire. A part of him yearned for martyrdom, like his hero Savonarola.

There was a jostling to one side, and then a woman approached through the crowd. She was in her late thirties, attractive, dressed in a simple down jacket and jeans, and in one hand she clutched something that had the gleam of gold. The woman held up the item, as if to toss it on the pile, then turned to Swope.

"Are you the Passionate Pilgrim?"

For the last ninety minutes, people had been coming up to shake his hand, embrace him, thank him tearfully for his vision. It had proven a most humbling experience.

He nodded gravely. "Yes, I am the Pilgrim."

The woman looked at him a moment, awestruck, holding out her hand to shake his. When she did so, she opened her hand to reveal, not the piece of gold jewelry or watch that Swope expected, but the gold of a police badge. In that moment, she grasped his hand with her other and he felt the cold of steel latch around it.

"Captain Hayward, NYPD. You're under arrest, shitbird."

"Wha—?"

But the woman, who did not appear particularly strong or fast, suddenly grabbed him with some kind of martial arts movement, spun him around, pulled his hands behind his back, and cuffed the other wrist. It was all done in a second.

All of a sudden, the Great Lawn blazed with light. High-intensity lamps hidden in the trees along its perimeter had snapped on, illuminating the bonfire. And now, a large battery of official vehicles—police cruisers, SWAT vans, fire trucks—began rolling across the grass toward the group, light bars flashing and sirens whooping. Other police in riot gear trotted forward on foot, talking into their radios.

The brethren around Swope, looking around in surprise at the sudden raid, wavered, broke—and then began to back off and scatter. The police let them go.

It all happened so quickly that Swope could not process it at first. But as the woman pushed him forward through the chaos, toward the line of police, he began to realize what had happened. The cops had gathered themselves, quietly, in the trees. Instead of provoking a riot by moving in force to arrest him, they sent in one undercover officer, in plainclothes. And now, with him in cuffs, the cops were at last coming out, with bullhorns, calling on every-one to peaceably disperse, while a fire crew came over, dragging a hose, and sprayed water on the heap of smoldering valuables, putting it out.

Ahead loomed a wagon of the kind used to transport prisoners. Its rear opened and the plainclothes cop grabbed Swope by the el-bow and lifted him onto the metal step. As the woman cop helped put him into the paddy wagon, she said: "Before we leave, you might want to have a good look at your followers."

Swope turned to give them a farewell gaze, but what he saw shocked him. What just moments before had been a peaceful, prayerful assemblage had suddenly escalated into bedlam. De-spite the police bullhorns, a large number of his followers had not dispersed: they had become looters, clustering around the pile, pulling things out and pocketing them, while the cops, surprised, yelled and chased them. Hundreds, perhaps even a thousand, followers now surged onto the dead pile of vanities, so many that the cops were temporarily overwhelmed. They grabbed fistfuls of money and silver bars and bearer bonds and jewelry and watches and shoes, frantically looting the very heap of vanities they had come to burn, and then scuttling away into the darkness of the trees with their swag, hooting in glee and triumph.

59

Ozmian waited, the echo of the shot slowly fading away, until Pendergast opened his eyes once again.

"Oops. Missed."

He saw no corresponding reaction in the man's eyes.

"Shall I give you another ten-minute head start, or shall I end it now?"

He waited, but Pendergast made no answer.

"All right. I'm a sport. You get ten more. But *please* try to muster a little more cleverness. There will be no more second chances." He glanced at his watch. "One hour and thirty-five minutes left in the hunt." He gestured with the barrel of his gun toward Pendergast's Les Baer, lying in the debris. "Go ahead. Pick it up—two fingers only—and be on your way. I'll remain here for ten minutes to give you another head start."

The quarry bent down, reaching for the gun.

"Easy now. Don't make the mistake of thinking you can get off a shot before I blow your head apart."

Picking up the gun with two fingers, Pendergast slid it into his waistband.

Ozmian pulled a key from his pocket and showed it to Pendergast. "I used some of that downtime, while you were out there on that ledge, retrieving a key to these rooms from the orderly's desk." Gun still trained on Pendergast, he unlocked the door and pushed it open, then tossed the key out of the window into the night. "There. Once again, we're even; no advantages. And now: on your way. Ten minutes."

Pendergast walked silently out of the room. At the door he turned and briefly locked eyes with Ozmian. To Ozmian's surprise, the look of defeat had changed; there was something even worse in those eyes now, a kind of existential despair...or was it his imagination? And then the figure was gone.

Ozmian waited, taking the ten-minute break to concentrate his thoughts and ponder where Pendergast would go next and what he might do. He was sure that, this time, his quarry would not waste a precious ten-minute advantage staking out his presumed exit point. Would he lead him on a fast chase through the building, trying to arrange a double-back? Or would he try to set up another trap? Ozmian wasn't sure what the man's next move would be—animals under the pressure of a close stalk sometimes behaved in unpredictable ways. His only certitude was that Pendergast would try to upend the game, change the assumptions—and the thought gave him a tingle of anticipation.

Pendergast raced down the hallway and plunged down the stairwell, intent on putting as much distance between himself and Ozmian as possible. He could run faster than Ozmian could track, so the key would be to lay down a long trail and buy himself even more time. He emerged from the stairwell and ran along dark corridors, up stairs and then down again, from floor to floor, creating a long, random and maze-like tracking problem for his opponent.

As he ran, he made a supreme effort to suppress an uncharacteristic feeling of desperation. Even though he had anticipated the second chance, he had also been finessed twice now. He may have gained psychological insight, but how could he turn that to his benefit? He saw that his fundamental mistake had been to think he could play Ozmian's game and beat him at it; that he could out-ratiocinate his opponent. He was playing a game of chess with a grand master, and he now realized—halfway through and fatally down by pieces—that he was surely going to lose.

Unless...

Unless he changed the game entirely. Yes: changed the game from chess to a game of...*craps*. A game of chance.

He remembered noting on his approach to Building 93 that the west wing had partially burned and was unstable. That would be an environment that offered the very unpredictability he sought.

His irregular journey carried him into a large space, and he stopped to catch his breath and consider his next move. He was somewhere in the back part of the hospital, once again on the first floor, and as he looked around he realized he was in some sort of arts-and-crafts room. Long plastic tables were strewn with half-finished projects, ravaged by time and rats. Pendergast quickly scanned the room for anything useful. A weaving lay decomposing on a small loom; childish watercolors were pinned to a corkboard; shriveled lumps of modeling clay half formed into grotesque shapes lay arranged on one table; warped plastic knitting needles with half-completed scarves lay on another. At the far end of the room, chairs were arranged around a bulbous 1950s television set, its picture tube exploded and lying in shards on the floor.

Pendergast swept up several half-finished scarves, pulled the knitting needles out of them, and tied them around his feet. As he walked on, he could see an improvement in the track he made: though still faintly visible, it was now more difficult to read amid the comings and goings of earlier travelers. He had no illusions: Ozmian could surely follow even this track, but it would take more care. That would buy Pendergast a little time.

Now he headed west, toward the ruined wing, moving as lightly as possible. As he passed room after room, one corridor after another, turn after turn, he began to pick up the acrid scent of an old fire. And then, passing a kitchen, he came to a hallway leading unmistakably into the burnt wing. He was now far enough from Ozmian to dare his flashlight; he flicked it on and aimed the beam into the blackened interior.

What he saw gave him pause. The walls were leaning and crooked; some had partially collapsed. Ceilings had caved in, leaving piles of charred wooden beams and spalled concrete pillars, exposing twisted snarls of rebar. And this was just the first floor—nine stories of building were stacked above, barely held up by these unstable walls. As he surveyed the damage, he realized the fire was not ancient—it had probably happened in the past year.

A homemade sign, written in silver marker on a blackened piece of plywood, had been hammered to an adjacent wall.

HAIL FELLOW CREEPERS!
LISTEN UP, DUDES: IF YOU THINK EXPLORING
WING D OFFERS A UNIQUE CHALLENGE, THINK
AGAIN. THIS PLACE IS SERIOUSLY DANGEROUS.
IF ANYONE GETS KILLED IN HERE IT WILL
IMPACT ACCESS FOR ALL OF US. SO PLEASE,

ENJOY THE REST OF BUILDING 93, BUT STAY
OUT OF WING D. DON'T FORGET THE
IMMORTAL WORDS OF THE GREATEST CREEPER
OF THEM ALL:
<u>ABANDON ALL HOPE, YE WHO ENTER HERE</u>

After a moment's hesitation, Pendergast stepped into the dark, foul-smelling labyrinth.

60

Oᴢᴍɪᴀɴ ᴛᴏᴏᴋ ʜɪꜱ time following the trail, savoring the pleasure of the stalk. There was no rush: time was on his side. Even though up to this point his quarry had disappointed him, the man was clever and dangerous and it would be fatal to underestimate him. And he was learning. He was getting better.

The long, meandering wild-goose chase of a trail eventually led him to the arts-and-crafts room. Strangely enough, he had no memory of this room, or of doing any crafts during his time at King's Park. Even so, the space was highly unsettling, with the tables still displaying the last unfinished craft projects of the patients—half-knitted scarves, clay heads, atrocious watercolors, the pathetic productions of misshapen minds. The tracks passed by the table of scarves and instantly Ozmian divined what had happened: Pendergast had swiped some of the scarves to wrap around his feet, thus leaving a fainter, more diffuse trail.

A clever move.

And from that point on the trail became more challenging to follow, requiring frequent pauses when it intersected the tracks of earlier explorers. He continued along the hall, in and out of several rooms. Pendergast was gaining time with this diversion, slowing him down. He was planning some sort of trap or ambush—one that would take time to set up.

The general trend in the trail was westward toward Wing D, and Ozmian wondered if that was where Pendergast was headed. That would be a most unexpected move.

Another few minutes of tracking did indeed bring him to the burnt section. At the point where the track entered the tangle of debris, he examined it closely with his flashlight. It could be a diversion, an attempt to lure him into this dangerous area, but a close look revealed that Pendergast had indeed entered the unstable wing himself. There was simply no way to fake it. He was in there—somewhere.

And now, peering into the scorched interior, Ozmian felt himself taken aback. He could actually hear the entire wing groan and creak with every gust of the winter wind. It almost looked as if the walls were moving, and the unceasing sounds made him feel as if he were in the belly of some foul beast. The walls were crumbling and the floors burnt, leaving great gaps and diagonals of fallen beams. It had been a hot fire, so hot there were puddles of glass and aluminum on the floor and sections of concrete wall that had crumbled and fractured. It was truly insane for Pendergast to venture into a place like this—an indication more of desperation than cleverness.

But no matter: if this was where his quarry wanted to continue the hunt, this was where the hunt would continue.

Ozmian shut off his light. He would have to move forward now by moonlight and by feel, making his way over the sagging, gaping floors with great care while at the same time maintaining high alert, trusting in his almost supernatural sense of peril. He was sure Pendergast had set up an ambush for him. He was like that wounded lion waiting in the mopane brush to spring upon his tormenter.

Moving past a heap of concrete rubble, he came into a huge open room that had clearly once been a communal dormitory. The beds, still lined up, were now rows of blackened iron frames. The far wall had collapsed, exposing a bathroom of heat-cracked porcelain sinks, scorched urinals, and exposed shower stalls, many of the fixtures warped and melted.

Pendergast's track led him to the main stairwell of Wing D. It was a perfect nightmare of destruction; Ozmian found it hard to believe it was still standing. Naturally, seeking the most dangerous area, the quarry had gone up the stairs. Again stealing forward with extreme care in absolute silence, expecting an ambush at any moment, Ozmian worked his way by feel up the noisome and crooked staircase. The trail exited at the second-floor landing into another ruined hall, a veritable labyrinth of charred and twisted beams. A fire hose lay stretched down the length of the hallway, evidently left by the firefighters who had put out the blaze. The end was still screwed to a standpipe. He paused. Something had been lying on the ground near the hose, and fresh scuff marks in the char and dust indicated that Pendergast had picked it up. What could it have been?

His preternatural hunting senses began to tingle. In his previous life as a big-game stalker, such a feeling meant he was getting close; that his quarry had decided to turn and face him; and that the charge was imminent. He paused, tensing. A particularly strong gust of wind caused a flurry of creaks, and it seemed to Ozmian that the whole edifice might come tumbling down at any moment. When was the fire? Only last year, he recalled. The building had stood since then; he shouldn't be overly concerned that it would happen to collapse just now. Unless given a little help.

Ah! The thought was a revelation. He had been pondering what sort of attack Pendergast was planning—and from what direction. But would he actually bring the building down upon them both? That was a crazy idea, far too unpredictable, as likely to kill him as his pursuer—and yet as he considered the possibility he became sure that this, indeed, was what Pendergast planned to do.

Ozmian took a silent step forward, keeping to the darkness of the outside wall, positioning himself behind a heap of concrete rubble. He was in excellent cover with a clear field of fire, near the outer skin of the building, his own figure hidden in darkness, with just enough indirect moonlight ahead and behind to see. He was exactly where he wanted to be. Still in darkness, Ozmian reached out, grasped the unrolled fire hose in his free hand, and slowly and silently drew it toward him.

Every cell in his body felt alive. Something was about to happen. And he would be ready for it.

61

ONE FLOOR ABOVE, braced against two wobbly beams with an exposed section of corridor visible through gaps in the floor below, Agent Pendergast waited for Ozmian. The fireman's ax was slung over his left shoulder, the Les Baer grasped in his right. Either his pursuer would continue tracking and come into range on the second-floor corridor, in which case Pendergast would have at least a modestly reasonable shot; or he would sense a trap, stop, and wait.

The minutes ticked by and Ozmian did not appear. Pendergast wondered if, once again, he had been outfoxed. But no—not this time. Ozmian would follow him into Wing D; it was a challenge he would not be able to resist. Even though he couldn't see or hear him, he knew Ozmian was out there, following his trail. *He must be there, and very close.* And evidently, he was waiting for Pendergast to make the first move.

The wind gusted outside, generating a chorus of creaks and a perceptible movement in the beams Pendergast was balanced upon. Wing D was a house of cards, a heap of pickup sticks, a wobbly stack of dominoes.

There was no point in waiting any longer. Sliding the Les Baer into his waistband, he grasped the fire ax with both hands, raised it above his head, focused his gaze on the point of impact, and swung it with tremendous force into one of the main load-bearing beams he was standing on. The massive blade bit deeply into the unburnt heart of the beam, charred bits spraying out, and a crack as sharp as gunfire signaled the breaking of the beam, instantly followed by the machine-gun fire of other load-bearing beams, supports, and concrete walls as they gave way in series. The floor lurched downward, not in free fall but in a sort of chaotic, semi-controlled descent, as Pendergast dropped the ax and whipped out his firearm; for a split second, as the debris heaved down, he had a clear field of fire at a suddenly exposed Ozmian, who was himself thrown off balance; Pendergast got off two shots before his own downward movement and the structure collapsing around him obscured everything in a great cloud of dust.

Leaping free of the slowly imploding mass, Pendergast projected himself out from the crumbling first floor, falling half a story and landing hard on the frozen ground, bricks and debris thundering down around him. The outcome was unpredictable...and that itself was its beauty, a dramatic transformation of the game. Ozmian was deeper in the building and thus more likely to be crushed—or so he hoped.

The rumbling collapse came to a halt. Incredibly, the rupture was only partial, the far corner of Wing D now a gaping hole directly in front of him, but the rest of the ten-story wing still intact—if barely. The entire edifice complained loudly, emitting a volley of cracks, screeches, and groans as the load-bearing walls and concrete pillars settled to accommodate the shifting burden of mass. Pendergast tried to stand, staggered, managed to get to his feet; he was battered but essentially sound, with no broken bones. The dust cloud billowed up around him, obscuring his view.

He had to get out of the dust and falling debris and into the open, where he could take advantage of the chaos and press the attack on Ozmian, if indeed the man had survived. Feeling his way through the chaos of rubble, moving away from the zone of falling debris, he emerged from the thinning dust cloud and into the moonlight, hard up against the chain-link fence that surrounded the building.

And that was when he spied Ozmian: unhurt, partway up the damaged façade, rapidly lowering himself from the gaping ruin by a fire hose. At the same time, Ozmian saw him. Dropping to one knee, Pendergast aimed and fired, but Ozmian simultaneously kicked himself away from the building, swinging sideways, even as Pendergast got off another round before Ozmian had released himself and dropped into the dust cloud, vanishing from sight.

Pendergast fired four quick shots into the cloud in a pattern surrounding the place where he judged Ozmian to have landed, knowing the odds were long but taking advantage of even this slight opportunity. The shots emptied his magazine.

Racing away, ignoring the pain, Pendergast sprinted alongside the outer building wall, leapt over a low windowsill and inside, then continued running down a corridor, which debouched once again into the arts-and-crafts room. As he ran he ejected the empty magazine, letting it clatter to the floor as he slapped in the second one, past the rotting tables, through a doorway, and down a nearby stairwell, heading for the basement.

He did not know if his four shots had caught Ozmian or not, but he had to assume they had not. His third plan had failed. He needed a fourth.

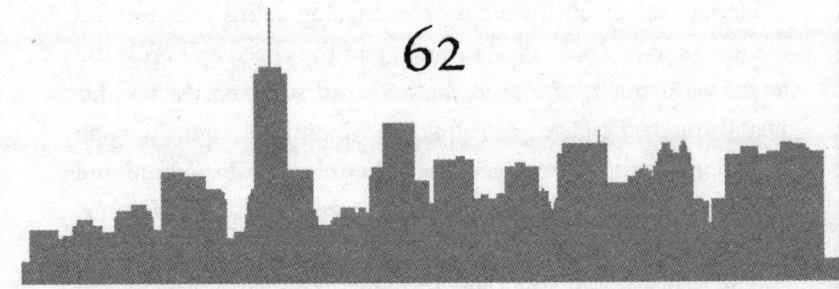

62

Ozmian emerged cautiously from the rubble, keeping to cover.
Those shots Pendergast had fired into the dust cloud had seriously
unnerved him, due to their random nature and his inability to anticipate them. One of them had come so close he felt the snap of
wind as it passed his ear. For the first time, Ozmian felt a twinge
of uncertainty. But he quickly shook it off. Wasn't this what he'd
most wanted—a supremely cunning, able opponent? He knew,
deep down, that he would prevail.

He moved alongside the ragged edges where the corner of
Wing D had collapsed, keeping to the darkness and the brushy
overgrowth at the edges of the abandoned building. Switching on
his flashlight, he scanned the ground for signs of Pendergast but
could see nothing. Coming to a broken window frame, he gave
the interior a quick recon and then ducked in, proceeding down a
vacant hallway. The tracks in the hall were old, and again he could
find no sign of Pendergast.

He needed to find his quarry's trail. That meant executing a
maneuver known as "cutting for sign"—moving in a broad circle
at right angles to the quarry's track, attempting to pick it up.

Reaching the end of the hallway, he started down another, cutting for sign, expecting at any moment to intersect Pendergast's tracks.

In the basement, traversing almost the entire length of the building, Pendergast passed a heating plant, storage rooms, a small block of padded prison cells, finally stopping in a vast archive full of rotting files. It was pitch black belowground and he had no choice but to use the flashlight. Despite everything he had passed, he'd found nothing and no place that would help him escape or turn the tables on his pursuer. There was something stupid, if not futile, in continuing this farce: running randomly through this vast building, hoping for a fresh idea. He was up against a savant, a man who could not be beaten. And yet no one was unbeatable; every human had a chink in his armor. He now had some insight into Ozmian's psychology, his vulnerability, but how could he turn that to his advantage? Where was that fissure in his armor and, even if found, how would he stick in the sword? The man was perhaps the most complex and ingenious opponent he had ever come up against. "Know your enemy" was the first dictum of Sun Tzu in his *Art of War*. And the saying contained within it the obvious answer: if there was anyplace in the entire world where he could learn about this man and his deepest weaknesses, it was right here: in the basement, in the archives.

Pendergast paused for a moment, collecting his thoughts and taking in the vast room with his flashlight. It was almost uncanny that he was there, in this immense space stuffed with tales of madness, misery, and horror: the archives of a gigantic mental hospital. He understood now that his own subconscious had led him here.

The archives consisted of racks of filing cabinets on a scaffolding of metal shelves, rising from floor to ceiling. Each aisle had its own pair of rolling ladders, necessary to reach the upper level of cabinets. As Pendergast moved through the space, trying to understand how it was organized, he became aware that the hospital, in its century of operation, had accumulated a staggering quantity of data in the form of patient histories, notes, Dictaphone recordings, diagnoses, correspondence, personnel files, and legal documents. Over the course of its lifetime, the hospital had housed tens of thousands of mental patients, perhaps even hundreds of thousands; the numbers only confirmed Pendergast's belief that there were vast numbers of mentally ill people in the world. If anything, he thought, the archive was rather modest, considering the collective insanity of the human race.

The aisles and rows were laid out in a grid, the aisles marked with letters and the rows with numbers. Moving down several aisles, consulting the numbers and rows, Pendergast located what he was looking for, seized the rolling ladder, slid it into place, and climbed, flashlight between his teeth. He yanked open a drawer, pawed through it greedily, got to the back, then opened another and another, pulling out folders and tossing them, until he realized that what he was looking for was simply not there.

He slid down the ladder, paused a moment to recalculate, then moved down the aisle to a second place, opening another series of drawers. The screech of rusty metal echoed in the space, and he was acutely aware that the glow of his flashlight would make a perfect target. He had to complete this search before Ozmian picked up his trail and entered the room.

He moved to the next aisle, then the next. He was running out of time. In one drawer he unexpectedly found a rolled-up set of reduced-size building plans. Flipping through them, he extracted one and stuffed it in his waistband. Useful, but not what he was looking for. He moved on.

Ozmian had cut for sign across half of the building's first floor, from one side to the other, to no avail; but now, as he moved to the staircase, preparing to climb to the second floor, he finally hit Pendergast's trail. It was remarkably faint—the man had been moving with the utmost care—but there was no possible way to completely erase it, especially to Ozmian's keen eye. To his surprise, the tracks were headed not upstairs, but rather down...into the basement.

Ozmian felt a surge of satisfaction. He had never been in the basement and had no idea what was down there, but he felt sure the presumably maze-like space and absolute darkness would be to his own advantage, and for Pendergast a dead end. On top of that, he retained a single overwhelming advantage: he was on the offense and his quarry in continuous retreat.

He headed down the stairwell into the darkness, one hand tracing along the wall, moving cautiously and silently, his heart thumping in anticipation of what was to come.

Pendergast had searched all the expected places without finding what he needed. Of course he hadn't found it, he reflected bitterly; *it was no longer there.* The records had been removed years ago. A man like Ozmian wouldn't leave dynamite like that lying around, even in a decaying and abandoned archive. He would have sent someone in to find and destroy it.

Pendergast's search had revealed the organization of the archives, and it now occurred to him that, at the time when this part of King's Park was finally investigated for malpractice and cruelty and subsequently shut down, there might be an appendix of files that escaped notice. They would, logically, be at the very end, rather than in their normal alphabetical and date-related places. He moved quickly to the last row of cabinets, in the farthest corner of the archives. Although still encrusted with rust, cobwebs, and mildew, these were slightly newer and of a different model. The drawers were also labeled differently. Evidently, the files within lay outside the established archiving system. After a quick search he came upon a drawer labeled:

RESTRICTED
INVESTIGATIONS / REPORTS / PERSONNEL GRIEVANCES
PENDING AG ORDER OF CLOSURE

It was locked, but a sharp twist in the keyhole with his knife broke the flimsy bolt. After sliding open the drawer with another loud screech of rusted metal, he riffled through the contents, his spidery fingers flying over the tabs and raising a small cloud of dust. Halting, he seized a fat file with some paperwork clipped to its outside edge. Suddenly he crouched, switching off his light and listening. When he had entered the archives, he had closed the rusty door at the far end of the room. It had just opened with a creak.

Ozmian had arrived.

This was catastrophic; he simply would not have the time he needed. Nevertheless, with infinite care, keeping his light off, he rose and moved through the blackness by feeling the cabinets as he went, making for the rear exit. A short journey across open space brought him to the cinder-block outer wall of the archive room, which he again followed by feel. There was a closed door somewhere along this wall, and he was not far from it. He waited, listening acutely. Was that the faint, whispery crunch of footfall on grit? Another faint sound, at the very limit of audibility, reached him; then another. Ozmian was creeping toward him in the dark.

Aiming the Les Baer, he waited. If he fired at the sound, he would probably miss, and the flash would give Ozmian a target for return fire. The risk was too great. The man had surely heard the opening of the last cabinet and knew Pendergast was in the room, but he probably did not know exactly where.

Pendergast remained at the wall, unmoving, hardly breathing. Another faint crunch of a footfall. This one was closer. He might just chance a shot, risky as it was. Aiming the gun into the darkness, he placed his finger on the trigger and waited for another sound; and then it came—the whisper of dust being compressed by a foot.

He fired two rapid shots even as he threw himself sideways, the double flash illuminating Ozmian about seventy feet down the adjacent aisle. Ozmian instantly returned fire, but the rounds slammed into the wall above Pendergast's prone body, peppering him with concrete chips. Into the dark he fired five more times at Ozmian's last location, again spacing his shots in anticipation of the possible ways he might move—but each flash showed Ozmian at a place where his shot was not, even as the man returned fire, forcing him to dive for cover into the next row of cabinets. In the vast echoing and re-echoing of shots in the cavernous space, Pendergast took the opportunity to sprint down the aisle, running in the dark; he found a row by touch, ran down that in turn, then wheeled into a new aisle and another row before coming to a halt, crouching and catching his breath when silence returned. Moving again with the utmost caution, he headed via a roundabout route back to the rear exit, feeling his way along; within minutes he found it, and—easing the door open with a creak—ducked through and slammed it behind him, even as he heard Ozmian firing at the sound, a round hitting the thick metal door but not penetrating it. There was a bolt here, and he thrust it home; that, at least, would buy him another few minutes to do what he had to do.

Flicking on his flashlight, he looked quickly through the files he had gleaned, page after page, until he stopped at one particular sheet. He slipped it out, tucked it in his pocket, glanced at the building plans...and then proceeded down the hall, not even bothering to tread lightly. At the far end, he came to a small green door, which he pushed open and then shut and locked behind him, even as he heard Ozmian trying to get through the archive door.

He had a great deal of work to do to prepare for Ozmian's arrival.

63

Sᴛᴀɴᴅɪɴɢ ᴀᴛ ᴛʜᴇ door, Ozmian turned on his flashlight. This was a seriously fortified steel door, as was merited to protect these once-sensitive archives. Examining the lock, he saw the only recourse was to shoot through it, despite the expense of rounds that might necessitate.

He ejected the now-empty magazine, slapped in the second one, then positioned himself and aimed with both hands for the cylinder, letting his heart slow down. His quarry had once again put several rounds within inches of his head. That fusillade unnerved him, but it also meant—if his count was right—that his quarry had only one round left to his eight. He believed the man was now fully on the run and out of options. An ambush with only one shot was close to suicide. He checked his watch: twenty minutes until Pendergast's pal D'Agosta was nothing more than hamburger on the walls of Building 44. No wonder he was losing it.

Bracing himself, he fired—and the round punched out the cylinder. He examined it, tried the door, found that part of the lock was still jammed in, and used a second shot to blast it free along with the bolt. The door swung open to reveal a long, empty basement hallway.

Six rounds left.

He headed into the hall, following the tracks into the very back wing of the basement. Pendergast was no longer even bothering to step lightly or try to confuse his trail. He simply didn't have any more time. This was the point in the chase when the hunted animal began to feel really pushed. Hunting a man, he mused, was really no different from tracking a wounded lion; the more he pressed and worried the prey, the more it panicked, lost its ability to think rationally, and became a reactive bundle of nerves. Pendergast was now in that stage. He was a man who had run out of ideas as well as rounds. At some point he would do what all hunted animals did in the end: stop running, turn, and make his final stand.

As Ozmian moved down the aisle, following the trail, he noted how grim this part of the basement was, how strangely unsettling, with unpainted cinder-block walls streaked with damp, regularly punctuated by lime-colored windowless doors along both sides. Each door was numbered in order, with a dirty label:

ROOM EECT-1
ROOM EECT-2
ROOM EECT-3

What did they mean? What were these rooms?

The tracks came to a halt at the door marked EECT-9. He examined the floor in front of the door, reading the spoor: his quarry had paused, then opened the door and gone in, still making no attempt at deception, shutting it behind him. While

Ozmian had no idea what was in the room, he sensed it was small and almost certainly a dead end, with no escape for Pendergast. It was like shooting fish in a barrel. But then, Ozmian reminded himself, his quarry was exceptionally clever and must not be underestimated; anything could be awaiting him on the other side of that door. And the man had one round left.

With infinite care, standing to one side, Ozmian gave his quarry a little test. He touched the door handle and eased it down, knowing Pendergast would see the movement on the far side.

BOOM! Just as he hoped, Pendergast had wasted his final shot firing blindly through the door. Now his quarry was unarmed, save for the knife. He looked at his watch: eight minutes to go before his partner was blown into bits.

It had been a memorable hunt, but the end was nigh.

"Pendergast?" said Ozmian, speaking through the closed door. "I'm sorry you wasted your last round."

Silence.

No doubt the man was waiting with knife in hand, like that wounded lion crouched in the mopane brush, ready for a final desperate struggle.

He waited.

"The minutes are ticking by. Only six minutes left until your friend gets turned inside out."

And now Pendergast spoke. His voice was shaky and high. "Come in and fight then, instead of hiding behind the door like a coward."

With a sigh, but not lowering his guard in the slightest, Ozmian raised his gun and gripped his flashlight against the barrel with his left hand, so that it pointed where the gun was aimed. Then, with one ferocious kick, he slammed open the locked door and spun inside, covering the room in a split second, expecting a desperate and futile knife attack from any quarter.

Instead he heard a voice speaking gently and kindly from the darkness:

"Welcome, brave little man, to the room of happiness."

The unexpected words were like a knife driven into the deepest part of his brain.

"How are we today, my brave little man? Come in, come in, don't be shy! We're all friends here, we love you and are here to help you."

The words were so instantly familiar and yet so grotesquely strange that, like a great earthquake, they split apart the bunker of his memory and a hot flood of recollection came pouring out: boiling, incandescent, forming a whirling maelstrom inside his skull, obliterating all in its path. Ozmian staggered, hardly able to remain upright.

"All of the kind doctors here want so much—so very much—to help you and make you feel better so that you can go back to your family, go back to school and your friends and live the life of a normal boy. Come, come, brave little man, and take a seat in our happiness chair…"

And at that moment a light snapped on and he found himself staring at a sight both outlandish and weirdly familiar: a padded leather reclining chair, unbuckled straps on the arms and legs, with a swiveling steel table next to it. Laid out on the table were special accoutrements: a rubber mouth guard, rubber sticks, buckles and collars, a black leather mask, a steel neck brace— all softly illuminated in the pool of yellow light. And looming over all, disembodied, was a stainless-steel helmet, a gleaming dome festooned with copper nipples and curly wires, attached to a jointed, retractable arm.

"Come, my brave little man, and have a seat. Let the nice doctors help you! It won't hurt, not in the slightest, and afterward you'll feel so much

better, so much happier—and you'll be one step closer to going home. The best part of all is that you won't remember a thing, not a thing, so close your eyes, think of home, and it will be over before you know it."

Ozmian, as if in a hypnotic trance, closed his eyes. He felt the doctor gently remove something heavy from his grasp, and then those sympathetic hands guided him into the leather seat; he took his place unresisting, his mind a blank; he felt the buckles and straps go around his wrists and ankles, felt them tighten, felt the brace go around his neck with a click of the steel lock, felt the leather mask snugged over his face; he heard the creak of metal joints as the steel helmet descended upon his head, icy cold yet strangely reassuring. He felt the doctor slip something out from his chest pocket, and he heard a faint clicking noise.

"Now close your eyes, my brave little man, it is about to begin…"

64

THE LIGHT ON the detonator strapped to Vincent D'Agosta had gone from red to green just three minutes before the timer reached the two-hour mark. It had been damn close, and he felt his enormous relief mingle with annoyance that it had taken Pendergast so long to kill that bastard Ozmian. Over the past two hours of waiting, listening intently, he had heard several exchanges of gunfire from the huge hospital building to the south, as well as the spectacular and frightening sound of what must have been a partial collapse of that building. His worries had mounted when Pendergast hadn't dispatched Ozmian in the first ten minutes, and the collapse of the building shocked and concerned him, suggesting a fight of epic proportions. He'd had the scare of his life as he watched the time tick down.

But in the end it had gone green, and the timer had stopped, which meant Pendergast had finally killed the son of a bitch, taken the remote, and switched it off.

Five minutes later, he heard the door to Building 44 open and in walked Pendergast. D'Agosta was alarmed by his appearance: covered with dust, clothing ripped and shredded, with two deep scratches on his face on which the blood had mingled with dirt, leaving a crust. He was limping.

The agent came up to him and removed the cue-ball gag. D'Agosta took a few gasps of air. "You cut that one pretty damn close!" he said. "God, you look like you just emerged from the trenches."

"My dear Vincent, so sorry to have given you a turn." He began unbuckling the other restraints. "I'm afraid our friend put up an admirable struggle. I must tell you, frankly, I've never come up against a more capable adversary."

"I knew you'd smoke his ass in the end."

Pendergast unstrapped his arms and D'Agosta raised them, rubbing the flow of blood back into them. Gingerly, Pendergast unstrapped the vest with the packets of explosives and eased it off, laying it with infinite care on a nearby table.

"Tell me how you exterminated the scumbag."

"I'm afraid I've developed an unfortunate reputation at the Bureau as an agent whose perps end up dead," Pendergast said, now unstrapping D'Agosta's ankles. "So this time I performed a live capture."

"He's alive? Jesus, how'd you pull that off?"

"It was a matter of choosing what game to play. We started with chess, in which he nearly checkmated me; switched to craps, but I had a bad roll of the dice. And so we ended up playing a mind game, one that my opponent lost rather dramatically."

"A mind game?"

"You see, Vincent, he actually caught me and put a gun to my head. And then released me, like a cat releases a mouse."

"Really? Wow. That's crazy."

"That was the insight I needed. He had already admitted this 'hunt' was more than just that: it was an exorcism of his experience here. When he spared my life, I knew that Ozmian was exorcising a far bigger demon than even he himself was aware of. Something terrible had happened to him here, far worse than sessions with a psychiatrist, drugs, and restraints."

D'Agosta, as usual, was uncertain as to where Pendergast was going, or even what he was talking about.

"So how'd you get him?"

"If I may be allowed self-congratulation, I'm rather proud of my final stratagem, which was to expend all the rounds in my weapon, thus fostering a false sense of security in my opponent, encouraging him to rush headlong into my final setup."

"So where is he?"

"In the basement of Building Ninety-Three, in a room he once knew very well. A room where the doctors made him into the man he is today."

D'Agosta's feet were finally freed and he stood up. He was freezing. Ozmian had tossed his clothes on a chair, and now he went to retrieve them. "Made him into the man he is today? What does that mean?"

"When he was twelve, our man was the guinea pig in a course of brutal and experimental electroconvulsive shock treatments here. The treatments wiped out his short-term memory, as is usual with those treatments. But memories, even the most deeply buried, are never quite extinguished, and I managed to nudge his back—to spectacular effect."

"Shock treatments?" D'Agosta pulled on his coat.

"Yes. As you may recall, he claimed not to have received them at King's Park. When he released me, I knew differently. I knew he'd gotten them but didn't remember. I found in the basement archives an investigator's file outlining the experimental treatments—and in it was the actual script, every word written out, of how the doctors would calm the poor boy down and persuade him to sit in a forbidding-looking shock chair. It turns out Ozmian got a particularly robust course of treatment. The normal dosage is four hundred fifty volts at zero point nine amp for half a second. Our fellow got the same voltage, but at triple the amperage for no less than ten seconds. In addition, the electrodes fired in sequence from front to back and side to side of the cranium. He was immediately sent into extreme convulsions during the process and for many minutes after it ceased. I would speculate the treatments did considerable damage to the right supramarginal gyrus."

"What's that?"

"The part of the brain that is responsible for empathy and compassion. That brain damage might perhaps explain how a man could murder and decapitate his own daughter, as well as take pleasure in the hunting and killing of human beings. And now, Vincent, there is your radio: please call for backup from your people, and I will do the same with the Bureau. We have the brutal murder of a decorated federal agent to report, as well as the perpetrator under restraint, who has, unfortunately, now descended fully into madness and will need to be handled with great care."

He turned and gathered his own clothes and equipment, which had been piled in a corner. Pausing, D'Agosta watched as Pendergast gazed at Longstreet's remains, making a slow, sorrowful gesture, almost a bow. He then turned back to D'Agosta. "My dear friend, I almost failed you."

"No way, Pendergast. Ditch the modesty. I knew that bastard didn't stand a chance against you."

Pendergast turned away, to hide from D'Agosta the expression on his face.

65

Bᴙʏᴄᴇ Hᴀʀʀɪᴍᴀɴ ᴛʜʀᴇᴀᴅᴇᴅ his way through the vast, busy newsroom of the *Post* and stopped at the far end, before Petowski's door. This was the second unscheduled meeting to which he'd been summoned in as many weeks. It was not only unusual—it was unheard of. And when he'd gotten the message—summons, actually—all the relief he'd felt at being suddenly, unexpectedly released from jail had evaporated.

This couldn't be good.

He took a deep breath, knocked.

"Come," came the voice of Petowski.

This time, Petowski was the only person in the room. He was sitting behind the desk, swinging his chair from side to side and fiddling with a pencil. He glanced up at Harriman for a minute, then glanced back down at the pencil. He didn't offer the reporter a chair.

"Did you read about the news conference the NYPD gave this morning?" he asked, still swinging back and forth.

"Yes."

"The killer—the *Decapitator*, as you branded him—turned out to be the father of the first victim. Anton Ozmian."

Harriman swallowed again, more painfully. "So I understand."

"You *understand*. I'm so glad that you do...finally." Petowski looked back up, fixing Harriman with his stare. "Anton Ozmian. Would you call him a religious fanatic?"

"No."

"Would you say that he was killing as a way of, *quote*, 'preaching to the city'?"

Harriman cringed inwardly as he heard his own words being flung back at him. "No, I would not."

"Ozmian." Petowski snapped the pencil in two and threw the pieces into a garbage can with disgust. "So much for your theory."

"Mr. Petowski, I—" Harriman began, but the editor held up a single finger for silence.

"It turns out Ozmian wasn't trying to send a message to New York. He wasn't singling out corrupt, depraved people as a kind of warning to the masses. He wasn't making a statement to our divided nation that the ninety-nine percent wouldn't take anymore from the one percenters. In fact, he was one of them!" Petowski snorted. "And now we all here at the *Post* look like damned fools, thanks to you."

"But the police also—"

A choppy gesture silenced him. Petowski scowled for a moment. Then he went on. "Okay. I'm listening. Now's your chance to explain away the pieces you wrote." He stopped swiveling, sat back in his chair, and folded one arm over the other.

Harriman thought frantically, but nothing came to mind. He'd already been over it, again and again, since he'd first heard the news. But there had simply been too many shocks thrown at him recently—getting arrested; being absolved and released; learning that the Decapitator theory was wrong—leaving his brain a dazed blank.

"I don't have any excuse, Mr. Petowski," he said at last. "I came up with a theory that appeared to fit all the facts, which the police also embraced. But I was wrong."

"A theory that caused an outlandish disturbance in Central Park, for which the cops are also blaming us."

Harriman hung his head.

After another silence, Petowski fetched a deep sigh. "Well, that's an honest answer, anyway," he said. He sat up briskly. "All right, Harriman. Here's what you're going to do. You're going to put that imaginative brain of yours to work, and you're going to recast your theory so that it fits Ozmian—and what he was actually doing."

"I'm not sure I understand."

"It's called *spin*. You're going to massage, pummel, and knead the facts. You're going to push your original theory in a new direction, speculate on some of Ozmian's motives that the cops might not have spoken of at today's presser, add some stuff about that riot in Central Park, and roll it all into a piece of reportage that will make it look like we had our finger on the pulse all along. We're still the City of Endless Night, with the boot of the billionaire class still on the neck of our town. Okay? And Ozmian's the very embodiment of the greed, entitlement, selfishness, and contempt the billionaire class has for the working people of this city, just like we've been writing all along. *That's* the spin. Got it?"

"Got it," Harriman said.

He began to turn away, but Petowski wasn't quite finished. "Oh, and Harriman?"

The reporter glanced back. "Yes, Mr. Petowski?"

"That hundred-dollar-a-week raise I mentioned? I'm rescinding it. Retroactively."

As Harriman made his way back through the newsroom, not a single eye rose to meet his. Everyone was studiously at work, hunched over notebooks or computer screens. But just as he reached the door, he heard somebody intone, in a quiet, singsong voice: "Ye one percenters, mend your ways before it's too late..."

66

D'AGOSTA QUIETLY FOLLOWED Pendergast around Anton Ozmian's home in the Time Warner Center. Like the man's vast office in Lower Manhattan, the huge eight-bedroom condo was practically in the clouds. Only the view was different: instead of New York Harbor, outside and below these windows lay the toy trees, lawns, and winding boulevards of Central Park. It was as if the man scorned the banality of a life lived at sea level.

The CSU team had come and gone long ago—there was precious little evidence of Grace Ozmian's shooting to be documented—and now there was just a small knot of NYPD techs on hand, snapping pictures here and there, taking notes, and chatting in low whispers. Pendergast had not spoken to them. He'd arrived with a long roll of architect's blueprints under his arm, along with a small electronic unit—a laser measuring tool. He had laid out the plans on a black granite table in the expansive living room—the industrial style of the condo was similar to that of the DigiFlood offices—and studied them in great detail, every now and then straightening up to peer around at the surrounding room. At one point he rose and measured the room's dimensions with the laser tool, moved through several adjacent rooms taking measurements, and then came back.

"Curious," he said at last.

"What is?" D'Agosta asked.

But Pendergast had turned away from the table and walked over to a long wall covered with polished mahogany bookcases, punctuated here and there by objets d'art mounted on plinths. He walked along the bookcases slowly, then stepped back a moment, like a dilettante studying a painting in a museum. D'Agosta watched, wondering what he was up to.

Two days ago, when Pendergast had reappeared mere minutes before he was to be blown sky-high, D'Agosta had felt mostly a huge rush of relief that he wasn't, after all, going to die in a most humiliating and ignominious way. Since then, he'd had plenty of time to think, and his feelings had become a lot more complicated.

"Hey, listen, Pendergast—" he began.

"One moment, Vincent." Pendergast lifted a small Roman bust from its stand, then replaced it. He continued down the row of bookcases, pushing here, prodding there. After a few moments, he paused. One book in particular seemed to get his attention. He reached for it, slid it out, and peered into the empty slot left by its absence. He snaked a hand into the space, felt around, and appeared to press something. There was a loud snick of a lock and then the entire section of bookshelf rolled forward, disengaging itself from the wall.

"Remind you of a certain library we both know, Vincent?" Pendergast murmured as he swung the shelf away on well-oiled hinges.

"What the hell is this?"

"Certain inconsistencies in the blueprints for this condo made me suspicious that it might contain a hidden space. My measurements proved it. And this book—" he held up a tattered copy of J. H. Patterson's *Man-Eaters of Tsavo*—"seemed too appropriate to be overlooked. As for what I've found—don't you think there is still a large piece missing from this puzzle?"

"Um, no, not really."

"No? What about the heads?"

"The police think—" D'Agosta paused. "Oh, Jesus. Not here."

"Oh, yes—here." Pulling a flashlight from his pocket and snapping it on, Pendergast stepped into the dark space revealed by the swinging bookcase. D'Agosta followed, suppressing a sense of dread.

A small alcove led to a mahogany door. Pendergast opened it to reveal a tiny, odd-shaped room, about six feet wide by fifteen feet long, paneled in wood with a Persian runner. As Pendergast's flashlight beam licked over the room, D'Agosta's gaze was immediately transfixed by a bizarre sight: the right-hand wall held a series of plaques, and mounted on each plaque was a human head, beautifully preserved, glass eyes gleaming, the skin a fresh, natural color, the hair carefully combed and coiffed, the faces waxwork-like in their strange stillness of perfection—and, most grotesque of all, each head had been given a faint smile. There was an odor of formalin in the air.

Beneath each plaque, a small brass plate had been screwed into the wall, engraved with a name. Revolted, yet fascinated despite himself, D'Agosta followed the FBI agent down the grisly corridor space. GRACE OZMIAN read the plate under the first head: a bleach-blond girl with a remarkably pretty face, red lipstick, and green eyes; MARC CANTUCCI read the plaque beneath the second head: an older, graying, heavyset man with brown eyes and a queer, wry little smile. And so it went, the procession of mounted heads leading to the rear of the secret room, until the two arrived at a single, empty plaque. There was a brass plate already in place below it. ALOYSIUS PENDERGAST read the legend engraved on it.

At the very end of the room stood a leather wing chair with a small accent table beside it on which sat a cut-glass decanter and a brandy snifter. Next to the table was a standing lamp of Tiffany glass. Pendergast reached over and pulled the cord. The room was suddenly illuminated in soft light, the six mounted heads throwing ghoulish shadows across the ceiling.

"Ozmian's trophy room," Pendergast murmured as he slipped his flashlight back into his pocket.

D'Agosta swallowed. "Crazy son of a bitch." He couldn't tear his eyes from the empty plaque at the end of the row—the one that had been intended for Pendergast.

"Crazy, yes, but a man with extraordinary criminal skills—in breaching security, hiding in plain sight, disappearing almost without a trace. Take, for example, the very expensive silicone mask he must have used to impersonate Roland McMurphy. Combine those skills with extreme intelligence, a perfect absence of compassion and empathy, and a high degree of ambition, and you get a psychopath of the highest order."

"But here's one thing I don't understand," D'Agosta said. "How did he get into Cantucci's place? I mean, the town house was a fortress, and that security specialist Marvin and everyone else said only an employee of Sharps and Gund could have gotten past all the alarms and countermeasures."

"Not so formidable for a computer genius like Ozmian, with a stable of prize hackers—not just extremely well paid, but some being blackmailed by Ozmian for their previous hactivist crimes—at his beck and call, in one of the most sophisticated and powerful dot-com companies in the world, with access to all the latest digital tools. Look what he and his people did to frame that reporter, Harriman. A diabolical piece of work. Having a brain trust like that on hand would make getting inside Cantucci's residence not so difficult."

"Yeah, that makes sense."

Pendergast turned to leave.

"Um, Pendergast?"

The agent turned. "Yes, Vincent?"

"I think I owe you an apology."

Pendergast arched his eyebrows in query.

"I was stupid, I was desperate for answers, I had everyone from the mayor on down climbing up my ass...I bought that damned reporter's theory hook, line, and sinker. And then I mouthed off at you when you tried to warn me the theory was bogus—"

Pendergast raised a hand to silence him. "My dear Vincent. Harriman's story seemed to fit the facts, it was an attractive theory as far as it went, and you weren't the only one taken in. A lesson for all of us: things are not always as they seem."

"That's for sure." D'Agosta glanced at the grisly row of trophy heads. "Not in a million years would I have guessed this."

"And that's why our Behavioral Science Unit wasn't able to profile the man. Because he wasn't, psychologically speaking, a serial killer. He was truly *sui generis*."

"Sweet generous...Him? What the—?"

"Just an old Latin phrase. It means 'of its own kind; in a class by itself.'"

"I gotta get out of here."

Pendergast looked at the blank plaque with his name on it. *"Sic transit gloria mundi,"* he murmured again in Latin. And then he turned away and quickly stepped out of the little chamber of horrors.

They returned to the vast living room of Ozmian's apartment with its sprawling views. D'Agosta went to the window, breathing deeply. "Some things I wish I could unsee."

"To be a witness to evil is to be human."

Pendergast joined him at the window, and they gazed out for a moment in silence. The wintry landscape of New York was suffused with the pale-yellow glow of the dying afternoon.

"In a strange way, that jackass Harriman was right about the one percenters ruining this city," said D'Agosta. "It's also kind of funny that the killer turned out to be a one percenter himself. Just another super-rich, entitled bastard, getting his jollies at the expense of everyone else. I mean, look at this place! It makes me want to puke: these arrogant assholes in their penthouses, lording it around town in their stretch limos, with their chauffeurs and butlers..." His voice suddenly trailed off and he felt his face go red. "Sorry. You know I didn't mean you."

For the first time he could recall, he heard Pendergast laugh. "Vincent, it isn't the content of one's bank account that's important, it's the content of one's character, to paraphrase a wise man. The divide between the wealthy and everyone else is a false dichotomy—and one that obscures the real problem: there are many wicked people in the world, rich *and* poor. *That* is the real divide—between those who strive to do good, and those who strive only for themselves. Money magnifies the harm the wealthy can do, of course, allowing them to parade their vulgarity and malfeasance in full view of the rest of us."

"So what's the answer?"

"To paraphrase another wise man, 'The rich will always be

with us.' There is no answer, except to make sure we wealthy are not allowed to use our money as a tool of oppression and subversion of democracy."

D'Agosta was surprised at this uncharacteristic bit of philosophizing. "Yeah, but this town, New York, it's changing. Now only the rich can afford Manhattan. Brooklyn and even Queens are going the same way. Where are working people like me going to live in ten, twenty years?"

"There's always New Jersey."

D'Agosta choked. "You *were* making a joke, right?"

"I'm afraid the trophy room of horrors has provoked in me an inappropriate levity."

D'Agosta understood immediately. It was like those M.E.'s, with a murder victim opened up on the gurney, who cracked jokes about spaghetti and meatballs. Somehow, the horror of what they'd just witnessed needed to be exorcised by unrelated banter.

"Getting back to the case," Pendergast said hastily, "I must admit to you I feel personally distressed and even chastened."

"How's that?"

"Ozmian completely took me in. Until he tried to foist Hightower as a suspect on us, I hadn't the slightest inkling that he was a possible suspect. *That* will trouble me for a very, very long time."

EPILOGUE

Two Months Later

THE SETTING SUN gilded the flanks of India's Outer Himalayan mountains, casting long shadows over the foothills and stony valleys. Near the base of the Dhauladhar range of Himachal Pradesh, some fifty miles north of Dharamsala, all was silent save for a distant boom of Tibetan long horns calling the monks to prayer.

A path rose up from the cedar forests, winding its serpentine way against forbidding rock cliffs as it began the long climb toward the summit of Hanuman ji Ka Tiba, or "White Mountain," at 18,500 feet, the tallest peak in the range. After about two miles, an almost invisible track separated from the main path and—heading away from the peak—hugged the cliff face, chiseled into the rock, as it made several narrow, heart-stopping turns until at last it reached a rocky promontory. Here, a large monastery—built out of the living rock and barely discernible against the mountainside that surrounded it—had stood for many hundreds of years, the carven decorations of its sloping ramparts and pinnacled roofs almost completely worn away by time and weather.

In a small courtyard high up in the monastery, surrounded on three sides by a colonnade that looked down upon the valley below, sat Constance Greene. She was motionless, watching a boy of four play at her feet. He was arranging a set of prayer beads into a pattern of remarkable complexity for a child of his age.

Now the horns issued a second mournful blast, and a figure appeared in the darkened doorway: a man in his early sixties, clad in the scarlet-and-saffron-colored robes of a Buddhist monk. He looked at Constance, smiled, and nodded.

"It is time," the man said in an English inflected with a Tibetan lilt.

"I know." She opened her arms and the boy rose and turned to embrace her. She kissed his head, then each cheek in turn. And then she released him and allowed the monk named Tsering to lead him by the hand across the courtyard and into the fastness of the monastery.

Leaning back against one of the columns, she gazed out over the vast, mountainous vista. Below, she could hear a commotion: voices, the whinny of a horse. Apparently a visitor had arrived at the monastery. Constance paid little attention. She looked listlessly out at the woods far below, at the dramatic flanks of the White Mountain as it rose beside her. The smell of sandalwood wafted up, along with the familiar sounds of chanting. As she gazed out over the vast expanse, she was aware—as so often these days—of a vague sense of dissatisfaction, a need unfulfilled, a task undone. Her restlessness puzzled her: she was with her son, in a beautiful and quiet place of meditative retreat and contemplation; what more could she want? And yet the restlessness only seemed to grow.

"Lead me into all misfortune." She murmured the ancient Buddhist prayer quietly to herself. "Only by that path can I transform the negative into the positive."

Now voices sounded in the dark passage within, and she turned toward them. A moment later a tall man dressed in dusty, old-fashioned traveling clothes emerged into the courtyard.

Constance sprang to her feet in astonishment. "Aloysius!"

"Constance," he said. He walked toward her quickly, then stopped just as suddenly, seemingly unsure. After an awkward moment, he motioned for them both to sit upon the stone battlements. They sat side by side, and she simply stared at him, too surprised by his abrupt and unexpected appearance to speak.

"How are you?" he asked.

"Well, thank you."

"And your son?"

At this she brightened. "He's learning fast, so happy and full of gentleness and compassion, such a beautiful boy. He goes out and feeds the wild animals and birds, who come down from the hills to meet him, quite unafraid. The monks say he's everything they hoped for and more."

An uncomfortable silence fell over them. Pendergast seemed uncharacteristically hesitant, and then he abruptly spoke.

"Constance, there's no easy or graceful way for me to put into words what I have to say. So I'll phrase it as simply as I can. You must come back with me."

This announcement was even more of a surprise than his arrival. Constance remained silent.

"You have to come home."

"But my son—"

"His place is here, with the monks, as the rinpoche. You've just said he's filling that role admirably. But you're not a monk. Your place is in the world—in New York. *You have to come home.*"

She took a deep breath. "It's not quite so simple."

"I'm aware of that."

"There's another matter to consider..." She faltered, at a loss for words. "What exactly will be—what does this mean for us?"

Quite suddenly, he took her hands in his. "I don't know."

"But why this decision of yours? What happened?"

"I'll spare you the details," he said. "But there was a night, not so long ago, when I knew, with utter certainty, that I was about to die. I *knew*, Constance. And in that moment—that last extremity—it was you who suddenly came into my mind. Later, when the crisis had passed and I realized I would live after all, I had time to reflect on that moment. It was then I realized that, quite simply, life without you is not worth living. I need you to be with me. In what way or relationship, precisely, as ward, friend, or...I don't know...remains to be worked out. I...I ask for your patience in that. But regardless, one fact remains. I cannot live without you."

As he'd spoken, Constance had stared closely at his face. There was an intensity in his expression, a look in the glittering ice-silver eyes, that she had not seen before.

He grasped her hands more firmly. "Please come home."

For a long moment Constance remained silent, holding his eyes with her own. And then—almost imperceptibly—she nodded.